DEAD GIRLS WALKING

To Grandpa, who asked me to split the check
before I wrote a word

CONTENT WARNING: As a horror novel, there will be things in this book that not all audiences are comfortable reading. Below, I have listed content warnings for anyone who needs them.

STRONG PRESENCE OF: body fluids like blood and vomit, bones, branding, emotional and physical child abuse, death, fire, gore, hallucinations, murder, profanity, PTSD flashbacks of abuse and horrific situations, skeletons, violence, abuse in the name of religion

BRIEF MENTIONS OF: ableist language, bullying, cannibalism, recreational marijuana usage, gun violence, the occult, police brutality, suicidal ideation, supernatural interpretation of terminal illness, transphobia

Cataloging-in-Publication Data has been applied for and may be obtained from the Library of Congress.

ISBN 978-1-4197-6676-3

Text © 2024 Sami Ellis
Book design by Chelsea Hunter and Becky James

Smoke images by rawpixel.com on Freepik; tree image by lifeforstock on Freepik; paint swash image by macrovector on Freepik.

Printed and bound in U.S.A.
10 9 8 7 6 5 4 3 2 1

Amulet Books® is a registered trademark of Harry N. Abrams, Inc.

ABRAMS The Art of Books
195 Broadway, New York, NY 10007
abramsbooks.com

DEAD GIRLS WALKING

SAMI ELLIS

Amulet Books • New York

CHAPTER ONE

Temple comes to camp alone because a crowd makes it difficult to go corpse hunting.

Her fingers ache around the wooden shovel, and pattering droplets hit her ears as light rain slicks over her back. She's losing steam. Her feet trip over themselves as she weaves through the pines.

Her dad's confession echoes in her mind over and over:

"You asked."

"Of course I did it."

"Why don't you dig up her body and find out for yourself?"

Damn. She can't have nothin' good.

She recalls staring back at her dad blankly. Hoping he'd crack a smile. His chapped lips splitting and bleeding before he guffawed like *You should have seen your face!*

Her dad didn't used to be like that, but he's changed since prison. Maybe he developed a sense of humor. The serial killer thing hadn't worked out for him; no harm in switching things up.

But apparently asking her dad to develop a personality overnight is asking for too much.

Temple slows her steps on the path as she finally reaches the Midpoint Tree. The branches twist and curl all the way up, reaching the canopy of the woods coated in thick, dark leaves. The rough leaves of the kudzu ruffle against her ankles as she hoists the shovel over her head once again.

A chickadee chirps overhead, waiting for her to get on with it. It clearly doesn't understand inner turmoil.

And honestly, she shouldn't be wasting so much time on it. She needs to hurry up—before she gets caught. She didn't want to believe her dad when he confessed, but she's here now. In the thick of the woods, ankles out. Sap-sticky and ready to bury a shovel deep into the soil.

This camp is private property. No one can see her here.

Temple puts her whole back into the first swing down. Her gloves grate against her palms as her hands tremble, even with her windbreaker beneath her raincoat.

You know the drill, she tells herself. Ain't nothin' to do but wait for the chime of the "coins." That's not what they are, but she's called them so since childhood.

She dug around the woods as a kid, too. Whenever she found a coin, she knew she was close to something. Something ivory, curving deep among the roots of the Midpoint Tree. She could climb to the highest branch that would hold her, yank the thinnest branch like a sword.

But Temple had perfect sight. She could make out the ivory, no matter how far she was.

The white smoothness was something dirty, something smelly. Something bloody that she was never supposed to find.

"But it doesn't matter." This time Temple speaks aloud, shaking off those rancid feelings that remembering always gave her. "Because you're supposed to find it this time."

What else would her dad expect after telling her *"I chopped her head off."*

Temple puts everything in it as she swings the shovel down. Closes her eyes.

Opens them again when she sees her dad's face.

Clink!

The sound of metal on metal makes Temple pause, her muscles going rigid. The finches beatbox over her head, finding no reason to hold their breath like Temple does. She leans down to the ground, pressing her hands into the damp soil. It squishes at her fingertips and lodges underneath her nails in thick globs. She presses through.

A second later, her fingers wrap around something cool—actually, quite freezing—and she pulls the iron charm out of the soil and thick, entwined roots. A solid disk, about the size of a medallion. A coin.

Branded iron.

That's what the coins are really called. The only time she's ever heard them referred to like that was in the courtroom. It's heavy. The design on the metal is intricately curling, with woven diamonds that twist around the edge of the coin.

It makes a weird symbol in the center—almost like a crudely drawn tree—overrun with snakes and leaves that Temple thinks is way overkill. Her dad didn't have style, but he killed with the Versace of brands.

Temple pockets the little disk, heart pounding in her chest.

"You asked."

She was onto something now.

"Of course I did it."

So the confession wasn't bullshit.

"Why don't you dig up her body and find out for yourself?"

Temple slams the shovel into the ground with a metallic thud, her fingers clenching around the bar as she groans. Rain drips into her eyes, filtering through her eyelashes. The October air is crisp. Chilly.

Another slam into the soil.

"*You asked.*" She never fucking asked. She never wanted to know.

Her windbreaker flutters in the breeze. She dumps another pile of dirt to the side. The coin weighs heavily in her pocket.

Thunk!

Her mind goes blank.

There's the sound of the light rain. The thuds of her shovel. The hiss of squirrels dashing through the bushes. The swish of synthetic material as her jacket sleeves rub against her stomach.

Temple digs until her arms hurt.

Crunch.

She freezes.

The heavy metal of the shovel head stops on something—not hard or solid, just . . . different. It's been hours of searching like this. Temple's big enough to admit to herself that desperation's only fifteen minutes away.

She looks at the walls of the hole she's dug so far—the top just above her waist. Then she looks downward to the base of the hole, where her feet are crooked over the uneven dirt. Her eyes run over the varied browns in the soil that has and hasn't soaked up rain to a patch of black. Her heart skips a beat.

Burlap—just what gets any teenage girl going.

With renewed strength, Temple clears what she can from around the bag. Her jacket's drenched with the light rain and her sweat.

The blackened bag is buried deep, but Temple knows it well. Burlap's somewhat of a staple for her dad. Temple crouches down, running her hands over the fabric and enjoying the rough feel on her palm.

"He wasn't lying," she says aloud. Anticipation hums through her veins, along with a thicker, tougher feeling. A feeling like flesh, like mush rushing in and out of her throat. She's not afraid of crying; she's afraid of screaming. It rocks through her so fast, she sways and drops her shovel.

The metal hits the bag, and it huffs. Rustles. *Splat.*

Temple takes a step back, her brow furrowing. That sound isn't right.

It's not like Temple would brag about it, but she knows the sound a corpse makes when something heavy falls into its slop. When the bones of the skeleton crack. She doesn't have any choice *but* to know . . . so what the fuck?

With no longer hesitant fingers, Temple grips onto the sides of the bag and braces herself. The body might just be bones at this point. The vinyl lining could hide the reality of the inside. It could be half-molten, decomposing and filled with writhing maggots by now. The smell alone could take her out.

She rips the bag open, nails easily snapping the threads before the cloth pulls back completely. It's no longer in good condition after years of wear.

The scent is faded, delicate. It's much like old meat, like rotten, spoiled flesh—but it's subtle.

Still thick, though.

She gags, but only once as she stands to full height and glares down inside the bag.

The low light of the woods hits the inside, and she finds piles of white paper flutter in the gentle wind, fragile and covered with smudged ink scrawls. The rain lets up a little, sending Temple shivering.

Nothing.

She grabs one of the sheets, and it crumbles in her hand. The writing is illegible, chicken scratch even more shameful than her dad's. But there's nothing there. No body.

No skeleton. No flesh.

Not even parts of it.

"Fuck!" Temple swears aloud. The echo bounces back to her, along with the obnoxious chirp of robins.

The body bag is empty.

And her mother's corpse is nowhere to be seen.

CHAPTER TWO

Temple sinks to the ground, ache rolling through her spine. She looks around the hole, filled with paper she can't read, and hisses through her teeth.

"*Fuuuuck!*" she screams again.

She let her dad launch her on another wild-goose chase.

One of her twists falls into her eyes as she tries to get control of her breath. The clouds have moved out of the way, and the sun is beaming down now. She remembers the weather being temperamental here—sitting in front of her window, looking into the shadows of the trees. Wondering when the sun would return so she could climb up on the roof and jump into the hay.

Shit, she's remembering a whole bunch of things now.

This can't be why he made her come all the way back out to the old farm.

"*Hide in the bathroom and count to twenty, sweetie.*" She hears her dad's voice flit through her mind, and she pictures his grin as he'd said it. How his lopsided shadow would crawl over her when she sat in the corner of the living room.

"*I've got a surprise for you,*" her dad would say. His eyes would gleam, and she knew it was joy. With other people, it was hard to tell, but Temple could tell when her dad was happy . . . and when he was deadly. *"But you've got to find it first."*

Temple shakes the memory away, but there's no doubt he played her like a fiddle again.

"Why don't you dig up her body and find out for yourself?"

After refusing to return to the farm for three years, he got her there with the promise of learning what happened to her missing mother. But he never knew where she was in the first place. He just wanted her to do his bidding.

Whatever that is.

She huffs out a breath.

Just what she needed. A macabre scavenger hunt.

Temple digs her claws into the walls of the shallow grave, the damp soil coating her skin. Her shoulders burn as she hauls herself out, grinding her teeth from effort—or anger. It's a toss-up which, and she's not a gambler.

When her back finally hits the grass, she's a huffing, puffing, drenched mess. She keeps the shovel tight in her hand as she looks down into what should have been an easy mission before she heaves up the shovel again. The thick mud slaps over the bag.

She knows this pointless shit is going to take forever. The rain has stopped, the clouds parting slowly. The sun is already starting to come back out when she gets through about a half-hour of re-filling the hole with dirt.

Before she hears a noise.

Another snap sounds from the path, and Temple freezes. For a breath, there's nothing but the sound of squirrels dashing in and out of interwoven leaves. Her shovel is half raised over the hole, her hand clenched on the wooden handle.

Then, a giggle.

Temple clenches tighter, her grip matching her jaw.

"You're lying—really?!" A voice says. "I can't believe you caught her in the act."

That's an omen if Temple's ever heard one.

Because that means the girls are coming.

Oh god, the girls are coming.

"Yeah, Cali *tried* to spray paint TRANS RIGHTS BITCH on the principal's door, but I caught her on camera so she didn't finish."

Temple looks down into her half-filled hole, her heart pounding in her chest as she runs a hand over her face. Apparently, time flies even when you're not having fun.

It's time for camp to start.

With a flurry of her shovel, Temple begins hauling slop over her feet as fast as she can, and her gray boots turn brown in her haste. The sound of the girls' chattering gets closer, making everything more difficult.

Her palms are sweating.

Her heart is pounding.

Best-case scenario would've been she found her mom's body and got to ditch the rest of camp. It's only right—she signed up for one reason, and that's to get access to the premises.

She doesn't want to be here all weekend.

Her dad isn't even here, but still, he's ordering her around, pulling her strings like a puppet.

The sound of footsteps is now audible. The girls' voices are so close, Temple can feel the vibrations of their timbre through her back.

Shit, that's on her—she spent too much time on indignation.

"We got off fucking lucky, 'Nae. Imagine if the Virgin Mary didn't switch cabins with you."

"If I was in Cabin Bey, I honestly would have stuck my hand in the garbage disposal."

Temple curls low to the ground slowly, silently. She had thrown her backpack against a tree early in the morning before she started digging, and she grabs it now, clutching tight on its straps. Her shovel drags against the soil, only shushing along the paste of the dirt. She can feel her heartbeat in her ears.

"The 'B' absolutely stands for bitch—all those girls *and* the new girl?"

"Temple as a camp counselor is a WWE ring and circle of hell all at once."

Before she can even think, Temple drops her shovel. It makes a loud *pop*, and the girls shriek as it echoes through the trees. She's hidden behind a curtain of branches.

If Temple just stays quiet, she can get away with this. Sure, it's the punk bitch way of doing things—but Temple never cared to be brave. She's not above running away, not even in her good boots.

But then her feet are already heading toward the open path. She pops out of the trees. Leaves and brush hiss around her, raining debris like confetti as the two girls scream their heads off.

Their shadows trail toward her, and she watches them clutch each other in terror.

It would've been bad if they'd gone to investigate and found her with a shovel. In the silence of them gathering their wits, Temple sizes them up. They have brown skin and dark-colored braids— fraternal twins to Temple's twists. Aside from the fact that one wears glasses and one doesn't, they look the same.

They look like half the girls she's seen her last eight months at North Prep . . . and she hates that she immediately knows exactly who they are. She hates it so much she can't even form words. Her mouth pops open and shuts closed again.

The girls take a moment to realize she's not moving. Then they realize *they're* not moving either and go on the offensive.

"What the fuck?" Glasses One snaps at her.

That gets Temple back to earth. She stares them down, towering over them by a couple of inches and a few pounds of muscle, though she hasn't quite perfected the right glare.

"Looks like you're missing the head Barbie," she says with a sneer. "Don't you horses turn back to mice without her?"

Janae and Wynter gawk back, and they're angry even though Temple's practically being nice. Well, maybe not nice—but just the right amount of mean.

At least there wasn't any violence this time. It wasn't as disastrous as their last meeting.

But *no*, the Wonder Twins don't know how to be thankful.

"Why are you even here?" Janae snaps. She's a mini-me with a neck problem—she can't stop rolling it. "Shouldn't you be in, like, juvie? Or maybe a mental institution?"

Temple turns away without answering. It makes them as mad as she wanted it to, but she'd also rather focus on why she came here. She begins down the path, her heavy book bag weighing down her shoulder.

This place will be crawling with girls soon. She's blown her chance to be covert, but she's still got a mystery on her hands.

What does her dad want from her? Why did he send her here? And where the *hell* is her mother's body?

A hand grabs Temple's elbow. She's yanked back and whisked around to meet Janae's scowling glare. "You can't just ignore us," she hisses. Behind her, Wynter says nothing. She was always the quietest.

Made it easier for Temple to pick at her.

She peels Janae's fingers off her jacket, raising an eyebrow. "I can't?" she asks Wynter.

The girl pushes her glasses higher up her nose. "You're an employee," she says matter-of-factly, as if Temple forgot.

Which Temple kind of *did* forget.

Shit.

"And camp counselors were supposed to arrive at Jigsaw Grounds an hour ago. If you're still all the way out here, you're running very, very late."

Double shit. Temple tenses but tries to keep her shoulders relaxed. Her alarm didn't ring, even though she *knows* she made her aunt set it. This is why cell phones are the devil—fucking unreliable.

But she doesn't let the terrible two see her sweat.

Without even an exhale, Temple hikes her book bag up higher over her shoulder. "Ooh, this is gonna be fun," she says sarcastically. "If you two know my schedule, that can only mean one thing— the head Barbie's a camp counselor, too." The smile that stretches across Temple's lips is insincere. Another goddamned thing to worry about. "I haven't seen that bitch since she got me suspended."

North Point Farms Scholarship Weekend of Horrors!

IN PARTNERSHIP WITH NORTHERN GIRLS' PREPARATORY SCHOOL AND THE PRIDE ROCKS FOUNDATION

The Pride Rocks Foundation supports five schools in the greater Fairfax area by awarding LGBTQ+ students a sponsored trip to a seasonal location. This year, we have rented North Point Farms for your Weekend of Horrors on October 16–18! Thanks to generous donations from North Prep alumni, the students below have been selected as this year's scholarship winners! If you have questions before the festivities begin, contact a camp staff rep: Brenda Thomas (director), Vivian Lam (assistant director), or Dawntae Brown (coordinator).

STUDENT ASSISTANTS

Anysaa Washington, Camp Counselor A
Temple Baker, Camp Counselor B

CAMPERS

Natalie Brennan, Cabin B
Sierra Morris, Cabin B
Janae Richards, Cabin A
Mickaeyla Rodriguez, Cabin B
Wynter Santos, Cabin A
Yaya Sidibe, Cabin B
Cali Wilson, Cabin A
K'ran York, Cabin A

CHAPTER THREE

As the campgrounds fill the horizon, Temple steels herself. Jigsaw Grounds—or JG, as the camp website called the main cabin—is an old school building that stretches from one end of the trees to the other. The path cuts through the rounded bundle of forest, a straight line all the way to the main building. There, the crops were plowed over back in the seventies for Cary Lauren's school—a writer's guild for queer Black writers coming up from the South.

As far as Temple's concerned, that was a way better use of the fields.

Temple had never been allowed this deep into the woods growing up, but she knew about the school building and what happened there. After the school closed down in the eighties, the farm was cut in half, and then into quarters. By the time Temple was born, North Point Farms was a shadow of its former self. Now, even though the land is mostly dense forest, there's still enough for the camp's layout: the school and the two cabins at the school's feet—Bey and Aye from closest to farthest.

The camp's land is about the size of half a football field and just as flat, with the new cabin additions on the left side. Cabin Aye is only a few yards from the pathway, looking too modern against the rugged brown woods.

The pines that surround the clearing are thick with leaves, the curved trees leaning over the roof and brushing against the back bricks. The shadows twist in odd shapes that reach all the way to Temple's feet.

Because it doesn't want her going any farther.

I'm not glad to be back, either, Temple tells the trees. Only in her mind, though. She's always been worried they listen.

Temple looks at Cabin Aye's wooden planks for walls as if it's the girl of the hour. Camp Counselor A. But of course, the building didn't do anything.

She turns back to Jigsaw Grounds.

Janae and Wynter haven't popped back on the path yet. Temple's at least made it there before them.

With a deep breath, she walks up the steps to the main door and pushes it open before she can talk herself out of it.

The interior of the cabin is like another world—one made of all wood and fluorescent light. Tables, chairs, floors, walls—all harsh, finished wood that reflects the overhead lighting right into Temple's face.

The kitchenette is filled with old appliances—white ones with a yellow tint. Even the lone sofa, the only fabric present, is a dingy color. It sits in front of the fireplace, which is—of course—wooden.

Damn.

City folk hear the word "cabin" and don't know how to act.

Temple has to actively hold her hands at her sides so she doesn't slap them over her eyes as she closes the door behind her.

She doesn't make it one step.

"That you?"

The deep, smooth voice comes from the left of the door, and Temple turns to see one of the adults. Lithe and relaxed, the woman's perched up on the windowsill. She glares down at a walkie-talkie clutched in one hand, the other holding a cigarette out the window. When she sees Temple, she puts it out on the sill and tosses it into the dirt outside. Her rod-straight posture deflates a little when she makes out it's Temple.

It's the stern glare that clues Temple right into exactly who she is. According to her bio on the camp's website, it's the former marine-turned-babysitter: Assistant Director Vivian Lam.

Temple smiles, because that's her natural response to disappointment. "Director?" Temple pauses, unsure of where to stand. "Were you expecting someone else?"

Lam shakes her head, making no move toward Temple. "Intern's still out—and no one calls me 'Director.' Everybody calls me Lam." She turns back out the window without offering to help Temple with her massive book bag or even pointing out where she's supposed to go.

At least Temple's not the only one who's late. She never met Dawntae, the chipper coordinator-slash-college-intern, but when Temple was selected as a camp counselor, her congratulations email had words of encouragement and an irresponsible amount of exclamation points. That was Temple's only interaction with her, though.

"She's not here?" Temple asks.

"No."

And that's it.

If Temple's honest with herself, Lam is much better at this whole aloof thing than she is.

"Is it finally her?" Clomping footsteps follow the voice, and the other director makes her way into the main room, her arms filled with tattered books of various yellows and creams. The frayed paper covers entangle with a ratty, knit cardigan that looks like she found it on the sidewalk. When *she* sees Temple, her brilliant grin makes Temple uncomfortable.

Temple tries to smile back. "Director Thomas."

"Temple!" she greets brightly. "You're late. So glad to have you!" Nobody's that "glad" to have Temple. "Are you ready for this weekend?"

No. "Sure."

Brenda's smile stretches tighter, showing all of her teeth. "And where are the spare keys? Where's the fire safety supplies? The emergency food?"

"You're panicking, babe," Lam says.

It brings Brenda back to earth, and she blinks, snapping out of it. She turns to Lam, then to Temple. "Sorry," she says sheepishly.

"Is everything OK?" Temple asks.

Slithering up beside Temple, Brenda shoves the mess of books into Temple's arms. The flopping sound of pages hums around the room as Temple juggles to keep them off the floor. "Take care of this, will ya? Our intern is late, and she was supposed to organize these for the read-aloud—god, you girls are gonna gray my hair out."

Brenda's head is shaved completely bald.

Temple isn't sure whether this is something she should comment on, but Brenda pauses as if waiting for her answer.

"The girls at school say they're into that sometimes. It's cool now." She has no clue if that's true, but she offers it up anyway.

There's a moment of quiet between them. Temple panics, for a breath, that somehow out of all the things in the world to say, she said the wrong thing. But then Brenda starts to laugh, a grin breaking out as she raises her brows at Temple.

"I like you," she says. "I'm not quite old enough to be a 'classy gray,' but I appreciate that you recognize I could pull it off."

Temple almost smiles. No one's said they liked her in a long time. Then the books in Temple's hands demand her attention

17

again, and she remembers she's most liked when she's not heard. She goes back to her production of struggling to carry the pile.

"Did you—" She stops herself. Words she doesn't even recognize nearly fly out of her mouth. She almost offered to help contact the missing girl—wherever she is.

But she's not here for these girls. She's here because her dad sent her. It's all a part of some plan that will lead to answers about her mom, if she can solve it.

And that takes precedence.

Temple straightens her back, looking over at Brenda with the mission in mind. Brenda's waiting for her to speak, watching her hold the wobbling books with a slight smile.

"Yes?"

"... Did you ... did you ..." Temple darts her eyes back down. The acceptance email is on her mind. All those damned "!!!!"s.

Temple looks back up. "Did you mean all those rules in the email?" They scroll over the back of her eyelids like movie credits. "The curfew and the buddy system for leaving the cabins?"

Unsurprisingly, Brenda laughs like Temple can't be serious. "Of course I meant them, Temple. You think we're letting a bunch of teen girls run around five miles of forest unsupervised? Especially *this* forest?"

"Even the lesbians would find a way to get pregnant," Lam calls from her seat by the window.

Brenda laughs, putting a hand on Temple's elbow. She tilts it up, and the books right themselves.

"What about us?" Temple asks. "The camp counselors—cabin leaders."

"What about you?" Brenda asks.

"Do we have to follow the rules, too?"

Everything about Brenda's joy wipes away. Her eyes turn stern. "Camp counselors are held to the same standards as the other campers." She crosses her arms, raising an eyebrow. "Don't think of this as a weekend getaway. You have rules and responsibilities."

Well, that's gonna suck.

While Temple has no plans of actually *following* the rules, it still sucks that she'll be breaking them. Brenda and Lam seem like good people.

Maybe they can see reason.

Temple opens her mouth to protest, but the sound of thudding footsteps fills her ears. She shuts her mouth again as the two girls from the woods finally catch up, popping the main door open with a squeal.

"Hey, Brenda!" Janae screams in greeting.

The room bursts into life and laughter and movement while Lam and Temple inch toward the walls. Their silence is unbefitting the mood, like the dark clouds have taken to the corners.

Brenda's stressed expression wipes away as she turns to the new girls, that soul-melting smile back and almost genuine. Almost.

"Girls!" she squeals. "We're *so* excited to have you here—for our inaugural Weekend of Horrors at North Point Farms!"

CHAPTER FOUR

Temple already hates nighttime in the woods, but she's extra edgy tonight. A gnat filters in and out of her vision, and she doesn't bother swatting at it. She's got to find a way to sneak out later. The problem isn't getting past her own girls; it's getting past the other cabin.

She looks across the fire, over to Aye, which sits right at the crest of the path. She tries to ignore the sound of the read-aloud happening a few feet away.

"Bell was more than familiar with death," the reader says. "With the last breath of a loved one. She thought she'd accepted that it would kiss her again—but she was mistaken."

The North Point Farms layout is pretty simple: The path stretches from the highway to the clearing. All the buildings are to the left, save for the bathrooms on the right. JG borders the back end, while Cabin Aye and Temple's own cabin—Cabin Bey—curves around the edge of the campsite firepit.

So in order to make it out undetected, she'll have to creep past Aye. Without getting caught.

"'Don't come around here anymore, Eric,' Bell cried at her husband. 'If you do, I swear I'll kill you.'"

A cliché of herself, Temple looks up at the word "kill." The girl in front of the campfire reads with her nose in the book, clutching it tight like it'll run away. She's chubby and cute, wearing a pink sweater that sits just above her jeans and a gold chain that nestles in her cleavage.

"'I don't care if you kill me,' Eric said. 'You already killed our son.'"

Over Temple's shoulder, the light from JG glows and warms her skin. She stands by the rocky gravel around the fire, right beneath the window with a hip-height stack of books next to her.

The book covers are all different colors, the tower of them haphazardly twisted by their covers and backs. If she had a friend, maybe they'd be betting on how long before it all fell down. But alone, she just watches it warily as it teeters, sure it'll fall over any second now.

Gasps sound around the circle, and Temple looks back at them. She's missed something.

The passage is particularly grisly. "His blood dripped down the walls, the sour stench of his flesh burning in Bell's nose. She had done that. Her fingers shook. Chunks of flesh had somehow burrowed beneath her fingertips."

The enthralled faces around the circle are highlighted with the flickers of the fire, bathing them in gold like a good Instagram filter. Overhead, the sky fills with stars this deep in the forest but somehow still seems so cold.

And then she feels eyes on her, and she turns her neck.

One girl stares back.

Big hair. Freckles that don't wipe in the summertime. *Anysaa*, her mind tells her. Temple has no problems ignoring it, though—she'd much rather pretend she doesn't know her.

Anysaa's two little friends are flanked at her sides, but they're just as gripped by storytime as all of the other toddlers. Janae and Wynter haven't talked to Temple since they ran into each other on the path—but they must have snitched.

Because the way Anysaa's looking at her, it's clear the Head Barbie knows Temple's been misbehaving. And she doesn't punish in the fun kind of ways.

"Stop making eyes at the girls and pass me that book."

Temple starts at the sound of Brenda's voice, right in her ear. But she turns and finds the woman snapping absent-mindedly at Temple. "The copy of *Hill House*? It's right there, Dawntae." Brenda halts for a moment, clenching her eyes shut. "Fuckin' *balls*," she hisses. "I mean, *Temple*."

Temple just stares at her.

"Language," chastises Lam from across the fire. She's got bat-hearing, apparently.

But Brenda is appropriately embarrassed, dropping her hand with a look of panic back to Lam, then to Temple. "Sorry. Uh, friggin' A. I meant Temple." She bites her lip to keep it from quivering.

It all becomes clear to Temple right then—Brenda's jokes from earlier, that faltering smile. She's really worried over this intern thing.

Temple's hand pauses over the twisting stack of books for a second too long as she catches the director's eyes before flicking her gaze to the ground. *This is none of your business*, Temple tells herself.

She can brush this off completely—some intern skipping out on their duties is nothing to dwell on. And Temple's fine with ignoring what she's seen, what she's realized. That Brenda cares.

Temple can ignore it all.

But . . .

Brenda likes her.

"You got Dawntae on the brain?" Temple asks before she can stop herself. She narrows her eyes at the titles on the spines as if it'll help her see better—but really it's so she doesn't burst into flames. "She's the intern, right?"

Temple searches for the book in question, and after she finds a book with a much *longer* title than just "*Hill House*" near the bottom of the pile, she plays Tetris to get the books arranged right so they don't fall over.

She hands Brenda the book. She looks out to make sure her voice isn't carrying, but there's a new reader up front. Sweater Girl has returned to her seat on a log, watching, just as enraptured as the others.

Temple flexes her fingers, looking into Brenda's glossy eyes. "I mean, she's ditched before, right?"

Brenda casts her eyes down. "Yeah. She has."

"College kids do shit like this all the time. Parties. Finals." Temple trails off, reaching the end of her knowledge of what normal college kids go through. "Whatever. She's fine, I'm sure."

She's fine. I'm sure.

Temple's heard those words all of her life. It never made her feel better. She looks back at Brenda, and it shouldn't surprise her that the woman returns an unconvincing smile.

"Is there something else that's got you so worried?" Temple asks. She swears she doesn't mean to. She doesn't care about wherever Dawntae's lazing around, about Brenda's concern.

She doesn't care at all.

But just saying "she's fine" doesn't sit right with her. Not when she knows from experience that that's not helpful. It doesn't stop you from worrying. It doesn't stop you from waiting. If anything, it makes you obsess.

The shaky smile Brenda provided slips a little. For a second, her hand twitches up to her waist, where her radio is clipped to her pants. She almost says something—but then she drops her hand. When she leans close to Temple, she turns her face away from the flames so no one can hear her low voice. "I'm just saying this because you're one of the student assistants. You know—make sure you know the situation. I'm a worrywart—so it's probably nothing. But . . ." She trails off. "We're here because the girls pushed for this, y'know? Even though they know. About the land. About the legends."

Temple tries not to nod. She remains stiff, eyes frozen on Brenda's.

"And I know they just want to have a thrill . . . but sometimes people go missing around here. It's always *just* far enough that it's not on the farm. 'It happened near King's Dominion.' 'Oh, it happened in Ashland.' 'It's probably the Klan.' "

Temple blinks back at her. She didn't know about any of that. But she tries to keep the shock off her face, as Brenda's eyes bug out.

"And now Dawntae's not here . . . I can't help but have doubts. At some point, I guess it's hard not to. What if it's not all that other stuff? What if it's what we're all secretly afraid of and we're really in danger? What if all these people went missing . . . in the woods?"

Temple zones out for the rest of the readings. She stands beside the pile of books, eyes frozen on the twisting fire.

"Why don't you dig up her body and find out for yourself?"

Missing persons. Multiple.

There's supposed to be just one body she's looking for. But she knows her dad.

This isn't a coincidence.

From the head of the circle, Lam pops up with a clap of her hands—somehow louder than the claps of ten girls. Finally,

Temple can snatch her eyes away from the hypnotizing sight, watching Lam's teeth gleam in the firelight.

"Alright, y'all," Lam shouts. "Now that *Hearts Stop* has officially been voted the definitive, best damned horror book to ever exist"—laughter breaks out around the circle—"it's time to get your jackets, stretch your legs, and toss your trash. The last activity of the night is one that I thought you'd all appreciate."

The girls all burst up at the tail end of her words. The sounds of trash and bags and the swish of jeans starts sounding around the circle. One girl groans so loudly when she stretches her legs that all the others automatically huff out a breath.

"Make sure to get all your trash, girls," Brenda calls softly. "You don't want a squirrel choking to death on your bag of Doritos."

Lam effortlessly speaks over the bustling. "We've got our big-ass TV set up in the mess hall, and we're gonna watch *It: Chapter One* on Blu-ray."

Some girls clap while the others half-whisper in affirmation. Temple can't take another book, but if there's a TV involved, it must be some show they have to watch. She stares at the pile of books beside her, wondering just who is taking all that shit inside.

She turns back to the open door of JG, glittering lights hitting the gravel. She makes out a darting shadow above.

Pop! Pop!

Girls shriek and duck. The monstrous clap overhead vibrates in Temple's ears as her eyes dart back up. She looks for the twist of darkness she'd just seen.

"Fucking nutsack!" Brenda cries.

Lam's laugh is breathy and light. "Watch your language, babe."

"Oh my god, what was that!" one girl shrieks.

"Was that a gun?" Brenda hisses. "Did somebody find our g—"

Pop!

More screams. Temple watches Lam's spine straighten, her back to the still-burning fire. Temple follows suit.

If Lam's not worried, Temple won't be either.

"It's not a gun," Lam says. "It's fireworks." Her words are undercut by the sound of a scream, the kind that pierces the night and raises bumps over Temple's skin. Then, another pop.

And it all becomes clear.

Light blasts across the sky, a brilliant arc that sparkles and hisses in reds and greens. It bathes everyone's faces in a nice glow before sputtering into nothingness, falling behind the trees, into the grass, into the dirt. It's pretty.

But it's also a bad idea.

"Fireworks?" Temple mutters to Brenda.

That lip Brenda's been biting is turning red now, and Temple can feel the fear pouring off her.

"In the woods? That's a recipe for disaster," Temple says.

Another stream of smoke catapults into the air, and Temple follows the curve with her eyes, right to its source. A bleed of pitch black in the blues of the night sky, blocking out the stars and the clouds. The shadow on the roof jumps up and down, sparkler sizzling at her midsection.

"Girl," Temple says finally. The figure cackles. Carefree and light, and so blissfully stupid that she must not know what this much fire could do to trees, clothes, books. Her purple yarn braids fly behind her with each jump. "Up on the roof."

Everybody looks up at JG at the same time, holding their breath.

"Is that Cali?" someone asks.

Temple takes a step forward. No matter her mixed feelings, she can't just let North Point go up in flames. The campfire warms her back as she stomps over to the scratchy brick, fingers grazing the wall before an arm stops her.

It's Lam.

Lam glares up at Cali like it's just the two of them in the boxing ring. "I've got it," she says.

Temple almost argues. But the words die on her tongue when Lam hops up on the windowsill in one leap, curling her muscular arms around the edge of the roof overhang and lifting herself up with pure core strength.

Whoa.

Temple was planning to do something similar, but much more akin to slowly crawling up the wall using the grooves in the brick. She's skilled at climbing trees, and sometimes a wall can be just as forgiving as a good trunk.

But—seeing it in person, that's not similar at all.

"One more!" Cali shouts as Lam approaches. Whatever Lam says back is lost in the wind, and Temple backs away from the wall with a tight feeling in her chest.

Lam grunts, snatching the sparkling firework from the girl's hands and stomping on it with her thick-soled boots. She glares at Cali like a cat that has to deal with people.

"*Please*," Cali whines.

"No."

"What? Why? I just—*hey!*"

A baby-blue bag comes flying over the side of the building, and Temple catches it with an easy step back. Encompassed in her arms is the whole arsenal of fireworks and sparklers.

"Holy shit," she says aloud.

"I love you, Cali, but you have to stop pulling this shit," Brenda shouts up to the roof.

Of course, now the peanut gallery has deemed it safe to approach and Temple is no longer alone. Eyes all peer into the dark sky at the shadowed silhouettes of Cali and Lam, but it still makes Temple tingle. The eyes feel like they're on her.

She feels like she's shrinking, like she can't breathe. Some unexplainable pressure claws into her, and she fights the urge to lash out with her nails like an animal.

"I thought you'd like it!" Cali shouts back.

Brenda pushes through the crowd that now is at Temple's back. "I did like it," Brenda shouts up. "But now I like that it's over, and that you're not going to do it again." And then she laughs, stepping back as Lam tosses over more wrecked paper from the used fireworks.

She *laughs*.

The sound burrows into Temple. Turns her inside out. And the voice rushes in one ear and out the other:

"Why would I like this? It's tainted. Just like everything in this family."

She blinks her mother's voice away, and then she looks around to find the girls are making their way through the campsite, into JG. Some girls rub their arms in the cold, while others carry armfuls of garbage. Brenda hangs back.

When she makes eye contact with Temple, she sighs. All business again. None of the light that shined in her eyes when she spoke to Cali. Brenda nods to the book bag Temple holds in her arms.

"Find a place for that, will you?" Brenda says. And she disappears into JG just like the rest of them.

Temple clenches her biceps around the firework guts, the jagged pieces on the inside pressing into her skin. It feels just a little bit colder than before.

RE: TRANSCRIPT COPY 0926—THOMAS BAKER MEDICAL RECORD CHECK-IN

On 20 September at 18:05, Joshua Boyle <j.boyle@evcon.com> wrote:
This is the selection I removed from the previous transcript (RE: Lawyer visitation regarding the health condition of Thomas Baker). It has been transcribed upon your request. Find the invoice attached.

Cheers,

Josh

JOSHUA BOYLE

Head Paralegal and Records Officer

Evcon Legal Services

EXCERPT:

[removed at 01:49:45]

TEMPLE BAKER:	What the—will you stop trying to slide me your wet envelope?
THOMAS BAKER:	Why do you insist on being so difficult?
TEMPLE:	Why did you wait until the lawyer guy left to start being weird?
THOMAS:	Charlie has a name, Temple.
TEMPLE:	And why would I care? [paper rustling] Yes, Temple. Of course I did it . . . What the hell is this? Did someone send you another threat?
THOMAS:	I wrote that.
TEMPLE:	You're not trying to give me a will again, are you? Don't. Steve's always listening.
THOMAS:	It's Charlie.

TEMPLE:	Whatever.
THOMAS:	[pause] You keep insisting I didn't kill your mom, right? You think I'm crazy?
TEMPLE:	Yes. A thousand percent, all my life. And if you'd play along better, it'd be easier to get you transferred.
THOMAS:	They're not gonna let that happen, sweetie. I killed twenty men.
TEMPLE:	Allegedly.
THOMAS:	I confessed.
TEMPLE:	Yeah, to *fifteen* of them. Besides, you're . . . [pause]
THOMAS:	Temple.
TEMPLE:	You don't even know where Mom's buried. You barely remember the killings. Really, it's more likely you imagined the whole thing. It doesn't matter what you think I'll find. I'm not going back, Dad.
THOMAS:	I swear she's buried there.
TEMPLE:	Prove it.
THOMAS:	You won't let me. [pause] Just go back, baby girl.
TEMPLE:	I'm not gonna. Even if I wanted to—North Point's a camp now. It's private property. Belongs to the school district. If I take one step there I'll get arrested.
THOMAS:	You could go to the camp.
TEMPLE:	[scoff] Wow.
THOMAS:	If you go to the camp, you won't get arrested. You'll just be another one of the campers, like all the other girls at that school of yours.
TEMPLE:	I'm nothing like the other girls at my school.
THOMAS:	None of them? Not even your friends?
TEMPLE:	Prison must have really gotten to you if you think I have friends.

THOMAS:	[pause] You're a brilliant girl, sweetie. A natural-born leader—you should have all the friends in the world.
TEMPLE:	I'm none of that, dad. I'm Black Boo Radley. Squirrel eater. And friends are just mistakes with good PR.
THOMAS:	[coughs] You can't— [coughs]
TEMPLE:	Dad? Maybe I should leave.
THOMAS:	There's no vomit this time.
TEMPLE:	Your hands are shaking. You're sick. That's why I want to get you out of—
THOMAS:	I killed her.

[silence until 01:53:09]

THOMAS:	She bled more than I thought she would, but it was outside so who cares? I killed her. Chopped her head off.
TEMPLE:	Stop lying.
THOMAS:	I'm never getting out of here, Temple. I killed your mother. Chopped her head off. Drained her blood. Branded her bones. Chopped her head off before I drained her blood and I—
TEMPLE:	Why are you saying this?!

[crash]

THOMAS:	You always wanted to know why she went missing, didn't you?
TEMPLE:	Yeah. I did. But then I realized that it didn't matter. Because you didn't do it.
THOMAS:	[whispering] I did.
TEMPLE:	I'm not a little girl anymore, Dad. I know exactly the kind of games you like to play, with your warning letters and your fake mental breaks. You didn't kill mom. You just didn't. And if I have to go to the farm to

get to the bottom of what you're *really* trying to hide, I will—

[creak]

CHARLES GUNNER: Sorry about that—the call took longer than I wanted. [pause] You ready to continue?

[silence] [unidentified noise] [paper rustling]

THOMAS: I think it's better if we stop here, Charlie. [pause] Temple isn't feeling well.

CHAPTER FIVE

"W*hy mutilate the bodies, Mr. Baker? Why go to those lengths?"*

"*I don't mutilate them.*" *Her dad's crackling voice was quiet, but he said the words unashamed.* "*I brand them.*"

Temple shrugs on her sleepwear in the corner of the bathroom building, the shower fogging up the mirror as two more girls get dressed across the tile.

She'll never forget her dad's trial. The lawyer that stalked around her dad on the witness stand. The lights that flashed right in her face.

This is where her mind needs to be. She spent her time in the shower making some much-needed adjustments. The whole room is over-lighted with fluorescents, bathing the blinding tile in bleached white that feels like it's overcompensating. Temple can barely even hide or avoid gazes in such harsh light. She manages, though, as her thoughts whirl. Now her head's clear and she knows *exactly* . . . what she doesn't know.

First of all, she doesn't know what the hell is going on in her dad's mind. That's normal, but things aren't adding up more than usual. If people are going missing around North Point Farms, it doesn't matter if people place blame anywhere else. That's not how North Point Killer fanatics work.

If anyone dies in the area, there are blog posts about it. Theories. And where there are theories, there are letters. There's no way her dad doesn't know about the missing people Brenda was talking about.

So the real mission is becoming clearer, even if she's not sure what it is yet. He didn't mention it for a reason. If the answer isn't at the Midpoint Tree, there's only one other place.

Temple's thoughts halt when she hears a gasp.

"Temple . . ."

She turns, her shirt half on while she scowls around the stark white room. In the time since she started putting on her clothes, the other girl left. Now it's just Temple and Cali, and Cali's eyes are saucers, looking at Temple like she has two heads.

"What?" Temple asks.

"Your back? What . . . what happened?"

Oh.

Temple pulls her shirt all the way on. She doesn't see it often, and she doesn't hide it on purpose. But she supposes nobody at North Prep would know about her scar. She pushes her arm over her shoulder, rubbing the glossy skin on her back tenderly. The burn scar covers almost all of her angel wing, rough and smooth simultaneously.

"I was burned as a kid," Temple says sharply. *Mind your business. Ignore me.*

Cali keeps staring. The sound of a match strikes, and it feels like it's right next to her ear. Temple closes her eyes.

"If you'll excuse me," she says, and she's snatching up the rest of her shit as quickly as she can.

"It looks like it fucking hurt," Cali says as Temple passes.

No shit.

Temple shoves her way out of the showers, passing the toilets while her back feels like it's burning with every drag against the cotton of her T-shirt. Before the memory can crawl over her, her sandals hit the soil, and the night air fills her lungs, calming her pounding heartbeat.

Temple crosses the empty clearing, past the firepit in its center. After a while, the wind chills her neck and goose bumps rise around her damp collar. She climbs her cabin's steps with a bounce like that'll shake it off, but nothing can stop that chill. Her sandals clomp against the wooden steps as she hops up, and she throws her towel over her shoulder.

Temple opens the door to her cabin and stops short when four pairs of eyes dart to her.

The girls are all over her own bed, leaning over her bag. Different shapes and sizes—variants of brown. And they're blinking. Fast. One girl has her hand on the suitcase's front flap that's nearly fallen off, and Temple feels herself heat up as red tints her bronze cheeks.

Her heart drops to a pit in her stomach. That dread you feel when all your secrets have been discovered.

She swallows. "What the fuck are you doing?" Temple asks, closing the door behind her with the back of her shoe. She keeps her voice hard. Cold. Because that's what she needs to be.

Nobody speaks up.

They *do* step back in unison as she takes a step forward, though. Like they could pretend they were never there. Temple looks beside her pillow, and her small leather case is still safe in the corner. Untouched. It's dingy and old, like most of her things, but it belonged to her dad—small as a glasses case, with worn leather and a bright orange zipper pull.

It's stuffed with three knives and a box of matches.

It's safe. It's untouched. To Temple, that's all she needs to breathe again.

Her reputation as a mean-but-OK camp counselor is still intact.

She doesn't care about them stealing anything else—not the confiscated fireworks she shoved under her bed, or her phone, or even her little pouch of dollar bills. All of her fear and anger floats away, rushing right out of her when she needs it most. She has to remember—she's not one of them. She's an outsider.

Even without the anger that catapulted her into the room, Temple marches up to her bed, slamming the suitcase shut. Drops her towel onto the mattress. "What. The fuck?"

One girl pops out from the line, and her short little blonde 'fro curls over an impressive scowl. "You're not gonna scare us!"

Temple glares back, stepping closer. "Is that why you were looking through my stuff?"

"We weren't looking through your stuff," she says.

"Yeah, you left your shit open," another girl chimes in.

"So it's open season on it, then?" Temple asks.

And then *another* one chimes in. Probably—there are way too many girls all against her at once. They all blend together.

But this one speaks all in a single breath. "Yaya saw a mouse, and then Natalie tried to find it, but we couldn't, so we didn't know where it could hide and thought that if your bag stayed open it could get inside, so we—"

"You're all pathetic," Temple says hotly. "You think I give a shit about a fucking mouse? Keep your hands off my shit and just call me next time, or else I'll—"

Her words—wherever she'd go with that, because the only part of her that knows is the blood rushing through her ears—are interrupted when one of the girls just starts cackling. Right in her face.

Temple glares over at her with narrowed eyes, but the laughter doesn't cease. It's the kind of laugh that bounces off the walls, that makes the other girls smile a little.

It makes Temple frown harder. She just got laughed at. This has to be some kind of new bullying tactic. Hysterics-driven bullying.

"What are you laughing at?" She tries her damnedest to keep her tone even.

"Oh my god, I think I get it now," the girl says.

Temple furrows her brow but can't bring herself to speak in the face of this nonsense. She turns her eyes up to the lights, the girl's laughter echoing in her ears.

Giggles is still trying to get her words out in coughs. "I get Temple now!" she says excitedly, pointing to the offending counselor. "I get how she's such a bitch, and the Anysaa thing. And why she never talks. And those *boots*."

Another girl blinks. *The reader*, Temple remembers. Her thick, fuzzy sweater has to be much too warm even in this cool weather, but Temple doesn't blame her for wearing it. Her body fills it nicely. "Oh my god, Mickaeyla," she says, and it's like they're multiplying. She starts laughing too, shaking her head as she goes back over to her own bed. "Oh my god, I know what you mean!"

"She's like a mini-Lam!" Giggles—Mickaeyla—shouts.

The room erupts in a laughter that makes Temple's insides curdle. She doesn't even dislike Lam, but she certainly isn't a mini-anyone. And she's not one of *them*. If she was, she'd just stick her head in an engine. Same level of tolerable.

But when she opens her mouth to argue, Mickaeyla puts her hand up. "Whatever mean thing you're gonna say, choose silence," she says through a big, wide smile. She's got a gap between her two front teeth that draws Temple's eye. "Y'all, don't you see? Lam's awesome. This weekend might actually not suck," Mickaeyla says.

Temple narrows her eyes. "I'm not anything like Lam." For some reason, that makes the others laugh as well, and they disperse from crowding around Temple's bed.

The air seems somehow clear, even though Temple doesn't want it to be. She wasn't supposed to fight with the girls—she knows that. But now that doesn't seem like such a bad idea. One of these girls could take a punch.

"Y'all were riffling through my stuff!" she whines. She doesn't mean to, but it comes out that way. She's lost her powers of intimidation.

The girls just go *normal* on her.

"Oh my god!" Sweater starts. "Did you see the *ring* Lam got Brenda?"

"Don't they get married in, like, a month?"

"Yes! They're so cute! I heard they invited Cali and Anysaa *both*."

"That's gonna ruin things."

They're now all at their own beds, ignoring Temple as if she's not a threat at all.

She zips her suitcase closed in a production kind of way, making too much noise and throwing it beside her bed. "Whatever. I don't care anymore."

When she hops onto the stiff mattress, the girls are looking at her again.

"What?"

"Nothing," Mickaeyla says. "Just ignore us."

"I planned on it."

A snort.

Temple leans back onto her pillow, staring at the ceiling as the girls' words fill the room.

"Tell us about the bi life," someone says to Mickaeyla. "Tell us about your boyfriend troubles."

Temple closes her eyes.

And then they launch into the most cyclical nonsense, filled with gossip about people Temple doesn't know or have any interest in.

"So instead of telling my mom about the camp"—Mickaeyla zooms through another half of a story Temple only half-follows—"I told her I was sleeping over Cali's house. Then I went and hooked up with my ex-boyfriend so he could drop me off this morning."

Temple shifts to lay on her side, watching the girls all seated together at the edge of their own beds. Mickaeyla points in the general direction of the path that leads to the highway.

"Why didn't you just take the shuttle?" Temple asks. She doesn't want to contribute. The words are out before she can weigh the pros and cons.

From the collective sigh the room blows back, Temple obviously didn't say the right thing.

Mickaeyla looks up at the ceiling for support before slamming her chin back down. "Because then I couldn't piss him off. Obviously. He was so mad when I told him I'd be gone all weekend. He got all *straight*, you know?"

"I'm a giant lesbian," Temple says.

"Me and Cali still hook up sometimes." Mickaeyla throws a look at Sweater, who laughs. "But he acts like since I'm bi he *has* to be involved. Like if I want to fuck a girl, I have to fuck a girl *with him*."

"Disgusting," Sweater says.

Nothing has been cleared up for Temple. "How did this come up for a ride?" she asks.

"He thinks me and him are, like, *together* together." She stretches her hand out. "But it's not like everybody else says. We're just talking, fooling around."

This gossip is harder for Temple to keep up with than when she tried to read that Cary Lauren book—and those have magic in them.

The girls stop speaking, watching Temple and waiting for her to say something. Comradery. Temple's doing it—she doesn't know how she got roped in this, but she knows that's what's happening. All of a sudden, she's deep undercover.

When she waits too long, Mickaeyla supplies a prompt. "What about you, Temple?" she asks with a grin. "Who's your ride of choice?"

Temple blinks at her, her mouth scrunching up. "My first time fooling around with *anybody* was in an empty stall at the Farmer's Festival, and I realized I was gay the second he took his pants off."

The girls look back at her in silence, so Temple pushes on. "He tried to make me feel bad about it so I kind of . . . I don't know. Shoved him into the next stall over and all their apples ended up spilling into the street. It caused a traffic jam, and Aunt Ricki had to cuss out Ms. Potts—the apple lady—because she threatened to call the cops."

She looks back at them. This time, Mickaeyla breaks first. The sound of her laugh is like a bursting balloon, and then all the girls join in, until the sound of it is echoing off the walls. Temple can't hear the comforting sounds of night anymore—the brush of leaves, the croaks of crickets—all because she made them laugh.

She clenches her fists, watching them all laugh at her. It didn't feel funny at the time *at all*. Temple doesn't smile and presses the pillow over her face.

Temple fakes sleep until 3 A.M., when finally all she hears is soft snoring. The whispering and giggling stopped once half the girls fell asleep. She opens her eyes, lifts her head. It was Mickaeyla and Sweater—or Yaya, as Temple soon found out—that stayed up the latest.

The silence of the cabin is welcome. Without the girls talking, without their stories and laughter, it's much easier for Temple to remember that they're not the same. What brought her to camp and what brought the other girls are very different things.

Temple crawls from her mattress as silently as she can, feet padding onto the floor as she swipes one of her knives from her leather bag. She only needs one—but Temple also has her family knife, and a standard 4-incher.

The family knife isn't the kind you can play off as Girl Scout shit—it's unique. The handle has the pattern of the vines that loop around her dad's coins. Not the full design with the symbols and diamonds—just enough to dip in and out of the intricate designs. The four-inch blade is hooked and sharp—exactly the kind for carving patterns in wood.

And flesh.

And bone.

She drops her pajama bottoms, her jeans right beneath. She drags her boots from under her bed and shoves them on silently, then stuffs her knife into her hoodie pocket along with matches and the radio they gave her as a counselor.

Can't be too cautious. While she doesn't consider herself "one of the girls," she's not above calling for help on a solo mission.

The bugs buzz from outside, and the sound presses into the walls. The cabin settles around her, low and groaning. But it can't scare her away. Nothing can scare away someone who knows what fear is.

Her flashlight is the last thing she pulls from her pillow, keeping it off as the moon shines in through the cabin windows. The corners of the room are bathed in soft, white light. Temple's fingers shake on the door handle.

She throws a look over her shoulder. The uneasiness that tightens her chest tells her there should be someone staring at her, reaching for her, something.

But there's nothing. Just the shadows of the cabin's six bunk beds in the dark, and the swaying trees bending in and out of the window.

Temple inhales and exhales, pulling the door open and finally slipping out of Cabin Bey. The door creaks closed behind her.

For the first time in three years, she sets off to go home.

CHAPTER SIX

At first, her return to North Point Farms was almost nostalgic. In the daytime, the leaves look like they have all her life. They're the same ones that brushed her shoulder in the summertime, tangled in her hair in the fall.

Nighttime is different, though. It reminds her so viscerally of her dad.

Temple hasn't been to North Point Farms since she was thirteen. The urge to hum a song is overwhelming as she moves through the northern woods. The muscle memory that was such an integral part of night strolls, easy games.

It's a routine she's been forced to forget. But her body can't help but remember.

She and her dad were a duet. They sang through the woods for hours on end, peeking through the leaves and going so still, squirrels would climb on them. They did it for fun. They were half animal—they had to be. And only they understood. Only they understood *each other*.

Back then, she was good enough at climbing trees that when she and her dad played hide-and-seek, she'd rarely get found. They used birds, song, and the rustling of the wind to catch each other. If she peeked from the high branches of the Midpoint Tree and listened closely to where his song moved, she didn't need her eyes. She knew exactly where he was—where the birds were running away from.

And when they weren't singing or playing hide-and-seek, she was following him close behind, right at his heels.

"*What bird is that?*" she'd ask.

"*I think it's an owl,*" he'd say. Look up, squint. "*No, it's a falcon.*"

"*How old are you?*" she'd ask on a different day.

"*I don't know,*" he'd say. "*Forty?*"

The leaves would crunch beneath them if it was fall. The grass would soak her soles if it was spring.

"*Dad, where'd mom go?*" she'd ask.

He'd freeze. His eyes would dart to her, and he'd run his fingers over his forearms. Scars. The blood that had long-since dried was now faded on his skin, not quite healed.

Not quite fresh.

Then, he'd cast his eyes down.

"*You're it this time.*"

He'd toss her a grin that he showed no one but her and then crack into the trees in one leap. She'd squeal and forget her question, because Temple wasn't a good daughter, and chase after her dad, pretending she didn't care about anything else.

She forces memories of her dad away as she makes it past the half-hour mark of her walk. The Midpoint Tree should come up on the horizon, and while Temple can't explain why she can tell it from the other identical trees that line the path, she can.

The stars beam above her, framed in the tips of the silhouetted green, and she inhales deeply as if they can fill her chest. The sounds of crickets press over her papery footsteps.

She should've worn a watch.

She has no idea where she put her phone, either—she never uses it in the first place. Breakfast starts at seven, and making it is her first job of the day. She's got like three hours until dawn.

Temple trudges forward, inhaling the crisp night air. Breathes it out just to see if it'll fog yet. Then she reaches the two-mile mark. A clearing finally comes into view, inching over the horizon.

As she gets closer, a small house towers over the overgrown grass in the center of the break in the trees.

Its front wall is overrun with moss and the door is half broken off, opening its contents to the woods. It's almost in motion, like green is crawling out to be free from whatever's inside. A chain hangs loosely around the threshold, clanging against the wood like a bell.

On the roof, a thin antenna pokes up to the top of the trees— the newest addition to the centuries-old structure.

A few dozen yards farther, Temple makes out the Midpoint Tree. The house and the tree are like twins—they orbit close by one another. Without them, the farmland has no center point. The highway is the northern border and the campgrounds are the southern border, but without the house and Midpoint Tree, there is no telling how far deep into the woods one could go. They could swallow you whole, and probably would if given the chance.

Tilting her flashlight, Temple waves the low glow over the etched words scrawled over the doorway.

THE NORTH POINT HOUSE

The dilapidated building lurks in the shadows. Its slanted wooden walls hide the moonlight and cast her into thicker, deeper darkness, forcing Temple's shoulders stiff. She's not surprised it fell into disrepair. The house was centuries old. It barely held up throughout her childhood.

But if she has her way, the state of the North Point House will never be any of her business. All she has to do is find her mom and she'll never have to see her old home again.

⌐

The North Point House has had a complicated past life. For about a century, Baker Farms was the only farm that would hire Black folk with good pay. It was owned by some white family who loved money more than Jim Crow, and they eventually sold the land to Temple's grandparents. Temple's grandparents rented it out to a local writer—some rich bitch making her money off gay horror—and then her grandparents took it back and gave it to Temple's dad. Arguably, the worst owner of the house.

Now it's a communication tower—the phone line to the outside world. It's way too expensive to build new lines deeper into the forest. Temple remembers her aunt talking about that when she first took her in. Might as well repurpose the old cabin as something useful.

The sound of the wind creaking through the wooden boards that line the walls brings Temple back to herself. She feels the soil beneath her feet and watches North Point House stand before her, silhouetted deep black at the tip of its roof.

The old wooden doors tilt crooked on their hinges, banging in the wind against the wall every few seconds. The carvings in the grooves that once told the story of Temple's growing height have turned a smudged color, seeping with green. The windows are gone—shattered. Even the colored glass ones she used to trace her fingertips along are unrecognizable. As the vines and leaves twist at the base of her old home, the kudzu fighting its way up to the roof and into the crevices of the wood, Temple blinks.

Three years make a hell of a difference.

Now that she's here, she's not exactly sure what her plan should be. Temple was just imagining . . . searching for the body. But that plan didn't work out so well for her the first time. And it's not only about the body anymore.

If she wants to get somewhere, she needs to think beyond her dad's bait. She's got to think of the *trap*. The missing people he must have wanted her to find out about.

If her dad knew about the disappearances, then he sent her back to camp for a reason.

And that reason isn't her mom.

Temple wipes her dampening hand on her pant leg as she raises the flashlight in her other hand. Her fingers tremble. To most people, the chill would come from knowing who used to live there. The North Point Killer.

The man of lore.

But Temple doesn't feel that fear. She's afraid of what awaits her inside.

Temple climbs the steps, holding her breath. She has no clue what he expects her to find. The door creaks as she steps in, the sound grating on her already-withered nerves.

Her dad had said something strange when he confessed. "*You always wanted to know why she went missing, didn't you?*"

Temple acknowledges that her dad always says strange things—but she "always wanted to know why she went missing"? Temple never wanted to know *why* her mother was missing. She always asked what happened to her.

As Temple pushes deeper into the room, a chill sets into her bones. She resists the urge to wrap her arms around herself—only because she wants her flashlight steady.

Halt, the house seems to tell her. *You don't wanna do this, dumbass.*
What an astute house.

She *doesn't* want to risk an asthma attack going into some moldy old building that probably has *at least* one rotting corpse. But she's on a mission.

Temple walks in farther despite her foreboding, and once she crosses the threshold, the shadows gather around her. The floor creaks under her weight. The rush of cold air blows against her face. Her fingers form a mask over her nose and lips.

Inside, North Point House smells mossy and thick, wrapping around her throat when she steps deeper into the grime. And even with all the dirt, all the mold, all the grit that slides against the soles of her boots, it's nothing compared to the cold.

She looks around, trying to take in everything as her breath billows before her. Her eyes adjust to the darkness as the gray mist spreads and fills the space. It's all mostly unchanged.

There are three open rooms and a single door to the bedroom. Each is tiny, with high, thin windows to the outside.

More like a prison than a cabin.

The front room is the living room, with hardwood floors and a single desk, which holds a phone—a new element in the room. Its blinking light bounces around, bathing everything close by in red, then back in shadows. Over and over again.

She slides her feet across the grimy hardwood, the floor crackling and groaning every third step. The books that clump together on top of the desk have wilted, basically. They gleam a little but mostly hide all the wood in crooked, uneven piles. Dust coats their covers, and lighter shades of brownish gray indicate years-old fingerprints.

Temple closes her eyes, imagining it's five years ago. If she looked up, and she was eleven, she'd find her dad cooking dinner. If she made it known she was watching, he'd smile back at her. It's all exactly what she pictures when she pictures "home."

But it's no longer her home. It's no longer allowed to be.

She opens her eyes, pressing her fingertip against one of the book's pages' edge. A Bible. Temple's mom always kept them on the table. The cover squishes to the touch, but she can make out the little glimmer of gold-edged pages. Even if they're covered in gunk.

She pulls her hand away. The house isn't so out of use that the ceiling is falling in, but it's clearly been a few years. Most of what once was there for her family—and for her grandparents—has been moved somewhere else. It could be in storage, sold off, thrown away. Temple will never know.

The chair beside the desk is rotted and flipped over. The walls are painted in some places and not in others, mismatched colors revealing where old appliances once were.

The bedroom is in the far back. An old mattress with an iron frame, barren with no bedding, is crooked against the wall. The bathroom's yellow tile reflects moonlight over the hardwood floor.

Now that she's older, it feels as small as a closet. Hopefully, its size means it'll be easier to tear apart and search through.

So it's time to get to work.

Arm resting on the wood of the door, Temple stops her fidgeting. She'll play her dad's game the only way she knows how—and that's looking for coins.

Damn it, she's about to look silly as hell.

Ever since childhood, Temple's dad would play the coin game with her. It was the only way he could distract her. Bury some iron brands in the yard and send her out after them. Tape one on the ceiling and see if she can get it down. Hide one under the book-shelf, hide one between the Bibles.

And no matter where he stuffed them, Temple never failed to find them.

If he wanted her to find something other than her mom's body—say, for example, an empty body bag—Temple was sure to find a coin with it.

She turns her eyes back out to the living room. The sound of the wind whistling through the loosened wood bounces around her and makes her grind her teeth. She should move confidently. The darkness could never overwhelm her.

And yet, Temple still hesitates before stepping deeper into the room. The cold air rolls over her shoulders and she shivers, hands shaking from more than cold. It's with such a force the batteries inside the flashlight rattle. At least it pushes away the silence that seems to coat her. She takes another step forward.

Bang!

Temple shrieks. Her flashlight bounces and she nearly fumbles it, catching it inches above the ground. She peers into the darkness wildly as the stream of white light flits to every corner.

"Why don't you dig up her body and find out for yourself?"

Temple takes another step forward.

The deep dark of the cabin stares back. There's nothing there. Just silence. Empty rooms. The fog of her breath.

In any other house, any other farm, any other woods—maybe that would be enough. But she's on North Point Farm, and Temple Baker is her dad's daughter.

Bang!

She only flinches this time. Clenching her jaw, she begs herself to stay in control. She has no clue where the coin is, but she has to find it. That's the only way she can leave.

Cracking begins to echo throughout the entire house. Like the walls themselves are snapping. Like ice is shattering.

As long as the bangs stay bangs, Temple doesn't need to panic. Her dad was known to say a lot of nonsense. Rambling, nonsensical musings that she was convinced were just crazy talk.

But he always said bangs aren't real. That they're not something to be afraid of.

Even if it means she may no longer be alone.

CHAPTER SEVEN

Flexing her fingers, Temple runs her hand over the little box in her hoodie pocket and relief flushes through her. The matchbox she stuffed in is still firm, and her knife is wedged in right beside it.

With the matches alone, Temple's got enough firepower to Fourth of July the whole damn forest if she has to. Honestly, she's willing to be creeped out to do her dad's bidding, but she's not going to die for it.

A scream whispers through the house, like it's miles away and between the walls at the same time. Temple blinks in the direction of the noise. Waits for it to escalate.

When nothing happens, she moves forward again.

The room stays quiet. Temple creeps deeper inside, her arms close to her chest as the walls seem to stretch over her. Almost as if they're in time with her breathing. But they're just walls, Temple tells herself. They're still; they can't hurt her.

Somehow, she keeps going until she reaches the back doors. Even though it feels like the house is watching her, she keeps putting one foot in front of the other.

The bedroom door swings softly and creaks. There's no wind that Temple can feel. She peers into the room, still feeling as if she can't enter. The floors are completely clear. She can see the shadows of the bed reaching outward, but there's nothing but dirt on the hardwood beneath. Leaning over it, a stand-up mirror's silver lining peels, overshadowed with dust.

The cabin's insides are exposed to the outdoors, but the temperature varies from room to room. She grips her flashlight tighter. With her hands occupied, she won't be tempted to run her arms over the goose bumps that spring up on her skin.

Her ears catch a distant muffle—she pauses. The floor stops creaking. The sound goes away.

She turns toward the other door, the bathroom. The yellow is softer in the dark, flashing orange with the red beaming from the phone behind her. Part of her feels like she's in a sci-fi movie—and the ship is begging her to evacuate.

But nothing's happened yet. Temple isn't ruled by fear. At least, not outwardly.

There's no toilet in the bathroom anymore. Just a bathtub that's filled with leaves and grime, from even before it was abandoned. A blooming scar of black coats the tile on the back wall, from the fire.

Temple stares at the mark. The room feels just a little cooler. Her skin starts to itch, and she ignores it—she can't get freaked out. This room is much more familiar to her than her parents' room.

She takes a step inside, the soles of her boots grinding into the wet sediment on the floor. Past rains and intrusive vines have over-taken what used to be clear, white tile. Now, everything is covered with green and soil.

Plump gnats fly and smack her. Crawl on her skin. Flutter up the walls.

In the tub, the old bed of leaves has broken down over the years. Now, it's basically a garden. Weeds wrap around the lip of the browned ivory, curl beneath the rusted spout. Temple crouches beside it, running her hands through the looser brown that lines the bottom. It's cool to the touch. Filled with some bugs, some thicker twigs.

Brown darts through her vision as a mouse sprints out of the room.

"Shit," Temple hisses, standing back to her full height. The moonlight is at her shoulder, beaming through the missing window. She narrows her eyes at the windowsill, which has also been worn down by time. In the corner, where sanded glass is scattered in the crevices of the wood, a brown stain clumps together like liver.

Temple turns her head toward it, unable to look away. Maybe because when the window light hits it just right . . . it's red.

"*Shut up!*"

Temple freezes.

She heard the voice so clearly, her skin pimples like it felt breath on her shoulder.

A voice.

Words.

Her dad's bloodstained face pops into her mind. Staring down at her. "*Listen to your father, baby girl . . .*"

Now Temple's a lot more than shaky. She slips her knife from her pocket, holding it in front of her as she creeps toward the bathroom door. The curved end of her family knife knocks against the wood, scraping off a thin line—doesn't even look lethal. Temple narrows her eyes, her dad's voice ringing in her ears.

"*Don't ever ignore the voices again.*"

Bang!

Bangs are fake. But voices are real.

That means it's time to go.

Temple darts through the bathroom door, ramming her arm on the jamb on her way out. When she gets to the living room, the temperature's dropped about ten degrees.

Slam!

The bedroom door slaps shut. On its own, right before Temple's eyes. Her heart pounds in her ears. The room's darker. Her feet are slowing. Changing directions. She doesn't have time to be afraid. Doesn't have time to be shocked—shock can get you dead.

Slam!

The bathroom door slams shut behind her.

If it's possible, it gets even colder. Temple grips her flashlight tighter, sliding the light all across floor so that she doesn't trip again. She's not going fast enough.

She's still sprinting for the front door.

The muffled noises come in again, clearer.

They get louder as Temple moves. She pauses—and the voices quiet. They're still there, just . . . lower. The sound crawls over her skin. Sends goose bumps rippling across her neck.

Temple moves forward again. The voices gain volume. Screaming.

Her flashlight shakes as she tries to steady her breath. She can't give up. She keeps moving forward until the sound is clear. Voices . . . a woman. Screaming.

Whispers and voices are real.

Her hands scrape against the rusted metal door handle, something sticky rubbing off on her palms. She tugs. The metal groans.

But it doesn't budge.

"*Shut up!*"

Temple tenses at the scream again. It burrows into her, and she trembles. She tries the door again—it *should* open. Its hinges are barely intact. But it's as if something seals it shut.

A line of frost curls its way over the clear windowsill, twisting like there's fresh snowfall.

Everything goes oppressively silent as the room darkens further. The blinking red mixes with the blue ink that spreads over the wooden floorboards. Purple. Black. Purple. Black. She nearly closes her eyes against the light. The chill of the darkness burns, and Temple's breath floats in a graceful bloom before her.

It's oppressively silent—even the screams stopped. But she'd heard voices, and she has to get moving.

Creak . . .

The bathroom door drags open again. Shadows dance across the yellow walls. Forms. Figures.

Temple turns back to the front door. It still doesn't budge.

Bang!

Temple feels the flutter of wind on her face. That sound is too close. The dark in the room seems like it's moving. It's halfway across the table.

It's coming for her.

She can't just stand there trying to get out the door all day.

Temple darts away. She won't be a sitting duck. She runs for the bathroom just as another bang sounds behind her. The footsteps . . .

Thudding.

Stomping.

Running.

Temple screams, whirling around. A hand grabs her shoulder, and she rams the heel of her palm out, connecting with bone. She sprints forward blindly, ready to slash her knife. Even if her eyes are squeezed shut. She makes it to the bathroom door, hand on the wood, when a voice calls her name.

"Temple!"

Drip. Drip.

Blood hit the leaves.

Drip. Drip.

Her dad cast his eyes down to the thick roughage that snapped at his ankles, blood dripping from his fingertips. Steady streams of red just missed his eyes. He probably wouldn't have flinched even if they went in.

Temple stepped closer. She ignored the sticking of the splinters, as if the Midpoint Tree was trying to grab at her.

"What is it, Dad?" Temple asked. Her voice was much more steady than her breathing. Even more than her vision, which seemed to tilt off center the longer she stared at him.

Her dad kept breathing, narrowing his eyes. His boots thudded against the path as he stumbled forward, falling to his knees before Temple. He dropped to her eye level, so close she could make out the thin red veins bolting through the whites of his eyes. "Listen to your father, baby girl," he said.

The way his hands gripped Temple's shoulders made her grind her teeth.

She knew a lesson was coming. Her dad always said "Listen to your father" before he gave her a rule, gave her an order.

"Listen to your father, baby girl. Never go past the Midpoint Tree."

"Listen to your father, baby girl. Don't leave your room."

"Listen to your father, baby girl. Cover your ears."

Temple looked into her dad's eyes, forcing her breathing calm, presenting herself as she should be. A good girl. Good girls didn't die. Temple was a picturesque child—better than a real child. Picturesque children looked unafraid at all times.

He opened his mouth. Teeth were missing. The blood cleared from some of his brown skin, and she could make out new scrapes that lined his cheeks.

His grip tightened. His words came out fast, all at once. "Pay attention to how goddamn cold it is out here, Temple—you hear me? It's cold, *and it's dead—and it's banging and it's screaming, and it's fake." His grip got even tighter. Temple knew she'd bruise.*

But he wasn't finished. "If them voices call you ever, ever again, you come get me. Bangs are scary. Ice is dangerous. But voices are real." That gaze of his stayed firm on her. "Say it back to me."

Say what, start from where, she didn't know. He probably didn't, either. The fear that possessed him in these moments was fleeting, the warnings he gave her hastily fabricated.

"Voices are real," Temple echoed flatly.

That satisfied him. His face still dripped in a layer of fresh blood, while a second layer of crusted gore beneath already began blending into his dark skin.

"Good girl," he said, letting go with a slight smile. Red fingerprints got left behind on her nice dress, on her goose bumps.

CHAPTER EIGHT

emple halts. Slowly, she turns to the familiar voice, her heart still pounding.

"Cali!" she shouts. This time, it's in unquestionable rage.

Cali Wilson's crumpled on the floor, holding her arm and hissing through her teeth. Temple can see the fluorescence of the purple yarn in her braids, even in the low light.

While they've never spoken before, Temple definitely remembers this oak-skinned girl from glances-at-short-skirts past.

"Temple," Cali says through a breath. "Fuck!"

The fear she'd felt seconds before has evaporated. The room gets brighter, as if the moonlight swelled to chase out the darkness. Nothing is after her. Anymore.

Everything *looks* normal, but Temple isn't a fool.

With a chance to catch her breath, Temple crouches beside Cali and reaches for her cradled arm. It doesn't look that bad—even though Temple knows how hard she hit the girl, there's no doubt some dramatics involved in Cali's performance.

"You followed me here?" Temple asks. "Why?" As soon as she says it, a brief rush of fear washes over her—Temple doesn't like being followed. Whenever people follow her, it's never for a good reason.

She looks around the room, her heart in her throat as she searches for signs. Shadows hiding in the corners. People smirking at her, glaring at her. That feeling of dread that raised her hair just before she got jumped.

But there's nothing.

The North Point House isn't a trap . . . it's just a house.

Temple looks back at Cali, who's now writhing around on the floor like she's on her deathbed. Even if she was here for bad reasons, she doesn't seem to have anything planned.

As if to prove Temple's point, Cali sits up with a jerk. "Check your levels, you bionic bitch!" She puffs up, then wanes. "Did you break my arm?" Her limbs fly in all directions as if she can shake off the pain.

Nope. This isn't a surprise attack.

Cali may not be here to get the jump on Temple, but that doesn't answer why she is here.

"I didn't break your arm," Temple says. She cuts her eyes around the room, even though the floor's creaking has settled since Cali showed up.

Cali moves slow as she scrapes herself up off the floor—and Temple doesn't attempt to help at all.

Click!

The sound is low in the room, but Temple jerks her head up at the noise of it. A slow creak stretches beneath the silence as the front door drags open. It sways open inches before them as if it had never been stuck.

Cali takes ten minutes too long to get herself together. Even outside among the trees, it's still a little too dark and damp for Temple to be comfortable. Believing her dad's paranoia is one thing—believing in the banging and in the voices. Experiencing it for the first time is an entirely different story.

It makes her curious. Temple's been creeped out by her house before—obviously. But it's always been about what she knew went on in the woods, not in the walls. So if her dad had been right all along, and the voices were real, she can hear them now, too.

Whatever that means.

"I think this is gonna bruise," Cali says from beside Temple.

Shit.

Temple realizes she's been frozen for the past few minutes, staring at the old house like it could jump out and grab her. She forgot the other girl was there.

"Can you just think positive?" Temple says.

Cali glares back at her.

If Temple left a bruise, that's bad for her. Lam will fire Temple over something like that, and she can't weasel out of it—even if she thought that Cali had been something . . . dangerous. She crossed a line. It's not like she can defend herself by saying she thought it was ghosts.

"What are you doing out here?" Temple asks once she's focused again. "Campers are supposed to stay at the campsite!"

Cali tests her arm out again, lolling it around like it's made of licorice. "I followed you," she says as a matter of fact. "Well, at first I was just stealing food. And then I was gonna sneak into Cary Lauren's grave." She does a couple of squats—this makes even less sense. Temple didn't hit her legs. "I'd maybe pray to it, you know—get weird. But then I saw you leave your room at ass-fuck in the morning, and I knew you were up to some shit."

Temple can't even think up the words. She watches Cali do her little exercise routine, mouth popping open.

Cali has proven that she doesn't need cooperation to keep talking. "You're on the basketball team, right?" Temple can't answer before Cali's rolling her eyes. "I'm head cheerleader? You recognize me, don't you?"

This time, Temple's supposed to respond. The quiet stretches as Cali watches her, and Temple's almost scared to confess. "Yes?"

Cali dusts her hands off on her pants. "My dad works in tech," she says. "You know, software design and coding?"

"Is this a conversation? Is this how conversations work?"

"I mean, you could have just said you don't know," Cali says.

Embarrassingly, the answer *is* no. Temple doesn't know anything about cell phones, and she doesn't know anything about "tech," whatever that entails. She blames it on growing up on a farm, but that's a lie—she's met other farmer kids before, and they handle phones just fine.

"Well, my dad taught me a *lot* about computers. Even the bad things like finding stuff you're not supposed to find." Cali continues, "Since I see you don't catch my drift, I'm going to tell you a secret. But you have to promise to keep your mouth shut."

"Can you promise the same thing?" Temple asks.

"No." Cali shuts her down, and Temple can't decide if she was joking or not. Her chest puffs out beneath her crossed arms. The moldy, muggy smell of the cabin drifts on a breeze and burns right into Temple's nose. Her throat tastes sour as Cali speaks: "I know who you are. Like. Everything."

CHAPTER NINE

There's an owl somewhere up in the trees. It calls into the night quietly. Temple's heart drops. "What do you know— what do you think you know?"

"Thomas Baker is your dad," Cali says. "Even if I let you play me like that, I saw your pictures in the courtroom."

"Son of a fucking bitch." Temple turns to the trees, running her fingers over her twists. There's no arguing with that. Temple even knows the picture Cali's speaking of—teary-eyed, preteen Temple reaching over the ornate, pine divisional bar, just to give her dad one last hug. Sometimes it still feels like the wood is pressing into her ribs.

Cali keeps going. "You know, even though they didn't put your name in the articles, they did a really bad job of hiding your identity."

"No shit." Right beneath a header where her dad was penned a monster, or the Devil, or a dead man walking, her face was crystal clear. Hugging him was a stupid thing to do, and so she ended up in the papers.

Temple holds her breath, her lips refusing to ask the question her pride wants to ask.

As if she knows anything about Temple, Cali smirks. There's some real sadism to it. "Yes, I *do* know your full name. I know that's what you wanna ask."

God damn it. Temple looks down at Cali, clenching her fists at her sides. She just might throw up. Then she deflates. "How did you find out? My name's really common."

A leaf falls and flutters between them. Temple almost misses the chickadees, the squirrels—anything to distract her with sound.

Cali mulls her words over with the stars. "Two reasons." She holds up a finger. "I know everything about everyone here. Hacking's not so hard when your allowance is more than a teacher's salary. I literally can pay for anything. I was gonna work at Apple next summer, but my mama thought it was 'unethical to unleash Cali on the masses.' Direct quote."

That's easy to tell from the way Cali flourishes her voice like an American forefather.

Temple quirks her head. "What's hacking? I'm guessing it's not the cutting vines kind."

Cali can't suck her teeth any harder. "It's like looking through your computer without having to have your computer."

"I don't have a computer, though," Temple says.

"It's accounts, too," Cali says.

"But—"

"It's not just hacking," Cali interrupts, then flicks out another finger. "In middle school I was obsessed with serial killers. The regulars like Bundy and Jack the Ripper or whatever. But your dad's trial got really big in seventh grade, and I didn't have anything better to do."

Temple's memories of her middle school years are hazy. She remembers sitting alone in the house, hearing the barking of dogs out in the woods. She remembers the sound of the door when Aunt

Ricki kicked it open, swearing about the condition of the only home Temple's ever known.

She doesn't know how much the news covered because she wasn't allowed to watch it, but she knows it was pretty bad. She tries to forget what it was like to be that kind of celebrity.

"You must know all about him, then," Temple says solemnly.

"I know Thomas Baker is one of the most infamous serial killers in history. That this was his land, and that when they excavated it two years ago, they didn't find all fifteen of the bodies he confessed to—and they found five he never mentioned at all."

Temple clenches her fists.

"I know his parents owned this land before Cary Lauren did."

"How could you—"

"Even with private property, the true-crime Reddit finds a way," Cali says, pushing past Temple's frown. "And I know you're his daughter." She moves her hands like weighted scales as she speaks. "Even if you lie to me about what you're doing here, I already know."

Temple says nothing.

This isn't the first time someone's found out about her dad. It won't be the last. For the years before, Temple moved from school to school, keeping her head down. The easiest way to tell she'd been found out was the stalkers. The pictures online. The police showing up at her door.

She'd get scared, she'd tell Aunt Ricki, they'd move, and it'd happen all over again a few months later.

Temple looks up at Cali, her stomach twisting. She thought it'd be safer here, the novelty of the freak having long worn off. It wouldn't get any more serious than a few whispers, and as long as Temple didn't get close to anyone, no one could scare her off.

But if Cali knows who Temple is, that means she's that kind of follower.

"You're one of them," Temple says softly. "A North Pointer."

The kind of people that searched her trash and sent her bloody pictures of corpses and didn't listen when she begged them, *"Don't follow me"*—

"Of course not," Cali says—but there's a hesitation before she says it, like the words were tough to get out.

Still, Temple's spiraling halts.

Cali looks back at her. "I'm not one of those freaks, though I see why you'd make that kinda connection. I'm obsessed with the dark and gritty, sure—but only in a 'how does a killer think' cause I'm not finna get serial killed' way. I'm not the kind that's tryna be a killer's wife. No offense to your daddy."

Temple's still unconvinced. But Cali isn't deterred by the silence.

"As your official sidekick now"—Cali beams between her words—"I gotta say, you need to be more communicative."

"You're not my sidekick," Temple says. "There's no sides to kick."

Cali scoffs. "A serial killer's daughter shows up on his old dumping grounds all mysterious-like and you expect me to believe it's all a coincidence? You're up to something. And I wanna help."

Temple really hates know-it-alls.

"Why?"

"Cary Lauren. *Duh.*"

Temple opens her mouth. Closes it. A mosquito bite on her arm that she didn't notice before suddenly aches and itches. "Cali, so help me God, I will scream in the middle of this haunted forest. I don't care who hears it; I want *anybody* to kill us."

Unfortunately, Cali just laughs. "Harsh. But I have a real reason, I promise." Walking toward North Point House again, she sits on the front step, folding her hands in her lap. Temple watches her, making no moves to get any closer.

"So, this is going to sound crazy . . . but I *swear*, this is all fate."

I've heard crazier. "Explain. Fully. Completely. Like I'm five."

Temple gets another of Cali's dopey grins, and it really would fit better on someone who's actually endearing.

"OK, so I read *Hearts Stop* when I was nine, right? And when I looked at Cary Lauren's author bio, I immediately got all obsessive because she's from here." She glances up at Temple as if she'll understand, but since Temple doesn't, the pause goes by unacknowledged. "So I beg and beg my mama to let me meet her because I'm nine and have no clue she died over a decade ago. Of course she ain't know what kind of book *Hearts Stop* was—didn't even find out until, like, last year when the movie came out. And now she's all pressed to act like she's a fan when *I'm* the one—"

"Cali," Temple hisses.

And it actually works. Cali stops talking. Blinks. And nods. "Right. Topic. OK. So since my mama felt bad about my hero being dead, she called her art connects and got me in at some kind of big-deal charity auction thing at a museum so I could see a bunch of rare items and shit. Long story short—I found a *leatherbound*, authentic Cary Lauren notebook with her real handwriting and everything. Just lying there in a stairwell I was hiding in. Fate, part one."

"Why were you hiding in a stairwell?"

"Because I put a shit-ton of these Polish laxative chocolates on the catering table, and I didn't want to look suspicious. Let me stay on topic."

No argument from Temple.

"So I see the notebook on the steps, defenseless. No guards around because it's in the staff area. No art curator people because they're out on the floor. I know it's probably priceless and I'm *definitely* not supposed to touch it—but I'm nine and I'm me so I *immediately* pocket it and get to reading.

"It's got her sexcapades and gossip and some poetry and even some diary entries that I'm sure were *never* supposed to see the light of day. But when I get halfway through, this little slip of paper falls out of the cover like the shit is booby-trapped. It's written all perfect and neat—so clearly it was *meant* to be read. 'If you find this notebook, burn it. Allow me to leave the mark I wanted and hide away the parts of me I needed to hide. Disregard this journal, ignore my writings, leave me alone just as it always has been. They are the rantings of a madwoman.'"

Cali lets the choir of the woods punctuate her words, giving Temple a nonsensical but meaningful look. "You see?"

No, Temple didn't see. She doesn't have the mental capacity to follow any of that—any of Cali's unhinged logic.

But the girl still looks at Temple expectantly, like this is the moment she's been waiting for. "Like, laying the secrets to rest once you've unburied them. Only one person was allowed to read the diary—and it was me! Fate. Divine intervention," Cali says. "To this day, I keep the journal on my nightstand."

Temple leans back against a tree trunk, not knowing where to look. She's actually exhausted just listening to her. If she were a little more sleep deprived, she might have cried from frustration.

"Cali . . . that . . . that wasn't some kind of sign to justify you violating people's privacy. You realize that, right?" Temple asks as tentatively as she can manage. A little ire bleeds in anyway. "You read her diary and stole from a charity."

Cali pops up off the steps, dusting her butt with another smile. "Of course I know that's wrong *now*—but I didn't as a kid. I'm not all that smart, you know."

"Oh my god." That's it. That's the quota. Temple stalks away, having wasted more time than she should have on Cali's nonsense. She's already cutting it too close for the walk back to the campsite. There's no way she'll make it in time to get any sleep.

"But I still think I'm right!" Cali calls after Temple, her footsteps close behind. "She may have wanted me to burn her notebook, but she didn't want me to *ignore* her. I think she wanted just one person to really know her. If that weren't the case, why didn't she just write the warning on the cover or burn the book herself, you know?"

"Because she didn't think a stupid kid like you would find it?"

"You're the same."

Temple stops. The swish of the trees sounds like rain, with the crickets just as ever-present and loud. Cali stops, too. She wasn't as left behind as Temple thought she was.

"How?" Temple asks. "How am I even—what's similar between us?"

"I mean, you're worse than her, yeah," Cali says, waving away the insult like it didn't matter. "Cary Lauren was so alone she put all she had in a notebook no one would ever find because she felt like no one cared. You're alone because you think everybody's out to get you. So you just shit on everybody that gets within a yard of you."

"It's better that way," Temple says through her teeth. "You wouldn't understand—you've never had a target on your back."

"I think it's *fate* that I caught you in that shack, Temple. Cary Lauren's buried here, you know—she asked to be buried near her school. Which means she's watching over both of us right now, guiding me to help other people like she was. And I'm gonna do her so proud."

"By bothering me and pretending it's all fate." Temple starts walking again, but now their steps are synchronized. She can't even pinpoint when they began moving in time.

"The bothering part isn't required," Cali replies with a grin. "It's just my favorite part."

If it were anyone but Cali, it would be easier to tell if that was a joke or not.

They start along the pathway with Cali talking at Temple more than anything. The distraction is what lets the cold sneak up on Temple, but when she feels a chill run through her, she's on high alert.

She remembers the ice of North Point, the blue creeping along the floor. She knows that cold is a part of her dad's warnings—whether real or all in his mind. So she keeps walking, saying nothing. Looking. Watchful.

Cali is clueless. "Wow! The woods are, like, actually pretty."

Temple knows exactly what she's talking about. "Yeah, they are."

"No, really. Like, we could sell views of this place."

Just as Temple suspected, she looks up and sees the Midpoint Tree glittering farther up the path.

The highway, the Midpoint Tree, the North Point House, and the old school. That's all there is to the woods and farmland. And all throughout her childhood, Temple was banned from the highway and the old school. She had nothing but the house and the tree to look forward to.

But the Midpoint Tree was always the best part of her childhood. It was the thickest, best tree to climb when she and her dad were playing hide-and-seek. It was close enough that she wouldn't get in trouble for wandering off but far enough that it took her dad longer to find her.

And the Midpoint Tree is gorgeous at dawn.

The sun only slightly paints the horizon as they approach the tree, and Temple looks over it, her eyes eating up every detail. It's nearly silver in the light. The vines that grip along its center glitter like blurred stars as they twist into the ground, dividing the leaves at the base that curl away from the trunk like rose petals.

Cali is enraptured by the sight. Temple remembers the countless mornings she spent on her roof, waiting for dawn. When she didn't watch the sunrise, she watched the Midpoint Tree sparkle. When the sun was full out, it would dim like its beauty was a secret.

There are other trees in the North Point woods that sparkle. She found one on a coin search as a child. Another's behind the school, not that she's seen it more than once.

Who the hell knows why it happens.

She's just happy that it does.

Her eyes rake over the glowing roots up to the canopy as the light lessens, the branches twisting one last strut before they turn solid again. Then a flutter of blue cloth floats on the wind, taking Temple's gaze with it.

And her heart drops.

Cali sees it, too. "Is that a bird's nest?" she asks, pointing.

Cali wouldn't know a bird's nest if it fell on her head. Temple can't breathe, and she definitely can't form words. Because that's not a bird. Temple can tell feathers from shredded satin and tulle, dangling over the branches. She can tell shelled eggs from sagging, mossy skin.

Cali may have researched the North Point Killer, but she's never seen a corpse in person.

And firsthand experience makes all the difference when it comes to dismembered bodies.

Temple knows just by the sight of the dress. It's the kind that floats behind a woman like a wedding train. That floats behind a woman that has always been Temple's mother.

Her mother's favorite dress.

In this neglected, Northern Virginia forest where all her dad's victims are laid to rest, Temple's mother is jammed into a tree, hidden like a secret.

CHAPTER TEN

You've seen dead bodies before, Temple reminds herself, but the words feel hollow.

This is nothing new. It all feels like a lie.

Her stomach lurches, and she twists to the side, spewing last night's dinner in one heave.

"What the fuck!" Cali shouts, jumping away.

Temple can barely breathe. She closes her eyes, exhaling through the stone in her throat. Trying to convince herself that the anticipation of this means it can't affect her.

You knew you'd find this. You've seen dead bodies before. This is nothing new.

But refrains don't work when the smell of vomit burns through her nostrils. When she's doubled over in the grass, vision crossing with her hands clasped onto her thighs.

Cali watches it all, taking a step forward like she's going to go on without Temple. Temple instinctively grabs her arm. Her fingers shake on Cali's bare wrist.

"Wait," she says feebly. The words feel like they scratch her skin.

But Cali hasn't seen it yet. She pulls away in exasperation, and Temple almost falls over.

"Girl, I think you need a doctor—or, like, Brenda or something." She gives Temple's trembling hands a pointed look. "Are you *scared*?"

Temple forces her head down. She'll never confirm, and denial seems just as weak. But her eyes fight to look back at the tree, and the flinch in her shoulders is honest and obvious. "Th-that—up in the tree. There's—"

"A bird," Cali interrupts. Doesn't let Temple stutter it out before she whips her finger toward the sky. "And it already flew away! Are you that scared of birds? Didn't you grow up on a farm?"

Temple's back cracks as she straightens her spine. Her eyes drift back up the tree.

It's empty.

And now's the time to really think she's going crazy. "It wasn't a bird," Temple says slowly. Her breath's not coming out right. She claws at the front of her shirt, like it'll help. She should have brought her inhaler.

Her mother *had been* there. She wasn't seeing things; she'd been there and—

"God *damn* it!" Temple screams.

The finches that have just begun their first songs spring away, and their wings clap loudly through the trees. Her puke is going to start baking once the sun is all the way up. The sky is already blending pinks and blues for the sunrise yet to come.

What Temple needs right now is to punch something.

"What the hell is wrong with you?" Cali asks.

"I'm not losing my mind," Temple shoots back. She grabs Cali's arm, holding so tight she might be hurting her. But the anger's starting to replace the fear.

She didn't hallucinate. Her mother had been up there.

"There was a body up in the tree. I saw something up in the tree—I saw—" Temple stops herself.

"What? You saw a *body*?" Cali looks at her with a questioning eyebrow, probably gleeful about her front-row seat to the freak show. Temple can't lose it. She can't afford to.

So, once again, Temple closes her eyes. She calms herself while the image of her dad's lopsided grin invades her mind, so entangled with Temple's unnamed fears it's almost the manifestation of them.

Her dad thinks he's absolutely sane, too. Even though he's clearly not.

Temple's nausea fades after a minute of woodsy quiet. The sound of crickets humming through her will keep her calm long enough to walk and regroup.

This time she gets her words out. "Let's go."

Cali's still squinting down at Temple's vomit, repulsed like a kid. Then she jolts her head up. "Go? But what about—"

"I gotta be back in time to make breakfast," Temple says. She remains still, not letting her gaze go where it wants to. Refusing to look at that empty branch.

Cali takes the hint. "Sure thing, boss," she says with a mocking salute. And they continue down the trail toward the campsite.

"Protect me from the evil one. Protect me from the evil one. Protect me from the evil one."

The floorboards groaned as Temple inched toward the bathroom. The crack of light that poured onto the tile let in a smell of metal so thick it was almost distracting—almost.

"Mother?" Temple called.

Nothing could distract her from the sound of her mother's chanting.

"Protect me from the evil one."

A silhouette blocked the door and cut off the light. Her dad. He glared down at her, shadow deep and bending with a scowl down between his eyes.

"Listen to your father, baby girl," he said quietly.

"Protect me from the evil one." Her mother's whispers persisted.

Her dad didn't seem to notice. "Stay in this room. Don't leave until I open the door."

CHAPTER ELEVEN

C ali mostly leaves her alone, and there's nothing Temple appreciates more than silence. When she's forced to be in the house at the same time as Aunt Ricki, she keeps to herself and stays in her room. Sometimes she'll play music. Most of the time she'll look outside and watch the roads, watch the woods.

The campsite appears before the sun's shown up. There's still time, even though it's probably after six—much later than Temple wanted to get back. Their feet crunch over the gravel and grass and soil of the main firepit, and Temple's arm bumps Cali's lightly.

"I won't tell anyone, you know," Cali suddenly says.

Temple looks over at her, but Cali keeps her gaze trained before her. Her eyes are nearly closed and the dark color underneath promises some cartoonish bags.

If Temple were a different girl, maybe she'd believe Cali. But she's not, so she says nothing.

"I mean it," Cali insists. "You keep that shit a secret for a reason. And trans girls ain't in the business of outing people."

We'll see, Temple thinks. But outwardly, she nods. "I trust you," she lies. And from the way Cali glares over at her, it's an obvious one.

By the time Cali disappears into Cabin Aye, the sun is visible. Temple heads to JG without changing—she's already late to cook breakfast.

Wind blows over her skin, and she rubs her arms while she walks. A crow whizzes by, just a little too close—its caw seems right in her ear. The rustling of swirling leaves sounds beneath Temple's boots, thumping up the steps to JG.

The door opens on its own.

When she looks up, she's not surprised to find Anysaa there, smirking at Temple. She has on her camp shirt, a bright yellow T-shirt with the logo in the center. Looks entirely too put together for six in the morning.

She is, however, surprised to see Brenda—frowning, right beside Anysaa.

"I can explain," Temple lies. The words all come out in one breath.

But it's no use. Brenda's eyes narrow. "Temple." Her tone is foreign, so low and steady Temple's suddenly on edge. "You and I will talk later."

The Talk is all Temple can focus on. She stares into space throughout breakfast while the girls gush about movies she's never seen, monstrous villains she's never heard of.

And she spaces out just long enough for Lam to put her to work. "I've got an idea that might be up your alley," she said to Temple about an hour ago. "But it might get you punched in the face."

The "no thanks" on Temple's tongue died when Lam glared at her, so now Temple's hiding in the adults' quarters hunched beside the closed door, barely able to see.

The mask Lam told her to wear is sheets of plastic-looking beige skin crudely sewn together beneath a poorly done wig, fit for a cafeteria lady. Plus, it smells bad—like someone threw up in a Chuck E. Cheese and they immortalized it in rubber.

This is what Lam thinks is Temple's element.

She presses her hand against the flexible, sticky skin while her breath rises back up hot against her nose, her eyes. She doesn't remember breathing this hard before. Now it's all she can hear.

The muffled sounds of the girls' voices on the other side would be clear without the mask, but, well, one must suffer for art. She may be having some version of The Talk later on, but apparently, she could go out with a bang.

"Do you have to be so into this?"

The floorboards creak, and Temple turns the eye holes over to Anysaa, who pops out from the closet. Whatever she's got clutched in her hands claps against the door as she stumbles out.

"I don't like you. You don't like me. But Lam's scary, and she told me to help you," Anysaa says. "I don't know why she's acting like this is a two-person job."

They're alone in Brenda and Lam's room, which is absolutely spotless. It's made entirely of the same oppressive, harsh wood that fills the rest of JG. But this room is very simple: two twin beds—one holds their luggage while the other they clearly share—a desk, a mirror, and a closet.

Anysaa leans against that closet's door, hands clenched around a clunk of brown and black plastic. Neither of them has killed the other yet. Though if looks could kill, Anysaa's very close.

"Because teamwork makes the dream work?" Temple tries. No chuckles from Anysaa, though Temple's not sure robots *can* laugh. She drops her shoulders, deciding they're on the same page. "I don't know, Anysaa. Maybe they want us to make up because we're employees and all the girls are gossiping about us. Can't we just . . . pretend we're on good terms?"

Temple's not ready to get back to her normal snapping—not when Viola Davis here might decide to go for the Oscar again. She doesn't think she can take a breakdown from Anysaa right now, and the mere possibility of it happening again is a giant red sign to BACK OFF.

Not because she's guilty.

It's because . . . because Temple has no idea what to do with her hands when people cry.

And she'll tell Brenda exactly that when she asks.

As if she can read Temple's mind, Anysaa rolls her eyes, stomping closer and shoving the toy into Temple's hands.

"Here's the chainsaw," she says quietly. She turns it over, pointing to a little red button on the underside. "That turns on the noise."

She takes another look at Temple, who's just staring at her from under the mask. Anysaa *tsk*s. "When you're finished playing around, we have to set up for the Cabin versus Cabin."

"You do understand Lam *asked* me to do this, right?"

Anysaa doesn't answer. She pushes past Temple with a wide swing of the door, and Temple has to duck to keep from being noticed. Head Barbie returns to the Mess Hall with the others, smiling and chatting like she belongs.

Temple is left behind to watch.

The door stays cracked open a little, the girls' conversation drifting in. She doesn't listen at first. She whines to herself about how much she *doesn't* want to listen, doesn't want to wait, doesn't want to do The Talk.

But then it gets weird.

"Am I the only one who heard knocking last night?" one girl asks. Temple just barely recognizes the voice, but she thinks it's Wynter. One of the Barbie's sidekicks.

"Knocking? Bitch, are you serious?" Mickaeyla. "Don't get me started on last night."

"Something weird happened to you last night, too?"

Temple smirks beneath her mask. They don't even know the half of it.

One of the benches scrapes, and Temple imagines a girl standing. When she hears the voice, she knows it's Cali. "Well, everybody knows it's haunted out here. Who do you think the ghost is? Is it Cary Lauren?"

"No way—she wouldn't go out like that," Mickaeyla says.

Another girl snorts. "*I* think it's a witch, like in *The Conjuring*."

"What are y'all talking about, 'haunted'?" Everyone goes quiet at another girl's voice—Natalie from her own cabin, Temple thinks. "This place is haunted?"

Temple can practically *hear* Mickaeyla's dropped jaw. She can hear it in the girl's scoff she huffs out before she speaks again. "You've never heard about it?"

"Tell her, Mickaeyla," Cali says.

Temple pushes forward an inch and reaches for the doorknob. This is as good a time as any to pop out—get them when they're on edge.

"Well, there's a legend about North Point Farms," Mickaeyla begins.

Temple freezes. Stops moving. Stops breathing. Her shaking hand returns to her side as she listens.

Mickaeyla continues to her enraptured crowd. "If you pore through the forums like I do, you'll get the real picture."

"Rest in peace NPK Truth!" Wynter interjects, and there are a couple of cheers in reply.

"Don't get me started with NPK Truth getting shut down—all these new forums is trash. You know, the other day I was on that new new one with all the rules and shit—"

"Cut out the foreplay, Stephen King," Sweater Girl—Yaya, Temple corrects mentally—laughs. "Get to the point."

Mickaeyla looks properly sheepish at the tangent, while Temple's thoughts don't go beyond a dispassionate *That's a thing?*

"My bad," she says. "My point: All the missing people and the videos and the news stories. If you really dig deep, you'll start hearing the rumor that's been around for decades—that the North Point Killer was, in fact, possessed by a *demon*."

Gasps around the table.

Mickaeyla continues, clearly proud of herself. "They say that he wasn't human when he committed those twenty murders—and that the demon that took him still haunts the woods to this day. They say it's what inspired Death in *Hearts Stop*."

"Holy shit," Natalie says.

Yaya chimes in, a smile in her voice. "You know he's coming when you feel the room get colder—so cold you can see your own breath. But by then it's too late. Even the Lord can't save you then."

"Wait," Natalie says. "So there's a demon just walking around here? Killing people? I mean, I love horror, but this supernatural shit is always so wack."

"*'Wack'?* Cary Lauren basically *is* supernatural! She had to be into freaky shit the way she wrote *Hearts Stop*." Wynter scoffs.

Now it's Mickaeyla's turn to laugh. "You can believe it or not, Natalie; it really don't matter. We're just telling you what the forums say. But you should probably know . . ." She trails off, voice getting low again. Even Temple leans forward, though all it does is press her forehead into the door and the moist mask into her cheeks.

This is it. This legend is exactly what she's been looking for—something to account for the missing girls. Something her dad definitely would have heard about, why he sent her on this chase.

Mickaeyla continues. "They say it kills everyone just . . . like . . . the North Point Killer!"

"Bullshit," Natalie says.

"They say the demon's victims are still trying to get warm," Mickaeyla's voice rises theatrically. "Their spirits wander the woods and try to get into buildings—away from the cold of the demon. So if you hear a knocking, don't let it in . . . or else!"

Temple shoves open the door then, and it slams against the wall, the cracking echoing around the room just when she presses the sound button on the plastic chainsaw.

"Ahh!" Temple screams. She runs for the table as a girl screams, leaping up before Temple's even fully in the room.

Then a biscuit hits Temple in the forehead.

"Ow."

It plops down to the ground, glistening with butter—a picture of sadness.

But she's distracted for a second too long.

"Temple!" Mickaeyla shouts, laughing.

Got caught because they recognized her voice—which is insulting. Temple swore she didn't talk much.

Mickaeyla keeps on with her cackling, turning to a short, stocky girl with tears in her eyes. "Oh my god, K'ran, she scared the shit out of you."

"I thought I'd have to change my drawers!" K'ran shouts back. Temple knows her from the basketball team. She's wearing loose basketball shorts and an oversize camp T-shirt, like there's a court to hop onto.

The girls laugh heartily as Temple pulls up the mask, cherishing fresh air as she reaches down and picks up the biscuit. She takes a hearty bite—because, really, how could she just leave it there—and she's surprised to find only half of the girls staring at her in disgust. Mickaeyla's still smiling, Cali and K'ran on either side of her with matching serenity.

Mickaeyla leans forward. "What do *you* think, Temple?" she asks.

Temple stares back. The mask is now deep conditioning her hair probably, but she doesn't remove it completely. "About what?" she asks around a mouthful of bread.

"Did you hear the knocking last night?" K'ran asks.

"Do you believe in the legend?" Mickaeyla asks.

Then, the three girls sitting side by side all raise their hands, wiggling their fingers in time with each other. "*Ooh!*" they chime like little kids, and Temple stares back.

Of course she doesn't believe any of those stupid legends.

Her dad isn't haunted by some demon. He's a run-of-the-mill *human* monster. But Temple takes the stitch-face-guy mask off all the way, thinking carefully about her words.

"I didn't hear any knocking," she says finally. "And didn't they catch the guy that killed all those people?"

The girls look down at the table, clearly disappointed that she isn't playing along. She has no clue why they thought she would— oh, well, probably because she was standing there with a plastic chainsaw.

But Mickaeyla doesn't let up. She leans forward ever so slightly. "They caught the North Point Killer. But people are still going missing."

"So?" Temple asks. Her hands start to sweat.

"*So,* something freaky has to be going on! Take Lara Michaels, for example. If you didn't see her live, then you didn't see it. But those of us who were in the chat know what we saw."

"A branded dead body," Cali supplies. "Branded right on the bone."

Holy shit.

"What?" Temple chokes out.

And Mickaeyla knows she's got her. She smirks, crossing her arms as she stares Temple down. "A little over a year ago, Lara Michaels went on Instagram Live to document the haunting of Cary Lauren's grave."

"But she never came out," Cali says next. "We don't know when exactly she died—"

"Or even *if* she died," adds Yaya.

"But on the video, you can clearly see two bodies in the background," Cali says. "One body's naked, and there's *something* on its chest like the North Point Killer's brand."

"And the other body, that's the killer. *That's* the North Point Demon," Mickaeyla explains.

The girls clap around the table like this is performance theater, and Temple stares at them, trying to keep her heartbeat under control.

It's not like she believes the story. She turns her eyes out the window, looking at the woods that seemed to so doggedly stalk her the night before.

She definitely doesn't believe there's a demon out there.

But it might be what she's been afraid of. The obsessed fans, the bloody letters, the missing girls—someone might be going too far.

Her dad might have a copycat.

WATCH: INFLUENCER'S LAST MOMENTS CAUGHT ON LIVESTREAM

Transcript

LARA MICHAELS:	[laughing] The reddit says the grave's supposed to be at the three-mile mark, or something like that . . . I've been walking in this fuckin' dirt and grass and shit for like a damn hour.
@niecyinibihh:	Why didn't u bring nobody with u luv?
@mrsmrjungkookbae:	Where did you get that fiiiiiiiiit (0_0) u lookin THICK
LARA MICHAELS:	You not supposed to follow the path—that's all I remember. Do you guys think I'll see something? Do you think the ghost of the North Point Killer is still around?
@bigbitchtim:	It don't work like that he still alive boo
@bratatatheghetto:	she fine but she dumb hahahaha
@niecyinibihh:	leave her alone lmaooooooooo
@mrsmrjungkookbae:	I'm soooo jhealous
@findmeatnorthpoint:	I can't believe you got on the land. Last time I tried they called the cops on me SKJDGPA;DSG
@mrsmrjungkookbae:	Is it cold yet
@9sd9f0ads:	follow back shu 49 49
@niecyinibihh:	I heard someone went missing up there last week
LARA MICHAELS:	It's kinda cold, Mrs. Not too bad—I'm not sure, really. I ain't bring no jacket—it's like July already. But it definitely don't feel like July. Oh, Niecy, I def heard about that too. Somebody posted it in the forum just this Monday. I was like "Well, if some shit pop up around my Black ass, I'm out." I won't die for the 'gram, you feel me? [laughs]
@mrsmrjungkookbae:	OMG

LARA MICHAELS:	All I really want to know is whether or not you can see him.
@mrsmrjungkookbae:	OMG
LARA MICHAELS:	I know, it's awesome right?
@niecyinibihh:	LARA
@mrsmrjungkookbae:	OMG
@bratatatheghetto:	OH MY GOD WHAT WAS THAT
@niecyinibihh:	did I see what i think i saw?
@mrsmrjungkookbae:	LAARA BE SAFE
@bratatatheghetto:	???????????!
LARA MICHAELS:	What are y'all talking about?
@niecyinibihh:	THERE'S SOMETHING BEHIND YOU
@bigbitchtim:	holy shit
LARA MICHAELS:	No there's not. There's—
[SIGNAL TERMINATED]	

CHAPTER TWELVE

At noon, the girls all gather around the unlit firepit. Temple's in the corner by the window, as invisible as she can manage. The girls sit before her in a circle on the logs, knees touching as they still giggle about the book-reading an hour ago.

Some girls try to motion her over, others ignore her. It's enough to make her hands shake. No one cares what she does—she knows that. But for some reason, she can't move.

She can't reconcile the fact that they're the same, that they're all here at this camp, alive. Their fathers probably just want them to go to college; her dad wants her to find some runaway murderer.

She's just some kid—she can't stop a damn copycat serial killer with her bare hands.

"I have an awesome idea, y'all!" Glinda the Good Camp Counselor, Anysaa, leans forward with her arm held out over the pit. "We've all got the same favorite book."

"*Hearts Stop.*" The group practically says it at once.

That book again. *Hearts Stop* by Cary Lauren, a book about a detective or a doctor or something killing people and being gay or whatever. Temple isn't sure what makes the book so special other than Lauren being a local author.

There must be some kind of chemical in their brain that likes to read, and likes to read mediocre, gay books about murder. While *Hearts Stop* is way more relevant to Temple's state of human condition than *The Great Gatsby* or *To Kill a Mockingbird*, she's satisfied enough with her mediocre, gay life about murder.

Besides, she tried to read the damn thing before camp started to prepare, but got so bored her attention dipped in and out the whole time. She only managed to absorb a couple of chunks of it before giving up. A fan, she is not.

Anysaa wears a long sleeve undershirt beneath her camp T-shirt, and rolls the tight sleeve up over her elbow. An inky, precise scrawl takes up all the skin on her forearm. At the lip of it, there's the trademark symbol of *Hearts Stop* that even Temple can recognize. The order of something something. A circle with a distorted cross piercing through it, like a futuristic power button.

"Anybody else have tats?" Anysaa asks.

It's as if she'd yelled at them to strip. Suddenly, the circle is full of half-naked girls and—shockingly—none of the puberty flares that often accompanies it. Every girl but one has a symbol tattoo. Some of the girls have whole paragraphs written on their bodies, too. Curly, loopy handwriting that's half-toddler, half-doctor.

Cali beams at the other girls as she whips up the sleeve of her T-shirt. It's just a brick of text on brown skin. "I didn't get the Mark yet. I'm saving that and a red balloon for my eighteenth."

Another girl leans forward, her sleeve half off and her shoulder bare. "Opening of *House of Leaves*." A long quote is scrawled over the skin, looking like the bites of scars. "I got my mark first. As soon as I got a fake ID." When she darts her forearm before her, the girls go apeshit.

"It's so tiny!" one girl says.

"How'd you get it that small?"

It's the size of a quarter, and when Temple squints she can see it's very clearly the Order-Something-Something's mark. The girl grins as she flips her arm over, in a very flexible display, to show it to the other side of the circle. "I had to go up to New York to get it, but it wasn't too expensive."

Without Temple, conversation flows naturally among them. They can get into book details that she'd just kill on arrival. She exhales, turning her eyes out to the woods. The girls are fascinated by things that won't get them anywhere in life. A hobby that's not useful won't do anything for their future.

But Temple doesn't have a hobby at all.

She doesn't particularly like to read or watch movies. She's *barely* on the basketball team. Whenever she does anything, it's just because time moves so slow, she needs something to focus on. She eats to live. She doesn't *like* anything.

So really, there's no need for her to ruin this. She needn't insert herself into this conversation with her nonexistent social skills.

Temple keeps her mouth closed, letting Anysaa be in charge up until Brenda and Lam enter the campsite. They're huddled to-gether as they cross over the gravel, whispering to each other like divorcing parents. Their mouths are turned down, eyes narrowed.

Temple knows the fear that crawls up her neck is irrational, but that doesn't abate it as her thought forms with conviction: they're talking about her.

Cali snitched. There's no way someone would find out about her dad and just leave her be. Cali told Brenda, Brenda told Lam, they're going to tell all the girls, and then Temple's getting kicked out. She knows she's spiraling, and it doesn't stop her for a second.

When Temple snaps out of it, she's eye to eye with Brenda.

"Temple," Brenda breathes. Her voice shakes as she looks over to the circle around the pit. "Anysaa," she calls.

That's Lam's cue. "Alright, y'all!" she yells. Her voice is deep and thundering, so every girl goes silent at the sound of it. Iconic. "Time for one-on-ones. Everybody get your Get-To-Know-Me sheets ready, you'll have thirty minutes to learn as much as you can about the most people." She looks around for a dramatic pause before raising a brow. "Winner gets my first-edition *Misery*."

Giddy screams sound around the circle, some girls even grabbing onto one another.

"Go!" Lam yells.

It's a flurry of rainbows and brown skin and braids as girls pair up the quickest they can. Anysaa stands from her log, looking over at Brenda and Temple with suspicion.

"What is it?" she asks, stepping before them.

Brenda's eyes dart every which way, like a coked-up squirrel. Her voice is so low as she leans in, even the wind can barely hear her. "Temple and I are going to go to the communication tower this afternoon," she says. "So you and Lam will have to watch the girls alone. We should be back before y'all finish that long-ass movie, though."

Anysaa scrunches her nose. "Why? And why Temple?"

"The walkies aren't working right," Brenda says through her teeth.

They barely have a lick of signal out in Wherever-the-Fuck Woods. Without the radios, they're totally cut off from the outside world. Which, sure, that's bad—but nowhere near as bad as she thought.

"Is it yours or Lam's?" Temple asks.

Even though Temple whispers it, you'd think she screamed by the way Brenda jumps. She grabs both Temple and Anysaa by the arm, dragging them farther away. Then, when it's absolutely certain that a college campus could fit between them and the rest of the girls, she speaks again. "We've been hearing someone's voice through the channel. And we don't know who, but it's not Dawntae."

"What are you talking about?" Temple asks. She doesn't like the way Brenda's shoulders clench up and her eyes dim. "There's interference?"

Brenda whips out her radio and holds it between them. "Someone's on our radio channel," she hisses. "And they're fucking with us."

"What the fuck does that mean?" Anysaa snaps. Temple's surprised at the harshness in her voice, but then again, she never knew Anysaa to be cordial. That's just what she shows everyone else.

Director Brenda narrows her eyes. "Before camp, me, Lam, and Dawntae decided on the specific channel we'd use for staff walkie-talkies. It's not necessarily private, but Lam said it wasn't likely we'd get interference. But now we are." Then she turns to Temple. She leans in close. "Next is the Cabin versus Cabin, and I know we'll need you both for that. But after that, me and you will leave as soon as Lam gets all the girls inside. We need to check if there are any radios missing from the inventory."

"You can't just change the channel?" Temple asks.

Rather than answering, Brenda swallows. Her lip moves, as if she means to say something—and then she just turns away from them, charging for JG. Anysaa glances at Temple, the corners of her lips turned down.

"That was weird, right?" Temple asks her.

But Anysaa has other things to complain about, apparently. "What's weirder is that she asked you. Why do you get to go?"

she asks. "You're the fuckup. You should have to stay and babysit, not me."

Temple could guess why—it's because Brenda and Lam don't trust her with the other girls. They can tell Temple's not normal. Also, she's pretty sure this is gonna be Brenda's opportunity to "talk" to Temple.

But it's obvious that Anysaa's only mad because she's jealous. So Temple shrugs. "Who knows?" she says simply. "I think this'll be a good opportunity to prove myself, though."

Anysaa scoffs and shakes her head, taking a step back. "I can't believe this shit is happening. You're getting over on everybody *again*."

The way her words lack any soul almost makes Temple want to argue. *No, I know what you're talking about*, she could say. *That's definitely not what's happening.*

But she likes getting under Anysaa's skin. Makes her feel better about her own issues. Sometimes, knowing Anysaa is just as big of a bitch as she is engages her.

"I won't let it happen a second time." Anysaa's eyes harden, and she stares Temple up and down with a set jaw. "I don't know *why* you're here, but I'm going to expose you for what you really are."

"I'm not hiding anything in the first place," Temple lies. "So go ahead."

Anysaa gives Temple one last look—the kind that would have taken down a less-experienced hater—and walks away with her hand raking through her gorgeous, perfect hair.

Even though Temple isn't offended, she is a little concerned. Anysaa could succeed in unmasking her. She could show everyone the truth: that Temple is actually terrible. Genetically. Culturally. Internally.

"There's only so much vile that can fit beneath the skin," her mother always said, *"before it finds a way out."*

SUSPENSION NOTICE

Northern Girls' Preparatory School

Student: *Temple Backer*

Student ID#: *265514*

Date: *05/20*

Principal: *Judith Washington*

To: *Richelle Baker*

This notice is to inform you that your daughter has been suspended from school for (*3*) days. This punishment is the result of the following:

Attacked a student with a pipe. Parents dropped charges after witness statements, but Temple did not accept community service. Did not apologize, even though the student is badly injured.

Please note that in order for your daughter to return to school on *05/24*, you must schedule a behavioral conference with the principal.

STATEMENT FROM STUDENT

yall spelled my name wrong, ricki's my aunt not my mom

her last name's not even baker or backer or whatever you think it is, it's smith.

you don't have to say sorry and you probably won't even read this so fuck you

the bitch had it coming

CHAPTER THIRTEEN

Temple, unfortunately, is not like other girls. They don't like her because they can smell it on her.

You're not a girl.

You're a monster.

And every attempt she makes to hide it comes out even worse than the last.

"Two minutes!" Lam's voice is so loud, Temple might have preferred a whistle. But it brings her out of her wallowing, back to the mess of paint and glue before her.

"Time's almost up!" Lam shrieks.

All the girls of Temple's Cabin Bey seem to flurry more while not moving faster. Temple's arms are covered in paste—flour and water—for the papier-mâché sculpture.

She looks down at the tortured slop they've created. With the sun beating down at them—fully, since it's noon—Temple can see the extent of this monstrosity. It looks like it's dying. It's a blob monster—that's all she can really call it. Maybe it's a character she's not familiar with, or from a book or something. But its rounded little teeth and agape mouth and closed eyes seem to scream "*Kill me!*"

"Is it just me, or are we doing really bad?" Yaya asks from the ground.

Temple nods, though no other girl sees her.

"Oh my god, we don't have time to worry about that!" Mickaeyla shrieks. She looks around, then locks eyes with Temple. "Get me the white paint, stat!"

Temple does so without complaint.

"I need more paste!" Natalie chimes, and Temple complies again. "God, this looks so unrealistic," Natalie says.

She'd rather be an errand boy than contribute to this crime against nature. Still, despite her lack of involvement, her camp T-shirt is covered in mud and spots. The only visible part of the original design is the jagged triangle pointing to her chin and PRIDE ROCKS FOUNDATION in a curved font.

"One minute!" Lam shouts.

Now the girls are really freaked out.

"Oh my god, oh my god, oh my god," Yaya mumbles, smacking on a palmful of red goop.

The other team isn't going through this soap opera. Temple looks over to them through her eyelashes. Anysaa and Cali practically gleam in the sunlight as they put the finishing touches on what looks like, to Temple, a buff Bob Marley. K'Ran and the other two girls from Cabin Aye run their hands over the cylinders that make up the man's locs.

Temple turns back to her own group as they slap on some more papier-mâché. The monster leans a little farther to the left, a thick glob slipping down into the gravel.

"Um . . ." She doesn't have it in her to warn them. It might not fall over. She's not versed in arts and crafts but—

The arm falls off and hits the ground. Every girl from Cabin Bey stops moving.

They all stare at it, the skinny little twig that twists at all angles.

"Oh my god, we're so gonna lose," Yaya whispers. She looks desperate when her eyes turn to Temple. "You're the captain, Temple—what do we do?"

"*I'm* the captain?" Temple asks. That's news to her, but the girls all nod as if they'd decided this long ago.

Even though she's been nothing but an absolute bitch to them, they still watch her. Like she's going to help them. And that's when something clicks for Temple.

She grabs the bowl of leftover papier-mâché clumps and splashes water and red paint over it.

Mickaeyla gasps, reaching past the sculpture and getting a chest full of paste on her shirt. "What are you doing?!" she shouts.

Temple doesn't respond. She tips the bucket of mess around the arm, the substance splashing back onto her jeans and the base of the slop. It turns it from a pathetic, chalky branch to a rotted mess of gore and flesh—just as Lam shouts "Aaaaand *stop!*"

The girls all step back, arms raised. Temple looks at their creation and her stomach turns. She looks back to Lam, who's very seriously considering what they've made.

"I have two beautiful sculptures before me," she begins in the center of the firepit. She looks at both sides, where the girls await the results as if it were the lottery. "And only one set of limited-edition *Exorcist* posters."

A tug at Temple's hand grabs her attention. Her cabin mates have linked arms with each other, staring at Lam with a challenge in their eyes. Like they could win if they wished hard enough.

"The winning team is . . ." The sound of buzzing bugs fills the silence of Lam's dramatic pause.

Temple swears that in the seconds they wait, about twelve crawl around her ear just to taunt her. They must want Anysaa to win. To be honest, maybe she'd wanted Anysaa to win at the start of the day. But now, just a little—she wants Lam to say Cabin Bey.

Lam grins, raising her hands above her head. "*Cabin Aye!*" she shouts.

Temple's shoulders slack just a little as Anysaa's cabin goes apeshit. They're jumping and hugging—and Anysaa definitely sends a pointed glare that Temple ignores.

Bey unlocks arms, murmuring. The disbanding only makes Temple realize that it's gotten a little chilly, and she wraps an arm around herself.

Mickaeyla leans over, a smirk playing on her lips. "I bet they slept their way to the championship," she whispers.

Temple didn't really care about winning, anyway. But still, she almost smiles at her girls.

They spend the next hour or so cleaning up and preparing for lunch. With the sun out, their creations will harden and the girls can bring them into the cabins as decoration. Lam steps in the center of the circle once again and looks over at all the girls.

"Alright, everybody, lunchtime," she says finally, and cheers sound around the clearing. "We'll watch our second movie afterward—*It: Chapter Two*. So be prepared."

Temple can hear Natalie whisper from behind her. "Don't talk this time, Mickaeyla."

"I will. You know I can't shut the hell up. I'm *gonna* talk."

The girls groan as they head into JG, and Temple stays behind. She waits for Brenda to come out like they planned, barely moving—Lam almost doesn't notice her.

But she stops before disappearing inside, frowning at Temple. Not in a mean way; Temple's pretty sure that's just her face. "Brenda must have forgot," she says solemnly. "I'll send her out—"

"No need!" The door slaps open and Brenda rushes out, flustered and out of breath. She puts her hand on Lam's shoulder as she passes, a smile spreading across her face. "I was trying to get our seating arrangements just right and lost track of time."

The corner of Lam's lips tilts. "That's why we should just elope."

They pause awkwardly, and then look at Temple. They probably would have kissed if she wasn't waiting in the wings like a stalker. But quickly, the moment passes and Lam heads inside.

Brenda pushes forward. "You ready?" she asks, and Temple nods.

When they stand shoulder to shoulder, Temple sees they're both dressed casually: Brenda in a pastel camp T-shirt that billows around her stomach, with light blue jeans. Temple put back on her black hoodie over some dark-washed jeans. They could be going in the woods or going to the grocery store, honestly.

Temple looks into the distance, protecting her eyes from the sun with her hand.

"This should only take about an hour," Brenda says. She takes a step toward the path, her voice low. "We keep all of our backups at the comm tower, with the phone." She wraps her jacket around herself, like just the thought makes her cold.

"Why don't you just keep them in JG?" *Then you wouldn't have to walk like five miles to check on a bunch of two-way radios.*

"Two words: Cali Wilson. Last year she took apart everybody's phones because she thought she could make a superphone or some shit like that." Brenda grimaces. "Don't tell Lam I said 'shit.'"

Brenda's already said way worse, but Temple nods.

She continues. "When we first signed the lease for this place, they told us that phones were a pipe dream. We thought it'd be fine since we could get some SAT phones or something, but those don't work either. There's really not a way to call out other than the landline." Their steps crunch beneath them. "So the fact that somebody's playing on our channel is fucking creepy."

Temple would have thought she worshipped the campsite, considering how much work they put into everything, but Brenda's young enough to bleed without a cell phone, too. It must be tough sacrificing her phone for her idol.

As they walk, Brenda puts a comforting hand on Temple's shoulder. "We're all gone tomorrow. It'll be over soon. I know you're probably missing your phone and your friends." Everything about that is fundamentally untrue, so Temple nods without comment.

Soon the misty woods cloak them in its shadow. The two of them walk in silence at a steady pace, combing through the thicket as quickly as the woods allow. The air around them cools and the atmosphere follows.

"This knife," her dad began, his teeth gleaming in the silver light of the Midpoint Tree, "is meant to rip apart." He ran the sharp end against the black hand side, drawing a thin, straight line that leaked in beaded red pebbles.

Temple couldn't hide her expression. It twisted, and her mouth soured—she knew it. She felt it. And when she met her father's eyes, playful and gleaming, he smiled wider at the terror in her own.

CHAPTER FOURTEEN

For the first few minutes, Temple hears only the crunch of her feet over the brush. It's thick enough that it could hide anything, and if her theory's right, it *is* hiding something. New bodies. Fresh kills.

When she makes it within a few paces of Brenda, she takes her mind off of all of that, though.

"Are you gonna lecture me or what?" she asks.

The birds are rampant, slamming into trees as they rush from place to place. Their tweeted calls are familiar—chickadees, finches, the usual suspects. But since it's the woods, some are downright alien. Birds always surprise her, no matter how long she's been around them.

"That's why we left Anysaa behind, right?" Temple says.

The way Brenda freezes up, it was like Temple proclaimed she killed Anysaa instead. Grass bends in soft pillows beneath their steps as Brenda looks around at the trees awkwardly. These northern woods aren't overcrowded like a forest, just a bit scruffy.

Brenda's pace is even as she chews her words. "I thought she would do better with Lam for the time being," she says slowly, her eyes everywhere but on Temple. "With the girls. And you'd do good . . . away from the girls for the time being."

Clearly Temple's not as good at pretending to be good at her job as she thought. "OK."

Not OK.

A chickadee whistles somewhere in the trees, and Temple swears it's a "whomp whomp." Even the woods aren't on her side.

She and Brenda walk without speaking for a little longer. Temple might be getting fired. Maybe Brenda's going to yell at her—that'd be interesting.

Instead, Brenda begins in an overly calm tone. "I know more about what's going on than you think. You know, I designed the camp with you in mind. The readings, the films—it's stuff the girls love, but it was also for you."

How so? Temple would love to ask that, but it feels like a trap. Does she . . . shit. She does.

"You know I lied," Temple says. "On my application."

"Temple, you misspelled *Dracula*." Brenda presses on like it doesn't matter. "But even if you're not the biggest fan, you obviously wanted to come. And I could tell you had leadership experience. A girl who gets things done—the perfect complement to Anysaa, the girl that gets people to act."

Temple looks forward without speaking. The trees they pass aren't packed together, but they carry through the rough dirt and breed good plants in thick batches. The dead mixes with the vibrant and green, and some leaves shake with hidden vermin.

"But you can't stomp around here with a chip on your shoulder. Or pick fights with the other girls," Brenda says.

"I don't pick fights—"

Brenda's loud inhale breaks off Temple's protest. "The only time you don't pick fights with the girls is when you're practically avoiding them," she asserts.

Temple says nothing. Mostly because there's no "practically" about it.

Brenda lets Temple catch up, and they walk together shoulder to shoulder. "Is it that you're being bullied?"

"Ha! No," Temple says. "I'm pretty sure it's the other way around."

"Why would you say that?" Brenda asks.

"I'm kind of a bitch," Temple says. When Brenda doesn't respond, Temple looks over to find her mouth agape. She realizes how hateful that sounds, and she forces a smile. "Oh, no—it's not that bad. It's just . . . you can ask anybody. I kind of have a hard time *not* being a bitch."

"I don't think so. Nobody has *everybody* dislike them. Like, I can be a little neurotic . . ." She pauses as if she expects Temple to contribute, but Temple says nothing and puts one foot in front of the other. "But my sister's way worse than me. She's always lecturing me about being too easygoing."

"She sounds annoying."

"She's not. She's my sister. But that's how family is. You think you're a bitch, but they think you're just fine."

Temple snorts. "'Fine' is a real stretch."

Brenda looks over questioningly. "I remember from your interview that you said you don't live with your parents."

"Nope. I moved in with my aunt after my dad went to prison. My mom's—" dead. "Well, she doesn't matter. She thinks I'm a bitch, anyway."

Oh no. Temple blurts it out without a second thought, but it makes Brenda give her the pity eyes. Temple hates those—the eyes that do nothing for her. She *loves* pity. Particularly when it gets her something, like an A in geometry sophomore year. Or free guac at a restaurant once.

But best-case scenario, Brenda's pity eyes will get Temple an uncomfortable pat on the shoulder.

She hastens to amend her words. "Well, that's not all that true. My mom doesn't think I'm a bitch—she doesn't even believe in that sort of language. She's the kind of lady that'd say 'Well, I never' if I even suggested it." She screws her lips, remembering the look of her mother's eyes on her. "She just thinks that . . . I'm not . . . good."

Brenda walks in silence for a bit. Temple's word salad is a little too rushed to take in anyway, but she seems to mull over her point carefully. Then, genuinely. "I'm sorry to hear that."

Brenda looks at Temple and smiles like calm in a storm. But she stops walking. Temple stops, too.

"But you can't take your anger out on the girls," Brenda says.

Temple scowls—but she's not angry. Just surprised. There's a depth in Brenda's tone that Temple hasn't heard before, and it's clearer than ever that this is Temple's boss. As much as Temple thinks Lam's the authority, it's Brenda who's in charge.

"No more fighting with Anysaa. No more snapping at the campers. Don't curse at them, lead them." Brenda narrows her eyes. "And *don't* sneak out again."

Brenda's gaze is hard, and she doesn't turn away—for a second, it's like she was never the bubbly counterpart to her surly fiancée.

Temple snaps out of it. Swallows. "OK," she says in a small voice.

"You find your temper acting up, do breathing exercises like the rest of us. Four in through the nose, four out through the mouth."

Before Temple can point out that mood control isn't that simple, Brenda's loudly demonstrating it. Her breath blows out so hard that her collar flaps against her skin, and then she looks over to Temple, expecting her to follow.

"Do I have to?"

"Four in through the nose!" Brenda yells, and Temple follows. "Four out the mouth." It goes by similarly, and as Temple's shoulders deflate, she resists the urge to roll her eyes. But she does, admittedly, feel less tension than before.

If only that was it for this feelings session.

"Why do you think you've been avoiding the other girls?" Brenda asks.

There wasn't a simple answer to that. She kicks a thick branch out of the way of the path. "I don't get along with them. With people in general."

Brenda puts a hand on her heart, smiling softly. "You get along with one person. Me. And this person is so confused. You didn't have to sneak out, but you did. I catch you and Anysaa glaring at each other every twenty minutes. You haven't even *pretended* to be interested in the group activities. Would you rather be fired?"

"Of course not," Temple says, her stomach dropping.

"I discussed it with Lam. She wants you out, but I think you'd do good if you stop thinking of these girls as *others* and promise to do better in the future. Can you do that?"

Of course not. Because the girls are fine. *Temple's* the other. But if she gets kicked off the island, they might call the cops on her if they find her digging around.

"I think so?"

Brenda smiles. "Good. I knew I liked you for a reason."

It won't last long. Temple ignores the words as she trails behind Brenda, her hands vibrating at her sides.

She has to sneak out, has to find what her dad sent here for—it doesn't matter whether or not Brenda likes it.

"There's no saving you."

No, mother. There's not.

NPKTRUTH.BOARDOM.COM Forum Post: "i never thought i'd post here, but . . ."

This is my first post.

Ten years ago, my mom went missing. I didn't know anything about the North Point Killer, or Cary Lauren, or anything when it happened—but it changed everything. I wouldn't wish this feeling on anyone, not even any of you. I hope you go home to your families that love you, and I hope you all live long lives.

I don't have that anymore. And no one else knows my mom. So I guess, in light of everything that's happening on this site, I wanted to leave a few words to those of you who show up at my house to talk about your theories and jump in front of my car on my way to work:

My mom was the kind of woman who packed me two lunches every day: one for me and one for the kid that sat next to me. She was the kind of woman who wrote out all her recipes on index cards so that her grandchildren would have something to inherit one day.

She was fierce. She would do anything for me, and anybody around me. If she was killed by the North Point Killer, she went down fighting. And if she saw you despicable monsters on our front porch—she'd shoot you. So stay the fuck off our property.

—Brittany

But you already knew that

Posted by *standwithvictims* at 11:48PM • May 6

CHAPTER FIFTEEN

In another half hour or so, they finally make it up to North Point House—or the comm tower, as Brenda calls it. As Temple needs to make sure *she* calls it.

"Oh. My. God," Brenda breathes. The feeling of the air brushing Temple's skin makes her shiver as the director looks at the house open-mouthed. "Does this place look haunted, or do I just want it to be?"

In the light of day, with sunlight hitting the worn wood of the walls, the house's disrepair is on full display. She can see the jagged edges of the busted-out windows. The caved-in, wet spots of the outer wood. It's pretty obvious why Temple needs paperwork just to be around it.

"It's gotta be haunted," Brenda continues to herself. "Like the coven's house. Oh my god—is this what the coven's house was based on?"

"You've never seen the cabin before?" Temple asks.

It's clearly visible from the path. And as camp director, Brenda probably should be as well-acquainted with the land as Temple is. Or *almost* as well-acquainted, at least.

"We didn't buy the farm, we just rent it," Brenda explains. "And they only let us do that much 'cause we offered up grant money to install some landlines. Otherwise, I just hired some movers to help Lam put the beds in the cabins and the equipment in here. We're supposed to come back in a few days to take it all out."

"And they didn't run into any problems?" Temple asks.

"Like what?"

Dead bodies. Corpses that the cops didn't find.

Temple shrugs. "I don't know. Termites?"

Brenda laughs. The sound winds through the clearing, and Temple's eyes are back on North Point House, which echoes Brenda's laugh back to them. Even though it's falling apart, the house is a little bit pretty—in a fairy tale sort of way. Its mossy wooden walls are accented by the few murky, stained-glass windows that still hold their place. If it were refurbished, it might be beautiful in its old charm.

Like a good knife.

Temple wraps her arms around herself. *And just like a knife*, she reminds herself, *it will kill you*. She has to remember that. Her back pocket strains with the matches and her trusty blade.

Brenda slides her jaw back in place, and Temple's heartbeat quickens. They creep up the steps to the front door. The sound of the insects that croak outside seems to go silent as soon as Brenda and Temple cross the threshold.

Inside, North Point's miniscule potential for charm is gone.

That faded red light bounces around the room and into the grimy corners. The built-up dirt is clear in the daylight, sticking to the walls and floor; footprints from last night are dense in the middle of the living room. Temple sees her own past footsteps darting right out the door. Her own, Cali's, old footprints from trespassers past.

There's even a swipe in the smudge by the bathroom, from where Cali fell into Temple's fist. Temple shudders, peering closer while Brenda crosses in front of her. That inky black substance is now somewhere on Cali's clothing.

Sunlight shines through the holes in the walls, highlighting the trickling dust and thick sediment swirling in the air. The smell's still stale and thick, and Temple covers her mouth with her palm like a mask. Even if it doesn't stink, there's something in the room that *festers*.

It's soaked deep into the sagging wooden floors, burrowing into Temple's bones.

"This house ought to be condemned," Brenda says. "Look like don't nothin' in here work but Mickey Mouse."

Temple's brought back to the task at hand, and she watches as Brenda approaches the desk with the phone. The turned-over Bibles gleam in the low light.

"Or it could at least be saged down," Brenda says.

"Salt and fire work pretty well, too," Temple mutters.

Without hearing, Brenda marches farther into the room, right up to the left wall where she runs her fingers over the mossy wood. There's no window, just a smooth, white-painted panel that makes a scratching sound against Brenda's fingertips.

"Lam said this part's a little tricky," Brenda says. Her voice is muffled, distant. "It'll take a second."

Temple turns toward her, raising a brow. "What part—"

A loud crack sounds in the room, and Temple stops short. The wood paneling groans as Brenda grips onto a chunk. She yanks it backward like plywood, snapping it at the base before it falls to the floor.

A wall of shelves lays behind it.

"What in the hell?" Temple breathes.

"I know," Brenda says smugly. "It's just a little hidden door for closet space, but—doesn't it feel so *spooky*?" She claps her hands in glee but then frowns within a span of a second. "Uh, but I definitely just broke it. Lam's gonna be pissed—don't get mad if I tell her it was you."

Temple can barely hear her. She's just staring at the hidden shelf she's never seen in her life.

In her own home.

What's unveiled is a graveyard of electronics. Clunky cell phones, neon-colored two-way radios. They clutter the shelves, dusty and turned over, like they'd been left there decades ago.

There are a few laptops, too. They look old and out of commission, cracked cases reflecting distorted images of the room back at Temple. Some are bent entirely at the wrong angle. Temple doesn't know much about computers, but that can't be good for them.

Everything's chaotically piled on top of each other. Temple's pretty sure that if Brenda pulls the wrong Jenga brick out, it'll all fall to the ground.

Brenda doesn't notice Temple's awe and keeps moving, beginning to tear her way through the stuff. She throws big chunks of plastic about, muttering numbers as she goes along.

"Four SAT phones that don't work." Throw. "Three laptops that glitch out." Toss. There's a distinct shattering sound when the last one hits the wooden floor. Brenda ignores it. "Lam told me there's something about the area that makes shit *break*. Of course, that's a North Point curse, too, but some people do just fine out here, so I thought it'd be OK."

How? Temple wants to ask, but she swallows. "OK."

"As long as *we* don't break, I don't think there's anything to worry about," Brenda says.

"Sure," Temple replies, unconvinced. She moves in closer to the shelves as Brenda continues clearing off electronic parts.

Brenda's voice can barely carry over the clacking and thunking. "When we found out walkies worked here, Lam took a hundred bucks to, like, twenty different pawnshops and got a whole stack for backup. We made fucking sure that if anything goes down, we're able to communicate."

Something groans deep in the walls. The wood creaks, but Brenda keeps going. "It's all we've got, pretty much," she says. She laughs easily, as if she's not describing utter dystopia.

"Twenty!" She finally straightens her back, pulling her head from the cupboard. She clasps a bright yellow walkie with some stickers on it—fandom things Temple will never understand. That phone booth, that peace sign, that weird lion from that show she'll never watch.

As she fiddles with the buttons on the side, Brenda begins migrating away from the closet. She walks around the room, the sound of static bouncing from wall to wall.

Temple is quiet beneath it, tiptoeing closer, eyes locked on the secret compartment.

"Hello!" Brenda calls into the radio. "*Hello!*"

It's echoed in Temple's pocket. "He-ell-oo!" Temple pulls her radio out, the choppy sound grating on her ears. She holds it for Brenda to see, and of course, Brenda shoots her a brilliant smile.

"All radios accounted for, save for Dawntae's. So, whatever's up with the radios, it's not because of a thief. Maybe some campers playing a prank," she says, pocketing the yellow radio for herself. "Just gimme five more minutes to try Dawntae on the landline. Then, we'll head back before my boo can miss me too much."

Temple nods as Brenda hustles over to the little table.

The Bibles that cover the desk crowd around the phone and the other knickknacks—a pen, some loose paper, and Post-its. General office supplies.

"Dawntae, Dawntae, Dawntae . . . where are you?" Brenda asks. Her fingers flurry over the number pad as the floorboards groan beneath her feet.

Temple turns back toward the shelves she's never seen, fingers rubbing over the thin wood absentmindedly. They've been closed up behind the wall and lack the same pileup of dirt that everything else in the room has.

Her fingers keep running over the grooves. They catch on nicks in the wood, little scrapes from paint, or from sanding.

And then, *click*.

Her hand stops on a notch. Temple freezes, finger pushed deeper into the wood than should be possible. Temple turns her eyes beside her, but Brenda's none the wiser.

She's still got the phone at her ear, eyes warily watching the dirty pile beside her. "With all these damn Bibles, this place is basically my grandma's nasty-ass, roach-ass apartment out in downtown," she says.

Temple's arm remains still. "Yeah," Temple mutters. Her voice is scratchy and dry, but Brenda doesn't seem to notice.

She just goes back to listening to the phone, swearing as she starts another call.

Temple turns back to the shelves and slowly wiggles her finger around. A little sliver of the shelf puffs up beneath a laptop, jiggling the metal like there's an earthquake.

Click.

It sounds again before a wooden disk slides upward, and Temple slips the little chunk of wood into her fingers, gripping it tight. It fits right into her palm, flat and round, the familiar design catching the light.

Temple bites her lip so hard she tastes salt.

It's a coin.

A brand.

But not one like she's ever seen before; it's made of wood.

Temple runs her fingers over that gaudy, intricate design she's reluctantly familiar with, tracing the curve of the oval outline before flipping it over.

Only the wood is light and smooth—and there isn't a brand pattern on this side. It's something she's never seen before.

Temple stares down silently, eyes tracing the straight lines burned into it that create a simple picture. Three little boxes that fit into each other tightly like an "L." Each side has a short, black bar.

Windows. Doors. A floor plan.

One lonely box sits in the bottom corner. It nearly disappears into the edge, as if it were an afterthought.

She stares at it in silence, hearing the sound of Brenda's fingers tapping in Dawntae's phone number again. Hearing the sound of her own breathing getting rougher and rougher.

Main room.

Bedroom.

Bathroom.

It's a map of the North Point House. It's a picture of her home, of where she'd lived for most of her life.

And yet, down in the corner, there's a room she's never seen before.

CHAPTER SIXTEEN

S on of a bitch!" Brenda shouts.

Temple startles—she slides the wooden disk up her hoodie sleeve like she would a four-inch blade just as Brenda pops out of the half-rotted chair.

"The line's not working," Brenda says.

Temple stares back at her, bug-eyed as she tries to understand her words. Then she remembers—the call to Dawntae. She and Brenda are in two different headspaces.

"It's not?" Temple asks.

Brenda shakes her head. "I can't get through at all."

With the way the light beams red in and out, in and out, it can't be that the phone doesn't work. It's connected to the line, and the line is connected to electricity.

Temple furrows her brow. Her fingertips press into the hard disk of wood beneath the thick fabric of her sleeve hem. "Is it one of those dial nine things?" she asks.

"That's a good idea," Brenda says. She darts back over to the phone but then slams it back down seconds later. This time, Temple doesn't jump. Brenda's too unpredictable for Temple to focus on her new questions now. She'll have to wait until she's alone, wait until after all the other girls are asleep.

Because she got her hands on her dad's next clue. Which means she's on the right trail. Whatever this room is, it's going to help her find this killer that her dad irresponsibly wants his sixteen-year-old daughter to stop. Well, *possibly*.

This is all made up because your dad is crazy is still a compelling option.

"Damn phone still isn't working," Brenda says. Her eyes dart back and forth around the room as if she's pacing, but she's not moving. The room's too small to roam around much, but the amount of energy pent up in Brenda's bunched shoulders could maybe power a home.

Temple does actually know the feeling. She's searching for something helpful to say, but she's not good with words. She gives a weak smile. "Well, you tried."

It seems to help a little. Brenda looks over to her and sighs. "Thank you, Temple." She clips the new, yellow radio onto her pants, shaking her head. "Lam doesn't even seem to think this is weird—I mean, sure, Dawntae's ditched before. But I feel like she'd get back to us *eventually*. She wouldn't just ghost."

"We could try the highway," Temple suggests. It's another two and a half miles. They won't be able to make it out there and be back to the camp in an hour. "Isn't that where the signal starts?"

Brenda hesitates. "Lam would get worried about us going alone . . ."

Yeah, but you're *worried*, Temple thinks. Outwardly, she shrugs. "If we head up to the highway now, we can get back to JG by dusk—which probably won't make her worry too much."

"But Sweets doesn't *know* I'm looking for Dawn—oh god, why am I arguing when I'm considering it," Brenda says, completely running past the pet name for Lam she let slip. The air shifts around her as she huffs. Makes the decision. "There are no missing radios. It's a straight shot to the highway. We'll update Lam about the change of plans in a bit and walk on double speed."

That's way more commitment than Temple had been offering, but she can't seem to say no to Brenda.

It's gotta be, like, mind control or something. ". . . sure," Temple says. She tries her damnedest to keep it from being a groan—though "tries" is the key word there.

"First sign of trouble, we're out of there. No wolf-fighting or whatever it is you girls get excited about."

"There aren't any wolves in these woods," Temple says, but it just earns her a glare.

With their plan set, they're out of the cabin in no time. Thank goodness North Point House didn't decide to kill them. And Brenda seems more at ease.

But now Temple has even less time to pore over her new clue. Side by side, Temple and Brenda speed down the path with the sounds of their footsteps shushing a rhythm beneath the chirps of the birds.

So there was a fourth square on the map, detached from the house—a part she's never seen before. If her dad could hide a secret compartment in the walls, he could hide some secret room or secret shed. She's just gotta find out what that means for her little scavenger hunt.

"Cary Lauren's grave is around here," Brenda says. They've made it only a few paces past the house, but it's already practically invisible in the thick of the interwoven branches.

The shadows make it seem like night is approaching, but it's still about three hours away.

"I know," Temple says. "Cali told me—uh, before. She was talking about wanting to see it."

"Ah—that's why she snuck out with you," Brenda says.

She just *has* to bring up the past that's destined to be repeated.

Brenda smiles, nodding. "Say what you want about Cali. She may be wild, but she's exactly the kind of girl this camp needs."

Temple keeps her eyes forward. A breeze brushes between the two, sending goose bumps over her shoulders.

Brenda continues. "I know sometimes it can seem a little loosely formed. Since we're a horror camp, I wanted to make sure we spent most of our time reading and watching movies."

"I don't think we just watch movies," Temple says.

The look Brenda sends back is unamused. "All of us girls are Black, gay, young. Virginians. I planned this camp for the kind of girl I'd been back in high school—and high school me? She'd shit herself if she could breathe the same air as local legend Cary Lauren."

"Local legend" is pushing it. A decades-dead niche author with *one* movie has to do a damn lot to be a legend. But then again, what did Temple really know about the woman every other girl here was obsessed with?

"What is it about Cary Lauren specifically?" she asks. "Did she, like, donate to a school or something?"

"You mean what did she do other than represent me? Giving me a story? She opened her school here in North Point—it used to be huge. It went defunct after she died, but it used to be the high-light of the town."

Temple recalls Cali's story from last night, about wanting to join the school. Being inspired by a woman she shouldn't have anything in common with.

Brenda clasps a hand on Temple's shoulder. "I know you think you don't get it, Temple, but you *really* do. I know exactly what it's like—feeling like you're on the outside. This camp's all about that. About being different and making friends anyway. Because you're with people like you, who love what you love, look up to who you look up to."

It sounds all well and good when it's put inspirationally like that. If only Temple were just misunderstood, maybe she would fit in. But she's not.

She's really just a bad person.

"Is that how you and Lam found each other? Because you both love Cary Lauren?"

Brenda laughs. "Lam found me because she says, and I quote, 'You were hot, and I'm not a pussy.' She's not as in touch with her emotions."

The laugh Temple lets out is quiet, then the woods fall silent again. They've only made it through five minutes more of walking when the path starts closing up. The shuttle road thins out, and the woods thicken with overgrown grass, bushes, and flowers. The flat land they were using to guide themselves is no longer clear.

And though Temple's walked this path just a day before—it still sets her on edge.

"Is it just me, or did it get dark as fuck?" Brenda whispers, and Temple feels her shiver beside her.

It did get darker. And Temple feels a pull on her, the atmosphere now thick and chilled. She recognizes it instantly.

Temple sniffs the air, the smell latching into her throat.

They're no longer safe.

Temple stops. "Hey," she whispers.

Brenda keeps walking, though her eyes are bugged out as they dart around the open woods.

"Brenda, it's weird here," she says a little louder. "I think we should turn back."

Temple knows she's lost. She can't explain the feeling that's settled into her bones. The feeling that mirrors what she felt when she was in the bathroom, when she was looking out the window. She's transfixed at nothing, at a speck—at a trail of dark brown that stains the path and—

Brenda slips.

"Oh my god!" Brenda's shriek is high-pitched. Annoyed. "My Timbs!" she moans.

Temple stumbles forward, ducking between the gate of curled-over trees and connected vines and wood. When she reaches Brenda, she's curled up by a tree clutching her foot upward.

Her boot is coated in a deep black mush, nearly up to her ankle. It matches the turned color of the path—the brown that Temple was too slow to recognize. The chips of ivory that curl up from the brush are a much starker image. Temple's heart stutters.

White against brown, like when she was just a kid finding coins.

It falls from Temple's lips before she thinks to hesitate. "It's a dead fucking body."

The leaves swish beside her and she catches Brenda watching her. Then Brenda looks at the mass of discolored slush, collected in the path, and her eyes widen.

And then she screams at the top of her lungs.

CHAPTER SEVENTEEN

emple doesn't move. She can't move.

Hide it.

She needs to find out what happened. There's a dead body out in the middle of the woods. It can't be one of her dad's. Or at least it shouldn't be. Her dad gave the cops the locations of all of his victims, and they dug out those bodies years ago. Any left would be bone now. Right?

"Go to your room, Temple. You're no help."

Temple tries to focus, shutting out her mother's voice as her eyes trail over what's left of the corpse. She wishes she could tell who it is, but the body has been through it. She notes how it's laid out—stretched across the feet of the trees. Flesh mixing with soil like fertilizer.

Brutalized.

Not decomposed.

Parts of the corpse are still much too intact for it to have been there for more than a month—and thank fuck for that. *It's definitely not my dad,* Temple confirms to herself. The rule of her childhood seemed to be that she was connected to any dead body she crossed paths with. Maybe that leftover guilt is messing with her.

Brenda's footstep is fossilized in the corpse's mushy abdomen, the structure caved where her weight hit. But Temple can tell that, before then, the corpse was already ripped apart. Its arm and a leg, just to the calf, have whole parts cut through messily; splatter hit the grass in deep black and brown chunks.

It has a whole head, too—*she* has a whole head. Temple can make out her long hair, which sticks into the leaves like a spider's web. Her chest, her stomach—both of those might as well be blasted open. But her disfigured face stares up at the sky.

Temple takes another step toward the body. Her feet move on their own, like she's entranced. She can't take her eyes away, but she can't swallow down the dread that's making her dizzy.

Oddly, frost coats the eyelashes like freshly fallen snow.

Brenda screams again.

Temple slams back into reality, whirling back to Brenda to catch her keeling over. She flinches in disgust, and Brenda's gag whips her back up.

"Oh god, oh god, oh god," Brenda murmurs through her choking. Tears stream down her cheeks. "Fuck! *Fuuuuuck.*" She glares upward, chin wiggling.

Temple shouldn't have said anything. No one else is used to this—why is that so hard to remember? Temple holds her hands out to Brenda like it's a hostage situation. It kind of is, if the corpse is a gun and Brenda's nausea is the assailant.

"I mean, I'm not really sure if it's a body. I could be wrong . . ."

Brenda doesn't listen. She clenches her fingers tight around her hair, a toe-curling scream whistling from the back of her throat.

Temple's arms remain outstretched. She debates which comforting words she can offer, but all that comes to mind are gems from her mother. "It's already dead; it won't kill you," is one. Also,

"Stop the blubbering. Do you want your dad to kill you, too?" Then there's "You should be an actress—all this time you've been supposedly crying as if you're afraid, but you haven't shed a single tear."

Those will only make things worse.

Then Temple remembers the normal thing to say. "We should call someone."

Brenda's hands are shaking so bad, Temple doesn't think she'll be able to hold the radio—but she does. She whips it out, snapping it up to her lips like it's her lifeline. "Lamlamlamlam, we've got an emergency," she says. "We've got a *fucking* emergency!"

Brenda gags again, and Temple holds out her water bottle. It's half empty, but Brenda takes it.

Then drops it right to the ground, as if her hands have ceased to function. Her whole body has begun to tremble.

"I'm sorry—I'm—I'm sorry," Brenda whispers. Tears stream down her cheeks as she shakes her head, turning away.

Temple tries very hard not to look at the body between them. She's already out of place—she forgot how to wear her never-seen-a-dead-body costume. As she watches Brenda panic, she's fighting not to seem *interested* in the body. Interested is freak behavior.

Brenda coughs something out, and Temple flinches at the splash against the branches. "Lam?" Brenda calls again. Mercifully, static clicks over the other side of the line.

A voice comes through. "Brenda?" Then clicks back out.

Brenda presses the radio even closer to her, making out with it. "Lam, *there's a fucking corpse in the middle of the path.*"

Lam's in an entirely different camp. Another world. The radio clicks back in, and their corner of the woods is filled with the sounds of laughter and normalcy—chatter and bustle and life hit hard in Temple's ears, when she's faced with the cold and dead.

Her gaze drifts back to the sunken pile of flesh, and her eyes feast over the sight. The clothing is discolored from whatever oils and fluids in a body make it disintegrate. Her eyes are gone, but there are a few still clear features. The skin of her forehead is colored nicely, a deep brown tone that had to have been pretty when life was still behind it. There are some spots of flesh already eaten away. Her jeans are dirty but still at least recognizable.

And not a dress.

Temple closes her eyes, clenching her jaw. It's not her mother. She never confirmed she saw her mother last night. It's silly to think anything lurking in the woods could kill her mother, considering who she married.

But *something* happened to her.

A scream rips through the radio, a shrill cry worthy of a horror film. "*Stop!*"

Chills travel down Temple's arm. She looks up from the corpse, her eyes darting over to Brenda, and their expressions match. Temple suddenly remembers the voice from the night before—the voices she heard at North Point House.

"*Shut up,*" the voice had said.

"Lam?" Brenda's voice turns unsure.

"*Stop it, Raymond!*" The pitch is higher, the words shorter. It's clearly not Lam. "*Let him alone!*"

"*For God's sake,* quiet!"

Then the static cuts out.

The woods go silent.

Temple closes her eyes. She notices the woods around them quieting, and the air chilling as they stand there. This is dangerous. Screams and whispers are real. They're real. And that wasn't Lam on the radio.

"We should go," Temple says.

Brenda isn't listening.

"Brenda, *come on*!" Temple shouts.

"It's happening again," Brenda says quietly. She stares at the radio as if it's the culprit, her hands trembling again.

Temple freezes. "What's happening again?"

Brenda meets Temple's eyes. Hers are frantic and scrunched. When Brenda speaks, her voice crackles. "It's just like last night—we thought someone was messing with the channel. I just . . . no one else should be out here . . . but I—I don't know—"

"You were hearing voices," Temple says slowly. She swallows, trying not to let her father's words resurface . . . but they always do. *"Don't ever ignore the voices again."*

Temple and Brenda stare at each other, and the pit in Temple's stomach grows. She opens her mouth to speak again. They have to go.

The radio crackles back to life.

"Brenda, it's me."

Brenda drops the radio. It bounces off of a rock, skittering into the corpse, and she crouches. Then, Brenda buries her head in her hands like it can make everything go away.

"It's me, Brenda." Beneath the pasty blood. The roughage. The painted leaves. The voice doesn't sound like Lam at all; all the static and distortion splits the voice apart. A feminine voice—but it's *not* Lam.

"Please, I can't—you have to—" The words are swallowed by static.

Then the line goes dead.

Temple's heart keeps time with a finch's chirps. After a beat too long, Brenda chuckles. It's long, drawn out, and without energy. She reaches the radio slowly, pinching the otherwise dry antennae between two fingers. Her hand quivers as she wipes it against a leafy bush, scratching it roughly into the wood.

"They must be getting too rowdy and can't hear us," she says. She laughs again, the edge in it sharpening. "What the hell!" Brenda screams. She stumbles down the path a little, only to turn back and stare at the twisted body in the soil. "*Fuck!*"

Clearly Brenda won't be handling this. And Temple would judge her if she had a clue what to do.

"Something *killed* this person," Temple says bluntly. The words feel like coal on her tongue and basically prove her dad isn't as crazy as he's acting.

This isn't an old body—it can't be her dad's.

There's another killer. And the girls might be next.

"We have to go back," Temple says. "We need Lam."

Brenda's an absolute mess—she needed Lam ten gags ago. "I don't know what's going on," she moans. Her figure sways against the trees like she might fall over at any second, shoulders slumped.

Temple tries to sort out her thoughts. "We can go on our own. I can't imagine the girls will react well—might be easier to just leave them behind and go for the highway. Get someone out here to help."

But, shit, that would tank Temple's actual mission. If they alerted the authorities, the cops would end up sniffing around the forest again—she won't be able to find her mother, or whatever else her dad has her looking for.

Then again, she doesn't want to die. The body still has tissue and flesh on the skeleton. Temple focuses on the preserved leg that's twisted at an unnatural angle.

Brenda stares at it with those empty eyes. Says nothing.

Temple's on her own. Brenda's a lost cause.

The body's jeans are ripped at the knees and ankles, partly in fashion, partly in decomposition. A stretch of brown skin is still in good condition. The color of the girl's calf has muted out, but in the low light of the woods Temple can make out a dark spot of black peeking underneath the stringy patch of the knee.

Foreboding bleeds through Temple, spilling over her like it'll take all of her breath. Something presses at her mind, but she blinks it away. Then, with the clearest voice she can muster, she points at the spot of black and asks, "Isn't that the Cary Lauren symbol?"

At the sound of the name, Brenda snaps back into herself. Her eyes focus again for what feels like the first time in hours, and she flinches when she looks back at the corpse.

Temple feels the jolt in her own body and lowers her hand. "Sorry, I'm a dumbass. *Don't* look. That *is* a Cary Lauren symbol, right on the girl's calf."

Brenda's sharp inhale is audible, but she still doesn't turn to investigate.

Temple leans over. "What is it?"

"If it's on her calf . . . it might be Dawntae." Brenda bites her lip. "I-I-It's *probably* Dawntae. She has one there, and she was . . . she's been gone this whole time." Her words ramble on as she works herself back up into a frenzy.

Temple remains silent and turns back to the body with that pit in her stomach growing again, churning inside her.

"Oh god, oh no, oh no," Brenda moans, and she slides to the ground, the tree bark crackling in the thread of her shirt. "Oh god, that's why she's missing."

MOST-WATCHED: 1992 CARY LAUREN INTERVIEW WITH DONNA HAYWOOD (QUEEN GOES OFF!!)

Donna Haywood: These are really crazy times. You've been very vocal in previous interviews about rights for the Blacks and the homosexuals—such as in last year's "Black Savior" speech for the *Times*. What, in your opinion, are the words the world needs to hear right now?

Cary Lauren: I don't have any words for the world. [laughs] I've fucked up half of my life already. No family, no love—I got a book that won't sell because my Black face is on the back cover. You think the world would even listen to me?

Haywood I'm not going to argue—but you've done pretty well for yourself. I mean, you've got award-winning, bestselling novels under your belt. That sure seems like the world is listening.

Lauren: I abandoned my kids five years ago. Did you know that?

Haywood: I can't say I did—

Lauren: Five years ago today. And six years ago, during my acceptance speech for the Oscar Wilde Honor, I said, "I got this award, but they paid me a peasant's salary." I said that up on stage, in front of all them white folk that could do something about it. "Help!" I basically screamed it at them. "I'm drowning." But people like me are . . . invisible. And no one helps a ghost.

Haywood: I'm sorry to hear that.

Lauren: They were both under ten years old, but nobody wanted to save them. I want to be remembered and to be "good," whatever that means. For respectable white ladies like you to know me for my "words for the world," as you say. As you expect from me. But what the hell does that matter, really? The world don't listen to me. You're not even listening to me right now. I could scream at the top of my lungs that I'm drowning, and I'll never get saved.

CHAPTER EIGHTEEN

They don't have much time before Lam and the girls will start looking for them, so Temple and Brenda start their hike through the woods toward the campsite.

The silence between them is heavier than before.

Brenda's behind her, and over her shoulder, Temple can see that Brenda's barely even there. She's still sobbing on and off, and Temple wishes she could tell her to shut up. Someone might hear them.

But she's worried that might freak her out more.

It's around three o'clock, and the sun is up high. It's not hot, still—the October air blows a breeze that actually feels kind of good. But she's paranoid about the cold.

"Slow down," Brenda says from behind.

Temple turns again, and she sees Brenda a few paces back. She's nothing but a shadow, the North Point House just over her shoulder.

She wonders if she should say something.

She keeps going. The trees spin and tangle over a knot, sagging branches dragging against the path. Even just looking at the shadows of the woods, Temple feels the past catching up to her.

"I can climb faster than you," she said to her dad.

He looked down at her, smiling. Nine teeth were missing now. "I'd like to see you try, sweetheart."

It's so odd, being here. Her memories bounce around, and she no longer knows why it's happening. It could be being on the farm again after all these years. Anyone could have a tough time returning home.

But Temple's pretty sure it's not just this place. It's the dread. The blood.

And the death.

Temple stops at a tree, running her hands over the scratchy bark and breaking off splinters with her rough touch. Her finger glides over something smooth and cool, like syrup, and she draws her hand back.

It's gooey and black.

She stares at the tree. "What is that?" she grumbles. The shadows hang over the trunk and she can't get a good look. She only sees a rough patch of darkness, right over the knot.

It looks almost like . . . Temple takes another step closer. Then she takes that step back again.

A handprint.

A single handprint, shadowed by the parting of the trees. How long has it been there? It's black now, so it's not blood—at least, it shouldn't be. Temple keeps staring, swallowing down her dry throat.

She should say something. Brenda should know about this. It might be a clue.

But there shouldn't *be* clues.

She looks up to tell Brenda before she can talk herself out of it—but there's nothing but brush and the curving trees.

Brenda isn't anywhere to be found.

"What the fuck?" Temple whirls to the other side. Still nothing. Her heart kicks up in her throat.

"Brenda?" Temple calls. No answer.

Temple skims the thinnest layer between the trees. There's no sign of Brenda's summery T-shirt. All that greets Temple is a croaking raven and the shushing of the path as snakes and rodents scurry through.

There's no fucking way Temple lost her.

"Brenda!" she calls. Her voice heightens in pitch. "Brenda!"

"Temple."

Her name is light in the air. She pivots toward the whisper, like it came from the trees themselves. There's nothing.

Her heart pounds against her chest. "Brenda?"

No response.

Goose bumps run over her arms. Temple may not know Brenda well, but she knows her voice.

That wasn't Brenda.

Slowly reaching into her back pocket, Temple clasps her hand around her knife. It's familiar to her touch, and her fingertips trace the geometric patterns etched into the metal handle.

As she pulls it out and grips it tight, she positions it away from her body, ready to strike.

She pictures her dad's smile when he gave it to her. The warmth of his hand on her shoulder.

"You're not normal."

Her step forward cuts through weeds. They swish and sway against the calves of her jeans. The voice came from the trees. Surrounding her, there's no movements of anything human. She doesn't see anything that could speak. Not in that tone of voice, and not so near to her.

Don't believe it, she tells herself. *Stop what you're thinking right now.*

But still her feet press on—slowly. Her muscles are clenched, ready for battle. Her breath is hitched, her lungs are ready to give out.

"Listen to your father, baby girl . . ."

Temple grinds her teeth.

A twig cracks.

A low branch shifts left.

Temple freezes.

"Cover your ears."

She stares hard at the offending branch, daring it to move again. It calls her bluff and shakes once more.

Then, light as a giggle, the voice speaks again. "Temple." It flutters on the breeze, harsh and soft all at once. "Come, now, before he finds what you've done."

Temple swivels and pushes off with her calves, using all her strength. The quivering branch is an arm's length away. The open path is before her. She keeps her knife tight in her hand and sprints for her life.

Her ears ring with the voice playing over and over again.

"Come, before he finds what you've done," her mother said.

Just now—that was her mother's voice.

Temple's feet pound in time with her heartbeat.

"Come, now, before he finds what you've done."

Exactly her mother's voice, exactly as her mother said it ten years ago. Temple remembers the moment perfectly, the way her mother's brown eyes lightened a bit in the sun as her shadow hovered over Temple, and Temple hovered over the blood-stained bathroom tile.

A few feet away, rolled underneath the bathtub spout, was a head. There was no body to speak of. Its forehead was branded with thick, bloody lines in a complex twisted vine pattern that Temple was too scared to look at for too long.

"Come, now, before he finds what you've done," her mother said. "If your dad finds out you messed with that man, he'll kill you like he kills everyone else."

Temple stumbles. The memory rushes over her, without her permission. Even though she knows she's running, knows she has to keep going. Her breathing goes erratic.

She remembers what she said.

"But I . . . I barely touched it."

A rock catches her toe. Her fingertips scrape the ground, but her heels keep moving.

You *did it, Mom*, Temple remembers thinking. *Why are you blaming me?*

She powers through the memory until she can't breathe. She tries to lift herself away, but it's so heavy.

Like the woods itself is dragging her under.

Her mother's voice.

And a trap.

It's the farthest she's ever run. Even in basketball practices, she never put in so much effort.

Her body rejects it.

Her feet slow without her permission, and Temple's knees give out before she falls to the ground, stumbling through the bushes. The brush and leaves snap at her until she slams into a tree. Her breath shoots out, and she chokes.

Whatever was in the woods knew who she was—and it was using her memories against her. Using her *mom* against her.

She closes her eyes, face buried in the soil.

A hand hauls her up by the wrist so fast and tight Temple's shoulder jerks and pops. "No!" she screams at the top of her lungs. She's lifted to her feet with no effort. Wind rushes by her ears.

God, she hopes she dies fast.

She deserves this death and this fear.

But she hopes it's quick.

"Temple!" Brenda yells. She shakes Temple by the shoulders with such force Temple's head lolls. "Temple!" she shouts again. Another shake.

Temple's mind clears only enough to register Brenda shouting into her face. Tears cloud Temple's vision and warm her cheeks as she struggles to control her breathing.

She's alive. Against all odds, she wasn't killed.

By all the memories that didn't kill her the first time.

Brenda's mouth turns down.

But Temple's probably scowling back. She knows she saw the tree move. Even if she panicked, there had been something there, and it wasn't her dead mother. She should definitely be dead. Something came for her—a murderer, a ghost, she didn't know.

"Why would you be dead?" Brenda asks.

Shit—Temple spoke aloud.

Brenda clicks her tongue, taking her in from head to toe. Temple feels the tickle of her twists against her forehead, and feels her sweaty palms clamped into her fist. She feels terrible. Can't look much better.

Brenda clicks her tongue again. "Of course you'd get scared," she says. "What the hell do you think you're doing, running off-path like that? I can't show up to Lam with another missing girl."

Temple doesn't dare glance into the distance. She focuses on Brenda's eyes, flashing with worry. The director continues her lecture for long enough that when she finally finishes, Temple's regained her calm.

The silence between them is much less ominous than before, though, and Temple plays with the hem of her shirt. "I'm sorry," she whispers.

Brenda blinks, because she probably hadn't expected any respect. She reaches for Temple's hand, clasping it like the sixteen-year-old is just a toddler. "We're almost at camp," she says. "Let's not get separated when we're so close."

"Temple."

The sound of her mother's voice is still fresh in her mind, but she shoves it away as she follows Brenda. Her mother may be missing, but Temple knows she died a long time ago. She saw the blood trail in the grass the night her mother disappeared.

"Cover your ears," her dad had said that night.

"9-1-1, what's your emergency?"

Temple couldn't speak. When her mother's screams stopped so suddenly, Temple left the bathroom without thinking. There was no one in the living room, in the bedroom—her hands shook as she picked up the cordless phone.

The smell of char burned her nose, and she burrowed farther into the nest of roughage in the moldy bathtub.

"9-1-1. Are you in any danger?"

The man on the other side must have been able to hear her breathing.

Temple pressed "end" and threw the phone onto the tile. She wrapped her arms around her calves, sunk her face into her knees. The bathroom window was open, letting in the breeze. But it also let in the silence.

The silence that felt like it lasted for hours, like she'd be left all alone in that tub—that room that was her room. But she wasn't left alone.

Finally, she heard the sound of the bathroom door open again. She kept her eyes down. Didn't look to see who it was.

Maybe she didn't want to see. She heard the heavy thump of the boots, and she already knew.

She felt her dad's hot, wet hand on her shoulder.

And Temple knew it was over.

CHAPTER NINETEEN

Breaking out of the thick watch of the trees gives Temple a chance to breathe, fill her lungs with clean air and smooth out that deep fear that seized her chest. Even though she's not sure what time it is anymore, the sun is still high in the sky.

At least there's that. Nothing bad happens during the daytime, she tells herself. It's a thread-thin comfort, but she lets it rush through her veins all the same.

The charred firepit smells fresh as they walk past it, the stink of the wood and kindling drifting over Temple once her feet hit that mishmash gravel spread through the campsite. The curve of cabins, awaiting—Aye, Bey, and JG—all dotted along the border of the circle.

Brenda and Temple trudge back to JG, where they belong—the door is closed, and the curtains are drawn.

"Thank you, Temple," Brenda says into the air, suddenly.

Temple looks over to Brenda, and the director's looking at the ground. "I don't remember doing anything so great that I should be thanked," Temple says.

"When we . . . up past the comm tower, you almost lost me. I lost it. But you kept me present. I don't know if I'd have made it back without you."

Of all the things that Temple expected, sincere appreciation wasn't it. It makes her chest feel sticky, like she has to fan her T-shirt to get the proper airflow in.

"It's not over yet," Temple says, turning toward the building.

It's time for her to take a fifteen-hour nap. So much is happening right now. And one look at Brenda lets Temple know the feeling is mutual, but Brenda wouldn't dare say so when she has a job to do. Brenda marches forward, jutting out one arm to JG's white-painted door and yanking so hard it slams against the back wall.

They enter to silence—even though all the girls' eyes snap to Temple and Brenda. Every camper is present, mostly crowded around the dining table. Cali's a few feet away, behind the kitchenette island, with her hands gripping the countertop. Lam stands over to the side, leaning against the wall with her radio clutched in her hands.

Brenda locks eyes with Lam, chest puffed out. "We need to talk," she says.

The eerie silence persists, even after Brenda speaks. Not a single person at Cary Lauren Horrors Camp looks glad that Temple and Brenda are back. At the center of one of the benches, flanked by her two faithful sidekicks, Anysaa sits, glaring down at the table. Salt crusts her cheeks, old tears long dried up.

Lam's frown turns grim. "You already did," she says, raising the hand that's clenched around the little plastic radio, tilting it for Brenda and Temple to see.

"'Just leave them behind,'" Anysaa says. Her tone is sharp, but she narrows her eyes at Temple with fire in her gaze. "'Leave them behind and go for the highway.'"

"We heard everything," Lam says, glaring over at Anysaa. "Is it true? Is . . . is Dawntae dead?"

"Please tell me you have pics," one of the girls chimes, and there's a hissing shush that shuts her up.

For the most part, none of the girls rushes to shout over each other. There's a low tension of excitement in the room—but Temple can feel the apprehension there, too. Ripples through like a rope, tying them all by the wrists they clasp atop the dining table.

Brenda is aghast. "How did you—what did you—"

"Your walkie was on. I tried to shut it off, but we heard pretty much all of it." Lam huffs, and her face cracks a little.

"She was ripped apart?" another girl asks. Temple realizes the questions aren't as gleeful as they sound. The curiosity that forces them out—she understands it well.

But they're definitely scared.

Most of the girls didn't even look like they're breathing. With all the movies and books about death, real death isn't fun. Temple respects the quiet ones more for their silence—death is a harsh truth to face. The process went better without any know-it-alls.

But of course, there's always one. Anysaa is the first to raise her hand. She doesn't wait to be called on. "You were just going to make us stay here?" she asks Brenda. The question should really be for Temple. "Were you going to abandon us and pretend nothing happened?"

"Not the time, Anysaa," Lam said pointedly. And Temple shouldn't have been surprised, but Anysaa backed off quickly.

It opens the floodgates, though. Yaya had been biting her lip until that point, but then she throws her hesitant voice into the ring. "Dawntae's . . . was dead?"

"Are *we* gonna die?" One of the girls from the other cabin tails onto Yaya's words.

Brenda answers confidently, "Of course not." Her words spread a warmth through the room that hadn't been there before. "If it's Dawntae, we could be in danger. But *we are not going to die.*"

"Are we safe?" Mickaeyla asks instead. "Even if we don't die, are we still *safe* here?"

Brenda halts at the worst possible moment. Her confidence crumbles in one breath. "I'm not sure," she whispers.

And the girls fall apart all at once.

"So we're gonna die?" Mickaeyla demands.

"Jesus, Brenda!" another girl hisses.

"Are we *leaving*, at least?"

The girls all scream and talk and panic at once, their voices a roaring wall while Temple and Brenda stand in the center of it all. Brenda doesn't last for a second. She's already blinking, glassy eyes focused on nothing and gleaming with tears.

The girls get rowdier and rowdier, standing from their seats with demands that aren't more than word soup. Lam is the one that finally puts a hand up, stepping between Brenda and the table. She takes the whistle that hangs from her neck and blows it hard. It's so shrill, half the girls cover their ears. The silence that follows is oppressive.

"Now, we will be civil," Lam instructs. "At this rate, Pennywise is more polite than we are. We have a serious situation here—an emergency. We all need to stay calm."

A hush falls over the room. The girls seem to listen, or at least reflect. And Temple is left to look on from the outskirts of the room. She sees the fear that rippled through everyone, feels that familiar anxiousness.

But she has more answers than they do.

She isn't afraid of the unknown.

"How do we know it's not one of us?"

Temple looks up from her reverie at Anysaa's voice. Once again, it's the lone one in the quiet, as the girl asserted herself with a smooth lean deep onto the table. All the girls look at her, even Brenda, while Lam glowers.

Anysaa continues. "Dawntae is dead, and whoever did it could still be out there. But what if the killer . . . is one of us." It's like a

Tyler Perry production the way she turns to Temple. "I'm just saying what everybody's thinking. There's no way to know we're safe when one of us is already a known psycho."

Lam sighs, her voice stern. "Anysaa."

Temple is much less a beacon of patience. She laughs. "Bitch, you know damn well"—she splays her fingers across her chest—"if I wanted to kill *any*body here your ass would be first."

"Temple," Lam hisses.

"I was actually there. I saw what happened to the girl—this ain't some cheeky little mystery," Temple says.

"Her name was Dawntae!" Barbie Incarnate Janae screams at her.

"Yeah, Dawntae. And that girl from Instagram. The other disappearances." Temple glares at her. "We're in the middle of a murder spree. And none of you cared about it because y'all were so excited to see the freak show."

"Girls!" Lam shouts.

Yaya, with a quiet swish of whispers, starts praying. Fear spills into the room thick like heavy cologne.

"We don't have time to argue," Lam orders. "I know you girls don't like each other, but it's all irrelevant now—camp is canceled. It was free, so don't worry about any refunds. We'll find a way to contact your families for the early pickup. Maybe me and Brenda can go back to the comm tower." She throws a wary look to Brenda, who's just about disappeared into herself, and rushes over to put her hands on her shoulder. They go off to the side, whispering at each other in soothing and panicked tones, but only Temple seems to notice. All the other girls are focused on the task at hand.

"Or," Cali interrupts. "I have another way."

Every girl in the room turns to her. Mixed emotions swarm as they wait for her to go on. Some girls wait with anticipation, as if

Cali can save them with a sentence. Others wait with scowls, ready for oncoming bullshit.

Cali: The wild card who's part cheerleader, part adrenaline junkie. The only one who hasn't given her unfiltered opinion—even though she *has* to have an opinion.

When she sees she's got everybody's attention, she holds up a cell phone. "We can use my phone."

With a kick at the table legs, Janae clicks her tongue like she expected as much. She's still got that attitude problem—but apparently it's not reserved for Temple. "Are you high? We don't have any signal," Janae says.

"Just stay out of this, Cali," Anysaa says.

"You don't know what I'm talking about, so shut the fuck up," Cali says with a sneer. She flicks out a thin piece of wire clamped into the phone's battery panel. It's poorly shaped and bending, the gleam from the overhead light making it flash white and silver.

Temple can barely see it from so far away, but Cali's clearly proud of it.

"I finally did it. I made the superphone," Cali says. The blank stares don't faze her at all. Her grin doesn't even falter. "I rigged my phone to get some signal this morning. Well, mostly the night before camp started—went through seven Androids on Thursday—"

"Your point, Big Brain?" Anysaa snaps.

"*My point*, Little Brain, is that there's a dead body in the woods, and camp is canceled. We have no shuttle, and no signal." She throws a pointed look to Lam's radio. "But we got my superphone. *I've* got signal. Three bars and unlimited data. With this, we can skip the hike and I can just ask someone to get us the *fuck* out of here."

Student Assistantship Application: Camp Counselor AB

Pride Rocks Foundation Camps at North Point Farms, October 16–18

PREFERRED METHOD OF COMMUNICATION (MARK ALL THAT APPLY)

(X) Home Phone ( ) Mobile Phone (X) Email ( ) Text

RESPOND TO THE FOLLOWING QUESTIONS TO THE BEST OF YOUR
ABILITY:

Why do you want to be a Camp Counselor at Pride Rocks Foundation?
What do you hope to gain from your experience at the camp?

> I love horror and scary things. I grew up on a farm, and every year I
> helped put together the hayride for the local farmer's festival. As a camp
> counselor, I want to be able to help people and get the creative feeling
> I got back then. I also like that the Pride Rocks Foundation focuses on
> queer youth like me.

What relevant experiences do you have that make you fit to lead your
fellow students (leadership experience, training [First Aid/CPR], other
jobs)?

> Like I said, I worked on a farm. I also was captain of my basketball team at
> my middle school. In my freshman year, I participated in a small camping
> program for local Girl Scouts. We toured the farmlands of the area, played
> baseball, and listened to records.
>
> Of that experience, I learned how to navigate the outdoors on my own. I
> am used to categorizing birds, berries, and plants based on my upbringing.
> I am fit to lead other students because I know a lot of the things they
> won't.

What value would you add as an employee of the Pride Rocks
Foundation?

> Even if everything is against me, I will get the job done. It's what I'm best
> at.

What's your favorite horror film?

> ~~Dracola~~ dracula

CHAPTER TWENTY

The girls crowd around Cali like her phone holds a link to that new new, unreleased IMAX Marvel movie—sequels, too. Not a single girl breathes as she swipes talk on a contact—one that doesn't even have a name. It's just a nonsensical series of emojis.

Cali's phone is turned up so loud Temple can hear the dial tone. The tension is thick as a tied game at the Super Bowl, but it isn't a lasting pain. The robotic voice is muffled, but the voicemail beep sounds loud in the quiet room.

"Hey, Dr. G, it's Cali. I got a message for mom that I want you to pass on. Kind of important. They found a dead body at camp, so send a helicopter . . . I'm joking. Not about the body, but about the copter. We couldn't *all* fit in one. But seriously, y'all need to bring y'all's asses out here ASAP, or I'll probably die. Call me back." Her signoff cues her audience to relax, and half the girls sigh when Cali hangs up.

Temple stares at the smart phone Cali palms between her hands, unable to compute what Cali did to it. She stuck a wire in and all of a sudden it worked. She'll sound like a bumpkin if she asks—but, hell, she *is* a bumpkin.

"How did you make your phone work? Is it more hacking?" Apprehension slips into Temple's tone.

"Life hacking, at least," Cali says, straightening the wire. "I paid a guy a thousand bucks off the dark web to show me how. Ended up being real easy—I just cut up some headphones I had back home, stripped some wire, and attached a new piece to the internal antenna. I didn't know if it'd work until I got here, though."

Mickaeyla's the first to lean over the table. She glances at Temple, and when she sees her expression clearly, she cackles, slapping her shoulder. The sound is a sunray amid the girls. "Oh my god," Mickaeyla laughs, pointing at Temple's face. "Have you never seen a phone, girl? Why do you look so lost?" When she laughs, her cheeks take over most of her chubby face.

The other campers join in after a moment, and the thick atmosphere dissipates a little as they all cling to the laughter. A chance to breathe, finally.

This is the other girls' first murder. Temple's OK with them laughing at her. It's a way for them to think of something un-murder related—or, at least, only tangentially murder related.

"I don't really use a phone or anything. I couldn't tell you where mine is right now." Her dad is all about nature, so phone service was never relevant. He'd never text when he could talk, so she never learned to watch videos when she could watch the stars.

Cali runs her fingers over the crinkly wire to straighten it once more and then tosses the phone to the center of the table. "If I didn't have ten thousand followers, I wouldn't deal with the shit, either," she says.

The girls all fall silent. Their eyes follow the little hunk of plastic as it skids across the wooden table like a rock in a river.

"We can text again," Mickaeyla says breathlessly. "Can I put this on my stories? Is that allowed?"

Natalie puts her hand on her shoulder. "This is an emergency, Mickaeyla—only a TikTok can handle the gravity of this situation."

Temple pokes her head up, hoping to find Brenda or Lam making their way over. Even though the girls don't have much faith in the former, the directors do a fine job of being the responsible adults as far as Temple is concerned. If anyone can stop these dizzy bitches off Instagram, it's Lam.

Unfortunately, Brenda and Lam are both tucked away in a corner by their quarters' door, Lam placating Brenda to try and calm her spiraling.

The girls' eyes never waver from the phone's screen. With Anysaa inexplicably quiet, Temple will have to be the responsible one. "We should call 9-1—"

"I'm going first," Anysaa announces, snatching the phone off the table. She's already half-dialed the number by the time the girls curse her, some scratching at the ghost of where the phone once was. But that doesn't faze the Head Barbie. She raises her chin. "I was supposed to go on that hike—I could have been covered in guts right now. And I'm the only one with the hookup to a truck."

The girls' arguing ramps up and devolves into phone swiping in a blink. Anysaa's justification is insultingly thin, but Temple has another reason to pause. *Nobody* mentions calling the police. She'll probably have to fight the girls just as hard for that. Yeah, fuck that—there's got to be a non-emergency park ranger or something.

Her legs ache from running, and her head hurts from crying and falling and hearing voices that weren't there. She and Brenda found a very real body, and her life may be in danger. Dawntae didn't just drop dead in the middle of the woods. An actual threat could come for them. Rather than wasting her energy worrying about memories and voices, she needs to find a way to get them to listen to her.

"Look for the emergency hotline, *then* we'll call homes in alphabetical order," Temple blurts. The girls quiet, somehow keeping one eye on her, the other on the phone. "We'll take turns."

"Sure, *Baker*," Anysaa spits.

"We'll go by first names. I'll go last. It doesn't matter to me."

Anysaa glares at her but says nothing else. It's a truce, of sorts. Anysaa will resume seeing Temple as her terrorizer once the Law of Common Enemy has passed—or Temple fucks up again. It's a toss-up which will happen first.

There's a silent negotiation among everyone, like they're on the same side now that Temple's given them orders. When the girls finally nod, the air clears. They resign to her agreement, and the phone is returned to the table.

Temple grabs it, holding it steady as the call screen appears. "First, we call an emergency number."

Mickaeyla sits forward, grabbing the phone first. "Not the police," she says. "If the police on some bullshit, I want my cousin to know something about it first."

"True. I don't trust no damn police," Cali agrees. "But not calling them seems kind of bad."

Anysaa scratches her shoulders, focusing on the wood of the tabletop. "They wouldn't just kill us . . . we're the victims."

"We get it, Anysaa—your dad's a cop," K'ran says sardonically. She's one from Cabin Aye—the one with the basketball shorts. She gestures to herself, all masculine posture and baggy clothes. "I'm the one that looks like I 'fit the profile.' Having witnesses makes me feel safe."

That solves that, and Anysaa plops back into her seat with no further input. Temple doesn't argue. She knows a bunch of Black girls—especially with the masculine split in the room—won't want to involve the cops. And when it comes to character judgment,

Temple's somebody that should keep her mouth shut, considering the company she kept. The cops are the ones that took her dad away—she can't hate them for that. But even if she loves her dad, he's a literal serial killer.

Temple is a very special case.

"There's a highway service number," Temple says. It's hazy, but she remembers it from her employee handbook. "They're an emergency service for people stuck out here. We call them. Then, we can get onto families." When Temple finishes, she nods to Anysaa.

Anysaa hurries her fingers over the number pad and leaves a frantic message for the emergency service number, then calls her for family and does it again. When she's done, she passes it off like a relay. They make it girl to girl with peace, more or less, down the line in alphabetical order. Temple listens to their messages and tries to keep track of who's named what: K'ran, Mickaeyla, Natalie, Yaya . . . Temple retains 50 percent. To her left, Cali helps with the names. She announces the next girl in order, making sure they keep with the rule and shuts down anyone who disputes it.

No one picks up. Whether it was Anysaa that called, or K'ran, or Mickaeyla—whoever. Every girl ended up leaving a message.

When the phone comes to Temple, she's at a loss for what to do. Everyone else called family . . . but all Temple has is Aunt Ricki. She didn't drop her off in the first place—Temple never told her where the camp was because she knew her aunt would flip.

Temple definitely can't say anything about hearing voices—not in front of everyone else. In fact, anything about the land is off-limits. Her dad taught her all she knows about nature and evil, and Aunt Ricki knows that.

Whether or not she calls her, she's sure she's on her own.

But Aunt Ricki doesn't want Temple bothering her. Temple takes the phone into her hand, pausing for only a brief moment as her fingers ache to do something. Closing her eyes, she finally just hands the phone back to Cali.

"I've got no one to call," Temple says simply.

Cali stares at her.

"Honest."

One of Temple's own campers narrows her eyes. "Don't you have, like, an uncle or something?"

"Aunt," Temple corrects. She turns to Cali, a little more forcefully. "But I said what I said. I don't have anyone to contact so *let it go*." A little more bite than she means.

Cali shrugs her shoulder with a jerk and brings the phone back up to her ear. She glares over, her posture loose but with a stiffness working into her shoulders. "I'm going to try calling the highway service again," she tells anyone still around to listen.

It's really just Temple and about three other girls. Mickaeyla. Yaya—who's praying *again*. And Wynter, a rare solitary Barbie without her boss. The rest seem to have resumed with their lives. On the surface. The fact that no one got through—everyone went to voicemail.

That's too much to think about.

There's nervous glances to the phone in Cali's hand every few seconds, sentences that start and trail off as girls try to take their mind off the fear. As they try to clutch to the little hope they have. After a moment, Cali hangs up with a scowl.

"What is it?" Temple asks.

Cali taps her finger on the table. Temple can feel unease drifting off her. It's how Brenda looked when she tried to call Dawntae.

"They didn't pick up," Temple realizes.

Cali nods, typing on her phone again. "I'm going to text everyone I can—maybe they can keep calling, too."

"But no one's responded yet," Temple says. No one answered a single girl's phone call. They have no idea if their messages were even received.

Cali smacks onto the back of the chair. "Yeah. So all we can do is wait."

CHAPTER TWENTY-ONE

It isn't the ideal break, but it's the break they need. The girls start separating, idling toward the door—but before the room empties, Lam takes a second to step away from Brenda.

The strings of conversation that flit from cluster to cluster die as she raises her hands.

"I know we're all a little stressed," Lam says, "but we're going to be strict from now on. I'll give you thirty minutes. Pack your things and bring them when we meet back here."

Two girls give a mere inch of protest, and Lam glares them down with the hard stare of an ex-con before speaking again.

"Dawnt—" Lam's voice cracks. "*Dead body* or not. I'm protecting us by any means necessary. We leave as a group—or we don't leave at all."

With that, the campers disperse. Some stick around the dining area to eat their feelings, but most go out to their cabins. They're a stumbling horde, all trudging across the left side of the campsite, their pastel yellow T-shirts soft in the dusk.

Temple barely even feels like Cabin Bey is really her own. She spent most of her time there pretending to sleep.

But after she steps inside, she realizes she actually knows everyone's name.

Natalie, Sierra, Mickaeyla, and Yaya sit on the floor together, their bags securely packed as if they'd done so hours ago instead of a few minutes ago. The door hits the wall, and they look up at Temple. Cards spread out before them in nonsensical batches.

For a moment, Temple almost considers doing her job—asking "Ain't y'all supposed to go back to JG when you finish packing? You know we're trying not to die right now, right?"

But that would be too ... too much. For her. So she says nothing instead, her only comfortable state when all of them turn their eyes to her.

They only pause for the quick moment it takes to decipher whether or not Temple's a murderer. When they find she's not, they turn back to their game.

"We started this game after the Cabin versus Cabin," Mickaeyla says, eyes on the cards.

"Winner was supposed to get an autographed *Hearts Stop*," Natalie says next.

"Mickaeyla said it would help us calm down," Yaya says. "You wanna play?"

Temple climbs onto her bed and sits cross-legged, then drags her gray suitcase atop the blanket. "Don't know how. Don't wanna learn."

They take that as her final answer and move on with their lives. She slacks against the wall, resting her hand on her suitcase wheels.

The coin Temple stuffed into her sleeve knocks against the plastic—and Temple's stomach drops. The others are too focused on ignoring her to acknowledge if they heard, but Temple knows hardwood on wood is not quiet.

It burns through Temple's hoodie, sending a crawl of paranoia up her neck. She can play this off. There's no need to spiral, Temple.

With a slow, shaking hand, she unzips her suitcase and angles its contents out of the girls' sight.

Her backup knife is still there. Good.

If one of the girls found *that*, they might have taken it to the fuzz. Brenda may have let Temple's bad attitude slide, but there's no way she'd get away with an *armed* bad attitude. The small pouch latches onto the front pocket of her suitcase, and she tucks both of her knives inside the pocket for safekeeping.

Matches. Cartons of salt. Some lighter fluid that she prays will last.

Temple reorganizes her suitcase in silence, idly listening to the girls play Tonk. She zips it closed just when the front door slams against the wall and Cali bursts in. The force blows some cards away, sending the girls scrambling on the floor to keep the game civil.

It feels like there's a sniper focusing right between Temple's eyes when Cali locks onto her.

"Bitch, Aye is hell," Cali says in lieu of a greeting. She stomps over to the nearest bed and plops onto the covers, bouncing as it creaks with her weight. "Anysaa and her backup dancers can't decide if this is God's fault, Brenda's fault, or your fault, and K'ran keeps bursting into tears." She cuts her gaze to Temple, as if expecting a commiserating eye roll, but presses on, even though she never gets one. "If I wanted to deal with that shit, I'd have stayed with Brenda."

Brenda's in for a long struggle after seeing Dawntae up on the path. Corpses are unforgettable. Temple still remembers her first as crisp as she remembers her dad's arrest. But she's got a feeling saying all that would only egg Cali on. So Temple just shrugs. "It's not like we'll have assigned cabins for long. Just ignore them."

Cali pulls out her phone and checks the screen. "I only got a few texts back so far, and all of them were just failure-to-send messages. I got nothing from your aunt." She tosses her phone over her head like it's made of rubber, unconcerned if it lands on the bed or not.

"My *aunt*? Why would my aunt text you?" Temple asks.

Rolling over, Cali puts her head on her hand. "Because I texted her, duh?"

Temple pauses. She closes her suitcase with a measured hand, wondering if she heard right. She couldn't have.

Before Temple can ask for clarification, Cali recognizes the look. "Don't even," she says. "You lost your goddamn mind not telling somebody what happened. I'm saving your life."

"I'm saving your life."

"Your afterlife."

The memory of her mother makes Temple grimace, but she doesn't have time to dwell on it. Cali needs to be dealt with now. She narrows her eyes at the girl, that stutter in her chest back and in full force. She feels nauseous.

And it's not that Cali didn't listen. Nobody listens to Temple, and for good reason—Temple's a shit source.

It's that Cali shouldn't know Temple's aunt's number.

Nobody would know that. Ever. Not even the school—Temple always put a fake number on the forms. Back when she got suspended, the assistant principal gave her an hour of hell for the lie.

"How the fuck do you know my aunt's number?" Temple hisses.

Cali blinks too quickly, then her eyes go wide. Temple's a trained professional at hiding her feelings, at masking her insides—even if Cali covers it all back up in a second, she knows exactly what it looks like.

It's *not* in Temple's head.

She's *not* paranoid.

"Hacking, dumbass," Cali says cooly. "I already told you, and you're *still* bitching about it?"

"Bullshit." Temple clenches her fist.

Cali glares back. "Believe what you want, girl. I know your social security number, too, and you ain't never get mad about that one." She laughs, up on her feet and raising her voice. "You're mad I called *your aunt*? What did you plan on doing, walking home? Catching the shuttle tomorrow?"

"I told you I didn't want to call anyone!" Temple shouts, rising from her bed.

No one's supposed to know *anything* about her. Nothing good *ever* comes from Temple being known. Be it pity, nosy counselors, or stalker North Pointers.

It always ends badly.

When Cali speaks, she doesn't mince words. "*Nobody likes you. You don't have any friends, no one's gonna give you a ride home. I'm keeping your dumbass alive.*"

Inches away, the other girls of Bey are still playing their card game but now with a much more concentrated effort.

Temple almost argues, but Cali holds up a finger to shut her up. She looks over to the others, eyebrow raised. "Did I lie? Y'all hate her ass, too," she declares for them.

Their quiet responses overlap with each other:

"I'm not in this; that's Anysaa's beef."

"I don't even have a class with that girl."

"We just tryna play cards, Cali."

"You bitches ain't playin' cards," Cali says. "That's a damn lie."

They don't confirm or deny. Cali's lips twist into a self-satisfied smirk. Not even in a mean way. Nothing Cali was trying to do is mean—but it still pisses Temple off.

"Just leave me alone," Temple says firmly.

Now the girls aren't bothering with the illusion of playing cards, openly staring at Temple and Cali both standing there by her bed.

Temple looks at the clock, rather than back at them. It's almost six, she notes.

Well, fuck it. Fuck her stuff, fuck these girls, fuck this camp.

She grabs everything in a rush, stuffing her suitcase under her bed and fixing her clothes.

"What are you doing?" Cali asks.

Everything's over, anyway. Temple's almost done with all of this. Her handy pouch lays across her mattress, the only thing she'll care about for now. Temple tucks it under her arm as she marches out the door, pausing with her hand on the knob.

She looks in the eyes of the others, and they're really staring now.

Front-row tickets to the freak show.

This never would have worked.

Her gaze lingers on Cali's before she sneers. "I hope each and every one of you bitches die," she says.

And she slams the door behind her, convinced she means it.

There ain't been nobody in five days.

And then, so quiet she thought she imagined it: "It's in here, dude."

The voice is deep, a man's.

Not her dad. He was gone.

"I swear. Pinnocents20 drew it out on Maps for me."

Temple lifted her head from her knees. Her back cracked, a dull ache beginning to spread from her shoulders down her side. The burn was probably infected by now. She had no clue how to fix that.

"Pinnocents isn't a real North Pointer, though—she's barely on the forums. And when she is, she's always lecturing us about what we post. How the fuck would she know anything with that stick up her ass?"

Temple stared at the yellow tile across from her, the tile she barely looked at since they took her dad away. Even the slightest shift in her body sent the rustling of the leaves beneath her into the silence.

But it wasn't silence anymore.

"Holy shit, this place is cool as fuck." A woman.

A tickle traced Temple's knee, and she flicked away the spider. She returned her head to her knees. She'd never heard these voices before.

She shouldn't leave the bathtub.

But it could be a survivor. Someone looking for help. A victim?

In a swift movement and a whirl of blackened green, Temple was on her feet and her toes touched the cool tile. The whispers from the other side of the door pressed on, getting closer. The floor settled just beyond the thin wooden panel that separated Temple from the strangers.

Who are you?

Her lips moved. Her throat was too dry, sticking closed, so she just stood there, wheezing. Just ask. Still nothing.

She couldn't order herself to do it. She took a step back.

"What was that?" the woman asked.

There's another creak, and then a pause. "What?"

"Are you sure this dude is gone? Because I swear I heard somebody."

"Bitch, there's only one North Point Killer—literally one house in these woods. We got the right person." Another creak, and they were walking again. Their voices got clearer. For some reason, Temple felt the vibrations of it on her skin.

"But what if—"

"He's gone," the man snapped. His voice was dry, impatient. "And from what I saw on the news, they're gonna execute him good."

Everything went cold. Temple swayed, her legs suddenly shaky as she clenched her fists, picturing her dad smiling at her from the kitchen table. Picturing him gripping her shoulder, his skin clean, free of blood. And him grinning, boosting her up to a branch.

He was going to die. The cops didn't just arrest him . . . they were going to take him away. For good.

The bathroom door blasted open, and light blared into her eyes just as Temple realized the truth—and then someone shrieked, and Temple couldn't see so she screamed, too.

Something sharp hit her on her side.

"What the fuck!" someone yelled.

She fell to the ground and heard clattering around her. Heavy breaths feet away. They could get her. She was weak. She was vulnerable.

She must protect herself.

"Listen to your father, baby girl. Strangers are a fucking problem."

"Holy fuck," the man shouted. "What the fuck is that thing?"

Temple screamed her head off so hard her neck twitched. Her voice bounced off the walls and whirred in her ears before—finally—footsteps thudded softer and softer.

She didn't move from the bathroom floor, but from what Aunt Ricki told her three days later, the North Pointers had chained the doors shut, sealing Temple inside.

CHAPTER TWENTY-TWO

Temple slips into the outdoor bathrooms, the signs gleaming in the lowering sunlight. The units aren't technically outhouses, but there's still an unclean feeling about them. Especially with those signature floodlights up on the damn ceiling. There are two stalls per gendered side, useless since there are only girls this weekend. Still a great place to hide, though.

Crouching into herself, Temple slides into a stall and tries to steady her heartbeat. The rhythmic thuds agree with her, telling her to go it alone. She doesn't need her aunt to pick her up because she doesn't need to be picked up. Not yet, at least.

She's the daughter of one of the most infamous serial killers of all time. She saw her first dead body when she was eight, and touched one when she was ten. She isn't like the campers. She can be by herself—needs to be. Maybe for now. Maybe forever.

"You should have all the friends in the world."

Nope. Her dad knows her so well and still got it so wrong. Friends are just voyeurs at a zoo, waiting to poke at the monster. Temple doesn't *want* friends, doesn't want anybody knowing that *she's* the monster. She needs to be left alone.

Temple let the woods spook her earlier; she's woman enough to admit it.

But she's over her normal girl façade. She's a freak. And she has freak shit to take care of.

The copycat.

The secret room.

Even the visions of her mother prove to her she's on the right track. Her dad's got something up his sleeve, and Temple's nearly there. But instead of thinking about the intentions of the slasher film wannabe, she needs to forget about her dad and focus on her. What she's going to do from this point forward.

She's definitely going to burn that bitch-ass North Point House down, that's for sure. The map tells her that there's a hidden room, but she can't see it from the structure outside. That means it's either detached or underground.

She's also gonna abandon this flimsy-ass camp counselor cover. She'll tell Brenda she's leaving—of course, Brenda will be all "you can't" and "you're not allowed." But Temple really doesn't want to scare her. If she leaves now, Brenda would probably do something crazy, like look for her—Temple doesn't want that.

But she doesn't have to play games anymore. She doesn't have to put up with everyone hating her, even if most of them only say it with their eyes.

With a sigh, Temple finishes up and flushes. For a glimpse of a moment, only about half of her exhale, she feels hope. Hope that it'll all work out. She'll find her mother's corpse, stop the copycat, save the girls.

But that's a betrayal. She stomps the hope down with a scowl. *No*, she tells herself. When Temple disappears, she's not going to save anyone. *Fuck the other girls.*

When Temple exits the stall, she stops short at the sight of Anysaa leaning over the sink, poised to wash her shaking hands. Anysaa jumps like Temple's stalking the bathroom bloody and with her knives on display. She averts her eyes, washing her hands frantically.

Temple washes her hands, too, but much more calmly. She shuts off the water, not even bothering to dry, and turns to the Head Barbie Counselor. Narrows her eyes.

"I wasn't aware I wasn't allowed to be in the bathroom at the same time as you."

Anysaa withdraws like a kicked dog but stays quiet. Her hands *have* to be clean by now, but she's stalling. The skin of her throat broadcasts her swallow.

"You know, it's kind of more annoying when you treat me like some mean girl," Temple accuses.

Anysaa looks up, her brows furrowed like she doesn't understand. "I'm sorry?"

"Your approach. I don't take your lunch money. I don't shove you into lockers. I've spoken to you, like, twice, and somehow each time, everyone finds out about it. Somehow, you're the innocent victim while *I'm* the 'bully.'"

Anysaa's eyes fill with challenge, but she stuffs it down quickly. She's back to averting her eyes, focusing on drying her hands like it's a math test. Now Temple realizes Anysaa *is* stalling. She's probably waiting on Temple to leave first.

"It's not like you're nice to me," Anysaa says. "I just match your energy."

"I'm a bitch to everyone. Not just you."

"But it *is* just me, Temple," Anysaa snaps. She keeps her distance, but her tone seems to spike across the room. "Unless you follow other North Prep girls home?"

Temple didn't follow her home, but Anysaa's too self-centered to consider her a neighbor. Her aunt's house isn't in the same housing development as Anysaa's—it's deeper, farther into the woods. Like everything about Temple's family.

But Temple's never cleared it up. She decided a long time ago that if Anysaa wanted her to be a demon so bad, she'd be one—but it sucks that Anysaa took the fun out of being bad, too.

"If this is about your knee then just say so, princess." Temple narrows her eyes. "But never forget that I know what really happened. *You* followed *me* home. Your 'woe is me' bullshit won't work on somebody that knows about your lying ass."

Anysaa pinches her lips, gripping the sink rim and glaring into Temple's eyes. Her entire wall of confidence is put up in just that second. Because—Temple had realized all those months ago—she would never admit the truth.

Anysaa would never admit that she started this.

"How about you just leave me alone? I won't bother you; you don't bother me." She gives Temple a look, one that says she's nothing more than a speck of dust. Then she starts to leave, bumping Temple's shoulder on the way out as if the conversation is over.

Despite all the attitude, it has the semblance of a truce. If Temple presses her, it'll be no better than picking a fight.

Of course, that's all Temple's looking for right now.

She whirls around and follows Anysaa out of the bathrooms, walking quick and keeping on her.

"Wow, you've got to teach me that trick," Temple says, her voice filled with a dark tint that she doesn't recognize. Maybe it's because she'd never known anyone besides her family this long. She doesn't think she hates Anysaa. Really, she doesn't know. But seeing her just adds to the fire Cali started. She nearly steps on the back of Anysaa's shoes she's so close.

Anysaa keeps her eyes forward. "Leave me the fuck alone; you're wilding, bitch."

Temple continues anyway. "It's like—you bossed up, but no one was around to hear it. How do you manage to be so consistently pitiful? Is it natural? Do you study?"

She steps on Anysaa's heel and Anysaa stumbles but keeps moving, determined not to look back at Temple.

Temple doesn't let up. "Maybe it's a pheromone? Do you use that? I mean, my life has been plenty shit and I still feel sorry for you. Does that make any sense? You've got the cool friends, the nice clothes, and you can afford a prep school while I only got into North Prep because I've been expelled from most schools in the county. It made for a super interesting application essay, but it wasn't pitiful. It wasn't pathetic."

"Just leave me *alone*."

Anysaa stomps into JG, where all the other girls are waiting. The room goes quiet when they see Temple walk in on Anysaa's heels.

Anysaa's eyes whirl to the other side, the one with all her cab-inmates. Her mini-mes, Wynter and Janae. K'ran. And Cali. Whispers sound around Temple as she glares at everything. At nothing.

It's clear Anysaa wants to scurry right into their corner, but she does that "boss-up" thing again instead. She turns on Temple, nostrils flaring. She grabs Temple's collar before Temple can put up a defense, and yanks her forward.

"Just leave me alone *for once!*" she screams.

"Oh, fuck off!" Temple yells back, and that rips through the room and silences the whispers. The girls all look at Temple, and it's the most attention she's ever had. It's in that exact moment that she makes eye contact with Cali again—and Cali's scowl speaks before she does.

"Temple, don't fucking take this shit out on Anysaa because you're mad at me," Cali says. "What is *wrong* with you?"

"This isn't about you," Temple lies. "I don't like either of you bitches." She whips her finger to Anysaa, taking a step forward. "Anysaa's always like this. She's always had it out for me and still got the nerve to play the victim!"

"I am so *tired* of you!" Anysaa says—she practically growls it.

Temple advances on her. Cali starts moving toward them, but Temple ignores it. She focuses on the one and only, keeping her voice low and menacing. "No, you're not," Temple says. "What you're tired of is remembering that I beat your ass the first time you stepped out of line."

"What the fuck did you just say?"

"You heard me!" Fire runs in her veins as she towers over this de facto leader. Stares down into her eyes. Temple remembers the pipe.

Remembers clutching onto it, screaming for dear life. It was so easy to convince herself to swing.

And it's like Anysaa can read it in her eyes. "We didn't even hurt you. Why do you hate us so much?"

"You think I hate you?" Temple tosses her bag to the side, taking another step forward. She can feel the girl's breath on her skin. "I don't think of you at all."

"You're a fucking bitch."

And finally, it's there. A desperation that only comes from giving up. Temple can see it in Anysaa's eyes that she's *tired*. She doesn't want this.

But Temple's just getting started.

She reaches forward. Anysaa's T-shirt twists in her fists, and there are gasps somewhere far away.

"You. Followed. Me. Home." Temple says every word clearly. Slowly. Anysaa can lie to everyone else—to security, to the principal, to her aunt. But she can't lie right to Temple. "You and your friends were stalking me. It may have been a coincidence the first turn, but not the second. And not when I saw you pick up that rock—so I fought back."

When it came down to it, Temple could only stomach one hit with the pipe. Only one swing. Only one scream. It ripped through Temple like a shiver, so hard and fast she dropped the pipe and ran. Until her lungs seized.

Still, it was enough. Anysaa's knee got permanent damage. And she also damn well got the message.

That Temple wasn't that little girl chained in the bathroom anymore.

Temple tilts her head, jerking the girl forward. "And I'll do it again. Every. Single. Time. You step out of line—I'll get you back in order."

Anysaa shoves Temple so hard Temple's back slams into the wall. Her teeth chatter. She gets back to balance, and Anysaa hits her. "You're a psycho!"

The girls crowd around for just a glimpse of Temple's blood spilled. For the long-awaited fight. Temple Baker's comeuppance at the hands of North Prep Royalty.

Anysaa whips her hand back for another punch, but Temple hits first. She knocks into the girl's chin. It's hard and loud, and Anysaa stumbles backward.

Temple takes the chance to launch on her. It isn't the fight she planned for, but she can only see red now. She tears into Head Barbie as quick as she can, as relentlessly as she can, but Anysaa gives it back just as bad. Temple fights until she's dizzy from all the blows to her head. They're tangled over each other, pulling, tugging, and screeching like birds.

Then there's feet pounding on the floor. Temple's world flips upside down as Lam snatches her off Anysaa. She tries to claw for Anysaa one last time but is held too far away. Everyone shouts. Blood rushes through Temple's ears.

Then Lam's screaming. "Separate, you two! Either side of the cabin!"

Cali drags Temple to the kitchen, and Anysaa and Cabin Aye stay by the door. Anysaa has blood streaming down her cheek, and from the warmth in Temple's mouth, she knows she isn't a much better sight. Her chest heaves as she tries to catch her breath.

Her heart rams. She feels on fire. She feels hated. She feels hatred. Blood starts dripping from nowhere, and Temple opens her eye. She makes eye contact with Anysaa, just for a second. That's where the hate is coming from. Anysaa hates her, Temple can see loud and clear in the way her eyes narrow, and Temple's glad. Anysaa can hate her. Temple won't be around for long.

She opens her mouth to say something. To join in the screams. To shun everyone else. But just as she does, the lights cut out completely.

Everything turns black.

CHAPTER TWENTY-THREE

At first, Temple thinks she's passed out. She's probably deserved to be punched a million times—and she's wanted a punch just as often—but the reality is, Temple's never been in a fistfight.

Losing consciousness . . . she can't tell if she's good or bad at fighting. If she won or lost. Nah, fainting is a clear sign she lost.

But then the girls all begin speaking at once.

Temple didn't pass out.

"What's going on?" Yaya's voice. Temple recognizes it even in the dark, its melody and its quivering. "Can somebody turn the lights back on?"

"I don't know what's happening." Lam. "Did anyone plug in an appliance? I told y'all those are forbidden because of all the shitty old wiring."

Bang! Bang bang!

Temple startles at the heavy thumps.

Cali lets go, stepping away. "What the fuck?"

It's loud and close, like a construction site just appeared over their heads.

A girl starts laughing—that loud cackling has to be Mickaeyla. "Oh my god, is this a prank? Where's Brenda? Is it Dawntae?" The excitement that always paints her voice sounds more hysterical. She's scared.

But not letting herself feel that fear.

Chills run over Temple as the banging continues, and she can't help but recall her dad's words. Banging is to scare them off.

But it's just the first step.

Temple slaps her hands over her ears as a pit grows in her stomach. All of her dad's advice is for the North Point House though. JG isn't even on the map—the main cabin, the school—it's new, not haunted.

Temple takes a step back, the rubber on her shoes dragging across the little grooves in the hardwood floors. Her back presses against the wall panel, the coolness bleeding through her shirt. As her eyes adjust to the dark, she can see all the girls in the living room, their worry blooming.

The hum of their concerns thickens into a fog of concrete dread, then grows into a roar. The bangs continue. Cell phone flashlights beam through the darkness.

"Is everyone OK?" That one's Brenda.

There's quiet for a moment, and then the shrill cut of Lam's whistle whirs in everyone's ears. "We need an answer!" Lam yells. "Is everyone OK?"

"Yes." The girls speak in unison, one dreary note together.

A sputter of light blinks in the room's center, and Lam's torso comes into sight—a big yellow flashlight clenched in her fist. "Visuals!" She's not yelling at the girls now. The light bounces around the room, fluttering on faces for half a second at a time. No one's looking anywhere directly. But fear and confusion paint their expressions.

"*Stop it.*"

The voice is distant. Barely a whisper.

But it's there.

"Who said that?" Lam asks. The light in her hand flickers on and off, over and over until she gives it a rough smack. It dies completely. "Shit."

Temple's frozen by the wall. Her ears tune in, listening.

Waiting.

It's muffled, far away. But it's still absolutely recognizable. It reaches into Temple, into her mind—into her memory of those nights long ago. Her first night here.

Goose bumps crawl over her arms as she clenches her eyes shut, as if that could block out the arguing.

It doesn't help that the girls are starting to heat up with panic.

"This isn't a prank, is it?" Mickaeyla.

"What the fuck is going on?" Anysaa.

"Lord, please watch over me." Yaya.

"Everybody stay calm." Brenda. "Let's make sure we're all accounted for first, before we start panicking." Her silhouette moves smoothly into the center of the room while Lam's cell phone lights begin to fritz and dim out.

In the midst of all this chaos, Brenda's more put together and human than she has been all day. "When I call your name, I need you to confirm you're here. Verbally." Her voice takes a hard edge, but there's a crack in that last syllable. The strange voices are no more. Just the ringing silence of the cabin. "When I say your name, you have to respond. Got it?"

"Yes, Director Brenda." The girls speak once more in unison.

"Good." Temple can hear the smile in Brenda's voice. Even as she gets started—in alphabetical order—with the name that can't have sparked joy. "Temple. You good?"

Good is fucking pushing it. "I'm here," Temple says. She feels Cali at her side, pressing a hand to her arm. Temple's still mad at her. But she realizes her voice is barely there. "I'm here," she says again.

"Natalie," Brenda calls.

"I'm here."

"Sierra? Janae? Mickaeyla?"

The girls all respond as the darkness deepens. That feeling of cold spreads.

Temple begins to tremble, reaching behind her to the wall. Pawing toward the window. The curtains tickle her wrist as she slips her fingers onto the windowsill.

She's played these games before. The woods will never fool her into thinking she's safe again.

Temple cracks the window open, just a little, and watches the room. Cool air breezes over her shoulders, running over her rigid muscles.

Brenda gets farther down the list of names. The girls already called move to the walls, clearing the center for the girls left. Temple watches them shift around slowly; losing the crisp light makes the air thick like water.

"Wynter? Yaya? Cali?"

The next set of girls confirm.

At the front, Sierra props the door open, and moonlight bathes the room in soft shadows and silhouettes. Cali's moved from Temple's side, now fiddling with the light switch with a knife she found who knows where.

Temple waits for her eyes to adjust. She needs to be able to see.

Something is wrong. This is wrong.

"Anysaa? K'ran?"

"Here." K'ran's voice is gravelly, but you can hear the fear through her breathing.

Anysaa doesn't respond. Temple watches her silhouette slide across the room with slow mysticism, passing from wall to wall. Her hair flows in its fluid shadow, drifting in the air.

"Anysaa," Brenda says again.

Anysaa's in the center of the room now. Brenda grabs her arm, concern in her eyes. "Hey, you don't look too good. You don't have a concussion, do you?" she asks. She tugs on her sleeve, checking for injuries.

Anysaa turns to Brenda. Her stare hardens as she peers back. Then her voice comes out scratchy and low. "Ah. *Another one!*" She raises her arm. The metal blades of the scissors gleam in the moonlight.

Temple can't even scream. She can't warn Brenda or yell "stop."

Anysaa slices down, and the blades burrow into Brenda's neck before Anysaa wrenches it right back out with a grin.

Brenda only gets a gasp out before a slit of red slides across her throat, like it's unzipping. She let out a deep gurgle, her feet staggering beneath her.

Everyone stops.

Brenda's hand reaches forward, clawing, clawing . . . at nothing. Her fingers don't even make it to her neck. She falls to the floor. *Thump.* Her body collapses in a heap.

All the girls scream.

"Oh my god!" Mickaeyla yells.

The push and pull grows fervent as Brenda's corpse lays still before them.

Anysaa swings her weapon wildly, screaming at no one as they scurry away. There's the thump of a girl falling to the ground.

Anysaa's eyes are dull and glazed, her voice a scratching echo. Not her voice. It's like someone else's voice.

Some other poor girl gets caught in the crossfire. Temple can't tell who.

The girls trip over themselves to get away. It's an immediate split, some spilling out of JG like the fires of hell are on their tail. Others disappear, dashing into other rooms and hiding places. They cry. They pray.

Temple is frozen.

She stays silent and just watches, paralyzed with fear. She can't move. She's going to die.

She takes too long.

Anysaa stops flinging her arms around and pauses when she notices Temple. She narrows her eyes, taking a threatening step forward before her face cracks into a harsh, tight grin.

"Honey," she greets. Her voice is distorted and distant, though kind for whoever that smile is for.

Because it couldn't be Temple.

But Anysaa crouches before her, reaching her hand out. She keeps her eyes on Temple's, like a challenge. "Come now—before he finds you."

It goes without saying, but Temple will not be accepting that invitation.

The eye contact snaps her out of her daze, though, and she whips around toward the window, slamming up the pane. Her head swims at the movement. A wave of dizziness stops her hands.

Anysaa's waiting for it.

She launches forward like a cat, grabbing Temple with her blood-covered hands, clawing her back into the room. Her tongue scrapes against her teeth in soothing clicks.

"Don't be scared . . ." she mutters.

She drags Temple away from the wall, unfazed by her flailing limbs and raspy shouts. Drags her toward Brenda's body. Toward the red splatters of blood spreading in all directions like branches on a tree. Anysaa's shushes get firmer with every step, and once they're in the center of the room again, she slams Temple to the ground, glaring down at her.

Temple struggles to crawl away. Her chest is tight. Her nails scrape against the floor.

But Anysaa snatches her by the ankle, dragging her deep into the cabin.

Brenda's corpse is twisted on the ground, sliced open. Her eyes stare at the ceiling.

"*Shut up!*" Anysaa yells at Temple over her screams. "If Raymond hears you, he'll string you up."

Temple keeps screaming. She grabs onto whatever she can. The sofa slides as she grips its leg, but Anysaa yanks her off it. Temple yelps. She claws around until she catches hold of fabric and she drags it along, her eyes squeezed shut. *Shit, shit, shit.* She's bathed in her fear. It stops in her throat and tenses up her hands. But intertwined with the fear, twisted around her spine, is a familiarity she can't suppress. That steel curtain of guilt that never leaves.

This is how her dad's victims must have felt. This is what they went through when they were caught, and she was eight, and they screamed for their lives while she did nothing.

Anysaa makes it to the door, Temple swaying in her grasp. Temple opens her eyes and sees the fabric she clutches—her bag. It catches on the leg of the sofa, vibration bouncing through the strap. Temple clenches, holding on like a prayer.

Anysaa tugs harder. "Come on," she hisses. "I'm not gonna tell you again. We gotta go."

Footsteps sound around the room, echoing like heels in a cathedral. For a second, Temple thinks someone's come for her—Lam, Mickaeyla—it doesn't matter. She'll even take a Barbie lackey.

Her neck creaks as she tries to look up, but her upper body strength fails her.

Then the lights flicker. White fills the room on and off, bleeding through Temple's skull and mingling with her headache. Then the lights flicker, cut back on completely.

Temple whimpers.

Blood streams through the room like a river, cutting the space in half. Two more slain girls line the floor. Her heart drops.

K'ran.

Mickaeyla.

Temple recognizes each of their faces.

The lights flicker again, and Anysaa stops moving.

Crack, crack.

Anysaa holds on to Temple's ankle, lowering her arm so Temple's back squishes into the wet floors. Anysaa's mouth has popped open, eyes darting over the walls. Body on guard, like death itself ran for her.

The metallic pool that splits the room crackles—white little bolts of frost burst over the surface. It freezes almost instantly, with the crawling movement of . . . cold.

Moving.

Approaching.

Anysaa's features brighten and darken as the lights flash. Her expression contorts into ugly hatred. "*Stop it!*" she screams. "Leave Thomas alone!" She yells it at the nothingness, at the frost that chips away at the wood.

Temple follows her gaze to the kitchen, just as veins of gray overtake the cabinets. The wafting crystals of ice condense. They drift across the floor—like footsteps. Huge, hulking footsteps that are coming toward them.

Temple's dad's words flash in her mind.

"Pay attention to how goddamn cold it is out here, Temple—you hear me?"

The lights steady, beaming down in the main room. Temple can see her own breath.

"Ice is dangerous."

Run.

Temple wrenches her body around on the ground, twisting her ankle and ripping out of Anysaa's hold. Her hand grazes Brenda's wrist as she drags herself along the floor.

"Honey! No!" Anysaa cries as Temple scrapes at the bag strap and loops it over her shoulder. She's knocked Anysaa off balance. "Thomas!" Anysaa shouts again. She casts Temple a weary look, opens her mouth to say something, crouching against the door to stay upright. "Y-Yo-Y-"

Temple kicks her in the jaw, and Anysaa flies backward. She knocks against the door and slumps into the threshold with her legs sprawled out. The crystal footsteps expand like a balloon and then half the room is enveloped in darkness.

Temple stares. Only for a second.

What is it?

It's fog. It's darkness. It's all compressed in a tight line that pushes through the room like night. As the cold spreads farther, ice grips Temple's chest. The tips of Brenda's fingers turn blue. Wood pops and chips as it freezes. Temple's body stiffens again, fear seizing her legs and keeping them still.

"*Finallyyy,*" a breathy echo sighs. It's the same voice as the distant yell she heard before. The deep vibration of the wail makes Temple shake.

She grips onto herself, refocusing on the room around her. Blood ... corpses ... cold. That's all that's left. Adjusting her bag over her shoulder, Temple takes a look at Anysaa's limp body, then to the crawling silver flakes that climb to the cabin's ceiling.

And then Temple slips away, running out onto the campground.

CHAPTER TWENTY-FOUR

Temple can't move very quickly. Her ankle, weak from where Anysaa grabbed it, throbs with every step. She limps, catching her toes in the dirt without looking back at JG. She can't stop.

Bey glides by, then Aye, and then she's at the edge of the campsite. Her breath rattles in her ears, her eyes locked onto the woods. JG. North Point House. Everything's so open and dangerous.

But Temple can always hide in the thick of branches.

The darkness of the forest overtakes her. The soft weeds that line the ground thump under her pounding footsteps. Her twisted ankle sends a knife up her calf with every step. But she keeps going.

A large trunk curves up the corner of the path—one thick enough to support her weight. Finally. Temple makes a dash for it, gripping its lower branches, huffing and risking a look behind her.

Which is a mistake.

Temple's vision swims and she loses balance. "Fuck," she spits as she hits the ground on her aching shoulder.

Shit.

Anysaa's hit from earlier, right on her head.

Temple's ankle pulsates. A snap sounds behind her, and all of her muscles tense. It could be a girl, another girl, looking for safety. Or it could be . . .

She hears it again, and she scrapes herself up. Twigs catch in her jeans as she sprints, the sound of her breath getting rougher. Her lungs getting tighter. She looks out for any shadows after her, any cold on her skin.

All she gets are the twisted green of the kudzu nipping at her boots. Branches hitting her in the face.

Her only chance is deeper into the woods.

Temple dashes off the path, onto the inner lining of the trees. She's wheezing now, and she really *should* have brought her inhaler. Without the loose gravel, it's even harder to walk. She has to keep her knees high just to move, and every time her ankle goes back down, she falters.

Crack.

She hears it again, this time in front of her.

She stops, staring into the trees. There's nothing but silent, still forest. No shadows creep through the breaks of moonlight in the leaves. No Anysaa, with her wide eyes and bloodstained clothes.

Temple presses her hand to the nearest tree, turning away anyway. It feels like she's surrounded. She left Anysaa behind, but Temple still feels eyes right on her shoulder.

She's already slowing down. North Point House has yet to come into view, but Temple's on shaky legs. She crosses the path, looking both ways, her chest convulsing with breaths it can't take. Her vision is spotting. Any longer and she'll have an attack.

There's no way she's making it any further. She tightens her fingers on the nearest patch of bark. She hikes one leg up, the other dangling, while her arms do most of the work. There was once a time she did this for fun. When she was seven, running through the woods and challenging and climbing trees with her dad was a great day.

Now, her heart slams in her chest with each branch she passes. She loses focus every time she remembers why she's there, in the forest, climbing a tree. Her hands stumble over the branch and her foot slips.

Temple holds in a groan as she swings by her shoulder joint. She feels something pop, then a sharp pain that dulls. But she must press on.

She grapples back onto the rough wood firmly. If she had a clock, she'd check it. Dinner was supposed to be at six, but they didn't even get to eat before everything. It's dark—the stars are high.

There's no way to know how long she was in Anysaa's clutches.

Temple reaches the highest branch thick enough to hold her—much like the one on the Midpoint Tree where she'd seen blue chiffon swinging from just a night ago.

There's no need to think about that. Temple grips it firmly. Her bag slams against her legs until she sprawls over the length of the branch. With her sides unevenly balanced, Temple teeters until she adjusts properly and leans against the trunk.

She takes a deep breath, and it comes out a cough as sobs rip through her, the branch wobbling.

The first time she saw a dead body, she was eight years old. She knew the woman she found nude, lying on the ground with red marks along her body. Her bloodied fingernails were tucked into her fists, and red painted her knuckles like broad brushstrokes. Cuts burrowed so deep into the flesh of her forehead they reached her skull. It was her classmate's mom.

But Temple's never seen someone get killed before.

Brenda ... right before her eyes. That isn't supposed to matter. She's supposed to be used to death. She *did* think Brenda was being dramatic when they found Dawntae's body earlier. Not on purpose, but she knows she did.

Now, snot spills out of her like a faucet and her wailing clutches up her throat, stopping her already choppy breaths.

Temple wraps her arms around herself as she tries to keep quiet, her eyes darting to any movement or a sudden chill. Both are threats now. She could seriously die.

She probably *will* die, and everyone will rejoice. *Ding dong, the witch is dead.*

When Temple's sobbing finally stops, the woods are quiet. Fog touches the branch just beneath her, lacing the trees with a twinkling mist she'd appreciate under different circumstances. The moon smiles down at her in its crescent, mixing in pearly light while the bugs and owls make the only sounds they know.

Even quieter still, Temple hears buzzing static, muffled. She furrows her brows, tensing up as she looks around. More threats. She clenches her muscles, ready to bolt. The static continues and she looks down. Nothing jumps out at her.

Then she realizes: the bag.

The black bag she carries is nice leather with brown accents over the back and sides, sleek and thin with barely anything inside. It's the successful fraternal twin of Temple's own old worn-down bag, and the sight of it makes Temple nauseous.

Shit. It's not hers. She got the wrong one.

She don't even got a fucking knife.

Temple rips the bag open, her skin pasted with sweat as she tears through the contents. The voice behind the static clears. At the base of the bag, buried under an empty wallet, is Brenda's radio. Temple throws the wallet to the ground.

"Someone please, help us!" Lam cries. "Four down—she-she might go after the rest. If you can hear us, we're on the North Point Campgrounds. We're in danger."

An understatement. Temple has never heard Lam sound so desperate, and it makes everything feel even more real. More real than her throbbing ankle or the blood slick on her skin.

Lam continues her calls, her voice strained and thick. "God, it was a slaughter—we need an ambulance. I'm all by myself out here. I had a girl, but I lost her and—"The radio cuts out and comes back in less than a breath. "Don't think we'll last a day. Next report at twenty-hundred hours."

Temple holds the device up to her lips with shaking hands. "Lam," she calls. "This is Temple."

"Temple? Temple?" Lam cuts out and clicks back on. Her side fades. Temple wonders if her own radio has the same poor quality. "Are you with any others?" Lam asks. "Are you OK?"

That isn't a question with an easy answer. She looks down at her ankle, and then out toward the campsite hidden by the trees in the night.

"Brenda's dead," she says. Her voice hitches on the last word, and she can hear Lam's whimpering on the other side. Temple keeps through it. "And Mickaeyla. And K'ran, too. No one was moving when I left."

She clicks off, and then there's silence. Even the buzzing of the nightlife fades. She finds herself shaking, holding her breath. Closing her eyes.

The sound clicks back on, and Lam responds. "Anysaa? Did you see what happened to Anysaa?"

"She wasn't moving, either." Sharp guilt fills her throat at the thought of Anysaa, and Temple swallows it down. An hour ago, she was ripping out the girl's hair. If Temple struggles and cranes and twists, she can see past the trees that block the main cabin and the firepit. She remains huddled into herself like it can make everything go away. She's so tired—from running, from fighting, hell she hasn't slept at all. She feels like she could fall asleep at any second.

The static comes again, and Temple snaps back to attention. "You have your radio?" Lam asks.

"No, it's Brenda's. I thought her bag was mine."

"Are *you* OK, Temple?"

Temple does a mental check—nope, not OK there.

But that's not all that different than usual. She looks down over her body, at the blood crusted over every inch of her—the urge to vomit surges through her. She's covered. That fake-Anysaa dragged her around in those girls' blood and—

Temple gags.

"Where are you?" Lam tries again. "Let's—"

Temple cuts the volume, shoving the radio back into the bag. Without the static, the sounds of the woods reach her, and she lets them wash over her as she presses her head against the trunk of the tree. She urges herself to breathe, as Brenda taught her, until the nausea passes. Four in through the nose, four out through the mouth.

This is all too much to handle. Temple just wanted to find a single corpse, and now there are four more to sort through.

They're all going to die here—and she can't do anything about it. Every gay for herself. Up against the unknown.

'Cause that wasn't Anysaa.

Whatever she was, she called Temple "Thomas" . . . and even though she doesn't want to think it, she can't help but think of her dad.

Thomas Baker. The North Point Killer.

She knows it deep down. Most of her wishes this is a random happening that she's just a victim to. Some weird tragedy in some isolated Virginia woods has happened before, and she can deal with falling into a stranger's trap more than she can think about being related to it.

But her dad *sent her here*. And she may not know why, but whatever the fuck just happened obviously has something to do with it.

Temple sighs, closing her eyes. Her ankle swells, throbbing with pain that she can ignore only with concentrated effort.

The night is plagued with intermittent, high-pitched screams that send Temple on edge, interrupting her thoughts and threatening to send her back into a panic.

Another killer in North Point . . . that could be one of them.

Temple can't stay, that's for sure. The moon and stars are still bright as she tries to wait out the pain in her leg. The night birds squawk just as good as the morning robins. They can't read the room.

There's a good chance all the other girls are dead. From what Temple heard, they didn't stand a chance. She hopes it's not true—even though she has little faith. Because if she's one of the only survivors, she knows who they'll pin the death on. And it won't be Anysaa.

She only has one thing she can do, really. And that's to end this.

Her attention turns to her ankle. She doesn't look forward to getting down from this branch.

She frowns at it. It aches all the way up through to her knee, but she's had worse.

When she'd just started high school, she cared about enjoying it. She joined the wrestling team because she thought it would help her in moving from the farm to her aunt's, and it seemed fun and badass to be the tall lesbian that could flip a jock over her back. One day she nearly tore her ankle in half attempting just that, and still helped movers haul hay that same evening.

Her ankle will hurt, but Temple will get by. She'll survive it.

Even if she doesn't know if she'll survive camp.

It's time to make her way to North Point House. Temple collects herself, waiting for her panic to fall away as she breathes in the fresh night air. Since she's on her own, she might as well finish out her mission in a blaze of glory.

Temple inhales again, loud and deep. Four in through the nose. Her mind clears as the harsh gaseous death becomes a faint memory. Four out the mouth.

A sigh follows her own, loud and thick from beneath her.

Temple tenses. Her muscles ripple so tight her shoulder stings.

"Dear Lord, please protect me. Please guide me and ease my fears and my pain." The girl's voice shakes as she speaks, cracking every time a leaf sways. "Let me and my sisters get out alive, in one piece, if you wish it."

A glitter of light dashes through the trees, making Temple lean over to find its source—a golden cross necklace dangling around the neck of the first survivor Temple's seen out of JG.

A girl from Temple's own cabin.

Yaya.

Excerpt of Goodreads Review of *Hearts Stop* by YaaYah (@ ScaryLaurenStan)

I CRIED reading this book. Cary Lauren said in an interview once that she stays away from "queer tears" (lol) but boy did she get a bucket of them for this:

"Fools anticipate forgiveness. You do not have to forgive your mother. You do not have to forgive your father. They are entitled to nothing. Not obedience. Nor mended fences.

"You are entitled your peace. Leave 'em hanging for as long as you want."

When I came out three years ago, my dad kicked me out of the house. My mom didn't do anything about it. I remember walking to my grammy's house with a bookbag full of shorts (fun fact: I always bought shorts in middle school because I thought they made me look straight). A week later, my mom shows up crying. "We changed our minds, we changed our minds," she says. "We're so sorry, we love you."

They were really sorry. I know they were.

I've lived with them for the two years since. They hug me, wish me a good night. We go to church together (plot twist, I'm a Christian). They've met my girlfriends.

They took me back in, right? Some people don't even get that. They kicked me out, but it didn't last forever. I should be grateful they aren't abusive and they're working on their homophobia.

But I cried like a bitch reading this, because Queen Lauren doesn't think I should be grateful.

Queen Lauren said, "fuck closure." I'm *entitled* to my peace.

CHAPTER TWENTY-FIVE

Temple listens in on Yaya's prayers. "I don't want to die, God. I know if it's my time, it's my time, but I don't think it is." Her words trip over themselves, tumbling out between her sobs. "Please let me rest and continue on the path meant for me."

It cracks at Temple. It's like that anger that spiked in her before, only this time she's not mad at Yaya. She wishes she had something to give her some resolve. All she has is herself.

Temple leans over the branch, stretching long until she can make out Yaya's shadow beneath her. She's in the pink sweater and jeans, filling them out with her thick, curvy figure. Kneeling at the base of another tree a few feet away, Yaya keeps her hands clutched to her chest and her eyes clamped shut.

Temple leans over a little more, and the branch rustles.

Yaya's head snaps up, her prayer trickling into silence.

"Hey," Temple calls out quickly. "Don't worry, I'm not gonna hurt you."

The girl freezes like it's Red Light, Green Light—and her life depends on it.

Temple leans a little farther, and there's an audible crack in protest from her branch. She calls again. "It's just me, Temple. Are you hurt?"

Lifting her head slightly, Yaya searches around for the source of Temple's voice. Her expression twists, her mistrust evident. Temple will have to climb down sooner rather than later.

"I'm up in the tree." Temple reaches over to her side, ignoring the pain, to shake the nearest branch.

Yaya's eyes follow, gaping up into the canopy. When she lays eyes on Temple, she gasps like a Georgia belle out of lemonade.

Temple nods to her. "Are you hurt?" she asks again.

Yaya's feet inch closer. She shakes her head. "When Mickaeyla got stabbed, Cali shoved me out the way. I didn't get anything but some scrapes. I . . . only heard."

She heard the screams, too. Like bombs going off, in every direction, but there was no boom. Just shrieks that vibrated beneath Temple's skin.

"I fucked up my ankle pretty bad," Temple says. She wouldn't have pointed it out if she didn't think the conversation would die on the route Yaya was taking it.

The clouds that cover Yaya's eyes clear. "Are you OK?" she asks. "Will you bleed out? Will you die? You can call for help, right?"

"No."

Yaya deflates, eyes flickering away. "Sorry," she says, fiddling with her interlaced fingers. "I was going to be the other camp counselor, you know. They chose you instead—I think 'cause I can be kind of . . ."

Yaya doesn't finish, but Temple winces. She remembers the phone call where they told her she beat out others for the position. Back then, it was just some loser figment of her imagination. She didn't bother considering the girl real. Now, here she is, watching Temple lay up in a tree.

"I'm sorry about that," Temple says truthfully.

"It's not your fault I'm pathetic." Yaya sighs, leaning against the tree's trunk and cutting their torturous eye contact. She kicks the roots with the heel of her shoe. "I kind of wish I hadn't come altogether now."

"So I guess we're even," Temple says.

The little huff of a laugh Yaya gives is small, but it softens Temple up enough she considers coming down again. Well, she has no choice. But she stops being actively against it.

Moving as slow as she can, Temple pulls up her knee, and her ankle drags against the branch. "I'm gonna come down," she announces. "After what happened, there can't be that many of us left. We should stick together." Her ankle radiates in revenge and gives Temple an excuse to let a tear fall. Her ankle got worse, definitely, but it's still manageable. Hours ago she could sprint, even with the fresh injury.

"OK," Yaya says.

Not even an argument. "You can turn me down, you know. I'm not gonna freak out on you and beat you up."

"I know."

And she sounds like she does, like it's obvious. She's just standing there, not even a little cautious of teaming up with Temple. Temple can't tell if that's her being good-natured or her being stupid.

With a cheer-up song from the crickets, Temple braces herself before shifting her weight. She throws her legs off the side of the branch, feet swinging and hips sliding off. She catches onto the thick part of its arm and hooks her fingers into the trunk bark.

As she goes down, she favors her good ankle. She's blessed with the common sense to know her other ankle is a sleeping dog, though. The few times she put weight on her injury, her knees near buckled. She hops onto the ground on one foot, huffing with the effort. She's in one piece, at least.

She catches Yaya looking at her warily. It's clear Temple doesn't hide her pain as well as she thinks she does.

Temple leans beside her on the tree. "What else did you catch earlier?"

Yaya swallows. The skin of her throat shifts with every move of her gulp before she looks away, toward the campsite. "Just a lot of screaming. It was silent for a bit, but then—" she stops, her words catching.

What happened can't be as horrible as Temple imagined. After all, Yaya's still alive.

"Then what?" she snaps, harsher than she means.

"Anysaa called out to a man . . . but there are no men here." They catch each other's eyes. Temple sees the same repulsion she felt.

Anysaa had said "Raymond" earlier. That's also a Baker name. But Temple keeps her mouth shut.

"You got caught. Cali shoved me into Brenda and Lam's room," Yaya says. "We got out the back, but then Cali said she heard yelling—arguing. So we split up and she went back in to help more girls."

Temple grinds her teeth. "I heard the arguing out on the path, too, with Brenda."

"It sounded like a *Real Housewives* reunion."

Temple wasn't familiar. The only housewife she knew was her own mom, and her mom had never argued with her dad. She feared him too much. Didn't want to lose what little domestic life they had.

"You see nothing else?"

Yaya shrugs. Out of her pocket, she pulls a hunk of plastic, shaking it and then returning it to where it popped from. "My phone ran out of battery, but I don't think it's midnight yet. No one's coming to help us. That's about it."

So they're caught up to about the same point.

"I didn't see where anyone went, or if anyone's alive. Cali . . . she—" Yaya stops herself. "I was too scared to look for other people or hike from here to the highway alone."

"So you tried to pray the fear away," Temple guesses.

"It worked better than just crying," Yaya says. "So I did both."

"You won't be alone now," Temple says, answering Yaya's unasked question. The highway is about five miles out. They can make it before her foot gets too bad. Before it's all over. She talks past her unease. "Unless you can carry me a few miles, we'll be going super slow. But I think we can make it before sunrise."

"I think I'm gonna need some food first," Yaya says softly. "I started this diet before camp, and I've been starving since last Tuesday. I think I might pass out."

Temple looks over at her, and even though her skin is a dark, burned brown, her lips are a lightened color.

Temple shakes her head. "We can last without food for a few hours. Then, when we get to the road we can hitchhike our way back to town."

"I was too scared to look for other people."

It's easier to just ignore Yaya even said that.

Leave the girls. Fuck those girls. That was the plan all along.

Yaya watches Temple steadily, as if she can see through Temple's thin resolve. As if she "knows" Temple won't abandon the other girls. But Yaya doesn't know the truth about Temple—that she's no better than her dad.

"You'll grow up to be just like him."

She knows this isn't her mother's voice for real this time. It's the way it always is—in the back of her mind, reminding her of the truth.

Temple can't wait to get out of these damned woods.

"We have to start moving," Temple says.

192

"We can't go," Yaya says firmly. A bird drops from a tree, hopping to another.

Temple blinks at Yaya, not even sure she heard right. "Excuse me?"

"Pl-please don't go," Yaya amends. "We have to go back to JG."

"You can't be serious. You were just praying for God to teleport you some spinach so you can Popeye punch your way through the bad guys or whatever the fuck. I can't even walk!"

"We can't leave our friends behind, Temple."

"*Your* friends. And I'm covered in your dead friends' blood." Temple winces at her own words but pushes through it. "If you're going to be like this, I have no problems leaving you."

"They're not all dead. There are some still at JG—at least, when I left there were." She clenches her eyes shut, real tight like the memories are pasted on the back of them. "I should have gone back already, to save them. There's no telling how many died because I was too chicken to go back by myself."

Temple rolls her eyes. This girl seems to think camp really is like the movies—that friendship is magic with the power to save the day. The only thing real camp and movie camp have in common is all the murders.

"I'm keeping my gay ass alive, Yaya," Temple says.

Yaya deflates, looking down at the soft grasses beneath her feet. Frustration bubbles in Temple's chest as she looks at the girl's forlorn expression. It's not fair.

It's not fair that Temple has to feel guilty for wanting to survive. Anybody would want to do that, not just monsters like her.

But she does, in fact, feel guilty. And she knows that's what she feels, or else she'd never say what she says. "But I guess I *am* kind of hungry," Temple says, narrowing her eyes. "We go back to the cabin, and if *anything* goes wrong—I'm leaving you to die."

CHAPTER TWENTY-SIX

Yaya is fighting back a shit-eating grin, and it pisses Temple off. As the leaves crunch beneath them, JG looming just beyond the curtain of trees, Temple recognizes that she had said at first that she would leave Yaya behind.

And here she is, not doing that.

It's all just because Temple's hungry. It has nothing to do with the other girls, or Cali, or saving anyone. If Yaya plans to tag along—as suggested by the way the girl pinches her fingers around the hem of Temple's T-shirt—that's her own prerogative.

JG has food, and it has her bag. Temple will at least get her knives and matches. At least if she goes back, she won't be defenseless when they head for the highway.

"Thank you," Yaya whispers again. She's done it about fifteen times since they started heading toward JG.

Despite all the big talk about saving her friends, Yaya makes it pretty obvious she's scared. Her eyes dart back and forth between the campsite and Temple, the campsite and Temple, before Temple eventually just sidles up to her and drags her by the hand. It's too dark to rely on sight, anyway.

Every so often, Temple has to glance back to make sure the hand warming her own belongs to Yaya, and not some blood-soaked demon taking advantage of the deep night. Given the last few hours, she has to check.

"It will be fine. The food will help us stay focused," Temple says, trying to make her voice light. She now understands Brenda's struggle of toeing the line between excitable and manic. "If we're hungry, we don't think clearly. Haven't you read an SAT prep book?"

"We also can't think if we're dead." Yaya grips Temple's hand tighter.

After that, they both go quiet. They cut through the trees with steady steps while the surrounding woodland creatures size them up. A late-nighter squirrel bounces around the two of them like they're out for its Lucky Charms. Bigger animals shake bushes and branches but never make themselves seen—equally afraid of the "demonic possession" possibilities that have presented themselves. However, as always, mosquitos are more afraid of the fires of Hell than ghosts—or Temple's poorly timed swats.

Temple and Yaya curve around the campsite, where the trees thin for the clearing. Temple can make out the patted-down soil of the firepit, the surrounding logs gray-tinted from the moonlight on their polished surfaces. The cabins are in their simple line—Aye, Bey, then JG.

Yaya's twitching starts again. It should be safe to speak—Temple has eyes on anything within hearing distance. But as they move across the interwoven vines and leaves, she'd rather they not risk it.

"Are you sure you can get Cali out?" Yaya asks—because she doesn't give a damn about what Temple wants.

But this, at least, is important. "It'll be easy. I opened a window earlier, right by the kitchen," Temple says. She tries not to think about what happened after she opened that window, or why she never got to close that window. Shivers rock her shoulders, but Yaya doesn't seem to notice.

"*By* the kitchen, not *in* it," Yaya says. "Are you *sure* that will work?"

Temple ignores her. "It's all part of my big plan. I'll slip in, throw the food out, and then slip right back out behind it."

"Temple." When Temple smirks back at her, Yaya doesn't look amused. "You're messing with me."

"Now you're getting it."

"Stop."

"Stop assuming I'm just gonna let Cali die in front of me."

Despite her quiet disposition, Yaya nods. For some reason, Temple believes Yaya decided to believe in Temple all on her own—not because of anything Temple said herself. "Is the window thing real, at least?" Yaya asks. "And how do you know the window is still open?"

"I don't think murderers get drafty. The window will be fine," Temple says.

When they make it to the perimeter of the campsite, right at the edge of her cabin—if she's still taking her job seriously—Temple stops. She watches the tranquil sight in the shade of the trees.

There could be up to ten other people—or bodies, since some are definitely dead—somewhere around here.

JG is fully visible from Temple's angle—she can see the front door still hangs open. Anysaa's red-painted jeans are black from the low light inside, her legs halfway out from when Temple kicked her.

Temple scowls to shut out the memory. Yaya stays right at her heels, examining her expression for a cue to run.

"We don't go *through* the site, we go around," Temple says. The campsite is a big circle that has a circumference filled with pockets they can't see through, but it's better to keep out of the pen where an enemy can confirm their location. They shift through the woods until they reach the JG. The siding is caked with black dirt that's never been cleaned off. She can make out the window, and the blue curtains shifting in and out.

When Temple comes to a stop, Yaya nearly rams into her to keep from getting left behind. "Sorry," Yaya whispers. She keeps her voice low, and Temple's glad—this girl at least has the sense to know when danger's afoot. Yaya's hand has soaked Temple's own, sweat sticking them together. With one of them near a breakdown, Temple figures it's better to fake confidence.

Temple drops to that same volume. "See, still open," she says. She wasn't actually sure it would be, but it was better for only one of them to be freaking out about it.

In the quiet, Temple's and Yaya's breathing sounds deafening. Temple eases beneath the window wordlessly. Her feet crunch and sigh over leaves and branches.

A twig snaps a few feet away, and it seems to echo throughout the whole campsite.

Temple and Yaya freeze.

Temple leans over, peering deep into the trees, where there's nothing to be seen. She calms her heart. As far as she knows, whatever is killing them isn't *hunting* them.

But it's already stupid to break *back into* the last place the girls were attacked—all for the sake of pantry snacks. *Not Cali*, Temple tells herself. She can't forget water—she feels a dryness creeping up the back of her throat.

Temple squints through the bottom of the window. She can't see anyone from the crack in the curtains. The window creaks as she slowly pushes it up, stopping it before it clacks against the frame. Waits. Nothing.

Then, hiking her leg up, Temple climbs in. Her heart pounds in her ears as the sole of her shoes hits the hardwood floor. She grips onto the sill to soften her step down. No sound comes from her landing. She has Aunt Ricki to thank for that—those three years Temple spent sneaking out to sit on the roof are finally paying off.

Once inside, Temple wants to jump right back out.

The room has transformed into a horrific shrine. Slain bodies and blood splatters overshadow the quaint cabin Temple first came to.

Thomas Thomas Thomas Thomas Thomas Thomas Thomas . . .

The name lines the walls and floors in deep red blood—some letters still wet and dripping, others caked and dried. Intermittently scribbled in the same ink, Cary Lauren's mark peppers the cracks in the pattern, filling in any blank spaces blood could touch. Temple's heartbeat kicks up. The symbol in blood makes her eye twitch and her head hurt—and there's nowhere to turn away from it.

JG's kitchenette stretches out before her, the dining table to the right, and farther down the sofa and fireplace. She can't see the living space around the corner of the adults' quarters, but she's frozen anyway.

Over everything keeping Temple from betraying a single reaction is a faint humming. She can't see the source of the voice, but someone else is in the room, humming a tune as Temple crouches, unseen by the corner of the kitchen counter.

The kitchenette is divided from the rest of the room by the breakfast bar—connected by the thick wall that separates Brenda and Lam's room. Their old room. But even as Temple takes a measured step, she feels like anyone could see her. Her calves tense up as she barely lifts her leg. Her ankle falters. She slides in something wet and catches herself before she slips.

The overhead lights are less bright than Temple remembers, illuminating the room in a dim glow. Temple studies the floor beneath her, following the dark-colored trail of blood that runs underneath her feet. It leads to a girl's body a few feet away. K'ran.

Mickaeyla's body's been moved.

She's not on the floor at all.

The bodies call to Temple, their twisted forms begging for a closer look. It's that sense of horror and curiosity that lured Temple to her dad's corpses every time. Before she can think about the consequences, she limps away from the counter. The full room expands before her, and she backs away from the table. All she can see, from the walls to the floor to the corpses *on* the floor, is blood.

Temple curls around the thick, separating wall. Her fingers avoid the dripping blood as she leans forward, covering her mouth to stop her bubbling cry.

Cross-legged before the fireplace is Mickaeyla.

She's facing the wall, one hand plunged into a new, gaping wound in Brenda's chest, the other holding her own lobbing head up. Mickaeyla—a Mickaeyla that is Not-Mickaeyla, Temple knows for sure—hums as she continues.

Her arm swings as she paints in blood, but Temple can't see past the wall. All she knows for sure is that Not-Mickaeyla is losing stamina. JG is dripping with the name, but as the panels get closer to the fireplace, the reddest, wettest ink gets less robust. Less "Thomas." More "Thoma" and "Thomm_____."

If Not-Mickaeyla can tire out, maybe Temple can force it to shut down. Maybe use salt.

No.

Fire, Temple remembers.

"Fire is best to get rid of evil."

Tiptoeing backward, Temple inches into the kitchen, cutting off her sight of Not-Mickaeyla and returning to the original task at hand. She can't move quickly—that would risk the floorboards unsetting. Not-Mickaeyla could catch a whiff of her at any moment.

Death is, for the first time in a long time, a reality. It was for Brenda and for K'ran. For Anysaa. Her body still, twisted half out the doorway, soaked with gore.

And even if Mickaeyla is moving right before Temple's very eyes, Temple knows that Death came for her, too.

Temple takes another step. Guilt springs in her chest, but she swallows it before she lets herself get overwhelmed. Crying is noisy.

Of course, she feels guilty about Anysaa. Temple never regretted her actions when she was berating her, ignoring her, or hating her. But now that Anysaa's dead, Temple will never be good. Everything between them is just . . . over.

Four in through the nose. She follows Brenda's imaginary orders, and circulation returns to her fingertips.

She feels guilty, because Anysaa's last moments will forever be characterized by Temple terrorizing her.

Four out through the mouth.

Temple's breath shakes, but her muscles relax as the fears go out with her sigh. She can obsess later, when lives aren't on the line. She forces herself to remember Mickaeyla. She won't let there be another murder, especially caused by her fretting. Get food for Yaya. Get Cali. Get home.

Temple focuses on her search for food first. She opens the pantry slowly, grabbing crackers and a gallon of water that she can toss out the window. She slides it onto the counter without even peeking her head out of the kitchen. She doesn't look behind her to the dining table. Doesn't peer back around the wall to the fireplace.

She just has to keep still, keep to her six feet of kitchenette while Not-Mickaeyla hums softly. Temple runs her finger over the counter, remembering what Yaya said happened before she escaped. If Cali hid her in Brenda and Lam's room, Cali might be there now. Temple might have to find a way to get past Not-Mickaeyla—maybe from outside?

Focus on food, she reminds herself. Cans. She flings open the low cabinet—and meets Cali's wide eyes.

Cali shrieks in a panic and slaps a hand over her mouth as Temple slams the door closed.

The humming stops.

Temple's hairs stand on end as the room fills with quiet, and Not-Mickaeyla's shadow stretches across the cabin floor.

CHAPTER TWENTY-SEVEN

It's as if she's running out of batteries—her body moves slowly, her shadow stretching and bending like a wilting flower. Temple keeps her eye trained on that elongating blackness, tenseness set in her shoulders.

"Thomas?" Not-Mickaeyla's voice is low and gurgled.

Hell no.

Temple turns on her heel, sliding across the floor as she hurries back to the window. She leans her back around the bar counters to stay out of view. Food can wait. She takes another step. The counter groans.

Temple isn't fast enough, and Not-Mickaeyla whips around, her head dipping unnaturally with the movement. They lock eyes.

"Thomas, you're not supposed to come here," she says.

The sound of the wind outside rustling the trees drifts in through the window, and Temple can only stand there. No words come out of her mouth. She just holds her breath.

Not-Mickaeyla's eyes glaze over as she stands up. "I specifically told you to stay in the house. It doesn't work if you're inside *here*." She sways from side to side as she walks toward the dining table. Temple isn't sure if she's all in one piece; blood dribbles down Not-Mickaeyla's arms and face like she's under a stream of it.

Her body is brutalized.

Like Brenda, her chest is cut open. Earlier, Temple saw only a single stab wound on Mickaeyla, but now there's blood seeping out everywhere. In some places, her limbs are jagged, in others they're uneven. Mickaeyla was torn apart.

This . . . this *thing*. Not-Mickaeyla is using the corpses to do its fingerpainting—and whatever else it's trying to do here.

Temple feels her heart harden, her legs refusing to move. She can't run like she planned—with her ankle, it'd be slow anyway. She just watches as Not-Mickaeyla approaches in a stuttering pattern. Two steps—stop. A turn at a bench. She steps over something that isn't there on the floor—stop. The movements are staggered and jerky, as if invisible obstacles block her way.

Then, finally, she's in front of Temple. A caring smile on her face softens her scraped-apart features.

"Are you scared?" Not-Mickaeyla asks. She reaches up and takes Temple's face in her blood-coated hand. Her touch is cold on Temple's skin. "Raymond's still at work. He won't catch us if we get back to the house." She squeezes, and Temple's jaw aches from the affection.

Temple stares back at her, trying to keep her eyes innocent. Her stomach twists as she raises her arm and holds Not-Mickaeyla's hand. Suddenly, she gets it. That voice. These touches.

"OK, Mom," Temple says softly. Not-Mickaeyla thinks she's talking to her child, Thomas. "Can I have some food first?"

Somehow the Mickaeyla that is Not-Mickaeyla . . . is Temple's grandmother? She's only ever heard her dad mention her in passing, but Temple knows it in her gut. Maybe Temple wouldn't have thought so with just being called Thomas—but Raymond was definitely her grandfather's name.

She's dealing with Grandma Ida.

Not-Mickaeyla—Grandma Ida—blinks, looking at Temple as she lets go of her face. Temple still feels the paste of old blood coating her skin. Grandma Ida doesn't speak. Temple's stomach drops at the thought of saying the wrong thing. Getting caught.

She'll be torn apart like everyone else—or worse. She imagines her body being dragged along as she murders the rest of the girls. Like Anysaa was. She can't let them possess her, too. If she's dealing with who she thinks she is, she can prevent it.

The moment drags on for too long, letting Temple spiral further and further into her doubt.

Then Grandma Ida grips Temple's face tighter. "We don't eat those anymore. I done told you that—don't let Raymond make you eat them anymore."

Grandma Ida points around them. At K'ran's body. Brenda's body. The gesture is big and wide, as if there's more than just two.

But that would make a lot of sense. Not that there are corpses Temple can't see. But that Grandma Ida doesn't see the same way Temple sees. That maybe the reason she sees Temple as who she isn't is because she can see the past—like how dementia works.

Grandma Ida smiles with a furrowed brow, a mirror of Temple's own. That ever-present scowl was actually inherited.

"When I finish, we can make some lunch. *Real* lunch, with more than just meat." Then with a twirl, Grandma Ida's eyes buzz around the room like an infant seeing for the first time. It bounces from each scrawl of "Thomas" across the room with awe. "We have to make sure he dies first."

Temple follows close behind. The floor opens beneath her—that sense of being trapped in a memory nearly choking her. That sense that she is, once again, trapped. Within herself.

She's back in her dad's courtroom, hearing him on the stand. Hearing what she thought was nonsense.

"I don't mutilate them." Her dad's crackling voice was quiet, but he said the words unashamed. *"I brand them."*

"You brand them?" the lawyer repeated.

"That way, until the marks fade from the bones, we can live together forever."

Temple raises her eyes to Grandma Ida, whose eyes still drift from panel to panel on the wall. It doesn't make any sense.

But she can't deny the resemblance between Not-Mickaeyla's mannerism and Temple's father's—the resemblance, even, to Temple. The kind that comes from living together, breathing together. Mickaeyla never looked that way—she was too full of her own life.

Grandma Ida flutters around the dining room table—stepping over what isn't there again—her eyes at her feet, at K'ran's corpse. Stressed. "I don't know how Raymond keeps following us. We were without him for so long, and now he won't leave us alone."

Grandma Ida catches something in Temple's own eyes, and her face hardens. She takes a tiny step toward the kitchenette. Her arms reach out for Temple, and Temple notices droplets of red falling from her wrist. Onto her bare feet.

"Listen to your mother, Thomas. You have nothing to fear from me."

Temple stops shaking. The words echo in her mind, and she finally swallows, dread filling her. "Yes, mother."

"Raymond is the one to worry about."

"I know," Temple says.

Her Grandma Ida smiles, satisfied, her grayed gums gleaming in the light. Her grandmother—a murderer just like Temple's dad. What was she like when she was alive for her to so easily slice into Brenda? Into even more, without batting an eyelash?

That dark feeling pools back around her shoulders, like an arm clawing her from beneath the floors. She tries to breathe, but it doesn't release her.

"You're still scared," Grandma Ida says. "You shouldn't be. I won't let him hurt you."

"I won't be scared anymore."

Another dripping grin. Now Temple sees the viscous drool curling over her bottom lip. "I know what will help you," Grandma Ida says. Her voice is light and melodic, bouncing over every syllable, even as foreboding as it is. "You need to touch one."

She's fast. Like a coiled snake.

Grandma Ida doesn't struggle to yank Temple to the ground. Temple's knees crumble and suddenly she's being dragged like before, like when Anysaa pulled her by the ankle. Only this time, the blood is so, so cold as she's tugged through it.

"Stop it!" Temple screams as she twists and wrenches.

Grandma Ida, of course, keeps pulling. Twisting and turning through the room as if there's a forgotten path there, as if the desks from the seventies still lined the floor. Temple can only see the ceiling fly by before K'ran slides past Temple's stomach. More hardwood. The sofa catches on her shoulder. More hardwood.

Then, finally Brenda, blood soaked and broken, lies facing the ceiling. The collar of her T-shirt has been sliced after her death, her shoulder revealed and coated in blood. The glistening red seeps over the curling tattoo on her clavicle—Cary Lauren's mark. And it makes Temple's throat close up. Grandma Ida stops, dropping Temple's leg as she looks up at the wall by the fireplace.

Grandma Ida snatches Temple to her feet forcefully. "Touch it," she instructs. "I won't be around to take care of you forever. You have to learn how to kill and brand them yourself. That's the only way you can live, son. But you can't do that if you're scared of them."

Temple can't breathe. She can't move.

Blood covers every bit of the wall, even the fireplace and the door to Brenda and Lam's room. Everything except the far right of the wall. The jumbled iterations of her dad's name were straight lines that curved upward, twisting around in even rows.

In between some of his names, that mark—the one so popular, so simple, it litters each of the girls' bodies—fills in the gap. Simple scratches. A circle. And a slash.

But to the right of the fireplace, her dad's name is completely absent.

Between the closed door to the adults' quarters and the dull brown brick of the unlit fireplace, Grandma Ida had drawn a mark in blood so large it nearly reaches the ceiling. It covers an entire yard of wood panels, seeming to tilt over Brenda's crooked body, seeping red into the floorboards.

The intertwined and twisted mark is no longer a simple series of slashes. The illustration is full of detail, vines twisting around the border as geometric shapes replace the center line. Clean lines etched in and out of the crusted red plunge down to the floor, another elaborate curl that was done by an artist's hand. Or at least, a practiced one.

Somewhere in between the simple sketches of the girls' tattoos and the ornate, heavy coins that signified buried bodies.

It all made so much sense, why seeing blood on the marks made her twitch. Why seeing Dawntae's bloody tattoo made her head hurt, like it could burrow inside her.

The mark was there all along.

She just needed to remember.

It's not just a mark. It's a brand. The Versace of brands.

The brand her dad carved into his victims.

CHAPTER TWENTY-EIGHT

G randma Ida is showing off her artwork. She's waiting for Temple to gasp, to admire it. To worship her. When Grandma Ida pats Temple's shoulder, she doesn't notice Temple flinch.

"If you're not going to touch the body, then at least be good and quiet," Grandma Ida says. "I need to concentrate."

Grandma Ida turns back around and gets back to digging for blood to scrawl more patterns into the leftover spaces of the mark. Grandma Ida hums louder than before with renewed strength.

She's moved on from Temple.

Temple takes a slow step back, as if it's a trick. Her Grandma Ida gestures to bodies that aren't there. She sees Thomas, but she's Temple. It's all things in the past. She avoids new parts of the cabin like there's a wall there—Temple needs to figure out how that works.

That's how she gets out of here.

Temple dashes back for the kitchenette.

There are safe spaces. She just has to find them.

When Temple reaches the counters again, she rips open the cabinet where she found Cali and freezes. It's empty. She must have escaped when Grandma Ida was distracted. Good for her—even if that means Cali used Temple as bait.

Temple grabs some canned beans and gets back to the other snacks on the table. She slides the bundle of food down the corner of the wood and lets them glide out the open window. The gallon of water lands on the other side with a deafening thud.

"Thomas, what are you doing?" Grandma Ida calls.

"Playing," Temple says. "Baseball," she adds. She pictures her dad's serene face as she says it, imagining his insistence on teaching her the game. She clenches her fist, hoping the good memories extend to her grandma.

"*Well, keep it down!*" Grandma Ida's voice bounces off the walls, half wail, half scream.

"*Well, keep it down!*" The words echo beneath static in Temple's pocket, muffled by the thick material of her jeans. Her fingers twitch—the radio.

With a slow hand, Temple pulls out the thick block of plastic. The stickers cover up some of the harsh yellow color, but she can make out the dark red light that glows whenever the radio receives a signal.

Brenda said someone had been talking to them. She thought someone had got ahold of the radio signal. Temple thought that, just maybe, it had been voices. The kind she had been raised to avoid. But if they were—is the signal coming from her grandma herself?

"Son of a bitch," Temple whispers.

Temple's family is a part of something evil, and it's breaking every rule of humanity. Even the rules of reality. Her grandmother just slaughtered a bunch of children and isn't any more haunted than Casper. Her consciousness infected one of her victims, and it's business as usual for her.

This family is evil. Temple had heard it constantly.

But even though she comes from a line of monsters, she will not die here with them. Whatever pity party grabbed Temple, she snaps out of it, pulling out more water and rushing it to the window.

The bottles disappear outside as Temple releases her held breath. Life now. Sad later.

She can't see Yaya, but she hopes it's because Yaya's crouched under the window snatching up every morsel like a rodent.

She swipes a loaf of bread. She doesn't want to think about it. The loaf flattens in her palm like it's made of cotton, and she slides it out the window. But she has to wonder . . .

Three years ago, if her dad hadn't been caught, it would probably be Temple out in North Point Farm. If he never went to prison, she'd be in the woods, lurking, dumping bodies of her own.

Temple grabs onto the breakfast bar. It's not surprising. Look at what she's capable of.

She throws another look over to Anysaa's body, facedown into the wood. She's no hero. No good person. Of course she was supposed to follow in her dad's path.

Just like your mother said you would.

Black jets out from beneath the dining table, just as Temple lifts her head. It's brown skin and the streak of yellow. Temple makes out the flutter of Cali's T-shirt a second later, as the girl darts toward the door.

Temple's teeth cut into her lip from biting in her shriek. She freezes as Cali's shadow overtakes Anysaa's body. The corpse's torso grays out; Cali stretches over the still body.

Cali moves calmly, her feet absolutely silent as they cross the parallel boards. Grandma Ida is *right there*, a breath away. If Cali breathes too deeply, Grandma Ida will hear.

But Cali spreads her palm on the doorframe like she's got all the time in the world.

What the fuck?

Cali, the whole reason Temple was in this godforsaken cabin, should have already been *outside*. Why the *fuck* is she still here?

Shit.

Temple lets go of the breakfast bar and slaps her wrists together, flailing with all the quiet she has left. Her forearms cross in an "x" over and over again as she prays silently.

Please let Cali hide. Go out the door. Run as fast and far as she can.

Temple never wanted to be left alone more in her life.

Cali catches the movement, jerking back. When she makes out Temple, she stiffens.

"Why didn't you stay hidden?" Temple mouths, pointing her fingers toward the cabinet. She then points to the entry window, miming every part of her and Yaya's plan with only her hands. It just makes Cali hesitate more. "We're gonna die," Temple mouths next.

Cali gets that part. She points to the wall by the door wildly and flicks her wrist. They both stop at the same time, and Cali cranes her neck around the door. She gets a direct line of sight to Not-Mickaeyla, now lying at the fireplace like a napping cat. Lazily, Not-Mickaeyla's index finger works around a crude rose. Its petals are jagged but loop into the round "o" of the mark.

Cali's eyes bug, and she slips her head back out.

"Get out of here," Temple mouths, waving Cali away.

This time Cali rolls her eyes, darting back into the room on silent feet. She slips right behind the couch—so close that if she wanted to reach out, she could touch Mickaeyla, still splayed out on the floor. Cali slides her hands underneath the couch, and with a stiff, heavy arm, she drags out a black pouch accented with harsh orange.

Temple's bag.

Finally, she'll have her knives. Cali must have snooped through Temple's things when Temple headed to the North Point House with Brenda.

Cali knows exactly what she's got, and she holds it up triumphantly with a thumbs-up. Temple gasps.

Not-Mickaeyla's slamming footsteps send Temple flying away from the counter, flinching when her ankle hits the floor. When Temple's eyes flicker back to the couch, Cali's shadow is already a thinning trail as she books it out of the cabin. Temple knows which cues to follow.

The staccato beat of mismatched stumbling lasts only a moment before Grandma Ida is there, leaning against the wall with her wide eyes rolling in her head.

"What are you doing?" she demands. "I told you no *snooping*!" Grandma Ida's gait is uneven as she wobbles over to Temple, her tilted head throwing off her balance. She half-topples with every step.

She reaches her hand out, impatiently flicking it for Temple's cooperation. Bile rises in Temple's throat. She doesn't want to touch that hand again. That's a corpse, overtaken by something that thinks it's a person.

"Come on, Thomas. I have no time for your games."

In Mickaeyla's face, right in that moment, her dad's stern frown emerges. Sometimes, when he made Temple mad, her mother said Temple did the same thing. Temple's only seen a single photo of Grandma Ida, but the mannerisms don't lie.

"Grand—Mom," Temple says, correcting herself. "Sorry. I was just playing."

Grandma Ida stares at Temple for a few more moments, and without her scratching and drawing, the cabin is completely silent.

Her eyes drop down to the cabinet. And her blank, grim expression expands into a sickly grin across her face. Her cheeks puff, flesh ripped apart by an unseen struggle. "I won't hurt you. I never do. But I told you not to sneak around here." Grandma Ida takes a step forward.

Temple blocks her on habit. She hadn't even wanted to move. "I'm sorry, Mom."

The cabinet wood digs into Temple's back, irritating her skin under her clothes. If it wasn't so deathly cold, maybe she'd start to sweat. "I'm sorry," she mutters again.

Grandma Ida scowls again. "You *are* afraid," she snaps. "You can't hide it from me." She cuts across the room, back to Brenda's corpse. Grandma Ida turns her bug eyes to Temple, curving her finger so sharply Temple can see the bone poking into the skin. "Come on. Come here."

Temple remains glued in place. She knows what Grandma Ida wants to do.

"We've gotta get used to them somehow," her mother said.

Temple throws a glance to the window. The curtain billows in the wind, screaming for her to make a run for it. It might give Yaya up. Grandma Ida might chase her out.

But Temple isn't about to touch that dead body.

She breaks for the window, hitting her side into the counter with a hard *thump*.

But Grandma Ida's quicker. She rushes, faster than Temple's ever seen her uneven gait. Temple can't even make Grandma Ida out before a cold, wet grip slaps onto Temple's wrist.

Mickaeyla's lopsided corpse wraps around Temple's arm, and Temple topples over, dragged across the floor again. It's some superhuman strength that Temple doesn't understand. No matter how hard she pulls, she can't get free.

"They can't hurt you, now," Grandma Ida says, running her finger along the wall. A pool of blood collects on her fingertips, dripping onto the floor as she grins down at her son.

CHAPTER TWENTY-NINE

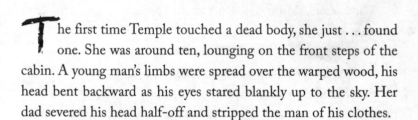

The first time Temple touched a dead body, she just . . . found one. She was around ten, lounging on the front steps of the cabin. A young man's limbs were spread over the warped wood, his head bent backward as his eyes stared blankly up to the sky. Her dad severed his head half-off and stripped the man of his clothes.

It's funny, thinking about it. Temple knows way more about sex ed and human anatomy than everyone else her age for a very odd reason.

Before this man, there were six others that she knows of, three she saw. This one, the fourth, was slashed across his chest and legs. His body must have been left to drain of blood somewhere else, as the patio was unstained beneath him. His bare skin exposed to the world, his genitals out for all the mice to see. Yet he didn't have the dark, freshly carved brand that she was also used to.

Temple knew her dad's schedule by then. She knew his ritual, even if she saw only the latter half of it. It's not as if he lived a double life—his life was a Venn diagram. Some days, he'd wake her up for lessons with her mother, make her breakfast, and joke around. When he came home from working the farm, they'd watch a baseball game or listen to records or go fishing.

Then, other days, he'd disappear in the morning and come

home with his pickup truck bed sagging with weight Temple wasn't allowed to poke through. He'd stay in the woods for about an hour, and Temple made her own breakfast. She listened to records alone and forced herself not to be scared until he came home, and they could work the farm, watch a baseball game. Listen to records together.

To find a body unattended on the steps was strange. Her dad was nowhere to be seen. Temple took a step closer, staring into the empty eyes of a man long gone. It was like he could still see her dad hovering over him, waiting for his lights to cut off.

The corpse's skin frayed apart at the foot, exposing a tiny sliver of bone.

"Palm brands are for family," her mother had said.

Temple jumped, turning to find her leaning on the door.

She glared down at Temple, as if waiting for her to do something. *"Ankle brands are for the bodies he saves for later."* Her mother raised an eyebrow. *"Are you afraid?"*

Temple's hands shook with a fear she couldn't let linger. She was a good girl; her dad was a nice man that would never hurt her. But her mother was always waiting.

Waiting for that to be untrue.

That day, Temple folded the young man's eyes closed before her dad returned.

She and her mother never spoke of the body again.

With Grandma Ida clamping down on Temple's wrists, Temple looks down at Brenda's body and can't muster up that same courage. The director's eyes stare up at the ceiling, deep red slicing over her neck.

A chorus of thoughts sways Temple on her feet. *I'm going to die.* She can't move, but her mind keeps running faster and faster. *You're petrified. You're going to die because you're a scared little shit.*

"Are you afraid?" Her mother again.

This time, Temple knows it's her imagination.

"Quickly," Grandma Ida snaps, and her slick hold on Temple tightens as she whips Temple's arm down.

Temple's knees buckle, and she stumbles to the floor, her arm smashing into Brenda. Someone Temple barely talked to while she was still fucking breathing. She couldn't be a normal person for one fucking day before Brenda got murdered.

Temple cowers at the cold touch of Brenda's blood, slicking over her skin as Grandma Ida yanks at Temple's strings. Even trying to remain rigid, Temple's eyes dart over to the fireplace, where K'ran's corpse awaits her. She doesn't have the confidence to resist again. Maybe she should just give up and die.

Grandma Ida coos as she makes Temple pet Brenda's blood-soaked top. The fabric sticks between her fingers as they drag over the fibers.

"See? They're staying dead. They can't get you," Grandma Ida says.

"Yes, ma'am." Temple's voice wavers, but Grandma Ida fails to notice.

"I won't let you go until you stop crying," Grandma Ida says. "Until I know I can trust you to behave. We *must* get rid of—"

The front door slams shut.

Grandma Ida drops Temple's hand and Temple plops into the corpse, a shriek flying from her throat. When she lifts her head again, she claps her dry hand over her mouth. She can feel her fingers trembling against her chin, as her eyes take in the white dust salting the base of the door.

Anysaa's body moves across the floor, dragged like a sack of potatoes by a force unseen. Temple can only make out the waxing and waning ice, silver coating the swirls of blood that now paint the walls.

Thick and a deep, deep blue, the ice creeps in front of Anysaa. The Cold. It pulls her by the arm, her form seeming to move on its own.

"As soon as you walk through the door," Grandma Ida grumbles. She clasps a hand over Temple's shoulder, rigid and sturdy. Temple looks up, and Grandma Ida's eyes are narrowed at the shadow—at someone who isn't there. "I thought you were at work."

A wave flits through the room, like the deepest note on a bass, and vibrates through Temple. She's heard this before—the arguing throughout the woods.

The Cold feels like pure evil, like ... like it had never been human at all. It has to have been a monster from the beginning.

Temple had never met her grandfather. But there's no way he could have turned into *this*.

She looks up at her grandma again, who tightens her hold on Temple.

"Go in the other room," Grandma Ida says through clenched teeth. Her voice wavers at the end. "I need to talk to your father."

Grandma Ida's afraid. Temple observes her features and can see the thick blackness of fear hidden in her eyes. Temple knows it well. It's fear only a loved one could cause.

"I can't keep this up. I have to save you myself."

When she wavers, Grandma Ida sucks her teeth and yanks Temple up by the arm. Temple's shoulder pops, and she flails to her feet with a gasp. She stumbles over to the bedroom door, where Lam and Brenda once slept.

Across the room, the stretch of ice crawls along the walls, still pulling Anysaa with it. Temple puts a hand on the fireplace mantel, her other on the doorknob. She stays there, watching. The Cold's muffled response rings through the room again.

"Don't yell at me, Raymond!" Grandma Ida screams. "I'm not afraid of you! I'll kill you, too! I'll kill you again!"

Anysaa jolts. The Cold throws her corpse, and she skids across the floor. The body hits the back of the couch and rolls onto the hardwood with a loud thump. And a whimper.

Temple freezes.

She stares at Anysaa's abandoned body and the veiny blue that crawls up her leg. Grandma Ida stalks a black corner of the room, her shrieks getting higher and higher. No words. Just mindless screams crashing around each other as they bleed into the room.

Anysaa's nose buries into the wooden floors. She doesn't move.

Temple keeps her voice quiet. She can't even hear it in the room over the arguing—but she doesn't dare move closer. "Anysaa?" she whispers. "Did you just make a sound?"

A chair flies across the room. It smashes against the countertop and a leg splinters off. Her grandmother's screams get louder.

"I'm not afraid, I'm not afraid—you do not scare me!" Grandma Ida chants, more for herself than for the dreadful Cold that moves around the room.

Anysaa doesn't respond.

Temple keeps her stare even. Another chair flies, and it hits the fireplace. Splinters of wood hit Temple's cheeks, but she keeps still.

Grandma Ida screeches.

Wood cracks.

The Cold howls.

And then, amid all the chaos in the room, Anysaa opens her eyes. "I'm not dead. I think my leg's broken," she whispers.

"Thomas!" Grandma Ida screams, and Temple turns to her. "You almost hit him, Raymond—I told you *never* to hurt him. Thomas was doing just fine until you came along."

The Cold's muffled voice gets deeper as the ice crawls along the floor to Temple. She runs her hands over her arms as the temperature plummets.

"Thomas!" Grandma Ida shouts again. "I told you to leave!"

The shrill scream echoes through the room as Grandma Ida marches over to her. She grabs Temple roughly, and Temple sways on her feet. Anysaa snaps her eyes shut.

"Next time leave when I say leave," Grandma Ida yells. She swings open the quarter's door, squeezing her hands as the ice plunges the room into deep, black silver. The wood door slams against the back wall. Grandma Ida pauses.

The window, the cabinet, Brenda and Lam's shared bed, and the unused one beside it. It's all the same. Everything is quiet.

Temple steadies herself by the wall and looks over Grandma Ida's shoulder, waiting to find the room covered in crystals—to see her death come for her. If she's gonna die by their hands, she hopes she dies instantly. That she's simply ripped apart—without any weird possession shit happening to her later.

Instead of the blue-tinted shadow blocking the threshold, Temple finds another girl. A girl from Temple's own cabin, Natalie—the one that didn't believe in demons. Natalie, who played cards with all the others just the night before. Temple slides closer, trying to see her face . . .

Then she sees why Grandma Ida paused. Temple slams back against the wall, yet again unable to untangle her arm from Grandma Ida's fingers.

She looks over to Anysaa, still playing dead on the floor, and hisses. "You need to get up," she says firmly. "Crawl, roll—whatever the fuck. We need to get the fuck out of here."

Bang!

A gun goes off, and Grandma Ida flies back. Temple's hand is free as Mickaeyla's corpse falls to the ground.

CHAPTER THIRTY

Temple can run, but she's not safe.

Bang!

The dining table freezes over as another shot goes off. It gleams in the light—a coat of thick ice settles over the surface. Temple drops to the ground and darts for the couch.

Natalie doesn't care who she shoots. She's got blood splattered all over her face, and her eyes are wide with fear. She's going to kill anything that gets in her way.

She screams and shoots again.

Temple darts for the front door, hopping over Anysaa in a smooth leap. Then she glances behind her.

Grandma Ida is still very much moving. She crawls forward as the gunshots get more frenzied. Anysaa's crawling, too, but her knees give out with every inch she gets. She's slow. She'll get herself killed—get them both killed.

You should leave her.

As soon as Temple thinks it, her body rejects it completely. She turns back to Anysaa, cutting through the living room with Natalie's screams burning her ears. No more dead girls.

Temple lifts Anysaa by the waist, her back exposed to whatever shots Natalie has left, and drags Anysaa to the front door. The main cabin has turned completely black. The indecipherable tones of the echoing voice fill Temple's chest, and she hurries, shoving the door open with her forehead.

They stumble out into the campsite, and it feels like they landed in a new world. Stars glitter indifferently above them, and the fresh air welcomes her in chilly, leafy wisps. Temple doesn't get wrapped up in it, though. She doesn't know what kind of gun Natalie has, but there have to be some shots left. She shot off five, maybe six.

Temple curses a little to herself. Distantly, she remembers Brenda saying something about a gun. Sure, this is Virginia, but a loaded handgun with a bunch of high schoolers is a fucking terrible idea. She wishes she could yell at Brenda—especially since she stored it where a camper could find it.

They creep around the front underneath the windows as they make their way to the back of the main cabin. Temple can still hear Natalie screaming. Anysaa trembles, but Temple has no words of comfort. They're in an endless stretch of open space. There's nowhere to hide. They have to disappear, and Anysaa's moving too slow for that to happen.

Temple shouldn't have brought her. She shouldn't have.

"Temple!"

Yaya's scream brings Temple back, and she swivels.

"Ow," Anysaa whines.

"Sorry."

From the side of the building, Yaya pokes her head out and waves. Temple forgot about it—the food. She rushes over, Anysaa only half moving. Her feet kick up dirt as they go, and when they reach Yaya, Temple pulls Anysaa into the thick of the trees. The leaves crumble and hiss with the weight, and Yaya's mouth pops open.

"Anysaa?" Yaya exclaims. "What—are you—"

"Did you not hear the gunshots?" Temple interrupts. "We need to get out of here!"

Yaya scrambles to the ground, picking up some of the food and glaring at Temple. "I wasn't going to leave you."

Temple's guilt and hardness return—just minutes ago she wanted to leave Anysaa and expose Yaya. "Where's Cali? Did she come this way?" she demands. She'll feel better when she has her bag. She needs her bag.

"She did. She said she was coming back but she had to go to the bathroom." Arms full of food, Yaya jerks her chin to point to the bathrooms.

Temple gawks. "The *bathroom*? We're in the woods. Piss on a tree!"

There's nothing but rustling from the woods. A knocking bird that Temple doesn't remember the name of, right overhead. Some slithering snakes among the bushes.

Yaya ignores Temple's tone as she gathers up the rest of the food with a flurry. They prepare to head back to their own corner of the woods, Yaya only pausing once to check if Anysaa's still OK. Temple looks up to the night sky, sighing.

She doesn't want to spend the night there.

Yaya notices. "I think it's around midnight," she says. The thickness in her voice lets Temple know they're afraid of the same thing. "Any word from Lam?"

"Not since I went in."

"I tried to check for other girls, but I think I scared them off." The way Yaya's eyes travel over her tells Temple she'll have to explain why she's soaked in blood.

Fresher blood.

Again.

But now, they have to get moving. If they want to get out of this camp before tomorrow morning, they're going to have to cut through the woods. If there's some sort of . . . *thing* Grandma Ida avoids, something that keeps her from moving freely across the cabin . . .

It's entirely possible the Cold is the same.

If Temple can find out how to get all of them through the woods in the places the Cold can't reach, all the girls might just survive. And while she's sure gonna miss some steps in her dad's grand scheme by just burning this bitch down behind her, she can't say she feels bad.

Just . . . unsatisfied.

That's better than dead, though.

So really, all Temple needs is her knife and her matches.

"Take Anysaa," Temple instructs, and she heaves the girl's arm over Yaya's shoulders. "Go back to the tree—the one we met at. But *not* any farther. We get out together."

Yaya falters a little but ultimately keeps Anysaa upright.

"Head back. I'm going to wait for Cali," Temple says.

"I'll wait with you," Yaya said.

"And what if they start shooting again?" Temple asks. "Only one of us needs to stay behind. I can warn Cali in time if I get to a high point. She can probably see me from the roof—if I climb up there."

Yaya still isn't having it. "My God got me this far. I'll die when I'm meant to."

Of all the times for the rabbit to boss up. Temple almost argues. They both know Yaya isn't as convinced of her survival as she puts on. But Yaya's stubborn expression stops her.

She admits—only to herself—that this shit will go a lot smoother with a team.

Without more to say, Temple approaches the side of the cabin. She knows the grooves in the brick are enough to give her hold, and she plunges her fingers into the spaces to pull herself up.

"I'll look from the roof," Temple explains to Yaya, who nods solemnly.

"I'll look after Anysaa," Yaya says.

The pain in Temple's ankle dulled through the hours, but she still favors her good one on the climb. It'll be a disaster if she falls.

About three-quarters of the way up, the JG door opens with a loud creak. Temple's breath bounces off the wall, right back to her, deafeningly loud. The slow sound fills the woods. Even the birds quiet as Temple moves along, onto the roof.

She can make out the shadowy tips of the trees that cluster for the miles-long stretch of woods. The darkened landscape is velvet and breathtaking as Temple's heart pounds in her ears.

From down below, over the groan of the door hinge, comes a deep, scratching voice. "Thomas . . ."

Temple scowls. It's almost Natalie's voice—but not. Like when Grandma Ida spoke through Mickaeyla, or Anysaa.

Temple peeks over the back ledge to Yaya and Anysaa, who are both looking up at her, bug-eyed. Temple waves them into the forest, finger to her lips. They have to hide.

The gravel clicks at Natalie's feet with every step she takes. The leaves that crunch beneath her sneakers freeze as she walks through them. When Natalie finally speaks, it's twisted and cracking. "*I know you're not Thomas . . .*"

Temple hides, too. She dips low onto the rooftop, out of sight. She may be stuck there, but at least she's out of the ice's path.

"*Where did you run to?*"

Temple peeks out to the campsite. A silhouette inches from the main cabin as Natalie walks out, her shadow stretching feet beyond her form. The voice and the figure don't match. That's not a girl anymore.

The deep voice has the belt of a smoker, thinly masked by whatever's left of Natalie's voice. When the girl fully steps into the campsite, Temple gets a good look at her. She holds in her gasp.

Protruding from Natalie's eye is a thick chef's knife. Blood freezes nearly white at the handle, trails of red sticking on her forehead.

There may still be a gun in her hand, but Natalie is dead.

The Cold has taken her over. Temple didn't even know it could do that, but seeing the ice . . . hearing the voice . . . Temple knows it in her bones.

The Cold moves through her corpse, its steps kicking on the rocky soil as it drifts through the campsite. Even if Temple finds a hiding space there, there's no chance it'll be a good one.

Temple follows the monster's path and freezes when her gaze lands on the firepit. The logs that circle it are thick for seating, but not very long. There are four in total, one each at the north, south, east. And behind the westward one, feet poke out.

Temple stands, getting a better angle, and she clearly makes out Cali's thin legs curled up beneath her. Cali squats behind the sitting log, her head buried into the ground as if not seeing the approaching corpse can make it go away. A yard away, the possessed corpse is very real. It advances toward her with its gun poised.

The Cold will get to her; it will see her; it will kill her.

CHAPTER THIRTY-ONE

The Cold keeps walking. "Come on out, before it's too late. I'm not gonna eat you," it says.

Temple swears she hears a smile in its voice. It makes her close her eyes and hope when she opens them that things will be different.

They aren't. Cali's still ass out by the firepit, and a monster's going to kill her.

Everything's bathed in blue and dark purple, even the gray gravel around the pit. Temple can only wait for the inevitable. Shit. Cali's going to die right before Temple's eyes. Cali doesn't deserve to die.

Cali helped Temple at the house and kept Temple's secret. She'd tried to get the girls out. She wouldn't abandon them or ignore them like Temple ignored the screams last night. Cali made one mistake because she doesn't trust the woods—doesn't see them as a free toilet—and she's going to die for it.

All Temple's done is argue with the other girls. Suspect them. Attack them.

Cali doesn't deserve to die.

Temple does.

Temple's heart rams and she punches her fist into her chest like it'll help her digest the thought. The monster in Natalie's body closes in. Cali's very still, but if it comes for her, Temple can't do anything. Worse, she hid with her head down. Cali can't see what's coming for her. Temple steps forward.

Temple can't just watch this. She has to do something.

She backs up from the edge of the roof, swallowing. A moment's hesitation rocks her as she thinks about what she's doing. She isn't the kind of girl that helps people. That's good people, and Temple isn't good people. She's like her dad, and deep down she knows so.

But she does care about Cali. Temple cares about all of them. Even if she's not *good*, she can pretend to be until they get out of here. She doesn't want the other girls to die. She wants to live, but not if it means letting them die, too.

Something unlocks in her chest, like a dose of her inhaler after running a mile. The words feel wrong. But they also feel right. *Good girl for the weekend*, Temple decides. *OK*.

Mind clear, lungs full, Temple runs forward and leaps. The wind rushes over her as she recalls all the times she's done this before: hopping off her dad's barn, tumbling into the hay. It was fun once. But Temple remembers her injured ankle at the landing.

"Shit," she cries out, tumbling over and eating dirt as she collapses. She tumbles onto her back, tastes blood in her throat. It mixes with bile, her lack of lunch finally pushing her stomach over the edge. Temple curls up and hoists herself onto her knees, her legs cracking. She's been too stiff for too long. She turns just as the Cold does.

The stabbing feeling in her right foot spreads as a smile hits its expression. "*I know you*," it says. It trains the gun right at Temple, at her head. "*Or is that just a new corpse*, Thomas?"

Temple dips just before the shot goes off. That's as good of a distraction as she can give her.

"Cali!" she screams.

Cali pops up. "Jesus!"

"Run!"

She doesn't have to be told twice. Cali bolts without a moment's hesitation, throwing Temple's pouch at her as she goes.

Temple rises under the Cold's gaze. It only glances at Cali, its arms adjusting just slightly. To aim at her. Well, that can't happen, or Temple's ankle and all her screaming will be for nothing.

Snatching up the strap of her pouch, Temple lunges for the monster's midsection. With a kick at its foot, she throws it off balance, and it stumbles. She kicks again at its arm. It drops the gun.

"*Who are you?*" it hisses. Without a gun, the hollow shriek in its voice carries less weight.

Temple scrambles for the weapon, her body scraping on the ground. Dirt kicks up her T-shirt, into the leg of her pants. It doesn't matter. *Get the gun,* she orders herself.

But she's too slow. The Cold lifts her up by the foot, tossing her aside with a groan. Her fingertips graze the handle before she hits the cabin wall—but she grips it. Her arms swing. She claps her palm around the hard metal, raising the gun.

Bang!

The Cold stumbles, and blood explodes where the bullet hits. She got it in the leg, weakening its posture. Its footsteps falter. Temple watches, holding her breath.

It takes a step.

Its leg gives out, and the monster falls to the ground.

Temple pulls the trigger again. Winces for the bang. But nothing happens.

The gun clicks empty, because *of course* she got it when it's almost useless. Temple goes straight for her bag without any hesitation, tearing through its contents.

The monster's laugh sounds from the shadows, and the fallen girl's body shakes. Temple looks up. Cracking sounds ring out slowly, as the footsteps of ice begin to creep from Natalie's still form. Almost as if the Cold didn't need a body at all.

Nonsense.

Out of all the *"Listen to your father, baby girl"*'s Temple was forced to sit silent through, there was never nothing like *"Listen to your father, baby girl—those fuckers can go ghost."* Her dad never said anything about, like, astral *projection* or some shit.

She's panicking, and panicking will make her dumb. She needs to stay calm. Temple searches through her bag until she finds salt, and then rips open a carton, pitching it at the thing's footsteps like it's a slug. The cracking halts for only a moment, persistently inching toward her. She throws more salt. The steps continue their path. The Cold is stubborn.

Temple doesn't need any more time. She drops her bag when her fingers touch the lighter fluid and the matchbox, and she rips them out.

"Your father is a madman," she remembers her mother saying once. *"He thinks he can actually stop evil with fire."*

That's all Temple needs. Immortals. Ghosts. They're all the same thing in this family. Temple flings the bottle, and clear liquid splashes on Natalie's clothes. She strikes the match ablaze on the first try, and the shadow stops. Everything about Natalie's figure sparks out, and she's aflame in seconds.

"Temple," it whispers.

Temple cocks her head as it gets warmer around the fire, and the silver footsteps retreat. Her whole body seizes up. *Temple.*

Not Thomas.

In her stillness, she tries to picture her grandfather's face—but she'd never seen it. She'd never met her grandfather. And if his mind was trapped in the past, as her grandmother's seemed to be, then he'd never know the name "Temple."

"Temple," she hears again. This time, it's Cali from the side of the cabin. "Hurry up and let's get the fuck out of here!"

True. This is time-sensitive. Temple tosses another match onto the corpse, along with the rest of the lighter fluid.

The whirring screams of the flames sound as she collects her things. She slaps the strap over her shoulder and keeps the gun as well, holding it as if it's still loaded.

As soon as she gets close enough, Cali hits Temple on the arm. "Where were you all this time?" Cali demands. She looks over to the growing flame. "When I couldn't find you after Brenda, I thought you were dead."

Temple shoves the gun in Cali's hands. "Hold this," she orders, and looks over to the two girls crouched by the edge of the woods. "Yaya! Let's go!" Temple calls.

Yaya bursts up, arm wrapped around Anysaa's back. Temple starts moving, Cali following close behind.

Their breaths are heavy and loud as they help Yaya drag Anysaa along, all four of them endlessly tired. Cali has strength on reserve. "I looked out for you," she says. "I thought you'd died."

Temple catches her breath to force out a few words. "I just ran for the woods. There wasn't much else to turn to."

Cali stops short. Yaya and Anysaa are a step behind as Yaya drags Anysaa beside her.

"What's going on?" Yaya asks.

"The cabins are safe," Cali says. "Before I got all stupid and thirsty, I saw Sierra sneak in there without any issue. It's like they don't even see them."

Cali's words spark an idea in Temple, a theory she almost says aloud. Cabins Aye and Bey are new. The highway is new. JG, the path, and North Point House aren't.

And those are the places her grandmother's been. The places she's killed.

It could be that, just like her mind—how she sees Temple as Thomas—her *body* only moves through the past as well. Or, at least, she avoids all of the new parts.

Temple looks to Cabin Aye. Then over to Yaya and Anysaa. She knows Anysaa isn't in good enough condition to make it to the highway. She looks like she's only alive because she has nothing else to do. And Temple . . . Temple really misses a bed. She hasn't slept enough.

She narrows her eyes behind them and then wilts. Everywhere in the woods is dangerous. Might as well hide in comfort. "Let's go," she orders, and the girls follow.

They all dart to the cabin while Temple hangs at their back. She checks behind her and looks past the flames, to the open door of the main cabin. K'ran stands there in the doorway. Blood drips down her body neck to toe as she watches the fire like it's a normal camp night. Her eyes dance, entranced by the flames. Then she tilts her head. She catches Temple staring from the cabin.

"Thomas," she mouths.

Temple hurriedly hops inside Aye, slamming the door shut before she can see any more.

Excerpt from *Hearts Stop*

Her fingers shook. Chunks of flesh had somehow burrowed beneath her fingertips. "I . . . I-I killed him." The words were lodged in her throat, like she could choke on them.

From the shadows, the scent of lilac tickled Bell's shoulders. "Burn him," Anna ordered.

Her voice vibrated in Bell's ear. It would have been so easy to lean back—close her mind to the intestines filleted before her. Her hands shook around Anna's. "I can't," Bell said.

"Burn him," Anna said. "That's the only way to stop Death from finding you again."

But this wasn't about Death. Bell's husband drenched the walls. His blood flooded the floorboards. Bell collapsed to the ground, a sob ripping through her.

She couldn't look at Anna. She was a disappointment. She knew it—Eric wasn't a good man, and Bell was weak. She should have been able to just—

The warmth of Anna's hand pressed at Bell's back. Bell felt the fabric of her dress twist around Anna's firmly pressed fingers. "It's OK," Anna whispered. "It's OK, you're OK."

It broke her.

Bell gripped onto Anna so tight their collarbones fit into each other like pieces to a puzzle. If Anna touched her, Bell could be strong. If it was Anna, Bell could forget. Even if she knew she couldn't.

From the corner of her eye, Eric's brown skin leaked into Bell's vision like migraine. She couldn't help but meet his dead eyes. But then, those eyes met hers.

Bell's heart dropped as the man whose bottom half was currently wet wallpaper turned his head to hers, his lips moving slow and subtle. Anna gripped Bell's arms tighter. And Bell ignored the words spilling from Eric's lips. His voice scraped through his slashed neck.

"I want to die. I want to die. I want to die. I want to die. I want to die."

CHAPTER THIRTY-TWO

Temple presses her back to the door with a quavering sigh. Grandma Ida knows where they are.

"Are you sure it's safe here?" Temple asks.

"As safe as we can be," Cali grumbles breathlessly. She's busy on the other side of the room. She bends over one of the bunk beds, dragging off a cleared mattress. It dominates her short, thin stature, but she merely grunts as she pulls it to the door, leaving just a space so she can kick it out the way when she wants. "This way, anything trying to come in is slowed down, but we can still leave if something happens," she says.

They aren't alone, either. As Cali said, Sierra is there, too. She looks at the faces of all the new tenants with an even expression as Cali moans and huffs her way through blocking the door. Then Sierra turns back to her nails. She has a full spread out—nail polish colors that only turn up on sketchy websites and cutesy decals with equally dubious origins. She's practically running a salon.

When Cali's done, she straightens, out of breath. She looks at Temple. "It may be safe, but I'm still scared shitless I'm gonna die."

That makes two of them. "Are we all OK?" Temple asks. "All in one piece?"

Cali nods and Yaya follows, folding her hands in her lap. The room falls noticeably quiet, and Temple turns to the wall.

"What about you?" she asks Anysaa, but Anysaa's in a heap on the floor. Sweat beads on her forehead as she looks up toward the ceiling with a blank expression. Like she's dead.

Temple pauses, her heart pounding. "What's wrong?"

"I don't feel so good," Anysaa groans. Her breathing is strained. Her body slumps as she looks at nothing.

A wet patch forms on her shirt sleeve, pooling blood down to her wrist. Temple gasps. She grabs Cali by the arm. "Did she get *shot*?"

Cali looks over her, her eyes roaming until she comes to the bloodstain. "Shit!" Cali shrieks. She hops over the mattress corner and crouches by Anysaa all in one action, grabbing her roughly.

Anysaa whines softly.

Even though Cali's the only one taking action, she seems to be the most flustered. "I-I know some wound stuff. I worked at a hospital last summer."

"'*Wound stuff*?'" Temple asks. She looks around the room like a doctor will fall out of the sky. Anysaa's been shot. Fuck. This kind of shit isn't supposed to happen. "Can you fix it?"

"I don't know! I can try!"

Anysaa's breath gets quicker as the girls devolve into panic.

"Take the bullet out!" Yaya yells.

"Don't do that! Stop the bleeding!" Sierra yells.

Temple's at a loss—she groans in frustration. They're trying to handle something they've never had to handle before. At this rate, Anysaa will die.

"Give me a shirt, or something to cover it!" Cali screams.

That, Temple can do. She marches over to the other side of the room where an old trunk sits, antiquated and rusty, and pops it open. Inside is everything for an emergency: fire safety kit, glow sticks, ponchos, backup phones that don't work—a little first-aid kit in red plastic lays atop the emergency blankets. Temple throws the kit over, and Cali catches it with deft hands.

"Softball team, bitch," Cali says proudly, crumpling the gauze in her hands and ripping the kit open.

Temple sinks onto the closest bed, sighing as she gathers herself. *We're not going to die,* she tells herself. She looks to the others, and out loud says, "Enough of us are dead. The rest of us are getting out of here."

Cali continues to patch up Anysaa, her eyes squinting at her immobile patient. It's impossible to tell if Anysaa is crying or passed out. Or dead. It would be just like the universe to kill her as soon as Temple proclaimed no one else would die.

"Are you sure you know what you're doing?" Temple asks Cali.

Cali pokes through the first-aid kit with fluent ease. Her actual work is sloppy, but seeing as there's no longer a gushing red wound on Anysaa's arm, Cali's clearly the best person for the job. Temple for damn sure can't do anything. Her kind of knife work is only good for destruction.

Cali barely spares Temple a glance. "My uncle owns that county hospital outside of Richmond—let me shadow some nurses to help me 'build character.' My character's still sketchy, but I can keep her alive for a few hours."

Anysaa's eyes pop open. "*A few hours?*"

"Go back to sleep," Cali orders. She soothes Anysaa back onto the wall with a fist pressed into her chest. Then, after a pause, Cali releases her. "Wait, no, actually, don't sleep. Stay awake."

Anysaa jumps back to life. "Which is it!"

"I don't know!" Cali pleads. "We need to get out of here ASAP."

"Sounds like a good plan," Temple says.

"But there are other girls still out there. *Lam*. Wynter, Janae," Cali says. "Someone's in Bey—I saw the lights on when I went to the bathroom, but—but—anybody could be anywhere."

Of course Cali gives a shit about that. And Temple does now, too, apparently. They're going to have to go to Cabin Bey.

Just as Temple's thoughts nearly circle back to "fuck them hoes," the radio erupts in static. Everyone shuts up, their necks craning to Temple as the sound drags in their bones.

"Fire on the south side." It's Lam. "Temple? Are you OK?"

Temple fumbles the little radio out of her back pocket. The silence that befalls the cabin shows the other girls cling to Lam's voice as hard as she does. Temple clenches onto the button.

"Temple," she states, the mouthpiece right on her lips. "We're OK. Y'all are still alive?"

After a moment of quiet, the radio crackles again. Lam comes back on. "—need to start heading to the highw—." Her voice distorts as the radio cuts the sound off.

Temple recalls that anxiety she felt before she and Yaya left the woods earlier. That feeling of having to leave the place where you didn't die, and head onto a path where you might.

She shakes the nerves out of her stomach and presses the button again. "Cali says the cabins are safe."

"I don't think the cabins will be safe for long. They're watching you. You all need to—"

"*Thomas?*"

Grandma Ida's voice slices through Lam's warning, rattling the radio between Temple's fingers, and Temple throws it across the room. It smacks against the wall, falling with a clunky stutter before rolling under the bed.

"*Where's Thomas?*" Grandma Ida calls from beneath the bed.

Then the radio cuts out, and the static leaves the cabin empty and quiet. Around the room, each girl has a different contorted expression—terrified to shocked to exasperated. Then they look at each other.

If they're looking for someone to blame, this is Temple's family, her land, her legacy. Once they know how rotten Temple's birthright is, they'll leave her to die. The radio message leaves the room heavy with thought.

Yaya sighs heavily and slams backward onto one of the beds. "Now who the fuck is Thomas?"

There's a communal sound that sums up the room's vocal shrug, while Temple avoids eye contact. Cali turns away from Anysaa's still form, holding her tongue. That girl knows damn well who Thomas is.

"Thomas is her son," Anysaa says. Her voice is weak, barely audible over everyone else.

But all the girls turn to her.

Yaya pops up from her slouch, rolling her head on her shoulders. "You're kidding. How do you know?"

"There's only one Thomas she could be talking about around here. Thomas Baker." Anysaa's eyes drift up the wall, across the girls, clashing with everyone's gazes. But then she stops at Temple, holding her gaze a second longer than the others. "Or, as we all know him: the North Point Killer."

CHAPTER THIRTY-THREE

Temple hadn't expected Sierra to cackle. The thick smell of nail polish wafts throughout the room, undercutting her hissing laughter. It's honestly admirable.

Sierra paints her nails like they weren't on the cusp of death. "*The* North Point Killer? 'Death Row' North Point Killer? His mama's just at camp, what? Chopping it up?" The amusement in her voice is sharp against the pit in Temple's stomach. "Don't you think that's taking the whole *Friday the 13th* thing a little too seriously?"

Sierra's words don't even register to Temple. Anysaa knows. Fuck—can't a bitch keep *one* secret? Everybody don't gotta know her business.

Anysaa's voice is shaky and light, but her eyes are right on Sierra. "You can believe me or not, but that's what I heard when—" she stops talking, her throat bobbing. "When I was trapped in there with them. I heard everything. I *know* everything."

The girls hold their breaths. Anysaa's voice seems so far away, breathing might be too loud for it.

And in the silence, Anysaa is able to continue. "I used to be so into the killer forums when I was in middle school. Like, I was a mod, and I had all the theories memorized."

"We all were," Sierra says. "All North Point kids got into horror that way. Cary Lauren and NPK are, like, gateway drugs."

"Yeah, well, me and Cali got banned from the forum in ninth grade for posting his personal records," Anysaa says. "We were North Pointers, through and through."

Temple stares at Anysaa's form across the room, but her vision is already blurry. North Pointers.

Cali is—

"Anysaa." Cali says it breathlessly, so Temple doesn't even have to look her way. It's true. She isn't lying.

Anysaa continues. "Basically, these woods—this land. It all belonged to the North Point Killer's family for decades. It was his father's, and his father's father's. Up to, like, the turn of the century."

Temple has a hard time seeing straight, listening to her own family history from somebody else's mouth.

Yaya clenches her arms around her stomach, leaning forward. "So that thing that's killing everyone—"

"Is the North Point Killer's mother." Anysaa leans her head against the wall. "Died like fifteen years ago."

"Holy shit," Sierra says.

Cali stands. It's so abrupt, even Anysaa cranes her neck—however slow—to stare at her. Cali's chest rises and falls as she considers everyone. Tries not to look at Temple—fails. "Maybe you should stop," Cali says. "I mean, maybe it's better if we don't know. Maybe some things . . . we shouldn't know." There's a shade of guilt in her words, and her eyes flick to Temple just for a second.

But it's too late.

Temple fights back her urge to run away. North Pointers or not, this is bigger than her. Everything always is. It doesn't matter if Temple feels bugs all over her skin, or her breathing is starting to feel thick in her throat—

Everyone's safety is more important.

"No," Temple grinds out. The word is bitter. It tastes like coal on her tongue, like bile at the back of her throat. But the witch has to get burned somehow. Temple is just collateral damage. "Tell us, Anysaa. We should know."

There's no way this is a good idea. No way this won't bite her in the ass. Anysaa meets Temple's eyes again, for that same second too long. Then turns to the others.

"I was the first to be possessed. By his mother." She tilts her head to the other side. "She's trying to protect North Point from his father—and trust me, you'll know him when you see him. Everything suddenly gets cold. So cold, it's hard to breathe."

"Jeez, that's insane!" Sierra says.

Temple has no idea who or *what* the Cold is—but if it's supposed to be her grandfather . . . *then how did it know her name?*

But Temple doesn't interrupt Anysaa. She doesn't meet Cali's wide eyes across the room.

"Ida—NPK's mom—she keeps talking about killing him. Every time he shows up: 'I killed you, I killed you!' It's all she can say. But, I guess she's supposed to be dead, too—so who's to say? All I know is . . . those two are the ones that are killing us. Probably killed Dawntae, too—they've probably been killing people for a long time."

Yaya raises her hand, like they're kindergartners at story time. Anysaa rolls her eyes. "You can talk, Yaya."

"I still don't get it," Yaya says. "Why's she killing *us*?"

From the mattress, Sierra nods. "Yaya's got a point. We're about as irrelevant as they come."

"Y'all call yourselves fans?" Anysaa asks, rolling her eyes. "It's classic *Hearts Stop*."

"You mean, like, Cary Lauren and her occult obsession stuff?" Yaya asks.

"No. Literally like *Hearts Stop*. You know, what she did to Eric to bring her son back? The marks NPK's mother put all over the walls?"

"A killing cost," Temple says aloud. They're finally catching up to where she's at—her grandparents have been killing people on this land for a long time. And they're doing it to pay for something. The girls even got the Cary Lauren connection—and that took Temple shamefully long to put together.

But even though they're almost where she is, when Temple looks up she's met with a bunch of blank stares around the room that nearly slap her. Her tongue works around even *more* words. "Like . . . they need to kill . . . in order to stay alive. Kill even more to . . . get power." Shame twists in her. She sounds crazier than her dad.

"I don't want to hear that nonsense from you," her mother's voice says in her mind. *"Just for one day, before he kills us both, I'd like for you to be normal."*

They're going to write her off now, abandon her to her serial-killing grandma. The silence that presses into the room feels like walls closing in. Temple bites her lip harder.

It's Cali that breaks the silence. "So, like, *Fullmetal Alchemist?*" she says. Tentatively—so unlike her. "Weird witch movies where the goth at the beginning says they need a sacrifice?"

"They're literally killing for immortality," Anysaa says.

Temple clenches her fists at her side. She remembers her mother glaring down at her, blocking the bathroom door. The only way out.

"He needs to kill them. If he doesn't—well, he'll probably just lay down and die. You don't want him to die, do you?"

"It's still not OK to kill all these people."

"You'll say that until it's you. Until it's you dyeing the tile with blood."

Her dad killed people and branded them . . . and if he got that far, he knew what all this meant. He knew about this possession. This bloodshed. His pathetic justification for murder was to live forever. And it was a family business.

Yaya rolls her shoulders back. "Jeez, we're really trapped in a *Hearts Stop* sequel? Do you know how grisly that book ends?"

Sierra looks up from her nail polish. "It's not that bad—not as bad as some Stephen King shit."

"Don't always bring King into it, Sierra," Yaya snaps back, and there's a flame of an argument that flashes like fire in a skillet. It sparks alive, rises, and falls, all quicker than Temple can collect herself.

She's still in awe. They believe Temple. Maybe because they've already seen the impossible. Temple's not so sure that's *all* it is, though. And then, before she can get a fully whole idea of what the feeling is in her chest, the girls quiet. Back to the subject at hand.

Sierra's lips screw as she closes one of the more sparkly bottles in her arsenal. "They're, like . . . sacrificing us. Keeping death at bay by coming after us."

"That makes sense," Cali says seriously.

"But why *us*?" Sierra continues. "In *Hearts Stop*, Bell and Anna killed abusers. Monsters. What's this demon housewife think she'll get out of a bunch of teenage girls? I mean, we're no angels, and it's not like we're virgins, but—"

"Speak for yourself," Yaya asserts, flipping her eyes to the others. "I realized I was a lesbian before I was biblically taken."

"So you *want* to get killed?" Sierra asks.

Yaya looks unsure, holding her hands in her lap as she considers the question seriously. "I'm sure there's some virginal clause for lesbians in the occult. There's gotta be."

"That's not how that works," Cali says.

243

"It's how it's gon' work today," Yaya asserts. "I'm not getting killed. My mom's due date is in two months, and she told me I was in charge of the baby shower."

Cali scoffs. "Too bad you're getting sacrificed with your hoe ass."

Another flash of arguments and shrieks before it quiets, and Sierra looks between Temple and Anysaa with big, soft eyes. "Are they really going to sacrifice us?" she asks. Her voice drops into a quiet whisper. "How long do we have?"

Not very.

Temple doesn't say that, though. It's Anysaa that answers.

"The cost of immortality is to kill. But you don't stay dead if you're marked," she says.

From the confused looks on everyone's faces after it leaves her mouth, it's too shaman even for the Cary stans.

Temple steps into the center of the room. Her back aches from standing for so long, from being tense for so long. But she still meets all of their eyes. "They're a pair of ghostly consciousnesses. They *need* to possess us or else they can't do anything," she says. "But they need to mark us to possess us."

"Until the marks fade from the bones, we can live together forever," her dad said. As long as the mark was there, they were able to possess a body.

Temple points to her forearm, tapping her skin. She looks over to Yaya. "You and me are safe. No tattoos, right?" Yaya nods. Temple points to the other three in the room. "All of y'all and your weirdo symbol tattoos are basically giving them your explicit permission to step inside your skinsacks."

Sierra drops her nail polish bottle. "Inside my *where*?"

Cali, bending to clean up the remnants of Anysaa's mess, freezes mid-tissue-swipe. Anysaa keeps her eyes closed, but her brow furrows as she presses her head against the wall. By putting the mark in her book, Cary Lauren pretty much fucked them over from be-yond the grave. How ungrateful she is to her fans.

"If what you said is right, we just have to get off the land. Un-dead old lady can't keep up with a bus," Yaya says. She looks across the room at Anysaa. "But the shuttle doesn't come back for hours."

Cali gestures to Anysaa's wound. "Which we can't wait for."

"We'll think of something," Temple says, scratching her head. Of course, nothing will come just from saying it. "But for now, we need to *do* something. If the mark is a door that can seal you in . . ."

"And let you out," Anysaa adds.

"Then we've got to get rid of them ASAP." Her grandma hopped from Anysaa to Mickaeyla to K'ran. Possessing one after another, because their marks gave her easy access.

Temple reaches into her back pocket, sliding out one of her cleanest, least-threatening knives. "So there's really only one solu-tion," Temple says. No one makes eye contact. "Who's first?"

"I'd rather be possessed," Sierra says, shaking her head.

"Well, you don't really get a choice, since possessed people *kill* us. I'm just going to ambush you if you don't volunteer."

Sierra rolls her neck like Temple said she was ready to fight over her best girl. "That's the only option you got, because I ain't finna *let* you cut me—tuh. If I'm gon' die I'm gon' look good." She flashes her dried hand, nails gleaming in the cabin light, to prove her point.

"It's not a game, Sierra," Anysaa snaps. "I was alone out there, playing dead. They walk, when there's nobody around. The fresher kills do."

Anysaa's voice seems to echo in the room, bouncing from girl to girl as they watch the blade gleam in the light.

"They tell you . . . about who else is here. Who else is in the woods. About how the strong ones can possess you, possess any-body that lets them. They can make you kill, too. Kill others to give them more power," Anysaa continues. "You don't even have to be dead for them to possess you. Just weak. Because when you're weak, you can get trapped in your body. Not controlling it. But not leaving it. Just trap—" Her voice breaks, and Temple knows she felt it. She felt every moment of Grandma Ida's spree.

Temple wants to tell her it's OK, that Anysaa can just let it go. But she doesn't say it. They need to know all there is to know if they want to get out alive and intact. She needs Anysaa to continue.

Anysaa swallows, blinking away tears. "Ida said she killed her husband, said that she found his bones and cut his mark. And that hers are still somewhere around here. If we can find *their* skeletons— *their* original marks—I think we can get rid of them."

A boy needs his mama. Long after his heart has stopped.

On October 1, 1997, detective Roberta Bell became the first in her family to own land. Hours later, her only son died.

His death was preceded by visions of her son running in sterile white hallways. Preceded by doctors ignoring her concerns over his slowing heartbeat. Preceded by her husband drinking himself to waste. By the beeping monitor flatlining.

The only thing that keeps her afloat are her new neighbors, a pair of sisters who claim transcendent understanding of grief. As her husband drinks himself to death and tears Bell's life apart, it's shy, smiling Anna and her older sister, Emily, who invite Bell into their home. Anna, who pulls Bell back together with the promise of her son's memory.

And Anna who teaches Bell how to handle Death.

Twenty years later, the detective returns to the hospital with Anna in her arms. But this time, she won't let Death win. With all that the sisters taught her, Bell slaughters in the name of love, vowing to keep Anna alive by any means necessary.

But when she starts seeing visions of her son again, she realizes there may be consequences to taking matters into her own hands.

Her son is waiting for her—and so is Death.

CHAPTER THIRTY-FOUR

Bags snap and zip around the room as the girls prepare survival kits for their comb through the woods. Out of sight, Temple breaks down some of her things to make them easier to carry in her pouch—she brings only one pack of matches with her knife and pours some salt in a plastic bag. Then she stuffs the entire contents of an abandoned bag of chips into her mouth, swallowing it all down at once. It's a wonder she doesn't choke to death—save Grandma Ida the trouble.

"We're really getting out of here," Yaya breathes. Her voice is soft, but it carries.

All the girls stop, taking a moment. No doubt they're remembering the bodies they had to go through to get to this point.

While the girls cluster in the center, getting the things they can carry in their arms without struggle, Temple approaches the emergency supplies box again.

There's not much good left. An extra first-aid kit. The blankets can stay—they'll just slow them down. Same as the rain ponchos and the glow sticks. The fire safety kit gleams in the bottom of the bin. Blasting her way out of here is still a viable plan, if it comes down to her leftover matches. But it's less necessary than before.

Temple's little bag doesn't have much room left—the first-aid kit won't fit. There's a click on the floor, and Temple looks up—to find all the others staring at her.

She freezes, all her muscles bunching.

Sierra looks at Temple, then down to the ground. Her finger curls out, pointing to the floor.

"What the fuck is that, Temple?" Sierra demands.

Finally, Temple sees the gleaming silver at her feet. Shit. Her knife—the *family* knife—is there in the light, slipped right out of its holster. She looks back up, wordlessly. Her eyes are wide, caught. The hook gleams wickedly between them all.

There's no way for Temple to seem normal now—they've seen a knife made for monster hunting. Might as well drop the pretense. "It's to kill with. If somebody gets too close, I'll gut them."

Sierra's ever-present frown deepens, and she overlaps her index fingers into a cross. "Yaya, pray for this child."

"We're going to *need* weapons," Anysaa cuts in before Temple can respond. Parting the girls like the seas, Anysaa creeps through the room to lead them to the door—smooth steps, too. When Anysaa's adrenaline wears off, they'll be in trouble.

All the girls go silent. Anysaa's breaths echo around the room—but at least she's breathing. "Are we ready?" she asks.

Temple snatches her knife from the floor and hangs back. Like they're counselors again: Anysaa's open, and Temple's closed. There's no doubt about who's light and who's dark, with Anysaa's fingers around the metal doorknob and Temple's around a twisting knife.

When the door creaks open, the night is deeply set. The trees seem to seep gas, the fog thick and pooling at the ground like inching hands. The sound of thudding footsteps is hollow beneath them, the line of girls hopping down the stairs wordlessly.

Temple's heart pounds—the smell of charcoal fills the air, wrapping around her throat. Natalie's corpse stopped burning a long time ago. Maybe an hour. Maybe a few minutes—time isn't as sure a thing as it used to be. Temple turns her eyes away from the scar that lines the edge of the campsite, the blackened limbs stretching out flat like a starfish. Even if it's not true—if Temple wishes hard enough, not looking at it could make it go away.

"Let's go." Cali's whisper breaks Temple out of her thoughts.

When Cali moves to grip Temple's shoulder, Temple slaps her hand away, the *pop* loud in the quiet. This may be bigger than her, but that doesn't mean Temple's a bigger person. She's just tryna live.

"*Don't touch me,*" she hisses.

"Temple, I know you're mad . . ." But Cali doesn't say anything else. Probably can't, with the way Temple's breathing is already hitching.

A North Pointer.

Temple's stomach twists in on itself, remembering all the warnings she'd *thought*. All the excuses she'd bought, and why? Because Cali was nice a couple of times?

Cali was a North Pointer, and she's been pretending to care about Temple all camp.

She's *really* after Temple's dad.

The thought makes her nauseous. She got letters, emails through her school, sometimes even packages. People asking about her dad because they *love* him, have some sick obsession with him, shoving her into a cycle as predictable as the seasons. They stalk her home if they find her. Then her aunt finds out and they have to move again. Every year. Twice a year. Since she was thirteen.

The other girls are already jumping up the steps to Cabin Bey, while Temple stands alone, glaring at nothing. Trying to keep her breath steady while the world is swimming around her. The trees sway gently, closing them into the circle of the campsite. Brightness flickers in the line—

And a dash of yellow blinks onto the gravel.

Then back out.

Temple pauses. She turns, but the only person around is Cali—who still hasn't left Temple behind to join the others for some reason. Temple doesn't wanna reward her by talking to her, but she has to.

"Did you see that?" Temple asks, staring over to the opposite side of the cabins. The curtain of trees by the bathrooms in the far corner, where the lights are still on.

"See what?" Cali asks.

The girls' footsteps crunch and crack ahead of them.

It happens again—pale yellow. Darkness.

Pale yellow again.

Two clicks, and then the light is gone. Temple takes a step away from the cabins. It has to be coming from the bathrooms.

"Don't do this," Cali whispers. "I swear to god, Temple, I don't care if you're mad at me about being a North Pointer, if I have to drag you in the cabin by your paint splatter I'll—"

"Temple."

The girls both stop in their tracks. Their eyes catch each other's, stunned at the sound of Lam's voice etched in static, muffled by Temple's hoodie pocket.

"Temple?"

She scrambles for the radio, snapping it up to her lips with her thumb jammed on the button. "Lam?" she whispers. "You're OK?"

The line goes quiet again.

Temple looks up, to Cabin Bey, only a few yards away. To the radio, nestled in her hands. The light flashes again, highlighting the gravel in peppery shadows and stars and Temple finally sees it clearly.

It's definitely coming from the bathroom. From Lam, leaning against the opening to the girls' room, her back on the tile wall as she glares across the campsite. She's no longer wearing her camp T-shirt—she's in a dark shirt over some baggy pants. Her hair is slicked back into a tight ponytail.

The radio crackles to life again. "We need to talk. In private," Lam says, agitated and short.

Those words aren't ominous on their own. But of course, Temple's already spiraling. Twenty-four hours ago, all she had to worry about was getting in trouble. Now, she's got two potential stalkers, undead grandparents, and exponential potential dead bodies.

She and Cali exchange glances. This is very clearly a bad idea.

"We need to talk now," Lam says again. The line goes dead.

In the silence that follows, unfortunately, Temple's thoughts are loud as day.

"You're gonna cave," Cali says. "I can't believe you're *actually* thinking about doing this."

"Go to the others," Temple says. "I'll be fine."

"*And* you're going alone?" she breathes. The silhouette of her figure is a shadow, and she darts in front of Temple to cut off her steps. "No way. Absolutely no way—not after all we've been through. You can't."

Fake concern, just like a North Pointer.

"What exactly have *I* been through?" Temple snaps. It comes out harsh, even though she's trying to keep a level head.

But Cali's expression is determined—even as it falls. She swallows, and Temple can see her throat bobble. "Still," she says.

Temple's hands tighten around the radio.

She absolutely understands Cali. They're keeping each other alive. But they also have been each other's keepers. Even when they were separated.

Even when they were fighting.

Not on a level of fate, but—Temple can admit it to herself. She and Cali have been looking out for each other.

Now they're going to separate again.

"Lam's obviously not coming here and wants somebody to come to her. I'm the safest one to go—nothing is trying to kill *me*. You saw what happened at JG."

"Yeah, I saw you get *shot at*," Cali says. "Lam's obviously trying to lure you out by yourself so she can slit your throat. She's possessed and gonna pounce."

"She's not possessed."

"How would you know that?"

Temple knows no such thing—Cali's making some sound points. But Temple won't give it to her.

"*Thomas*," she whines, her voice mimicking Grandma Ida's ghastly tone. "*Thomas, where are you?* It would be like that if Lam were possessed. They don't know Temple, only Thomas."

Except for the one time.

Temple tries to hide her shiver, looking away from Cali for a moment. It's deep inside her now. The sound of her name coming from the Cold, reaching her like a whisper on the wind. She still doesn't know what that means.

"Somebody needs to meet with Lam regardless of how safe it is. It's not like we can leave her behind." Temple jabs her finger in Cali's face, which Cali promptly swats away. "Unless you were planning on leaving her here. How long do you think she'll survive?

They took Brenda out in seconds, but maybe Lam can last . . . minutes? An hour?"

"You could get killed," Cali says. "Of course I don't want Lam to die, but . . ." But it's easier to just let Lam slip through the cracks. Maybe they'd even manage to convince themselves—*we shouldn't worry about Lam, Lam can take care of herself.*

Temple knows that concept well.

They'll die anyway, Temple used to think. *No need to get involved.*

"If I get killed, you and all your friends can have a field day," Temple says, and Cali flinches. Temple's tongue tastes like copper, the words that want to come out are hard to bring up. She swallows hard. "Before my dad was arrested, I knew exactly what he was doing to those people." She clenches her fist, simply remembering the past enough to seep blackness into her again. "I didn't do anything to help them. I didn't even try. I'm not ready to die, but I'm never going to just let shit happen again."

It's honest. For once, it's the absolute truth that Temple's been holding back for who knows how long, and it's heavy with the guilt that she's going to drag with her forever.

Temple slips her bag off her shoulder and hands her supplies to Cali. At least with her, they'll still help people if Temple dies on the way. She knows Cali will. Even if Cali is a North Pointer, Cali's on her side. Even if silence hangs between them for a long moment. When Cali finally nods—no matter how reluctant—Temple exhales.

"But I'm keeping watch, bitch," Cali says slowly. "I swear if you abandon us, and I get killed, I'm gonna haunt you and torture you. And if anything happens to your dumb ass, I'm getting the girls and leaving you behind." She turns on her heel to Cabin Bey, looking like a flamboyant vampire. Her camp T-shirt billows around her like a plush cape rather than a cotton blend.

Sounds fair.

Temple rubs her hands over her arms as she begins her trek across the gravel. The cold, hopefully, isn't supernatural—but it's still enough to keep her trembling and looking over her shoulder. The shadows of the trees line the circle of the campsite like a void.

The bathroom awaits her with its light making pale white bells on the gravel. It's a surprise the fluorescents are still on—they may be yellower, duller, but they're on. The sterile smell hits Temple and gets stronger with each step. Her eyes water at the sharp and over-bearing scent. At the bit of normalcy. She may have never inhaled bleach so deeply before, but she does it now and clings to it with every step.

When she reaches the building, the white tile now looks brown and oily, like a strange substance has covered every inch of the walls. Temple bends into the opening, stumbling out of the gravel and into the dimming fluorescents.

Lam's there, standing still. The lights flicker over Lam's head—even if the lights are nowhere near as bright as they used to be, they're the brightest thing the camp has this late.

"Lam," Temple calls.

When Temple gets closer, she notices the sweat pasted over Lam's forehead. Lam's T-shirt clings tight. "You're a dependable girl, aren't you?" Lam says. She tilts her head, challenging Temple with eye contact, and it's like no time had passed. Lam just stands there, solid.

The lights darken again, then glitch back on. Temple's radio gleams in her hand. In front of Lam there's not death and chaos all across the land—there's only death. But Lam will make it orderly.

Damn, is Temple really glad to see her.

"Temple," Lam says. "You know why I called you, right?"

"Of course I don't," Temple says.

Lam crosses her arms. Her biceps bulge and Temple notices darkness—dirt, moist dirt, like freshly rained-on soil—lining the hem of her sleeves. Lam clears her throat, and Temple jerks her eyes back up.

"I'm going to give you some intense instructions," Lam says firmly. "It's very important that you listen to what we have to say. You're the only relevant one here. Aren't you?"

Temple has no fucking clue how to answer such a question.

"Anysaa's with you and Cali, right?" Lam asks. She leans against the nearest bathroom stall wall. "Do we know what happened to Yaya, Janae, and Sierra?"

"Sierra and Yaya are with us," Temple blurts. She blinks at Director Lam. "There's that many dead?"

"K'Ran and Mickaeyla went down right after Brenda," Lam says. "You know what happened to Natalie. I found Wynter's body in a closet."

Temple swallows. "They're all gone?"

"I don't know how to answer that," Lam says calmly. Because Lam is solid. Lam is who Temple needs to be.

She'd seen so many of those bodies and yet . . . it didn't seem real. And Cabin Bey—if Wynter's dead, and she and Janae had been together, Janae may have been alone all this time.

But before the thought can sink into Temple too deeply, Lam raises her hands—like she's washed them of the situation. She frowns even deeper than before. "Don't freak out, OK?"

Lam stretches her arms forward, like Temple could attack at any moment. The image helps Temple keep her emotions in check, and she remembers she's here for information. She knows girls are dead. She can't get emotional every time it happens.

She breathes in—four in through the nose; four out the mouth.

"I'm fine," Temple says. "I already saw the bodies. What is it you have to tell me?"

"Don't freak out," Lam says again. Then she tilts her head back, toward the empty stalls behind them. "Come out now," she calls.

Creak . . .

Temple's eyes jerk to the back of the bathroom, where the plastic stall door opens inward. The lights flicker as the knock of hard shoes hit the linoleum floor.

Brown skin peeks out, ashen and slick with wet—an unknown, unspeakable color. Her posture relaxed, completely—casual, even. And her shaved head is crusted red, even as her bright eyes bounce to Temple, full of life.

"Holy shit," Temple says.

Because even though it's already been explained to her, it's still unbelievable.

"See how helpful it is when you breathe through your emotions?" Brenda says.

And when her lips tighten, and her teeth sparkle in the light, her smile is as open and wide as the first day of camp. As it was a day ago, when Brenda was still alive.

CHAPTER THIRTY-FIVE

Temple blinks at the two, her legs too stubborn to move. The light flickers in time—on, off. Darkness, Brenda. Her breath comes out short, and she feels herself losing control. This has to be—

"Breathe, Temple," Brenda says firmly. "It's really me." Her voice is clear, even though there's no way she should be able to speak. Not with the red crusted over her throat. The open cavity beneath her clavicle. Not with the way Temple saw the scissors skewer her neck. Brenda straightens, her tennis shoes squishing on the tile. "The Bakers aren't the only ones who can possess a body."

The energy around Brenda twists and bends as she steps toward Temple, eyes unmoving and locked. "Lam called you here because there's danger," Brenda says. She grabs Temple by the arms. Her fingers clench so tight it's like her nails dig in. "You need to get out of here *tonight*. Just get out of here and go."

"What are you doing?" Temple asks.

"The physics of the dead are complicated, Temple—there are a lot of bad people out here. I was able to repossess my own body but . . . someone's taking over the other ones. They've killed. A lot. You need to get to the highway as quickly as possible."

"Listen to Brenda." Lam's voice is impossibly calm.

It keys Temple up a little bit more. "We already have a plan—we can't go too fast because some of us have injuries. But if we find the original bodies, that could buy us enough time to—"

"*No!*" Brenda's breath is loud and ragged. The front of her shirt melts into shiny stickiness, the wound crusted over her neck softening and bleeding again. "*You* need to leave, Temple. Your dad—" she breaks off, like the sentence clogs her throat. "They all remember your dad."

Temple freezes. She never realized how terrified she was of hearing those words. "You . . . you know—"

"I didn't before," Brenda says. "The others—the other victims that are still trapped here . . . they talk. They know." She runs her hand over her shaved head, the scratching sound echoing in the dark. "I didn't know anything before this shit show."

Temple still says nothing.

"Your grandparents owned this place before Cary Lauren did. Your father used to dump the bodies of his victims here. I don't have the whole story of how your grandma fits into it, or why she thinks you're Thomas, but I know this"—she narrows her eyes, leaning in—"all the dead are still around. The girls. Your grandparents. Your father's victims."

"But they're all marked," Temple says. "They can be stopped if their mark's destroyed."

"Then—don't you see what they want?" Her voice is pleading, like Temple has something she needs. Like Temple has the answer she wants.

Temple swallows. "Immortality?" It comes out like a question. Something she was so sure of moments ago slips from her fingers at the look in Brenda's eyes.

"They don't *need* immortality, Temple. They have it." Brenda's next step forward is halting—lopsided. "Your grandma has it. Your grandfather has it. It's not a subscription service; it's a criteria to meet. You hit a certain body count, and you've got it."

Temple's brow furrows. If they don't *need* to kill to become immortal, none of this makes sense. "But if they're already immortal—"

"Then why keep killing?" Brenda finishes Temple's thought. With the harsh undertone of her voice, it's clear she knows the answer.

And suddenly, Temple realizes it, too. *Power.*

"When you kill, you can preserve your own body. Not only that—you get stronger. And you can do whatever you want with that power," Brenda says. "There are dangerous people here, and you *cannot* let them find you. A lot of these corpses are your dad's victims."

Temple pauses. Yes, a lot of them probably are. Her dad's victims' bodies had been removed—but their souls are still trapped.

"We're dead," Brenda says harshly. "We only see what we know. If I meet your children, I'll think they're you. So if your grandma thinks you're Thomas, who do you think your dad's victims think you are?"

Temple's thoughts fill the silence, flittering as fast as a cicada's chirp.

"They're all still here," she says slowly. And finally it all makes sense. She remembers, from the trial, every word her dad had said about his ritual. If her grandmother's still here, so are the victims.

They're hanging around, too.

Damn it. Fuck, fuck, fuck. *She* needs to get out of here. "Shit," she says aloud. Temple takes a step away, just as Brenda lets go.

Brenda can't help her. Nobody can—Temple looks up to Lam, panic creeping into her eyes. "We need you—we need somebody to carry Anysaa to the highway. She got shot, and I think her leg's broken. She lost some blood, and—"

"No," Lam says. The calm in her eyes makes Temple's stomach drop. Lam's tone is absolutely final.

Temple doesn't know where to put her pounding heart. "But . . . but you have to help us. We have to get out of here, and we can't do it alone!"

Lam looks down at Temple solemnly. "I lied before," she says. She pushes off the bathroom stall and leaves behind a sticky paste like mashed paint on a paint roller. "I wasn't OK when I first called you. When I tried to head out to the highway."

An owl. Mockingbirds. They howl outside the bathroom, the night pressing on Temple's back. Gnats swirl in and out of her vision as she stares at Lam.

"You remember where you found Dawntae, right? By the comm tower?" Lam asks.

Temple could never forget. She was splashed across the pathway like sewage.

Lam goes on. Her eyes are unmoving. "After the gunshots from JG, before we talked again on the walkies—I went out looking for survivors. I saw where y'all found Dawntae, then." Her voice goes thick. "But—not just her." Temple's trembling now, as each word leeches the hope from her. "No one could have stopped this," Lam says, clutching onto her shoulder. Temple squints her eyes at the dark fabric, watching her boss crouch lower to the ground. "I wish I could have reached you—or told you. The walkie doesn't work so well on this side."

In the fluorescent lights, Lam pulls at her shoulder. The sound of slop and smacking fills the room as she reveals a gash of a wound tearing into her clothes. Her arm is nearly separated clean from her torso.

The iron smell of blood rushes into the air, the squishing sound of flesh with it, and Temple finally makes out that the black of her shirt . . . is red. Her shirt—her camp T-shirt, Temple realizes—is so bloody it looks black.

261

Lam looks at Temple, even-gazed. "There's no putting me back together. No regeneration, no magic spell. It's up to you now—and they know you. Whoever did this—they asked for you."

Temple's legs give out. The hard tile cracks against her knees as she sinks to the floor. "Lam," she gasps. "I hate this, I hate this, I hate this. Lam. You're—"

"Calm down, Temple," Lam says.

Calm down. What a thing to say.

Everything crashes onto Temple at once, and she finds herself swallowing a wall of tears. When she tries to speak, she coughs and shakes her head as her emotions surge. "I'm fucking *overwhelmed*, Lam," Temple snaps. "I'm the normal kind of bitch that freaks out at these kinds of things."

"I'm sure you are, but the situation—"

"If normal people couldn't handle this shit, why are you asking me to *calm down*? You're *fucking dead* and talking to me!" Her voice is now a hysterical shriek, and she doesn't know how to return it to normal volume. "I've seen girls kill each other, and ice people, and I heard my mom's voice the other day, and that bitch is dead." She gulps in air. "I set someone *on fire!*"

Lam's silent for at least a minute while Temple catches her breath. Mosquitoes buzz in Temple's ear. A birds squawks. Sinks drip. Lights flicker.

Then, Lam folds her hands over her belly. "Are you done?" she asks pointedly.

Temple's hollow breaths fill the silence.

Lam crosses her arms. "Temple. You're allowed to freak out. Nobody thinks you aren't. But you aren't the only one here. You're in charge now. Either you go AWOL or you nut up. Got it?"

"Do I have a choice?"

Lam snorts. She whips Temple upward, and Temple stumbles to her feet, tears glistening in her eyes.

"We hired you because you're a leader," Lam says finally. "You walked into your interview with your head held high because you've had to look out for yourself your whole life. And now you're looking out for the others. You can do it, Temple. I know you can."

Temple peeks up through her eyelashes at Lam, sobbing hiccups raking through her body. Through her blurry sight, Lam's blood-sticky hands cross before her, rotted cotton of her shirt slipping over her collarbone.

Temple shakes her head. "Sorry," Temple says, wiping her eyes. "I'm really sorry."

"It's not your fault," Brenda says softly. "You don't need to apologize to us. We just want you all to live."

Lam nods. "The cabins aren't safe. It won't stop a corpse possessed by someone who died after the cabins were built." She nods along with her given orders. She remains stone-faced, unsure of what to do with Temple's blubbering. "Just get out of here, OK? We'll try our best to buy you time."

"OK," Temple says through sniffles. She lingers, staring at Brenda before Lam shoos her again, this time with a shove. Before Temple turns out toward the cabin, she sees their expressions fall. Tears glisten over Brenda's eyes in the light.

She's trying hard to be tough.

Temple has no right to take that away from Brenda, so she turns around, saying nothing. Once she steps out into the gravel of the campsite, she feels cold seeping into her shoulders.

She can no longer tell if it's her own dread or something coming.

But it won't matter soon enough. She has a target on her back. She has to move.

North Point Tribune: "Families of North Point Killer victims celebrate answers by shutting down popular forum"

Thomas Baker confessed to killing 20 victims last Friday.

When the families of the victims of the North Point Killer came together to meet the FBI on the Monday following the serial killer's confession, there was little fanfare at the entrance of the crowd. However, they were there for an important reason.

"The confessions gave us new information, but we're all old friends at this point," Brittany Martinez, 16, said, gesturing to the 30 people behind her. "We've been working on this for a long time."

Before the community found out their loved ones' names were on the list of Thomas Baker's victims, they were already a family brought together in the most tragic of circumstances. "People go missing in North Point, sure. It just so happened that all of us were connected," Martinez said. The connection didn't stop at the murders, though. Harassment, stalkers, and violent attacks from strangers all plagued the surviving family members of the victims thanks to a doxing website called NPKTRUTH.

"My son loved that site," Lester Wallace, 53, said as he held up a note from his long-passed nephew. "But he knew it was up to no good. Left all his passwords and said to delete his account just in case. That the boards were a bad place we shouldn't mess with."

The names that the North Point Killer included in his confession have not been made public. The North Point Victims Alliance hopes it will stay that way, now that NPKTRUTH has been shut down.

"We're taking our lives back," said Martinez. "We could have built a memorial with the money we used on lawyers, and maybe we will someday. But I don't regret it. We need safety and respect for our families by any means necessary."

CHAPTER THIRTY-SIX

"The sins of your father will send us all to hell."

Temple hears her mother's voice ring in her ears.

"Atone while there's still the purity of childhood in you."

Temple heard snapping of wood, felt the tickle of a bug crawling on her thigh. "Mom?" she asked. "Mom, is that you?"

Temple gasps in air, as if her lungs had been frozen.

Cabin Bey comes into view, lights shining onto the gravel Temple walks on. Once again, she's faced with the reality of her death—it's almost guaranteed. She climbs up the steps to the cabin. A breeze flaps around the hem of her T-shirt.

A scream rips through the air just as she touches the door handle.

"Get back!" Anysaa yells.

As if she's fighting someone—something? Temple slams open the door, blinded by the light as everyone turns to her—the room is like a classical painting. All of the things Temple had left in the cabin are scattered about the room. Her clothes from her suitcase, her salt and matches from her pouch. Her coins.

Strewn across the floor, tossed aside like garbage.

On the far side of the cabin, Cali and Yaya kneel with their hands up, cowering like hostages. Sierra stands above them—fire extinguisher clutched in her hand. Anysaa's on the opposite side of the room, standing with a straightened spine beside the new addition—Janae.

And Janae's got one of Temple's backup knives.

"What the fuck is going on in here?" Temple demands.

Janae is quick on her feet—she raises her arm and Temple only sees her knuckles before pain explodes in her forehead. "Take her," Janae mutters, and another hand grips Temple and yanks her back.

Everything swims in her sight as the trees circle her and her words cut off. She can't see Cali anymore. Her arm is bent, wrist held tight against her spine.

And then cold presses onto her neck.

"Give me the walkie." Anysaa. Her voice is cool and demanding. Unruffled, but out of breath.

"What the fuck, Anysaa?" Temple whispers. Her eyes flicker to Anysaa's arm, bandaged up. Her leg she said was broken.

Anysaa tightens her grip on the knife. "I had a lot of time to think about how to get out of here. Lucky for me, I know exactly how to act when you can't walk."

The slightest gulp makes the cool metal hit her skin, but Temple can't help it. She closes her eyes for a beat, tightening them like it'll rid her of this headache of a situation. "Now's not the time—we need to stick together."

Janae is the one whose shadow dances across the wall. "Fuck you, and fuck togetherness."

Anysaa remains still, and Janae goes fuzzy in Temple's vision. "Radios glitched out," Janae says. "We heard everything."

Sierra turns to Temple, too, keeping the pointed end of the marked knife aimed at Cali. "You never noticed how this camp is one giant mark?" she asks. Her voice is smooth and quiet. "Like, literally in the shape of the mark. The whole campsite, waiting to trap us. That means there *ain't* no running away. There's no killing them before they kill us . . . unless we leave some bait."

"Ida Baker can't catch us if she's busy with the family reunion," Anysaa finishes.

Temple feels the metal blade tremble against her skin. Anysaa's other hand fiddles in Temple's back pocket, pulling out her family knife, too.

"Don't do this." Temple switches gears. "At least don't take my knives. Not both of them."

Anysaa laughs in Temple's ear. The sound vibrates in her shoulder as Anysaa's hold gets painfully tight. "No. They're my knives now." She drops her voice lower. "Do what I say or else."

"You won't cut me."

Anysaa pushes—Temple's skin splits open as the knife digs in. Not enough to kill, but she feels the hot rush of blood drip down, brushing the collar of her shirt.

"I will," Anysaa says. "These fucking monsters have already made me a killer. I can up my body count."

"We need to stay together," Cali hisses from the floor.

Sierra shakes her head and turns to Temple. "It's nothing personal. They follow you around, Temple. I figure we can get cover away from you."

Janae clasps her hand around Temple's shoulder. "It's personal for me—I saw that bitch tear Wynter to pieces. Fuck you *and* your family, Temple."

Temple tries to relax a little. Seem less . . . terrible. "There are *things* out in the woods. They could kill you. Whatever you're planning—don't do it alone—"

"Shut up," Anysaa snaps. The blade cuts just a little deeper, warning her. "You don't care about us. You're his *daughter*. You thought we wouldn't find out? That you lied about who you are?"

"What was I supposed to say?" Temple says desperately. "'Hi, I'm Temple Baker, and I come from a long line of serial killers'?"

"You made my life *hell*," she hisses. Temple feels her hand shaking at her back. "I admit—I didn't welcome you when you first came to North Prep. I didn't know you. I went to that school since the sixth grade, and I knew everybody. I didn't think it was that big of a deal to not like you. We were just playing around that day." Her voice quakes, and Temple hears her sniffle. "And now, because of you, I'm off the basketball team for good. My parents had to put a loan out for my medical bills—" And then she breaks down sobbing, her cries echoing in the quiet room.

It's odd. Temple feels a little coal in her throat—she's close to crying, too. And she has no clue why. "I was just scared when I saw you following me," Temple says. "I *saw* you pick up that rock to hit me." *Excuses.*

"I'm finally getting you back." Anysaa's voice turns to steel. "For everything—for all your lying, and your pretending. For that day."

"I thought you were gonna hurt me," Temple whispers. *Excuses.* The voice is harsher this time—sounds just like her mother.

"And what about after you saw it was her, huh?" Janae cuts in.

"What about when I begged you to put the pipe down?" Anysaa asks.

Temple swallows down the disgust at her own self. Because Anysaa's right—she's a monster. She beat this girl. Brutally.

She hadn't regretted it for so long, didn't even face the consequences of her actions. Not in any way that mattered. She just coasted by as a tragic figure whose father was a monster and mother was a victim. On her reputation as a "misguided youth."

Thick tears fall down her cheeks as Temple remembers her anger, her panic. She'd wanted to send a message to anybody else watching her. Wanted to seem so tough . . . and so she ruined a girl's life.

"I'm sorry," she says, finally. Temple sniffs, trying to keep her voice even. "I shouldn't have hit you like that—but I'm fucked up. You know that. Before I went to North Prep, North Pointers would follow me home and—"

"That doesn't make everything right," Anysaa says. "It doesn't. You can't be shitty and then just take it back."

Temple knows. Excuses and forgiveness don't complement each other.

"You're right, Anysaa—they're following me because of my dad. And I lied on my application. I don't care about horror, and I've only ever read like half of *Hearts Stop*." Temple's breath catches, and she lets out a shaky exhale. "I know that you have no reason to trust me. But you have to. I can get us out alive."

Anysaa makes one more cut, saying nothing.

Temple swallows, and she feels a hot bead of blood tickling the back of her neck. "I'm sorry."

Anysaa shoves Temple forward. "Take your 'sorry' and go to hell," Anysaa spits at her.

Temple jumps for her, reaching her arm out—she can't let them take her knives. But her ankle twists, and the ripple of pain sears all the way up her leg. She falls to the ground, wind hissing out of her chest.

"Got everything?" Anysaa asks above her. Two shadows join her, Janae and Sierra, out of focus for her. Three girls leaving. Three left.

"Even if you leave me behind, she'll kill you," Temple says. "She kills everything." She can't control her breath—it's all caught up in her fear. Her fear that she's fucking things up again.

"Protect me from the evil one."

When Temple stumbles back to her feet, her vision swims. Her eyes whip over the wooden paneling, to Cali's and Yaya's somber faces—to Anysaa's back, possibly for the last time.

But Anysaa's already swinging open the door. "We got enough to get through the path in about four hours, if we keep up the pace." Anysaa rotates her arm—her wounded one—with just a slight wince. "Then we're out for good." Their footsteps thump as they race down the stairs.

Only Sierra lingers.

Yaya scoffs from the ground, narrowing her eyes. Then, she pouts a little. "This effing sucks."

"Tell me about it," Cali adds.

"Anysaa's not the messiah she thinks she is," Yaya says to Sierra. "She's not Bell. She won't save everybody from Death."

Sierra bites her lip as she stares, and Temple remains silent. She always thought of herself as a human sacrifice anyway—but the sting that someone decided for her . . . and still left others behind.

"Remember how Bell lit Anna on fire to sever their bond?" Temple blurts out. "How she destroyed the one she loved to save herself? That's how this ends."

Not a single sound passes among them. All three girls just stare at Temple, jaws dropped.

"What?" Temple asks. "I told you I read half the book. It was the end half."

"Come on, Sierra!" Anysaa's shout from the campground pierces the room, and Sierra looks over her shoulder.

She turns back to the girls for a moment, and she really does look sorry. "Cali, Yaya, you can come with me."

"Excuse me?" The disgust in Yaya's voice is definitely a comfort.

"I'm just trying not to die—and it's all about Temple. Y'all don't have to stay with her."

"But we are," Cali says.

Sierra's face twists, genuinely distressed. "I *really* wish it wasn't like this. If we all make it out, maybe—"

Her words stop short, and she stumbles backward, blood spilling from her lips. When Sierra falls to the ground, the long spear of ice that sticks from her back cracks in two.

CHAPTER THIRTY-SEVEN

Blood spills along the floor, the lengthening pool crawling through the cracks in the wooden boards like molasses.

"Sierra?" Yaya calls. Her voice—it's so tinny and broken. Dulled. The death is in their bones now. They almost expect it.

Crack.

. . . Crack.

It starts as a whisper. The sound of chipping, of inching ice, hisses through the room as Cali, Yaya, and Temple stare at Sierra's fallen body. Then the blood begins to solidify. Winding webs of white burst into the thick red, and Sierra's corpse goes stiff and blue.

Crack, crack.

"Shit," Temple says. "Get her out of here!"

Yaya's the closest, and she springs into action, running over to Sierra in the doorway. Her fingers wrap around the dead girl's ankles, and her eyes waver only for a moment—a second of fear that she's completely allowed—before she drags her by her legs. Temple sees her breath wafting upward, and she knows it's close.

The Cold is almost there.

Yaya heaves Sierra out of the cabin.

"Hurry!" Temple screams.

Cali's voice is just as thick. "Close the door!"

Sierra tumbles down the steps and Yaya slams the door shut, pressing her back against it. Her eyes are wide, and they flicker from Cali to Temple. "It was moving. The . . . just . . . *darkness*. It was coming straight for me."

Son of a bitch. "It's not dead," Temple says.

Another scream pierces the night, and Yaya stumbles away from the door. Temple and Cali reach out to her, dragging her against them, and they huddle together. Only their sounds between the walls.

Then there's another scream. A different girl.

And another. Both. It keeps going.

It's the first kills all over again, hearing the girls. Hearing their pain. Never knowing how terribly they suffered. How lucky they are to be alive. A tear slides down Cali's cheek. Yaya's shivering. But Temple can only shake her head.

The screams stop after a few minutes.

The silence that fills the space is dead. It forces Temple's eyes shut, and she realizes her lips are trembling.

"We tried to help them," Cali says.

But it will never be enough.

She shakes her head again. "It never matters. I've 'tried' before," Temple says. She stands up, and Cali follows, matching her stance. Everyone's blurry—and her skin is hot.

Blackness seeps into her again, that hard stone that makes her shoulders ache. "It happened again." Turning away, Temple clenches her fist. "I didn't stop it *again*."

"Temple, I'm sorry I lied about being a North Pointer," Cali says. Her voice is thick, but no tears fall down her cheeks. She grabs onto Temple's hand. "Fuck—I'm sorry I was a North Pointer, *period*."

Temple says nothing in response.

"But we're not dying any time soon. Not me. Not tonight. So this feeling sorry for yourself shit?" Cali points back and forth between herself and Temple. "That's for later. Now—we have a very traumatizing trek ahead of us and a dead body just on the other side of that door."

The silence feels like it's getting even thicker as they take a moment to think.

"Yaya—you're a good runner," Cali says, leaning in close. "Temple's got the background info. We know we have to get to the highway for sure now. There's only forward."

Then the radio rattles with life. Cali jumps, nearly patting Temple down with excitement as the speaker crackles. Temple holds her hand up, waiting for a voice to come onto the line.

"Who is it?" Yaya asks hopefully.

They wait. Cali leans in. The static clears on the other side.

"Thomas?" Grandma Ida wails.

"Damn it," Cali swears.

"I should have known," Yaya sighs.

Temple pulls the radio out of her pocket, pressing the button. "Stop playing on the radio," she snaps.

"Thomas, *you have to hide*," Grandma Ida whispers, her voice supernaturally clear. "*He sees you.*"

Then the line goes dead again.

Temple has half a mind to turn the volume down in irritation— but that's a terrible idea. "How long do you think before she shows up?" Temple asks the other two girls. There's already so much to worry about. Her clothes feel dirty and sticky, her head dizzy from stress and crying.

But they have to keep moving.

Cali is already pulling together the remnants of Temple's emptied bag, wrapping the strap tightly around her shoulder. "I swear to

275

God, if one of these dead bitches kills me before we get out of here, I'm gonna be dead bitch in charge. I'm killing everybody left. You, your grandmamma, your cousins. *Anybody.*"

"Sorry," Temple says—because somehow she feels she needs to.

"Shut up, Temple," both Cali and Yaya say together.

Cali slaps her free arm around Temple's shoulders, doesn't even let go when Temple fights the hold. "Stop blaming yourself for shit that don't got nothing to do with you, and be optimistic for once. You're not alone. I mean, I'm pretty sure me and Yaya aren't going anywhere. And you saved Anysaa's life—even though she's an ungrateful bitch. Can't you just pretend we'll definitely survive? We—"

Knock knock.

The girls freeze.

Knock.

Knock.

Yaya looks at Temple, who looks at Cali, who shakes her head as if to say *Do you think that's somebody we wanna fucking see?*

Their teeth chatter as they lean against each other, facing the door in anticipation.

It hasn't torn down the door yet. It can see the cabins—at least, it can knock on them. Lam, maybe? Or Brenda?

Shit, she'd even take Janae at this point.

Temple raises the radio to her lips slowly, pressing the button and breathing silently. She doesn't know who she wants it to be. But she goes for it anyway.

"That y'all?" she asks.

"*That y'all?*"

Her voice echoes from the other side, and the girls turn their eyes to each other. Temple can taste the panic in the room.

"Fuck that," Cali mouths. She whirls around, tiptoeing to the back wall, where the trees in the window sway in the breeze.

The knocking turns into scraping.

It repeats rhythmically, knocking and scraping, scraping, scraping. Yaya grabs onto Temple's arm as they both follow behind Cali, but Cali is stopped at the back window. She holds a hand up, her eyes focused on the ground outside. Her hand presses against the glass and she slides the lift down.

Temple steps forward. "Let's go, Cali. That ain't nobody we know."

"I see two shadows," Cali says solemnly. She looks at Temple and Yaya over her shoulder. "There's someone out there."

"In the back, too?" Yaya gasps. "Are we gonna die?"

Cali shakes her head. She glares at Temple. "I told you what would happen if I died. I'm not gonna be cornered."

Fuck—they waited too long to leave.

Yaya's fingers are tight on Temple's sleeve, and when Temple takes a step back, Cali wraps her arm full around Temple's elbow. Feeling her tremor makes Temple swallow and think.

"Cali, Yaya, see if you find anything under my mattress," Temple orders. She pulls from their hold, looking around the room.

Cali runs over, Yaya close behind. They drag the mattress off the creaking wooden slats, sliding it to the floor.

"Confiscation?" Cali asks. Temple doesn't have to confirm.

Temple can't exactly remember everything she took—a blunt sticks out in her mind pretty clearly. But if they can't find any weapons, they're hopeless.

Temple focuses on the door while the others rifle through the stuff. She takes tiny steps toward the door, her heart ramming in her chest.

Cali gasps behind her. "Wow, is this—"

"Yes," Temple says, knowing what was found.

"Wish I knew about it a day ago," Cali says.

"What's this?" Yaya asks, even though Temple isn't looking.

Cali exclaims. "Shit, you got my fireworks? Maybe we can use these to signal for help." The giddy way she says it, though, Temple wonders if she isn't thinking more about lighting them for fun again.

Fire. Temple sprints across the room, bumping into the wall as she stops behind the door at Bey's fire safety kit. Its lid is askew after all it's been through. Temple flips it open, and it's just about ransacked—except for the emergency blanket.

And the line of fire safety tools.

Brenda only mentioned it briefly. She was much more worried about the girls making out and doing drugs. Temple's eyes roam over the toolbox, taking in what she can use: a fire extinguisher, a pair of gloves—and an axe.

She pulls it out, raising it like a baseball bat, and she looks back at Cali. "You think I can pull it off? It's a little short," Temple says.

The scraping overshadows Cali's quick footwork as she darts across the room. "Well, we've got to try," Cali says.

She presses against the wood of the door as she holds the handle with a tight grip. When she whips it open, she'll be out of sight.

"Ready?" Cali whispers.

Temple adjusts her grip. "Let's chop up a bitch," she says, feeling that rock in her chest that always forms before the first day at a new school. The chance to be somebody new. The chance to not be a monster.

She isn't going to die, Temple decides. If anything tries to change that, it's getting cut in half.

Cali pulls, and the door swings open, letting the night air in. Moonlight glows in a halo around the open door. Gnats swim in as the thick wet of outside fills the room, too, wrapping around Temple's quaking form.

She nearly drops the axe.

Anysaa is standing at the door. Clumps of blood and dead leaves mix into her curly hair, her clothes soaked red as she stares at Temple somberly. Her legs wobble like a newborn fawn. "Temple," she says.

Adrenaline keeps the axe clasped in Temple's sweat-slicked hands.

"Temple," Anysaa says again.

"What the fuck, Anysaa? Did you forget something after you stole all my shit?" Temple asks.

Anysaa falters, her prettily arched eyebrows raising. Wisps of her hair gleam in the light. "Temple. It's me. *You have to recognize me.*"

Temple pauses, slowly realizing the change in voice. Tears coat Anysaa's eyes as she looks up at Temple, flexing her jaw the way Temple does when she's stressed. The way that Temple got honest.

The way she got from her mother.

Temple loosens her grip on her axe, air leaving her lungs. "Mom?" Her voice wobbles.

When Temple speaks, an unmistakably familiar grin breaks over her mother's face like a sunrise. She steps inside, reaching out with her blood-soaked hand and grips the fabric of Temple's sleeve.

"Temple, you're here," she says. She wraps Anysaa's wobbling arms around Temple's body, sopping red through Temple's T-shirt. "I missed you so much."

CHAPTER THIRTY-EIGHT

Temple's mother always feared her dad. When he was away, she sprawled around the house as if she were laying roots. When he was there, she locked herself in the bathroom with Temple. Temple remembers many nights waking up in the bathtub and finding her mother awake and shuddering. Her face smeared with blood. Whispering for Temple to go back to sleep.

"You don't want to wake your dad," her mother would say, rubbing her hands together. They smacked with a wet sound like liquid soap. *"He's had a long day."*

When Temple's mother disappeared, Temple lost the only other person who understood what it was like to live in the cabin. Understood life with Thomas Baker.

Her mother was the one that needed to be protected, though.

It got harder to feel that way as the years went by, and her dad's words slipped into incoherent babbles.

Without her mother, there was no one to lock the bathroom door and keep Temple away from the leftovers of her dad's latest escapade. That task wasn't easy—Temple had been a curious child—but she'd only seen six bodies of his in her childhood. The court's estimate was twenty victims.

"I killed your mother. Chopped her head off," her dad said. Twenty-one victims.

Now, Temple's mother is right in front her, her arms wrapped tight in the kind of hug that feels so familiar—even though it's the first time it's happened. Even though the hug looks like it's from Anysaa. Temple sobs, rather than speaking, and her mother shushes her, rubbing her back as Cali and Yaya silently watch.

Temple's axe falls to the ground, and she wraps her arms around her mother.

"You're dead," Temple finally says. Her mother is gone. She isn't missing; she's dead.

Cali retrieves the axe, and the scrape of its metal bounces around the room.

Temple's mother pulls back with a grin. "What's all this crying? We're in a hurry. We need you safe."

Her mother's hold loosens, and Temple looks into her eyes through Anysaa's. She holds her breath, like it'll help her climb in and read her thoughts. That fails. "Did Dad kill you?" Temple blurts out. That question escapes on its own. It's festered in her chest for so long that saying the words feels like an exhale.

Her mother barely moves. With a craning, stiff hand she grabs Temple's chin. "Does it matter?" she asks.

Temple sniffles, wishing she could take her in—but it's just Anysaa's dead eyes that stare back. Whispers sound around the room, and she steadies her breathing. She pictures her dad smiling down at her, watching cartoons with her.

It kind of does matter. Wait, no—it *really* does.

Temple's mother wraps Temple back up in a hug before Temple can say anything, and Temple remembers all the hugs she's had to this point.

None.

Her family wasn't affectionate. And the last time she'd seen her mother—

"Repent. We all must repent."

Her mother sighs, pulling Temple from the memory that sends a shiver deep into her spine. "You must have been scared," she says, her hold tightening so hard Temple's ribs ache. "I'll protect you. But we have to go."

Behind her, Yaya begins to whisper. "Dear Father, our lord in heaven." Her prayer tumbles from her, and Temple tries to pull away, but her mother hugs her tighter.

"I won't let you go again," her mother says. *"I've been without my family for five years."*

Five years ago, she disappeared.

Temple pulls away, shoving her elbow between them so her mother can't snatch her up again. Her brow furrows. "Did he kill you, or didn't he?" Temple demands.

Her mother blinks at her, and Temple realizes the last time she saw her mother she was eleven. The last time she saw her mother, it was in the bathroom. When she couldn't move. When the grass was inside—sticks barring her in, down on the porcelain as her mother hovered above. Her arm outstretched, fingers clenched around a tiny box that bent with the force of her grip.

With a wave of her hand, Temple's mother pouts. Then she studies Temple's face and sees her resolve. "You know what he's like, Temple. It was a matter of time."

"So he did."

"Temple," Cali drawls. Evenness fills her tone, as unnerving as silence. "Look at the door."

Temple lifts her gaze, past her mother. At first, she sees only the blank space of night in the empty space. Gnats flit in the light of the cabin, buzzing in and out of sight. Then, Temple notices the door. Higher than brow level, half a circle is carved into the wood. A line cuts through the curve, stopping just short of a thin "I." Just underneath that . . . her name.

Temple stares for a moment, her thoughts in slow motion. She looks down at her mother's wrist. She grabs on and feels a hard slick in the fabric of a sleeve.

"Repent," her mother had said that final night. *"We all must repent."* Then she glared down at Temple, her daughter tied up in a tangle of weeds and twigs.

Struck a match. And let go.

"I've been hiding knives in my sleeves since I was six," Temple says aloud. She flips her mother's wrist over and pulls the knife out—the four-incher Anysaa took. "What were you doing, Mom?"

Her mother's eyes deaden, and she grips Temple back.

Clank.

Something falls behind them—it's Cali and Yaya, huddled together in the corner.

Temple's mom leans in, her words cutting with thickness. *"Who are your friends, Temple?"* For the first time, Temple can make out the conflicting tones of two voices laced together. Darkness creeps into her mother's edges. Temple's mother loosens her hold, her eyes narrowed on Cali as they shift. *"I don't remember them."*

The temperature drops. Curls of ice crawl from beneath her mother's feet like footsteps. It hadn't been this cold before—but this is her mother. Her mother isn't a monster, she—

The room chills another degree, and Temple swallows. She remembered the sound of its voice laced with Natalie's as the monster taunted Temple, searching for her hiding spot.

When Temple speaks, her voice gives away no fear. "That mark on the door . . . was it supposed to be a seal? Were you trying to trap me in here?"

"It's what's best for you, Temple," her mother had said that night, as ghosts of gold flickered against her brown skin. *"I'll always do what's best for you."*

Her mother was the only good one. The only one that cared about the evil Temple's dad did. That cared about the evil Temple would become.

But somehow, she's the Cold. Not her grandfather. All this death was because of *her*—which means her mother was never the good one at all.

None of them were.

There was no good for Temple Baker.

Her mother jolts up, light flashing in her palm before she scowls. She seizes Temple by the wrist. *"You never did listen to me,"* she says, and the curved hook of the knife gleams, the marked handle tight in her hands. When she runs it against Temple's palm, there's no blood—it just scratches at her skin. Her mother smirks.

"But that's OK. I'm here for you. Always." Her mother is so fast—she pulls the knife right from Temple's fingers. Her mother kicks Temple in the bad ankle, and Temple crumbles.

"You're just like your dad," her mother says in that dead girl's voice. *"You never know what's good for you."* She twists Temple's right palm upward, pressing her foot into Temple's ankle and plunging the knife into Temple's skin. *"Even though all I want to do is protect you, you two continue to disobey."*

CHAPTER THIRTY-NINE

Temple screams through the first piercing of the blade. Blood tickles her wrists as it slides down her forearm. Each slice brings tears to her eyes—tears, and the explicit fear of death.

The death of her nightmares. Maybe even the Death of Cary Lauren's book.

From elsewhere in the room, she hears Cali and Yaya yelling. She hears them call for her, and she knows that they can't get any closer.

Her mother intends to kill her—just so that they can be together.

She won't think twice about killing them.

Her mother holds steady as Temple struggles, twisting.

"You think your dad is the only one that loves you? When he was going to leave us behind? *This is the only way our family can stay together, Temple,*" her mother says. "*Your dad can't die, and I can't either. I won't lose you just because you're afraid.*"

Temple's mother begins another trail of the blade, curving it and bending it as she strips off the flesh. Like she wants to dig to the bone.

If Temple's bones are branded, there will be no escape. A memory of her mother's screams flashes through her mind, and she whimpers through her tears.

Her mother hears. She grins, a soft smile like Temple's just a baby. "I was scared, too. I thought that it would rip away any chance I had of living with you in the real world. But I was so, so wrong. It's not scary at all. *After the first kill, it's so much better than being normal.*"

The fourth cut lasts the longest. Her mother drags a hole in her palm deep and thick like a shower drain. The blood no longer keeps to her forearm, dribbling down off her skin and onto her jeans. She doesn't know how far her mother's gotten. She feels all the blood pooling over her elbow, her nerves like needles.

"Stop!" she pleads. She fights. She loses.

Cutting her eyes back to Temple, her mother smiles brightly. The tight muscles spurt a glop of Anysaa's blood from an unseen cut in her neck. "I'll keep you safe," her mother says. Her voice is clear now, like an old recording. "You trust me, right?"

Temple watches her mother's smile crack, falling at the corners as the temperature drops. Temple's own breath clouds before her as it leaves her lungs. The fog twirls above her, swishing and slithering like a coiling snake.

"*Right?*" she asks again.

Temple swallows. "Yes." Her voice is barely above a whisper.

And just as quickly as Temple's mother changed, she closes her eyes and returns to the version Temple recognizes. The one that hid with her in the bathroom, rubbing her back until the screams stopped outside. The room returns to a normal temperature, gradually warming and leaving goose bumps on Temple's skin.

Bang!

Cali and Yaya shriek as the back window slams upward. Temple whirls toward them in the dim light, the trees from outside swishing right near the opening. And a thin, gray leg curls inside. An unfamiliar corpse—a man, ripping at his seams—presses his face against the glass. His chest bulges around the metal windowsill, puffing up as he tries to push through the opening.

"I can keep you safe from them, Temple," her mother says, her eyes locking on the corpse as if in a trance.

It stops.

The monster simply pauses, like her mother has his remote. Temple looks at Cali and Yaya, clutching each other in the corner of the room, and then to her mother's still expression. Then to the mark on the door, halfway to sealing her inside.

"What about my friends?" Temple asks soberly.

Her mother blinks like it hadn't crossed her mind. Temple having friends is a foreign concept. Then her mother grips onto her tighter. "Temple, we don't have time for this. You have to hide. You can't go poking around or else you'll get caught."

"You've said all of this to me before." It's definitely her mother. She recalls those exact words from her childhood. Her mother's hands tight on her shoulders. Her eyes wide, a mirror of Temple's but filled with none of the tears. Back then, she was trying to help. But now there's something sinister in her words. They're being played back like a greatest hits album.

"Temple," her mother says firmly. "Forget what you've seen. You trust me, don't you?" Her mother's shadow bends beneath her, and ice reaches across the cabin, twisting and turning.

Temple snatches her hand away, stumbling back. "You said that when I found Brittany's mom dead on the steps. You've said this before."

"You love your mom, don't you? *Listen to your mother, baby girl.*" Her voice gurgles in a haunting tone. It shifts deep as she glares. The chill in the room dances as darkness inches in from the doorway. "Things like you, like your father—you aren't meant for this world. If you won't listen to me, at least do right to balance out the evil."

It's what Temple's heard all her life—it settles into her, and she almost lets it sink in. Lets the world return to the way it once was. Where her mother is good, and Temple is the evil.

But she remembers the look on Cali's face when she saw the burn scar on Temple's back. As if, to Cali, Temple hadn't deserved it. As if whatever had caused that scar *wasn't* a good thing.

"Is that why you tried to set me on fire?" Temple asks. Her head feels heavy as she raises it to meet her mother's gaze.

Her mother's expression doesn't change. Only the shadows that cast across her skin move, and they darken against her hairline. "That was to purify you."

"You're a murderer," Temple snaps.

For the first time, her mother doesn't deny it.

Her dad didn't kill her mother. He sent Temple here to stop her.

"You're the monster," Temple says aloud, still barely believing the words.

The whole window shatters.

Shards spray through the air like shooting stars, and the grayed corpse fully gets through the small window opening. Cali and Yaya claw backward to the bunk beds while Temple stands still. Cali holds up the axe.

Temple faces her mother again. "Stop it!"

Frost cases over Anysaa's bare feet, turning them white as her mother raises a brow. The chipping ice crawls beneath Temple, reaching in a thin line to the other side of the cabin, where another corpse creeps through the window.

Temple clenches her fist. "I know you're doing this—*stop it!*" She inhales through her nose to calm her quickening heartbeat. The frost, the voices . . . it makes sense.

The realization solidifies in her as her mother wraps her arms around Temple tighter, the blade forgotten on the floor. It's bathed in Temple's blood, gleaming red while the family knife beside it is clean, untouched.

"Temple." Her mother's voice is stone. "Enough of this. You're staying with me. *Forever.*"

Temple sinks to the floor, tears blurring her sight as lightheadedness finally sets in. The pain twists through her, and she writhes on the floor, crying out. For mercy. For forgiveness.

At this point, it doesn't matter.

Her eyes are so clouded, she can't make out the figure moving in the corner until it jumps over the mattress. Water rains down in tiny drops, hitting her forehead in short, cool splashes. By the time Temple looks up, it's over. There's only a putrid smell left over.

It's not water.

Her lighter fluid.

"*Hey, bitch!*" Yaya's scream is nearly indecipherable—half yell, half shriek.

And then the room explodes in a million pops of light.

Temple's neck jerks as Cali darts between Temple and her mom and yanks Temple by the collar, toward her bed. Temple's world flips upside down. The ceiling zooms by, the paneling of the wood in straight lines. Her numb arm flops against her thigh.

"Trying to keep your eyebrows safe," Cali says, lifting Temple by her armpits.

Pop! Pop!

Flames erupt from Temple's mother—her back goes alight. She screams, a shrill cry through the cabin. Temple's eyes widen as she stares at her mother's figure falling backward, beginning to turn different shades of red and orange and black.

Even the smell—Temple stops.

She's trying to survive, she remembers. Temple shoots up, grabbing the axe from Cali's hand. "Stand clear!" she orders.

Then she swipes Anysaa's midsection—a chunk of the axe buries in, knocking her mother over. The bed lights on fire. The bloody wooden axe handle slips around in Temple's wet fingers, but she keeps hold.

"Y'all OK?" Temple asks.

Cali and Yaya don't respond; they just run for it. Temple follows their scrambling footsteps, hard against the wood as they all tumble out the door. She snatches up her family knife on the way out. The sour smell of charring makes Temple's eyes water.

"Oh shit!" Cali screams.

Temple can't tell if it's fear or excitement. The cabin thumps back at them. Crackling sounds. And as orange lights their backs, her mother's wails follow behind them.

Outside, the air smacks against Temple's cheeks, twice as cold with her face still wet from blood and tears. And the temperature keeps dropping.

Cali stumbles, holding her arm and flailing at the pace. Temple looks to Yaya, who glances back. They have the same thoughts, and they stop at the same time. The cabin fire behind them grows, the whole building ablaze behind the windows.

But Temple can see clearly now.

"We have to go," she whispers. Her eyes bounce around the corners of the campsite.

They're all trembling. Temple's hands shake, but it isn't all her. Cali, Yaya—there's nothing between them but their inching footsteps and growing unease. Yaya clenches tightly to Temple's left hand so her fingers ache and bend.

They don't speak. None of them has a reason to.

The silence keeps a thick hold of the clearing, but it's nowhere near as bracing as all the eyes in the trees. The pressure of a million consciousnesses concentrating directly on them. Temple's heart pounds in her ears as she watches them over her shoulder, moving toward the path as quickly as they can.

Then, corpses begin to shift from the shadows of the woods.

And into the moonlight of the campsite.

CHAPTER FORTY

The three girls keep running, their breaths coming out in hiccups with every heavy step. They can't stop. If they stop, they'll be caught.

But Cali slows. Her breath goes heavy.

"Cali, we keep up speed or we die," Temple calls back to her. Yaya saves her voice.

Cali doesn't stop gripping her arm, even as she falls behind. Her steps lag, tilt, and her feet drag. As if she'll get left. As if Yaya and Temple even had it in them to separate from one another.

Never.

Corpses spill into the grass far behind, their pounding footsteps like the buzz of a beehive. Twenty—thirty corpses? There's too many for Temple to count with only risky glances over her shoulder. They all close in on the gravel, hobbling on uneven legs as they curl around the fire at the cabin.

Cali looks up in a panic, stumbling backward. The smell of Cali's blood mingles with Temple's own—as well as the smell of burning. She's injured, probably from when she pulled Temple out of danger. There's no time to check how bad it is. Temple clenches her fist, and the gash in her hand spills blood to the ground.

"We're not leaving you, Cali," Temple says firmly. "Not after all this. So either you suck it up, or you kill us all."

Cali swallows, looking between them. Temple reaches out as Cali and Yaya grab onto one of her arms, just like before. They support Temple while Temple supports Cali, cutting through the campsite like a four-legged race. Someone screams behind them.

Temple throws a wary look back to the campsite, and thick columns of smoke billow up to the sky. The girls keep moving forward.

"It's not looking great back there," Temple says.

Cali gags. "Good."

"Your mom's still out there, isn't she?" Yaya asks.

Temple nods. "At least until we get rid of her original body."

A corpse shoots from the leaves and the girls all scream.

"Cut it in half!" Cali shrieks, and Temple's brain isn't fast enough to comprehend—she drops the axe, muscles clenching. As if her goal is to be as useless as possible.

The corpse halts before them, howling and staring them down. They breathe each others' air for silent seconds—not even seconds. Shorter than that. But it feels like time is frozen. Like the silver in the air takes its sweet little time fluttering down onto the corpse's shredded puffer vest.

Like the rising sun, the flicker of the fire's light grows. Trees become golden, yellow, orange—and Yaya lets out one, tiny squeak. "Lara Michaels?"

The colors twitch between one another, and the corpse jerks its head upward.

"Hah," it grunts. *She* grunts.

Her breath is so close, Temple feels it on her skin for a moment. A blink of an eye.

Then the girl's corpse turns away from them completely. She twirls as if the girls aren't even there, staccato wailing wheezing from her open throat. She stumbles over the remnants of fallen trees. Her shadow guides her.

She makes her way into the campsite, curling soundlessly around the border. Then she walks through the open doorway of Cabin Bey, where the wisps of flames consume her.

Temple's blood slows, the trail of red curving along the skin of her thumb. Her thoughts are faster than her heartbeat.

"Let's go," she orders. Even if one's gone, others will come.

She can never escape this. Her family and their victims are all around her. Black dances in her vision, but she takes another step.

As the three girls' feet move over the brush and old dead trees, darkness engulfs them once again. The light of the camp closes behind the tree branches. It's still there, but it becomes a world away.

That still doesn't feel far enough, though.

"Lam was right," Temple says, her mind stained with the image of Anysaa looking over her.

She shakes it away. Temple always thought she was meant to protect her mother. She came here under the pretense that she could, one last time, come to her mother's rescue. But she'd been wrong after all. Her mother is just as bad as her dad. Worse, even— she's been getting away with her murders.

Cali's uneven breathing fills the quiet as she staggers at Temple's right. "About what?" she asks.

"The cabin wasn't going to last us forever," Temple says.

Yaya's the only one with strong strides. She barely falters with the weight of the other two. "What do we do now? Just head for the highway?" she asks, standing on her toes for a moment, as if that'll make her tall enough to see those three miles away. "Everyone else is pretty much missing or dead."

"And I've got a target on my back," Temple says. "But there are no safe places. And I've given up on ditching you two."

"You couldn't if you tried," Yaya says knowingly. She lets up her arm so Temple can walk alone a little. "Cali'd find you."

"You know I would," Cali says with a belabored chuckle. "Yaya—you would, too."

They say it like it's in good-natured fun, but from the way Yaya goes ahead without a glance back, Temple wonders if there's a true threat in their words.

Yaya stops short. When she glances back, she purses and tenses her mouth.

Temple limps upward, furrowing her brow as she and Cali crunch over the brush. "What is it—oh."

Once they catch up to Yaya, the feeling of eyes on her is immediate. It's as if Temple passed an invisible line, and once she crossed, the cameras turned on and she's on a reality show. They've finally hit the entry to the path.

"They're all still here," Brenda had said.

Temple finds she preferred the campsite zombies. At least she knew they were coming for her. But one thing's for sure: the official count of her father's victims is way off. There are more dead in this forest than Temple can imagine.

They have to get to the highway—through *this*.

Like clockwork, Yaya presses her hand to her heart and starts praying. Temple feels the calming effect she expects Yaya feels, just from the sound of her prayers. When Cali catches up and surveys the land, she says nothing. Then, when Yaya's voice drains to wordless whispers, Cali sighs.

"I'm an atheist," she says, "but damn it if I'm not believing in the power of suggestion right now."

This is their second night on the North Point Farm. By now, anything can happen. As Yaya's words work over her, Temple moves forward with her chin up, and Cali and Yaya trail as a unit. They glide through the path, their fear whittling away with each step. In the face of death, Temple believes in whoever gives her the strength to move forward.

And right now, that's these two girls.

They march on, their eyes trained ahead as they continue on the path. A figure in the distance steps on the path. Blocking their way, backlit in the moonlight as Temple looks on. The figure makes no moves. It stands there, still and settled.

It's as if she's been waiting for hours, right there in the center of the path. The corpse's mouth moves with her words caught up in the trees. She shouts with her volume down. But Temple don't need to hear to know what she's saying.

"Thomas!"

"Ida," Temple sighs. Her ankle aches at the sight of her grand-mother there.

Cali's just as tired. "Should we turn back?" she whispers.

"Thomas!" Grandma Ida yells again. The words clear up, and she shrieks more jumbled words, but they're too far to hear. The body she wears is older. She probably has fewer vocal chords to work with than she did with the freshly killed K'ran.

Temple narrows her eyes, taking another step. "What's she say-ing?" she asks. She can't hear it, can't read her lips. She can only get closer.

Grandma Ida points wildly, fretting in place. She makes no moves toward them. Beside Temple, Yaya restarts her hissed prayers.

"*Thomas!*" Grandma Ida shouts again. She cups her hands around her lips, hips bent forward. "*Thomas,* run!"

The trees behind them crack with an unseen weight. Temple looks behind her to the path, through the lashes of leaves that obscure it. She gasps. Silver bleeds out through the dirt, crawling its way through the brush and rock. Its corner of the woods is eclipsed in cracked colors—silver and blue and white and darkness.

The frost from her mother's shadow erases the dirt altogether.

"*Run!*" Grandma Ida screams again, moving back herself as terror transforms her features.

The three girls break into a sprint. No words, no plans, no hope. They just have to run.

Grandma Ida's the first over the hill, waiting every so often for Temple to catch up like she might lose sight of her at any moment. Cali's doing her best, but her breath verges on hyperventilation. The girls never lag far behind Grandma Ida. Temple's feet pound into the grass, Cali and Yaya's breath on her back. Her arm lulls beside her, hitting her thigh.

The shadow spills onto the path. Every leaf and vine dries and cracks as the line of sparkling darkness inches closer and closer.

"We're gonna die," Yaya states. Her voice doesn't shake. It's not fear—to her, it's the truth.

Temple agrees.

They pass the hill. Grandma Ida is a few feet ahead of them when the North Point House comes into view. Temple hiccups, needing air, watching as Grandma Ida's retreating form gets smaller and smaller. None of the girls speak anymore. They can't afford to. The house looms over them like a tombstone awaiting their return.

Grandma Ida doesn't approach it, though. "*Thomas,*" she hisses. "Thomas, this way!" She cuts between the trees. Just vanishes, off the path. If this were any other day, Temple would keep straight, leave that bothersome ghost to go on its way. But cold air flutters onto her back. Branches break with the icy gravity of her mother's silver stain on the woods.

The girls don't even debate it; they follow Grandma Ida. Branches smack Temple in the chest, the legs. She smacks back, knocking birds and rodents out of their homes. Wings burst around them as they clamor through, breath rattling in their chests.

Grandma Ida's before them, stopped. A mound of grass glistens with dew behind her, shadowed in the abundant shrubbery.

They catch up to her, heaving air into their lungs. Cali leans against a tree for support.

Grandma Ida crouches down onto the pile of grass and moss, running her hand over the leaves like it's a kitten. "We're back home," she murmurs to Temple.

Her breath is too short to form a response. She watches her grandmother with her legs shaking.

The snapping twigs get louder and louder as the Cold gains on them.

"We'll be safe in here," Grandma Ida says. She grips onto one of the twisted branches and pulls. A wooden door creaks as it pops up out of the matted mound. A mist of dust and mold puffs out, hitting Temple's nose with a thick, damp stink. "Go," Grandma Ida orders.

Temple's feet freeze in the dirt. "Go where?" she asks. The door leads to nothing but blackness.

She looks to Cali and Yaya, who're just as dubious but have their feet set to follow. This is a mess. Temple can't trust her grandmother—she's a murderer.

"Temple," Cali says. "C'mon."

Temple looks around again. The trees are the silver and blue of night, but dread is not far behind. She sees wooden tips shake with a chill as her mother overtakes them. Temple's hair raises.

She turns back to Grandma Ida, whose eyes bug as she bounces from foot to foot. Grandma Ida looks genuinely terrified as she glances behind them.

"Go!" Grandma Ida orders.

Finally, Temple grabs Cali and Yaya and tugs them forward. Cali gasps, her strong stance throwing Temple off balance as they stumble over hard steps. They scream all at once.

Grandma Ida hops in behind them and closes the door, plunging them into darkness.

OBITUARY:
IDA CRYSTALLINE BAKER

Ida Crystalline Baker (née Michaelson) was born on May 1, 1941, to Abraham and Ida Michaelson in Richmond, Virginia. The youngest of three, Ida quickly became one of the foremost minds in chemistry during a time when segregation kept her in some of the most underfunded schools in the state.

In 1970, she met and married Raymond Baker, with whom she had one son, Thomas Raymond Baker. She had a short but prosperous teaching career among brilliant Virginia educators before she moved with her family north, to Haverford County. There, they owned and operated the largest Black-owned farm on the East Coast for forty more years. It was there that Ida ultimately spent the rest of her life.

Ida was preceded in death by her husband, parents, and brothers, Jacob and Jonathon Michaelson.

She leaves with her love her son and her newly born granddaughter, Shirley Temple Baker.

Ida will be greatly missed.

CHAPTER FORTY-ONE

In the oppressive darkness, Temple falls for too long. Feet. Miles. She flails for something to hold on to until her fingers hit cold, solid wood.

The railing.

Temple catches hold of the wooden banister at her side and grips tight, her shoulder popping with the weight of the rest of her body. Her cut-up right hand slaps on a step, and she winces as it burns. Her good hand tightens. She freezes mid-fall, suspended in gravity.

Around her, the girls' breathing is loud and labored. Temple can't see them at all, the room a deep well of darkness. But she can feel them. Yaya's trembling fingers still clasp tightly around Temple's tensed forearm. Cali buries her entire torso in Temple's right arm. They both weigh Temple down, silent with adrenaline and fear.

Then, hesitantly, Yaya moves.

Cold and wind replace her body's warmth as she lets Temple go and holds on to the railing for herself. The wood of the stairs creaks beneath her footsteps.

"One," Yaya's soft voice says from nowhere. She creeps down once, then again, and again, until there's silence. Her breath shakes from a distance away. "Six more."

Cali's hold loosens a little to let Temple move, following Yaya's lead. Temple rights herself, feeling the edge of the steps with her shoes as she climbs down at a snail's pace. When she counts six down, her sneakers grind against grime.

Only when they're on solid ground does Cali fully let go. She steps away from Temple, her breath shivering and quiet. It's twice as humid at the bottom, and the room has a tinge of rotted life and soiled clothes.

Cali swears. "Fuck. It's pitch-black in here."

"Should we not have followed the ghost grandma into the scary room?" Yaya asks humorlessly.

"Should we have waited for the creepy snowman to just kill us like it did Natalie?" Cali counters. "I *know* how to fight a body. I don't know how to fight whatever that shit is."

"So when are you gonna start fighting bodies, Cali?"

"You know, ever since you started growing a spine you've been—"

"Wait," Temple interrupts firmly. Both girls go quiet, though from her gasp, Yaya is on the cusp of a retort. Temple imagines they're both looking at her, eyes wide with hunger for what they should do next.

At least, from luck and old habit, Temple has some matches. She roots around her back pocket, where she always shoves everything, and finds two little matchbooks. She knew she'd need them. Good to know even with all her mistakes, her instincts aren't shot to shit.

Swiping the stick against one of the boxes, Temple lights the match, and a dim glow spreads. The three of them breathe in relief.

"You can't light that in here." Grandma Ida appears next to them in a blink.

Cali screams, fingers digging into Temple's arm so deeply Temple almost drops the match. Grandma Ida doesn't bat an eyelash. Her face glows orange with the shadows clawing up her forehead.

Up this close, Temple can see Grandma Ida possesses a girl Temple doesn't recognize. Her eyes are almost fully intact, with patches of peeling and discolored skin over her brow and cheek. She's unfamiliar and older than high school, so the body's from before the camp.

Grandma Ida throws an annoyed glance to Cali before backing out of the light.

Temple regains her balance. "We need to see," Temple says firmly. She stretches out her arms, and the flame illuminates the corners of the room.

Grandma Ida stands a few feet away, her eyes locked onto the twisting flame. "Give it here," Grandma Ida orders.

Despite every fucking thing inside her that screams "fuck that," Temple obeys.

The cold of the corpse brushes against Temple's fingertips for a heartbeat as Grandma Ida takes the matchbook and swipes another match. She disappears around a wall dividing the room.

Temple feels Cali tug on her sleeve, and she grips Yaya by the hand in turn as the room darkens again.

Seconds later, the flame reappears. Grandma Ida lit a lantern mounted high on the back wall. The amber light hits them with warmth.

Temple, Yaya, and Cali flow to the light like moths, looking up into the tendrils of the flame with transfixed gazes.

"This is better," Grandma Ida says from beneath the lamp. She wanders away, the fabric of her skirt billowing behind her.

Stationed beside her, Cali finally turns away from the flame and runs her eyes over the rest of the room. "Where are we?" she murmurs.

Mold and slime cover the walls, murky and dampened with time and dirt. The fire lights only a small radius of space, close to the thick wall that separates the entrance steps and a step ladder, which Grandma Ida leans against and sits on. The floors are covered in old clothes and papers that smell foul and ancient, like the forbidden rooms of a museum.

Temple knows exactly where they are. The room from the map that she'd never seen before.

It's not a part of North Point House at all; it's a bunker.

Grandma Ida keeps her eyes on the fire, enraptured by it. She's unmoving.

"I suppose I'm not supposed to kill them, or you'll throw another one of your tantrums," Grandma Ida says. She takes a breath and turns from the flame, staring pointedly at Cali and Yaya. When she looks back at Temple, her left eye flips out of place and retreats to the white.

She pops off the rungs of the ladder and stalks over to Cali and Yaya with twining legs twisting in disharmony. Her other limbs go completely ignored, swaying behind her. It should slow her down, but she darts before Cali in a sprint.

"Or *should* I kill them?" Grandma Ida asks.

Temple steps between the two, her arms outstretched to her contorting grandmother. She pushes Cali aside. "No, Mom, I need them. They're . . . they're here to help us get rid of Raymond. Uh, Dad. Daddy." That definitely doesn't sound right. "They're, uh, cops."

Grandma Ida bristles. "*Cops!*" Her body twists like a snake about to strike.

Cali throws her hands up. "Crooked cops!" she shouts. She clenches her jaw as sweat hits her forehead. Yaya only peeks through her fingers. "We're interested in living forever and, like, we've killed, too—lots of people," Cali says. The words tumble out of her mouth and Grandma Ida stops, turning her head over to Yaya.

Yaya nods in agreement, tears in her eyes. "Yeah, we're giving her half our corpses," she says. Then she sniffs. Wipes a tear from her eyes. "So she can teach us how to live forever, I mean."

"He," Temple corrects.

"Yeah," Yaya says.

Grandma Ida stares at the three of them for a long moment. She takes so long, Temple's sure she's deciding how to kill them and in what order. They aren't the most convincing. But then, after a grunt from her throat, Grandma Ida brushes past them into the dark side of the room and disappears completely.

Cali, Yaya, and Temple all huddle even closer together. Cali leans into the middle, nose smeared with a swipe of black grime.

Temple follows her grandmother with her eyes for a moment before she speaks in a shaking whisper. "What is this room?"

"Our secret place," Grandma Ida answers from the blackness. "Raymond must have forgotten about it—even though he shouldn't be here at all. I burned his bones. He should be gone . . . but at least he can't hurt us in here."

Temple blinks, looking around the room. "So we're safe?" she asks, gesturing to the trash-covered ground. "*In here?*"

"It smells like ass," Cali grumbles, and Yaya agrees.

From the darkness, there's a snap. Grandma Ida lights another of Temple's matches. It burns yellow before her as she stares at Temple. "You don't remember, Thomas?" she asks. She circles behind them, carrying the match and lighting another lamp. More golden light spills into the room.

With the darkness receding, Temple can make out the steps a lot better. They're far down, the wooden door a smudge at the top of the stairs. The mark is very clearly etched on it, like the one Temple's mom was carving into the cabin door. Just like in the main cabin, iterations of "Thomas" litter the wooden walls. Finely drawn and neat, it's a much older scrawling made with dense ink. Grandma Ida's name is also scrawled in between the cracks that "Thomas" leaves.

Grandma Ida joins them, looking up as well. "We claimed this room while we both were still mortals and you were finally ready to move on." She points higher, her fingers miming the shape. "No one will see the inside of this room. I sealed it after your consciousness left."

Temple scowls. "You're protecting it from all the others? The other . . . dead people?"

Grandma Ida doesn't answer. She turns away, looking down and twirling her skirt like a little girl.

"If the room is marked, can we leave?" Temple asks.

"Not your body, not since you're branded." Grandma Ida says, shrugging. "Just your mind."

Temple goes cold, her palm stinging like her eyes. Her mom branded the cabin, and then tried to brand Temple. She was trying to trap her in, to kill her. If she had succeeded . . .

"Together forever," she'd said. Temple has to find her own way to sever the tie.

Grandma Ida notices Temple's silence and observes her with a pout. "Don't worry, Thomas," she says smoothly. "Raymond can't find us here." She spreads her arms wide, spinning around the room. *"You've found your way back."*

Yaya shrieks. "Dear-Father-in-heaven-I-beg-you-to-protect-me." The prayer spills from her desperately as she rocks into Temple.

Temple shuffles, just as Cali gasps. Temple follows their gazes.

When Grandma Ida lit the second lamp, the corner of the room filled with light, the base of the stairs visible. On the floor, grayed out by time and covered in bug carcasses and spider webs, two skeletons wrap around one another—a big one with wispy cobwebs draped from her skull and a tattered dress: the mother. And a tiny one, about half her size: the son.

It was time for the Midpoint Tree's show. Temple and her dad sat camped on the roof, ignoring all of the house's creaks and snaps like they always did. The risk was worth it—the sight was one unique to the North Point woods. Her woods.

Sparse rays of sunlight peeked from the horizon as the sunrise began, tickling the tips of the Midpoint Tree's topmost leaves. Beads of silver spread where the light touched, like the glisten on freshly fallen snow. The more seconds that passed, the more the sun rose, the more diamonds sparkled and blinked from the tree's newly tinted silver leaves.

No matter how many times Temple had seen it, it was still breathtaking to watch.

"It's beautiful," Temple whispered. Her voice didn't carry, but somehow her dad heard it anyway. He always heard her.

He shifted beside her, and when he spoke, Temple could hear the smile in his voice. "When I was a kid, I thought it was the king of trees."

Temple snorted.

"Hey." Her dad pouted beside her, knocking her shoulder. "You're way less bumpkin than I was at your age."

For a moment, Temple turned from the Midpoint Tree. If it were as fiery as it appeared, maybe her face would light up like it did before a campfire. Her skin would glimmer, and she'd remember this moment for the rest of her life.

Instead, she smiled. "I'm still a little bit bumpkin," Temple said, and with all her might, she hit her dad in the shoulder.

He toppled over.

They both gasped as her father rolled off the side of the roof, hurtling toward the ground. Temple was too shocked to even scream—she could only watch the space where he once was, her mouth open and a high pitch whirring in the back of her throat.

Crunch. *The sound was definite.*

Temple sat there, still. So still a moth landed on her, stayed with her. Fluttered for a bit, and then moved on. The woods surrounded her, but they felt more like witnesses than friends.

Temple. What have you done? *She could already hear her mother's voice in her head. Feel her grip as she dragged her out of the house.*

Temple was shaking now, her hands trembling over her crossed legs. But then, she heard it—

"It's OK, baby girl." Her dad's voice.

Temple's throat caught, then her heart, and she scrambled to the edge. She looked deep into the dark, out on the ground where she found her dad smiling, looking up at her as the stars glistened in his eyes.

Somehow not dead.

Twisted at an angle. Something was broken, just from the way he fell—but it didn't look like his spine.

"I'm OK," her dad said again.

Didn't you hear that crunch? *Temple wanted to ask.*

But then he stood up. "I'm really OK."

His breath was heavy, labored. His steps uneven as he rose off the ground. His shoulders were lopsided, and the crunching began to sound again. Crack. Crack.

"See?" her dad shouted up.

Temple didn't realize she'd closed her eyes.

But she opened them, and they saw crystal clear in the dark. His figure, hazy in the low light, shivered and twitched. He pressed his hand at his left thigh, his right bicep bulging. Gave it a shove.

His leg let out a snap.

And his back was upright again. His spine never bent. And his bloody smile, unfaltering.

CHAPTER FORTY-TWO

The skeletons aren't more gruesome than any of the others Temple witnessed in the past two days. She thinks of Brenda, K'ran, Mickaeyla, Natalie, Sierra, Dawntae—she saw them all, stretched out across the ground and ripped apart with time or violence. Those made her retch, and just the memory of the sight twists her stomach.

This is still horrific, though.

Temple examines the skulls, taking in the embrace and the faded clothing. On the forehead of each, the symbol is etched deeply into the bone. Temple's eyes linger on the remains of her family.

Cali, to her right, finally processes what she's seeing. Her words come out in one breath. "Jesus fucking shit, fuck." She folds over, knocking Temple's shoulder as she gags.

Grandma Ida watches the three of them from her ladder like they're leads to a stage play she has no interest in. When she realizes there isn't much to the scene other than Cali's vomit, she glances back up toward the flame. Her gaze lingers, a ghost of longing.

"Don't touch," Grandma Ida warns, her lips tilting upward. She steps off the ladder and crawls to the bodies. She peers at the corpses with sad eyes. "You didn't have long before the disease took you, anyway. So I just put you to sleep. This room is small enough I only had to drain my blood to claim it." Her eyes dart over to Cali, who's still doubled over. "*Don't* touch it."

Temple stares at the skeletons, a little clog forming in her throat. Her dad's skeleton is so small. She's not an expert in bones—she's not an expert in most dead things, other than seeing dead bodies—but if she has to guess, she'd say her dad was older than ten, but not quite a teenager.

"*Why?*" she breathes. Temple closes her eyes, trying to force her thoughts to calm, but they won't. Why was her family doing this? Why was this happening to her?

Her mind keeps spinning until Grandma Ida's freezing-cold hands press against Temple's cheeks. "Do you still hate me?" she asks, her voice wavering. "She told me you would grow up normal. That all I had to do was get you older bodies as time went on, but—but I made you like *this*." The disgust in her voice was plain and undisguised.

About Temple's dad. About what he was. Temple swallows. "What did you do to me?" she asks.

"You had to move from body to body to keep yourself alive, and I made you kill them to keep me alive, too. When I can't even stop Raymond. When I *never* stopped that . . . that *monster*." Grandma Ida opens Temple's palm. Temple's wound has stopped bleeding, a sticky red burn puckering her skin. "I just wanted to be happy with you, together."

Forever.

The words roll over Temple's shoulders as she feels her posture sag. Her whole family just . . . they never considered the cost too much. Of any of it. Why did dozens have to die so that they didn't?

Temple wonders if her dad actually hates her grandma for making him immortal, too. Grandma Ida did it to save his life, but since he went to prison, he's been sick again. So what does it matter? What was it all for?

He definitely hates her. He *has* to resent Grandma Ida.

Because Temple has to resent her dad.

"It's all of us," Temple says. "We're all demons."

"Don't say that to me," Grandma Ida whispers, still holding Temple's face. Her voice cracks as it thickens. "I don't care what that Lauren girl told you—don't let her take you away from me. I don't want to be separated ever again. I can't make things right, but I don't want to be alone."

"Lauren girl?" Temple asks aloud. She stares into her grandmother's eyes, but they're a mix of white and faded pupils.

And then they narrow. "Don't act like you don't know her now," Grandma Ida spits. "Not after you said you married the wretch."

Temple flinches, trying to decipher the words as Grandma Ida's pleading expression fades into a sneer.

"You *can* make things right," Yaya interrupts, stepping toward them.

Temple didn't realize she and Grandma Ida were having a family moment until everything stopped, and they both look at Yaya.

Yaya pushes between them, taking Grandma Ida's hands in hers. With a look of concern, she stares into Grandma Ida's good eye. "An ill-fated innocent child. A lifetime cycle of bloodshed and repentance. From what I'm hearing, this is just like Detective Bell's story."

Grandma Ida blinks. The words seem to go in one ear and out the other, lost to the mangled brain of the undead ... until she tilts her head. Furrows her brow.

"As in *Hearts Stop*?" Grandma Ida asks.

Cali's head pops up, and Yaya's hands visibly tighten over Grandma Ida's. When Yaya speaks, her voice is half words, half shaken breath. "*Yesss.*" She nods slowly, looking at Grandma Ida like a bear would a hapless camper. "Are you a Cary Lauren fan?"

Grandma Ida twists her palms out of Yaya's hands. "Not necessarily . . . I didn't read too many of her books. But she was my closest friend."

CHAPTER FORTY-THREE

If the room can shit itself, it does.

The fan brigade already had trouble keeping focused when they were Cary Lauren adjacent—so Temple's not surprised when Cali almost chokes on her own spit.

She darts forward, voice high-pitched. "When you say Lauren girl . . . you mean *Cary* Lauren?"

Grandma Ida cuts her eyes to her, nodding curtly. "Her daughter. I let Cary and her girls live here for a few years, and she taught me how to keep Thomas alive. I never thought she'd write about it."

"Holy shit," Cali whispers.

And Temple very much agrees, though the hope in Cali's eyes twinkles brighter than the fire. They're on very different thought tracks.

The way Grandma Ida had mentioned her father married the Lauren girl. That would mean that . . .

Well, it would suggest that Cary Lauren was Temple's maternal grandmother.

She fails to keep her thoughts together as she considers the possibility that her grandmother is Cary Lauren—author of that weird horror book about those gays that Temple didn't like.

Cali, on the other hand, is practically buzzing with excitement. "She wouldn't happen to be one of the undead wandering around here, would she? And if so, does she have a hand that could sign my chest?"

"She made me promise to burn her," Grandma Ida says. Her voice goes stiff, and she turns down her eyes. "I did it before anything could get ahold of her corpse."

Though none of the girls says anything, it feels like they all come to a consensus on that one—that's for the best. Well, maybe Cali and Yaya's feelings are more complex. Temple's are simple: if Cary Lauren taught Grandma all this occult shit and how to make her dad immortal . . . this whole thing basically is *her* fault. And then she cremated her body so she didn't have to deal with any of the consequences.

Damn. It really be your own grandmas.

Temple keeps that thought to herself for her own safety.

Yaya grips tighter onto Grandma Ida's hands. "You've sacrificed so much for your son. I know that can't have been easy," she says with gravity in her voice. "Do you remember the story of Detective Bell? How she redeemed herself after she killed Eric and betrayed Anna?"

"She joined the church," Grandma Ida says. She looks up at Yaya with newborn hope.

"Are you religious?" Yaya asks.

Grandma Ida sniffles, wiping away a stray tear. "Would I be? *An abomination like me is destined for hell.*"

"That is *not* the case." Yaya pulls out her cross necklace from beneath her shirt, flashing it to Grandma Ida. It catches the light and reflects a glimmer around the room. "You and Thomas can be together and put all this behind you."

Grandma Ida can't hide her enthrallment. She twists her lips. ". . . How?"

"God forgives!" Yaya shouts. She grabs Grandma Ida by the shoulders, screaming into her face. "He forgave a sinner like me for . . . uh, sodomy! He forgave Judas for his betrayal! And he can forgive you if you just ask for his forgiveness."

"But I've done so much wrong, and Thomas . . . Will God—"

"Yes. He sees all circumstances and makes a way when there is none. Won't he do it? God is good!"

"All the time," Cali chimes in, almost as if on autopilot.

"And all the time?"

"God is good."

Temple's never stepped foot in a church in her entire life. Even Aunt Ricki keeps away. She probably fears her demon niece will burst into flames once they step over the threshold.

Yaya leans into Grandma Ida, her gaze welcoming. "What's your name, dear?"

"Ida," her grandma says.

With a yank of her palm, Yaya pulls her in even closer, like they're the only two in the room. She nods dramatically, her chin bobbing up and down and smacking against her chest. "Good name. It's in the Bible."

"It is?"

"Yes, Book of Job. She sold him goats as a charity. Shall we pray together?"

Temple can tell from Grandma Ida's fidgeting and the slump in her shoulders that she's a hair from saying "no." Then she makes the mistake of looking into Yaya's eyes again. They sparkle. *Convert*, they order. And they don't do it politely.

So Grandma Ida flexes the muscles in her fingers as she clasps Yaya's hands in return, and Yaya guides them both to kneel on the sediment-covered floor. She rubs her thumbs over Grandma Ida's skin—the skin of the girl who's being violated by Grandma Ida's ghost—her eyes closed and her voice breathy. "Let's bow our heads and close our eyes, Ida," she whispers.

Grandma Ida complies, blinking as she follows.

"Dear heavenly Father, our Lord and savior, we call upon You today to guide our sister Ida on Your path to forgiveness." Yaya snaps her eyes open, keeping her voice even. "We ask that You hold her hand as she finds her way to You, Father, and lays her burdens at Your feet." Yaya looks at Temple. "Take all her burdens"—she jerks her chin—"her sins." Temple looks at the skeletons. "And all her fears, and put them to rest, Lord."

Temple understands instantly.

"We ask that You allow her to find peace, Father, and wrap her in that peace."

Rocking her wrist, Temple flicks the old family knife out of her sleeve and leans over.

"Thomas."

Temple freezes at Grandma Ida's low tone. She pauses, the dull blade ready to dig in, and she glances up. Grandma Ida's white gaze is on her.

"*I told you not to touch!*" she shrieks, and she's on her feet at once. The flames flicker around them as her limbs curl forward—

And Temple dives the blade into the skeleton's forehead.

Grandma Ida's scream echoes against the wall as the sharp edge of the knife slices a line through the red mark, gliding through like butter—like it was fulfilling its purpose.

And then Grandma Ida crumples to the ground. Mid-leap.

Everything goes silent.

The three girls watch Grandma Ida slump, falling over her out-reaching leg. There's a few more moments of quiet, as if they expect the body to rise back up—scream at them again. End them for good.

But when that doesn't happen, Yaya releases a breath. "Amen," she says, and picks herself up. In the quivering light, she dusts off her jeans, sending clumps of dirt flying around the room.

Cali and Temple stare unabashedly at her.

"What?" she asks. "Did I get some corpse on me?"

"You're scarier than anybody in these woods," Cali says firmly.

Temple only sort of agrees.

Yaya puffs up. "What did I do other than pray?"

"How can you be so calm while you handshakin' Samara over there?" Cali asks.

"You religious zealot-ed her into converting so you could kill her," Temple says.

Cali shakes her head. "I mean, the bitch had to die. *Obviously.* But damn, Yaya. That was cold-blooded."

Yaya rolls her eyes and joins them by the steps. "I said Ida gave Jesus a goat—had no clue what I was talking about. I was scared shitless."

"And I still love it," Cali says.

"I did it, though, because I . . . because I knew I could do something. Even though I was scared," Yaya adds. "But the old lady could have easily found out I was bullshitting her."

"Doesn't matter now," Temple says.

"You make a great lieutenant," Cali says. She salutes Yaya, then Temple.

Cali bends over the skeletons. Their embrace still tugs at Temple, and she watches them silently. Yaya has no reason to feel guilty. Grandma Ida wanted to die; she just didn't know how. All of them do. Temple remembers the corpse that ran into the fiery cabin, driven toward it like a magnet.

The dead want to die.

"Y'all." Cali speaks from the ground, voice soft and hesitant. "Come look at this." She's still bending by the skeletons, tilting her head beside the little one, and the orange glow that licks the wall reflects on her profile. "Is that a mark?"

Temple sees the rust from the damp stony floor, and she moves to Cali's side. She recognizes it instantly.

"What is it?" Yaya asks as Temple picks it up. It's a deep brown, faded and old—but the gaudy twisting vines and snakes wind around each other in a familiar pattern. One they all knew by now, but one Temple was an expert in.

A coin.

Right at the wrist of her dad's dead body, a coin. He wanted her to find this place, wanted her to find his body.

Temple's breath rocks a little harder in the quiet room as she looks at her dad's skeleton. The dead want to die . . . and he's one of the dead.

Cali puts her hand on Temple's shoulder. "Hey, you OK?"

Temple hesitates to take her eyes off her dad's child-sized body. Her voice audibly trembles. "I guess. I mean, everyone in my family has murdered someone at some point, which is weird. And this is just . . ." She gestures to her dad's skeleton wordlessly. "It's all just weird. I can't believe—I always thought my dad was crazy. Always thought I was doing him a favor by listening—but nearly everything he said was true." Temple scoffs at herself, embarrassed. Her eyes flicker to the coin in her palm, then to his forehead, and that darkness resettles into her chest. "He's been dead since he was this little. Jumped from corpse to corpse because he had to."

She's poised before his body, blade sharp and gleaming. Her ears ring, her scowl deep as she focuses on her task. But, despite her set jaw, her hands shake wildly.

"Temple—" Cali starts.

"Give me a fucking second," Temple snaps. Her voice is breathy, too—not mean, but out of control.

Soon, she isn't breathing at all. Her lungs convulse, but she refuses to puff the air out.

"You don't have to do this, Temple," Yaya says. "If it's too much—"

"I can—I can do this," Temple insists, even as she lowers her knife. It's just for a second while she catches her breath. Her sight blurs.

The only way she can get past this is if she talks through it. She has to keep talking, or else she'll scream. "I can do this," she says again. "I'll do whatever it takes. I promised myself I would. That I'd keep everyone safe from him."

"Maybe me and Yaya can do it." Cali puts her hand on Temple's arm.

Temple shrugs her off. "I can do this, I can do this, I can do this. I have to keep everyone safe." Repeating it is the only thing that keeps her on her feet. She never thought it could get harder. She's supposed to hate her dad, and she can't. Her mom . . . now she's not allowed to love her mom.

This is why she hates the right thing. She resists it, like she did with her dad. Like she did with Anysaa. But it always comes for her in the end.

She hates the right thing because she always does it.

"When I was in eighth grade my dad killed my classmate's mom." She ignores the horrified expression that passes between Cali and Yaya, remembering the feel of hot leather on her forearm as she sat in her dad's truck. "I waited for him while he buried the body—for two whole hours. And I never said a word."

She clutches the knife tighter, blinking back the tears that threaten to fall.

"I knew he couldn't stop. I know he's a killer, but he would never hurt me like that. He just . . . he just wouldn't. Even though he's hurt so many other people, he'd . . ." She trails off, taking a deep breath. "So I called the cops on him. I didn't get the nerve for a long time. But I put him behind bars."

Cali and Yaya don't say anything. They don't even move.

"He's going to die anyway—I know that. This was meant to happen. He wanted me to do this. He sent me here because . . . because it's not right if I don't. Because he can't rest if I don't."

He wants to die.

Temple's throat clogs. She's on the edge of incoherency. *I can do this*, she tells herself.

Her hand begins to inch forward. A flash of her father's smile, mirroring her own, flits through her mind as she gnaws at her lip. Tears flood down her cheeks.

She can do this.

She's allowed to hesitate for a second, but she will do it.

Temple stretches out her arm, the tip of her blade reflecting her bloodstained face. Cali and Yaya watch somberly, too afraid to move and break her trance.

And with a flick, just a simple slash of the cold metal between her fingertips, Temple scratches apart the blood on the child's skull. She kills her dad.

Lights flashed around Temple as her good shoes clicked along the hardwood floor.

No. Not her shoes—her mother's shoes, left behind. She didn't have any good shoes.

The panic was settling in. This was the last time she'd see her father. He stood there, moments after his sentencing, with a tear trickling down the fat in his cheeks. He had to be scared. He had to be sad. He had to be tired.

"Dad!" she called. She didn't care that she was too old to do this. She ran across the floor, ignoring the buzz of shock and gossip. She didn't want him to go.

She'd just wanted him to stop.

Her father's arms wrapped around Temple the second she got to him, and she felt the rough fabric against her arms as he sighed around her. He smelled like ashes and soil, like a deep dark rotting that hid the good man. Only the shell was evil.

"Be good, Temple," he said. "I know you've got it in you."

Temple said nothing, gripping him tighter as she heard footsteps behind her.

She felt his movements, his chin coming down to her crown. "You were right," he said. "I'm tired. And I need to rest eventually."

Hands gripped the back of her dress as some stranger had the good sense to get the child away from the convicted killer. They were wrenched apart, and she was dragged away. She didn't scream. She didn't even cry.

CHAPTER FORTY-FOUR

Temple truly breaks apart for what feels like the first time in her life.

Miles away, in a prison cell, her dad probably just dropped dead. She allows herself to picture it for just a moment and finds comfort in the image. At least he won't be executed like some animal.

Her breath comes out in choppy heaves that bounce off the walls of the cellar. She's out of tears, but her wails are still clear as Yaya rubs her hand over her back in soft waves.

"It's OK," she whispers. "You're OK."

Temple doesn't know when her inhaler made it to her mouth, but one moment she's clawing at her chest and the next Cali is there. Cali's hands join Yaya's as she helps Temple take in the puffs, calming her breathing. Temple's eyes go spotty as she breathes in, holding in her breaths in a mix of doctor-ordered and Brenda-taught.

She's only able to talk when her breathing no longer echoes off the walls. And once her vision is no longer black at the corners, she doesn't stop herself from asking her burning question: "Why the fuck do you have my inhaler?"

Cali pockets it when she's sure Temple's done, shrugging. "I saw it on the floor when Anysaa tossed all your stuff . . . figured you might need it."

Temple doesn't even figure she might need it. She never has her inhaler when she's gasping for air, but Cali had the foresight to bring it even when Temple was smacking her hand away.

Temple bites her lip. "Thanks," she says. And she means it.

They don't speak for a long stretch. Eventually, Temple can hear her own breathing even out, the hollow room reflecting all of her agony back to her. She feels completely wiped out by the time she heaves herself to her feet.

Temple runs a hand over her crusted cheeks, wiping her nose with a deep breath. "I'm OK," she says finally. Firmly.

Cali nods while Yaya stands as well.

"No spiraling?" Cali asks.

It's maybe a joke—Temple's apologetic that Cali's become so familiar with her moods she can joke about them—but she does an earnest check of her emotions. She doesn't feel numb; she feels calm.

She hasn't made peace with everything, of course, but there's a relief that wasn't there before.

She sighs, flexing the wrist of her injured hand. "I'm not fine. I'll manage." She smiles bitterly. "My mom always told me I was just like my dad. That I'm evil, like him. A killer. She's actually kind of right."

"That's a load of shit," Yaya cuts in.

Temple blinks in surprise, turning to her while Cali nods in agreement.

Yaya narrows her eyes. "You're gonna listen to evil bitch mommy call you names after all we've been through? We managed to spend a whole weekend without you murdering someone. Not all Bakers were so kind."

"But I—"

"She's an asshole, Temple. A *huge*, seeping asshole who—from what I'm gathering—treated you like shit. And there you go. I used up all my bad words for the year. Cali?"

"I wasn't gonna say nothing, but your family's got shitty fucking manners. That's the only thing you got from them, honest, Temple." Her eyes darken as she gets serious. "And I'm going to say this right now. Once. Because we might die, and I don't want you to die thinking you're alone like your freakout last time."

Temple opens her mouth, but Yaya shuts her up with a look.

"You're not alone," Cali continues. "I am so, *so* sorry about *everything*. About being a North Pointer and playing even a little part in making your life shitty. But I will *never* do that shit again. I'm going to be right here. *We're* going to be right fucking here." She pauses for a beat as the words hit Temple, and Temple doesn't know what to say.

She's silent for too long, because Cali gasps in a breath like she's just getting started. "And another thing! Check out the guardianship laws in Virginia—your aunt didn't *have* to take you in. She accepted you. Same with me. Same with Yaya. Yaya didn't have to choose to stay with us, and I didn't have to make it an us. We're here because we want to be. Because we're friends."

If Cali's trying to make Temple cry again, she's going to succeed. Temple presses the heels of her palms to her eyes to try to suck back in the thick tears. She should be an empty faucet by now, but they blur her sight almost immediately.

Cali continues. "Also, I mean, you've got therapy and your thirties to figure all this shit out. But we've got an unknown amount of minutes to figure out what we're doing, like, *now*."

Very good point. Temple huffs, hoping the breath will calm her like Brenda taught her. Four on the inhale, four on the exhale. It works, just a little. Temple knows she feels sad, and that'll have to do until they're safe.

"We've got to get out of here," she whispers. "We probably don't have much time—she'll come looking for us soon enough. And I'll be damned if I die in these woods."

Cali smirks. "That's more like it. Hand still OK?"

Temple nods. She twists her wrist before her, the gash on her palm severe but the blood stopped by singed flesh. "I can't feel it. I'm pretty sure that's bad, but it's OK. Your shoulder?"

"Hurts like shit," Cali says, adjusting her shirt to cover it. They both turn to Yaya.

Yaya adjusts her sweater, looking over herself. She slaps her arms, testing their strength. "I haven't gotten hurt yet."

"You lucky bitch," Cali says.

Yaya smirks. "Blessed, thank you."

"So what do we do now?" Cali asks.

As if on cue, Yaya and Cali both turn to Temple.

Temple looks between the both of them. "Why are you asking me?"

Cali shrugs. "You're the general. The Beyoncé. Lead us, lead vocalist."

"Aren't *you* the Beyoncé, Cali?" Or Anysaa, maybe? Anyone but her.

Cali slaps Temple's shoulder with a sharp laugh. "You're the center of attention, girl. We know the occult stuff. You know the ins and outs of the killers. And the land. What do we do?"

Temple doesn't like where her thoughts are going. She knows they have to get to the highway, and all the options to get there aren't all that inviting.

"My mom won't let me out of here," she says finally. Now that she knows her mom wants her dead, no matter how deceptively noble the reason, she knows what she has to do.

If Temple doesn't take down her mom first, she'll be locked up in the woods, or worse—her mom will go after Cali and Yaya.

"She has to be taken care of," Temple says.

Cali nods. "We'll take care of it, then."

"We will." Temple closes her eyes, turning to face the other two. "But y'all're going to have to trust me."

Cali narrows her eyes. "What are you talking about?"

Temple snatches away the fire axe, holding it steady between them as she tightens her grip around the wooden handle. She looks at Yaya, then at Cali, making sure she doesn't waver.

"At first, I wanted y'all to kill me," she says. "You're at risk as long as my mom goes after me. So I could be a distraction, and she could—"

"Are you out of your fucking mind?" Cali shrieks. "You're kidding, right?"

Yaya huffs. "I can't believe we're going through this *again*. We don't have it in us to kill anybody. I was too scared to walk to the highway by myself, remember? And even if you do end up succeeding in your consciousness transfer or whatever—*we* won't be staying behind. There's no way to get rid of your own mark if it's on your bones, and waiting for you to decompose will take forever. You'll spend eternity as a bodiless ghost unless you start killing people." She narrows her eyes at Temple, the glower deeper than anything Temple's seen from her. "And that's just not going to be in the cards for you, sweetie."

Temple blinks back, holding her arms out. "I said I *was* going to ask that! I don't want that anymore."

Cali rolls her eyes, sucking her teeth. "Well, what *do* you want?"

Temple speaks over her, breaking through their grumbles of annoyance. "We can't hide down here forever. I have to face my mom." She looks them both in the eye, finally feeling their words. Believing them when they say they're friends. "Now, I have a new plan. And I think you'll like where I got it from."

326

Hearts Stop by Cary Lauren

Dedication

This book is dedicated to my darling daughters.

*Richelle, my fighter. My backbone. I can never
repay you for teaching me what it means to be loyal to yourself.
For showing me that forgiveness is a gift not owed, but earned.*

*And Michelle, my heartbeat. My conscience.
You taught me what it means to love. When you
gave me my grandchild, I truly understood what it
meant to be a mother.*

I am so thankful to you both for so many things.

I am so deeply sorry for not realizing it sooner.

CHAPTER FORTY-FIVE

With the tip of the axe, Cali nudges the cellar door open, and moonlight pools through the crack. The outside air swims in.

Cali looks back to Yaya and Temple, smiling over her shoulder. "Moonlight looks good, don't it?"

Passing the axe back to Temple, she climbs out to the open air. Yaya and Temple follow, pushing out into the woods as the fresh air rushes into their lungs and the moonlight hits their skin. The scrap of clothing wrapped around Temple's hand is probably rancid enough to infect her to death, but she feels safe. Even with death hanging low and high, all around in the air.

The trees of her childhood bend toward her. With two more friends than usual and a star-studded sky, it's easy to let her guard down. Once they reach the pathway, an oppressive silence chokes through the forest. There's not even the flap of a bird's wing to cut through the quiet.

Cali, Yaya, and Temple's expressions fall into wary frowns as they stare down the woods, their previous serenity tasted only for a moment.

The leaves crunch beneath their steps, crystals of ice chiming as they shatter. The leaves are frozen solid.

"This will lead us straight to her," Temple says. The words collect in the back of her throat, lingering even when she tries to swallow them down.

Cali, Anysaa, and Temple move with linked arms.

"I'm still grateful for moonlight," Cali whispers, throwing her eyes around the shadows that the trees make. "Even though I'd be more grateful for sunlight."

"Moon or sun, we've got to face her sometime," Yaya says. She grips Temple's arm tighter, bringing her to her side along with Cali. "If we die, we're at least gonna die like we've got ovaries."

Cali pauses. "Hey."

"An honorary ovary."

"No."

"We'll die like the real women we are," Yaya settles on.

"I'll accept," Cali says, shrugging her free shoulder. "But I'm not going to die. I already done said it a million times—if I die, we all got a goddamn problem."

Temple listens to the two of them while she focuses on the wrongness in the woods. The swirl of frost that sprinkles silver dust over everything.

Like the Midpoint Tree at sunrise, she thinks.

"Look, you two," Yaya says, "I'm not Miss Popular. I got more friends than Temple, but, you know, it's easy to beat last place." Temple's well-acquainted with reality, so she isn't offended. "These last two days have been the worst days of my life—but if they're the last days of my life, I'm glad y'all are the girls I tried to survive them with."

Cali tugs Temple closer to her, pulling Yaya closer to them both. "Aw, thanks, Yaya," she says. "You bitches complete me."

"Thanks, Cali," Yaya says.

Temple can feel their warmth through the sleeve of her T-shirt when then they both turn to her, waiting for her final words. Their theme seems to be friendship, something Temple is very inexperienced with. Her eyes dart between them.

She decides to be honest. "Y'all made a big deal about not killing me, and that's nice, even though it's annoying. You're my first friends ever."

"First friends ever," Cali parrots. "That's our reputation. You don't even have enough experience to know how blessed you are."

She lowers her grip to clasp Temple's hand, and Temple does the same for Yaya until they're all linked together like paper dolls. They walk on in tandem, the path to the highway glowing before them in shimmering grass and moss beneath their feet.

Yaya prays as they move. The walk taps along to a slow, lulling beat, and soon the crooked antenna over the cabin stretches before them, then behind them. Temple even feels less animosity seeping in the mist, and both Yaya and Cali cling to her a little less hard.

They follow the frost.

A few yards farther, Temple's the first to make out the twisted, overgrown weeds and the murky color that splatters against the trunks. She stops the other two from walking too close and stares at the tree's dark spot, thick clumping in the soil that wasn't in the path before.

Dawntae.

Jeans shredded at the calf in thick clumps of blue, black, and red. Fingers gripped tight into the soil, head twisted at an impossible angle as if she were frozen mid-writhe. She's different than before.

Temple swallows as she takes a step forward. In the hours past, Dawntae's corpse has somehow ended up this far down the path. The moonlight illuminates a deeper darkness that drags behind her missing feet—a stain of blood curling up the packed dirt.

A *trail* of blood.

"Jesus," Cali breathes from beside Temple. She's looking at the corpse, too—before she whirls so quick she almost takes Temple with her. "Jesus," Cali breathes again, and gags through each syllable.

When Yaya sees, she crumbles to her knees, tears springing in her eyes. "Dawn . . ." she whispers.

Sadness ripples through them both, stealing Temple's attention from the still corpse's new location.

Dawntae worked for the Cary Lauren Horrors Camp, and she gave Temple her application to the camp counselor position. A former North Prep student. A member of Pride Rocks.

She was the girls' friend.

Not just a body. Not just a victim. A person that the campers had been looking forward to seeing.

Cali gags again, and Temple hears the splatter of vomit as she evacuates her last meal. Yaya's sob is silent but her back jerks as she looks over her friend's body, ripped apart in the grass.

Temple takes another step forward, wiping a tear away. She stares for a moment while Yaya and Cali mourn her. The sky is less an opaque black and is beginning to show hues of blue, but the birds have not yet started their morning songs. It's silent enough that Temple can feel her friends' cries in her bones.

Then, Dawntae turns her neck.

It's slow—so imperceptible that Yaya doesn't notice. Only Temple looks head-on. Dawntae tilts her head, moving her neck so that it bends and she can face Temple. Dawntae opens where her eyes should have been. Left there is just loose hanging strands of dried, stringy flesh, vibrating with her every movement and words unheard.

Moving—Temple had suspected it. It's another thing to see it happen.

She can feel Dawntae's heavy gaze as the corpse peels herself up from the ground by a millimeter. She falls back down. Her mouth is half intact—her lips pucker like a fish as she gets used to the feeling of moving it again. No sound comes out. From her pocket, her radio clicks.

But she makes no other sound.

A ghastly voice doesn't press from her, like it does with her mom. That must be another thing only the murderers can do. Temple examines Dawntae's body, watching the miniscule twitching that the corpse can't help. She doesn't want to think about how long Dawntae's been here, trying to move forward. To escape to . . . anywhere.

Her top half has been through it all—attacked, flattened, bitten, and rotted. It's the portion she recalls the most, even though she knows there are other parts still intact. What's left of Dawntae's jeans is caked in dirt and leaves. The gaping hole in her stomach is, too.

Now, the sound of static rustles in her pocket, then cuts back off—a clear sign she's still in there.

Temple approaches her lower body, leaning over with her knife. Her heart pounds as she lowers the blade to Dawntae's calf. The Cary Lauren tattoo peeks out from just beneath her knee. Temple slices across it, and Dawntae flops back down.

She looks down to her hand, at the carved, wooden handle and all its grooves and twists. The knife meant to unmark. When Yaya and Cali notice Temple looming over Dawntae's corpse, their weeping ceases just for the spare glance toward her.

Of course they're grieving their friend, but they're out in the open now. They don't have time to mourn as much as they want to.

"Let's go," Temple orders. "We said we were doing this. Let's do this."

Cali straightens back up, slow and steady. She nods, wiping her eyes and looking to Yaya, who follows.

"Lead the way," Yaya says.

The shrubbery closes in as they move on from Dawntae's body. All the twisted vines and interlocked leaves are steeped in leftovers from a grisly murder they'll never see. Temple glances at the blankets of leaves and vines—the loop of the ice wrapping around and through a cut in the trees. The Cold could jump out at any second. They have to make it to the Midpoint Tree.

To where she *knows* now she saw her mother all those hours ago.

Temple stalks forward over the path, stomping in her ratty sneakers. The other two are right on her heels, climbing and dipping with their breath heaving as they clamor toward the clearing.

The trees lean against each other, gray peeling in from the shining moon and streaming over the ground in thin ribbons. Silver begins to dust the horizon line, the path widening as the North Point House approaches and an overflow of moonlight washes over her, actually warming her up like the sun in the summertime.

The statuesque tree glitters with silver and white, its sparse leaves emphasizing its dramatic shadows. The Midpoint Tree at dawn—the sun must be rising soon.

Temple takes a step toward it, called by the thick trunk that twists up to the sky. She hasn't thought anything about nature was beautiful for the past few days. She's in the woods, somewhere she loved all her life, and it had almost been tarnished. But now, at the sight of the silver, Temple remembers why she and her dad spent hours out on the roof, just up the path. Through the woods, even, walking and climbing until their legs were sore.

And then, with a deep sinking feeling, Temple looks past the beauty of the Midpoint Tree. Ice winds up the bark, curling over the branches. And at its highest point, stripped of their leaves, Temple can see the branches of the Midpoint Tree with devastating clarity.

"Motherfucker," Temple spits.

The trail just stops. Her mother's body is missing, yet again.

CHAPTER FORTY-SIX

There's no other explanation but possession. Temple swivels to Cali and Yaya, who are as captivated as she is but nowhere near as shocked.

If her mother is on the run in her own body, they have to get moving.

Temple searches through the arms of the tree as if a corpse could be camouflaged there, her feet skittering forward along the path. But she has her senses about her. She knows it's hopeless.

"What is it, Temple?" Yaya. She can tell something's wrong, even with Temple not saying anything.

Temple bites her lip. "It's no use. She's not there. She *was* here."

Maybe it's like before. She *was* there, she ... disappeared somehow. But Temple can only think of a few places to find her. And one of them is just down the road.

Cali takes her eyes off the trees for only a moment—to roll them. "Well, she's obsessed with you. She can't be far."

They continue their hike. The North Point House sits alone in the clearing of the trees, its shadows more warped and stretched than Temple's ever seen them. A twig snaps beneath Yaya's foot. She stops. Temple turns to Yaya, whose head quirks up to the sky.

Yaya watches the thin sliver of stars visible from where they stand. Silver glows at her back as she tilts her head back down, brows furrowed. "What's that sound?" she asks.

Cali and Temple pause to look at her, silence washing over the clearing. Distantly, Temple makes out the rumble of a voice—soft and quiet like a steady breeze. It gets louder with every second.

They all look up.

Splat!

A thick stump of a body explodes. A few feet away, blood and flesh splatter onto the path, splashing at the girls' feet and coating them instantly.

Yaya's shrill scream pierces the night. The kind made for panic, the kind that makes Temple grip her chest and Cali sway on her feet. Temple falls over, catching herself in a crouch before she lands in the thick chunks of gore.

Temple, self-proclaimed as "good with dead bodies," is filled with shivers.

"What the—" Cali starts gagging as the smell spreads.

The sour, putrid scent wraps around their necks, and Temple chokes. Nausea spreads in her stomach. It doesn't help when Cali succeeds in freeing what little bile is left in her stomach.

Yaya doubles over right after, her heaving dry but loud.

Temple scans the clearing, her eyes darting from tree to tree.

Branches shake by the house. It's close. Temple takes a step forward and winces when her sneakers smash into something soft and wet. Whatever it is, she doesn't want to step in it.

"We need to get to the house," Temple orders. She lifts the axe, eyes locked on the shaking leaves. Her heart pounds. The girls are right at her back, trudging forward through their laboring breaths.

Another corpse catapults from the trees, slamming to the ground at their feet. The girls break into a sprint.

"Jesus!" Cali screams through harsh gasps.

The body hadn't broken apart like the last one. It just fell to the ground with a thump, and when Temple glances over her shoulder at it, it rolls toward them, gazing at them with empty eye sockets, flutters of snow in its lashes and on its lips.

Yaya reaches the yard first, her eyes wide like she's mid-scream. "What is *happening*?" she asks the sky.

Temple clenches her teeth, trying to focus through the smell. She whirls around just yards from the steps, searching for the shadows of the trees. Anywhere she can find a wrongness. The trees sway in the night, bristling slightly in the breeze. Temple sweeps over them in a glance, once, twice . . .

Creeeeeak.

There.

The front door to Temple's childhood home sways open in a long drag of wood against wood. The interior is cloaked in shadow, only flecks of silver fluttering in the air like thick dust.

"My mom," Temple says. "She's controlling the corpses."

"But *why*, though?" Yaya replies. "That shit's just gross!"

"This bitch straight up *launches bodies*?" Cali shrieks.

She's trying to scare them. Trying to scare Cali and Yaya, at least. Temple never had friends, and any friends she'd made probably wouldn't stick with her to the death. Her mom just wants Cali and Yaya to run away, leaving Temple alone to face her.

Temple tightens her grip on the axe, whipping it before her like a golf club. Something drips from her brow—blood, guts, vomit, sweat—she doesn't know. She ignores it.

She never takes her eye off the door. Adjusting her stance, she nods over to Cali without turning. "You got your stuff?"

After a pause and a shuffle, Cali responds. "Yeah."

"Yaya?"

"Of course." The terror in Yaya's voice melts away.

Creak. Creak. Creak.

Footsteps this time. Temple takes a small step forward, looking up at the fine point of the North Point House's roof that cuts into the leaves dangling above it. A brush on her back tells her Cali and Yaya are right behind her, and she inhales.

"Let's get a start on Plan B," Temple orders.

Because Plan A hinges on her mom being reasonable.

There's a snap, and then a *whoosh*. The clearing illuminates in orange just as Temple feels the blazing hot of a fire at her back. She keeps her eyes trained on the dark doorway of her home, but she knows the tree behind her is engulfed in flames.

Temple takes another step forward. If her mother wanted to, she could cut a path through the grass with her instant frost, slither it up Temple's leg.

Instead, her mother waits in nothingness. But Temple's tired of waiting.

"Why are you still doing this?" Temple asks her directly. Her voice carries across the clearing, echoing around them as the fire grows and climbs toward the stars.

Her mom remains shrouded by the house. She doesn't respond.

"Why don't you just kill us?" Temple calls.

This time, there's a flicker. Thin blue peeks from the house, billowing in the roughening breeze. Her mom takes a step from the inside of the house, her brown leg grayed out in the night—then she stops. She's paused, half in the moonlight, half in the shadows.

But Temple sees her glare just fine. "*I wouldn't kill you, Temple,*" her mother says, her voice coated in that horrific echo. "*I love you, no matter what you think.*"

Temple's hands shake as her mother fully steps out of the North Point House. Silver ice coats her whole body, and trees and branches shake and hiss as if infested with creatures unseen. Her mother blinks at Temple. She's back in her original body. The corpse that Temple thought she'd never see again, that shouldn't even be in one piece at this point.

A deep, blackened scar divides her neck in two—harsh, jagged lines striking up her chin like lightning. The wound pulsates with her steps, crackling quietly as her jaw adjusts. Dirt, frost, and the old blue dress cover up what's left of her.

Temple's axe wobbles in her unsteady hand.

"Your friends . . . I can't kill them," she says. *"They're your friends."* Gray coats her by the feet, traveling up her legs as she glares through to Cali and Yaya behind Temple. *"I've never wanted to harm you, Temple."*

Temple swallows. "You seem to have selective memory," she says. Her breathing is choppy as the smoke begins to thicken. "I slept in the bathtub every night until . . . until you filled it with twigs and trash. Until the night you lit a match and decided to flambé me. I would have died if Dad didn't catch you."

"I wasn't myself that night." Her mom's voice wobbles as she meets Temple's gaze head on. *"The spirits of the farm became too much, and you got caught in the crossfire. That's what made me want this new life in the first place. On this side of mortality, no one can touch you."*

Temple risks a glance behind her, and Cali and Yaya have their arms outstretched like they're ready to jump to her defense. She can't let her mom touch them, though—none of them are all that ready for a fistfight.

Her mom has to get desperate. If any part of her really does love Temple, she'd do anything to protect her.

Hopefully.

"You always said I was evil. That I was going to hell, just like Dad," Temple says. And back then, Temple believed her with every fiber of her being. She believed her mom hated her. She believed she deserved that.

But she doesn't.

And every justification Temple uses to wave away her mother's hatred is simply that. Justifications. Reasons.

Excuses.

Each and every one, a concoction of Temple's own mind.

"Were you possessed then, too?" she asks.

"Does it matter?" her mom asks, basking in the moonlight. Even though she's a corpse, she looks serene. At home.

At home, at North Point House, in a way she never seemed when she was alive.

It nearly takes Temple's breath away. It's like her mom never left, like she never died. All those years, Temple suspected her dad was to blame for her mom disappearing. But obviously her mom is happier now.

"Does he know? That you're . . . like this?"

Her mom's laughter echoes across the clearing, a haughty chime that carries on the wind. "Your dad's the one that tried to get rid of me—it just didn't take. But he knows I've killed before." She turns her eyes away, sighing. "The body he's in now—the sperm donor, if you will—I killed him. Your dad knew. I'm not some hidden evil . . . he's just not as guilty as everyone thinks he is."

The twenty corpses they'd found. Her dad had only known where fifteen were.

Temple clenches her jaw, the muscle flexing against her skin as she tries to calm herself. "You set him up," Temple says. Her eyes flicker to the trees, then back to her mom. "Bell betraying her Anna."

Her mother cuts her glare back to Temple. "Enough. You're stalling. *Come and let me mark you so we can finish this.*"

"No way," Temple says.

"Don't argue with me. I told you—it will all be better once you join me." The air chills as the cracking sounds begin again. Temple can't even see the ice as it inches toward her. "Come home, Temple. With me." The North Point House looms over her open arms, the dense dim of dawn tinting its shadows in a deep purple. Its swinging door creaks its own welcome, as if it wants her back, too.

"Do you even love me?" Temple shouts. This is how she expected everything to go. Her mother isn't being surprising, given that she already tried to kill her back at the cabin.

Still, Temple finds tears pressing at her eyes.

She watches her mom consider the question, her eyes rolling upward. Never flustered. She never lost her cool—and Temple hates it.

"I've always lived for you, Temple," her mom says. "Even now, I only want to do what's best for you."

"But what you want isn't best for me," Temple argues.

"I said *enough*." This time, when her mom speaks, there's a whir of wind that cuts at Temple's cheek. She can't see the ice piercing through the air, but she feels it when it crystallizes on her skin. "Stop arguing. This isn't the time for us to fight."

"I'm not arguing, Mom—I'm . . . I'm *begging* you. Just let us go." She tries to raise her right arm, the blood crusted into her sleeve, but the piercing pain in her shoulder is so great she stops. "I'm injured. We all are, and we need medical attention."

Her mom grins at Temple's words, tilting her head.

"Just let us go," Temple continues. "I'll even . . . I'll come back. I'll visit—just . . ."

That lopsided grin broadens as her mom stares her down, eyes gleaming. "So you want me to give up?" she asks. "What are you hoping to accomplish with this little tantrum?"

Temple shuts her mouth. Her mom is so sure of herself—she isn't bothered at all. She doesn't care that Temple's hurt, and it's obvious but . . . Temple had hoped, a little, that her mom cared about her.

That she'd realize what she's done.

It's too late for that now.

Temple whips up the axe to her wrist, blade glistening white as she glares into her mom's eyes. The crack in them, that tiny chip in her cool, feels like fresh air to Temple.

"If you touch me, I won't let it go your way," Temple says. "I know I'm all you want. I'll chop my own hand off before you get that." She holds the edge tighter to her skin and Cali squeals, right by her ear.

"You—you were just supposed to talk to her! This wasn't the plan!"

Yaya stays silent, watching intently.

Temple's mom makes no moves. The patchy grass in the yard dies in a spiral around her, coiling to consume her. Her mom stares—taking in the axe, then Temple, then the two girls at her side—while silver wraps around her and glows against the wood of the house. Then she laughs.

Her hearty guffaw disrupts the woods, and the birds reappear like they're returning from migration. Temple hears crows caw and robins chirp, all watching her mother cackle like a witch in a fairy tale.

It takes a minute for the laughter to subside, and her sigh flows into a hateful glare as hot as the fire that spreads through the trees at Temple's back.

"I'll do you one better," her mom snaps, calling Temple's bluff.

Temple can't make her play more convincing—not without freaking Cali and Yaya out. She lowers her axe.

"*Temple*," she hears. The voice is soft. Distant. Almost like it's from within her own mind, but she knows it's not.

It's coming from the trees.

"*Temple, listen to your mother,*" another voice says.

"*Put down the axe, Temple.*"

"*Temple, Temple, Temple.*"

Her name sounds all around the clearing, melting in with the bird calls and just as hidden. The girls glance around the field with wide eyes as the voices blend into a chorus of her name.

Her mom relaxes, waiting until Temple faces her once again. "How about I surround you so you can't escape?" Her mother raises a brow, craning her neck to the woods with an even, unperturbed gaze. "Then I can beat you until you can't fight back."

Crack, crack, crack.

The black and silver that peels from beneath her mom's feet speeds through the grass—right at Temple.

CHAPTER FORTY-SEVEN

Temple doesn't have the chance to think. She leaps for the burning trees—and hits a solid wall.

Her breath gets knocked out by the tough flesh of a corpse, thrown at her from deep in the shadows.

Temple can barely stay on her feet.

"If only you'd listened to me from the start," her mother taunts from the tree. "Then I wouldn't have to kill your friends."

The hisses and whispers of her name still carry through the woods like the chirps of cicadas. She can't see the corpses—she can just hear them—and they're so loud she nearly covers her ears. Cali whimpers from farther back. Yaya's trembling prayer is overtaken by the roar that hums lower than thunder.

This isn't the time to be afraid.

Temple grabs the axe from the dirt, swinging at the corpse stumbling before her. It's too slow to dodge her, too dead to do anything but fall to the ground.

"Don't be difficult." Her mom is suddenly right in front of her. Her eyes charcoal and her grin gleaming. Her hand seems sharpened as she grips Temple by the crown. Temple feels the cold icicles press into her forehead. Her feet drift upward, off the ground.

"You know you're going to lose," her mom says. "Give up now, and I'll spare them."

Temple says nothing.

Her mom grips tighter, then slams Temple's head down to stone. Or patted dirt. Temple doesn't know what hardness she hit, but her vision peppers out and back, and she can feel the warmth of blood collecting in her hairline.

Her mom lifts her back up. If Temple hits her head again, it's lights out. She digs into her pockets, whipping out the wrinkled bag of salt and throwing it at her mom. Her injured hand burns, but she closes her eyes against it as her mom drops her with a shriek.

"You evil bitch!" her mom screams.

Temple grabs more salt off the ground, but her mom backs away in darkness and cold.

She swallows. In a second, dying becomes just about the only option.

"Here, Temple." Yaya walks up beside Temple's crumpled form, reaching down a hand to help her up.

Even though Cali and Yaya have made it clear they're in this to- gether, Temple still tenses. More corpses peek from the shadows of the trees. A few more from behind the house, hands running along the siding. Their uneven steps slow them down, but Temple knows her mom won't stop sending them.

"You two can still run," Temple offers, taking Yaya's hand. "While she's focused on me, you can make a run for it. She said she wouldn't kill you, but I'm sure she'll find a loophole somehow."

Cali doesn't miss a beat. She steps beside Yaya, crossing her arms. "I'm lazy as shit, and I ain't a selfish bitch. Running ain't in my blood."

When Temple's all the way up, Yaya puts her hand on her shoulder, squeezing slightly. "Whether I die here or tomorrow or in fifty years, God is with me. I have nothing to run away from."

Cali blinks at Yaya. Then sucks her teeth. "Hers is better. Pretend I said that instead."

Temple knew they'd refuse before she said it, but she'll never allow herself to regret staying quiet again. She inhales, her head going hazy and then sharpening again. She looks back at her mother, who glares from the ground.

"Let's go through with this shit, then," she says. "She said we're surrounded. She's probably controlling every corpse on the property by now."

Cali and Yaya nod.

Temple's legs are made of cotton, and her step forward quivers. A thin trickle of blood slides down the corner of her eye. She's bleeding from when her mom slammed her head into the ground. Without adrenaline, she probably would have passed out by now.

She's *terrified* of dying. It should be obvious, but it's something she just now realizes. She's spent so much of her energy on not dying, she should have known she was scared of it. But now, seeing her mom's eyes are black holes, she knows for sure. Suddenly, Temple's *very* concerned about dying.

The difference—what keeps her from curling into a ball and crying until everything's over—is that she knows Cali and Yaya are terrified, too. She's not special. She's normal.

But her mom is not.

She stares at Temple without an ounce of fear as she rises to her feet, ready for a fight. She probably doesn't even know fear anymore. She probably doesn't recognize it in her victims before she kills them. She doesn't care.

That's the only way you can brainwash your daughter for over ten years and then kill her with your own hands, Temple tells herself. Her mom doesn't care at all. She fakes rage just as well as she fakes compassion, but the reality is that no matter how much her mom yells, or how much the Cold fluctuates—

Her mom is in control of everything she does.

She's using *Temple's* fear. She's making *Temple* afraid. And she knows exactly what she's doing.

Her mom is a lost cause. The best Temple can do now is make it worse. To piss her off for real. They only have one shot to break her wall down. To snap that control.

Temple paces toward her mother, stopping once she can see her face clearly.

"Dad's dead," Temple says firmly. "I cut off his mark, the one right on his bones."

Her mother's face falls, a scowl pulling at her features. The Cold goes still. "Don't lie," her mother hisses.

Gotcha.

Temple grins, the blood that's plastered all over her tickling her face as her muscles move. "I killed him along with Grandma Ida. He can't come back," Temple says. "I'm doing what's best for us. He wanted this. He's gone. He's *gone*, and you're all alone."

Her mother's expression cracks. The crystals travel up her neck to her open mouth. "No. No, I'm not. Never again. *No one else will leave me!*" Glass breaks at her shriek, the remnants of the North Point House's windows shattering to the ground.

Her mother's eyes snap up. They're all white, and a whistle screams through the forest. "How *dare* you?" her screech echoes. Then she starts sprinting into the clearing.

Temple stumbles back. The ice spikes from her mom's arms like a porcupine's needles as she closes in on Temple, baring her teeth. "How could you—"

Her mom stops short.

Her feet hesitate, crunching on glass and solid snow that flows from her feet as sharp columns of ice spring from her skin. She takes another step toward Temple. The Cold mellows out. That brief, honest moment from her thaws and her fists tightly clench. She's restraining herself. "The both of you, ungrateful—" Her jaw slides from one side to the other. That dead look seeps back into her black eyes, replacing the red of anger.

Her crown of clear blades begins to elongate, stretching from her. "As soon as he couldn't handle living, he pawned everything off to me—killing for him and his mother, watching you. And once his conscience kicked in, he stopped. He would have left us eventually. Just like my dad. My mom. My sister." She glowers, as if he's standing between her and Temple. "Tom can rest now. We'll be together without him. *You're all I have left. And I will* not *be alone.*"

An icicle slices free, piercing through the air until it snaps around Temple's neck. She's brought to the ground in an instant, falling to her knees with her gaze frozen up to the sky. Her body slides closer to the house, dragged over the frozen dirt.

Temple grits her teeth, feeling shivers run through her.

"You're coming with me," her mother says. Temple can't see her. Only hear the crunch beneath her feet as she steps slower, feel the cold of her palm grip onto her ankle.

The shards of glass dusting the ground pop and creak as they freeze, inching along with Temple's mom. The chill around Temple's neck tightens with every step, her skin turning numb.

But she will *not* go back to that house.

"No," Temple says. She digs her fingers into the soil, feeling snow and ice and dirt bury into her nails. They go numb but stay put, gripping hard.

"*Yes*," her mother hisses, yanking. Temple feels a nail bend.

She's definitely made her mom angry. She doesn't stop fighting—kicks her legs in her mother's hold, yells at the trees.

"I thought you were afraid of him!" Temple shouts. "You were always whining about him, hiding away in the bathroom with me."

"*You* were afraid of him. I didn't like how he controlled you. You worshipped him so much like you thought he was perfect, but you were scared." Her mom drops Temple's ankle, huffing a breath. "I just acted a little so you weren't alone."

From the ground, the silver frost blurs at her mother's edges. Temple tries to catch her breath, her chest heaving as she turns over onto her back. "You really did pull a *Hearts Stop*, then," Temple says. Once again, she looks to the trees, avoiding her mother's eyes. "You think you're Bell, but you're really Anna."

"Are you babbling because you're so scared?" Her mother frowns. "Don't pick up that bad habit from your father or else I'll have to kill you more than once."

The way she grins after she says it, matching Temple's own bravado with such calm, Temple realizes—her mother isn't afraid of her at all.

Temple sucks her teeth. "Damn," she says. "Plan B failed."

She jerks her head back, jaw to the moon, and settles her gaze on her girls. The ice digs into her shoulders, but Cali and Yaya are in clear sight.

"Plan C. Cali," she calls. The responding snap sends her heart fluttering, adrenaline rushing through her veins. "Yaya."

"Got it."

Pop!

Fireworks burst in a sparking flash. Temple shields her eyes as they fly through the clearing, shrieking in a trail of light. Icicles spurt from the ground all at once, jolting her mother forward. She clears the firework in one leap.

The porch of the North Point House bursts into flames, the trail of fire catching on a patch of leaves that pierce a line through to a turned-over corpse.

Her mom's laugh is a roar and a shriek and a cackle all at once as her head lobs back toward Temple. "I won't fall for that twice!" she screams.

The fire behind her mother and the fire behind Temple climb but don't connect. They form a wall, cutting them off from the way they came in.

"You're locked in!" she shouts. Her grip is back on Temple's neck almost instantly. Temple barely saw her move, because her mother is just that powerful. She's been playing with Temple.

If she chose to, she could have gotten what she wanted easily.

With the fire behind Temple and before her, and the corpses everywhere else, there really isn't a way out.

But it's much more dangerous for her mother.

Cali and Yaya throw lit matches and sparkling fireworks over and over, tossing them into every corner of the clearing in a frenzy. Everything they have left.

"Fire," Temple says. She stares at her mom as she keeps laughing, and says nothing else—but a smile works its way onto her face as she watches the fires grow and claim her yard. The path. Everything that was once her entire world.

Fire. The only thing that destroys indiscriminately.

Finally—as the flames light every corner and spread behind them, behind her—she freezes. Her mom glances around in a daze, tamping down her panic. But Temple can see it. She hears ice crack. The hold around her neck loosens.

She can see the way the orange glow bends and flickers around her mom's grayed-out skin.

Her mother's never felt this trapped. Never been scared like Temple was, or Mickaeyla had been, or Natalie or Brenda. She fakes it well, but she doesn't know it.

She's only playing at immortality, after all.

When she was alive, she was a murderer. She felt powerful over her victims—not the other way around.

Of course someone like that will never see reason.

Plan C was always the best move: If the bitch doesn't back off, just blow her the fuck up.

"We've got you." Temple hears Cali before her legs block her vision, the gleaming axe swinging by her knees. Cali cracks it into the ice, only inches from Temple's shoulder. Her mother shrieks at the crunch, chips of glittering ice bouncing on the ground.

When the Cold finally releases her, Temple stumbles to her feet. The field sways around her, and when she swallows it feels like she's gulping down a marble.

Temple takes her last matchbook from her pocket, pausing to watch the ice drop away from her mother as she stares up at her in horror. Temple snaps it on the matchbook in one smooth motion, just like her dad taught her. Then she throws it across the grass, and it falls at her mom's feet.

The flame rises before her, still not exactly on her but closer than ever before. She can't escape this time. Whatever trick she used to get out of Anysaa and Natalie won't work here. Not on her original body.

"Don't do this to your mom, Temple!" she shouts. "I've done everything for you! For my family to stay together!" Her skin tints blue as cold overtakes her and the flames ravage the house. She takes a step forward, turning silver all at once.

Temple's heart drops. How many people *has* her mom killed? It has to be more than her grandmother. She's never seen this kind of power before.

Maybe she's too strong. Her mom can still—

The silver shifts, twisting around her body. Ice halts, honed in on Temple like a poised arrow.

"Stop this at once!" her mother screams.

Another corpse breaks from the trees, eyes darting around to pinpoint where everyone is—Temple, Cali, Yaya, her mom. The body is nearly beheaded. Ravaged by time. Decomposed far past the point she'd been the last time Temple had seen her, mostly skeleton. Still nude.

The first corpse she ever saw.

"Go ahead," Temple hears from deep behind her classmate's mom. The voice is soothing and soft—familiar. But she can't take her eyes off the skeleton of Ms. Martinez.

"*Temple*," she growls.

Voices around the clearing begin again, beckoning and whining. "*Temple, Temple, Temple.*"

And then Ms. Martinez breaks into a sprint, cutting through the hot, sparkling grass.

She rams right into Temple's mother with a howl, tackling her into the growing flames. They are both completely set ablaze.

Her mother's scream stops once they're consumed by the fire, and then all at once, the chorus of *Temple*s falls silent, too.

RE: TRANSCRIPT COPY, 0926 –
THOMAS BAKER MEDICAL RECORD CHECK-IN

On 20 September at 21:42, Loretta Hoppe <l.hoppe@shieldsandhoppe.com> wrote:

Josh. Sorry, but you can't just decide what information is added and what isn't. As per my LAST email, even if you feel a portion of the recording isn't relevant to Baker's health, you must send the transcription of the conversation with his lawyer in its entirety.

Please stop editing the convo and forward the full transcript, or else I will cancel the payment for your services.

On 20 September at 22:42, Joshua Boyle <j.boyle@evcon.com> wrote:

This is the selection I removed from the previous transcript. It has been transcribed upon your request. The invoice is also attached.

Cheers,

Josh

JOSHUA BOYLE

Head Paralegal and Records Officer

Evcon Legal Services

EXCERPT:

[removed at 02:05:17]

CHARLES GUNNER:	I understand if you don't want your daughter here. I can leave her next time—just let me know.
THOMAS BAKER:	[sighs] You won't have to drag her here again, if that's what you're getting at.
CHARLES:	I just don't like sending her off to the bus alone.
[pause]	

THOMAS:	I want you to take care of Temple for me. When she finds out. When she finds out everything.
CHARLES:	Tom.
THOMAS:	Richelle probably tells her all kinds of things about me . . . but she's never heard everything before.
CHARLES:	What do you want me to do?
THOMAS:	Clear my name from the records of the farm. I want it in Temple's name. She won't sell it. Not once she knows.
CHARLES:	[laughs] Why are you giving final orders? I promised you you wouldn't get the death penalty, and I mean that.
THOMAS:	Death is the only fate something like me deserves. Running from it is pathetic. I made peace with my fate the second I stepped on asphalt for the first time in my life.

[pause] [muffled noises]

CHARLES:	I don't understand—are you sick?
THOMAS:	Well, clearly. But that's not what I mean.
CHARLES:	Are you thinking of . . . of hurting yourself? I'm working on getting you off of death row, Tom. If you can get through the next year, just—
THOMAS:	I'm going to die by the end of next month.

[pause]

CHARLES:	Tom?
THOMAS:	I'm glad I lived to be a father. I want to die a good one.

CHAPTER FORTY-EIGHT

The woods sound like a normal forest again, the only disturbance the crackling of the weakening fire. The clearing's suddenly become unbearably hot, and sweat collects on Temple's forehead, heat sticking under the fluff of her twists.

A new corpse, the one with the familiar voice, steps into the light. And it fills Temple with—with *something*.

"Brenda," Temple breathes.

She's no longer the same Brenda they started camp with. Her body has become lopsided, one arm mush as she bends her knees and crouches. "Temple."

"Took you long enough," Temple says. She realizes what she's feeling—relief. Relief that it's over. That they didn't fail.

Brenda stands before the fire, looking at the girls with her back straight and gaze clear. "I would have done it myself, but there was a line to do the honors," she says. "How'd you know we'd be watching you?"

"The dead follow me around everywhere else," Temple responds. Her heaving breaths carry in the quiet.

The trees rustle again, to their far left. Another corpse steps out into the clearing. Her clothes are ripped off, her chest is eaten away, and her ribcage is exposed. She's only half put together but stalky and muscular like an athlete.

Yaya, Cali, and Temple grip each other as the corpse's eyes rake over them. Temple feels it in the goose bumps that spread over her forearm. With another faltering step, the corpse grins. Her browned teeth are still there but cave at the force of her stretching lips.

"The girl who gets things done," Lam says, her voice a deep, scratching gurgle. She smirks, the expression not quite a fit to Temple's memory of her but not quite out of place on her corpse. "Using *Hearts Stop* was cute."

The book where the hero burns her only love alive. "Your fave still sucks, though," Temple says.

Thank god she read the correct half of that book.

Cary Lauren needlessly *complicated* that half by making the deaths all a dream mechanism, but at the very least Temple powered through it for this moment.

But both Brenda and Lam get the gist of what Temple means.

"We don't know when everything will go to shit again," Brenda says, the flames behind her casting her in a silhouette. "Alla y'all should get the fuck out of here, ASAP."

"Language," Lam chimes. "Just because we're dead doesn't mean we're not still the adults here."

Brenda smirks at Lam, her gaze soft. "Get the *heck* out of here," she corrects.

Temple, Cali, and Yaya all nod and turn out toward the trees.

"There's more," Cali says.

Temple barely catches it, but when she glances toward the trees, she makes them out.

A few more corpses creep out of the woods toward the house, just as Brenda and Lam did but with less theatrics. They tiptoe to the edge of the fire, studying it. Different shapes, sizes, and degrees of rottenness swarm together toward their only source of peace and death. They fall over the fire, some lighting up instantly, others slowly withering away.

Lam turns to Cali. "How many more matches do you have?"

Cali holds up three fingers.

Temple takes one, lights it, and chucks it over to their left, away from the path. She spots more of the dead behind them, crowding around the flame.

The dead are all trying get this over with.

The dead want to die.

Lam and Brenda step closer to the fire. They both face the three girls. "Get to the highway," Lam orders. "The sun will rise soon."

"We will," the three girls say together.

More and more corpses push out of the trees in a solid wall, ambling toward the flames. There are branches and bodies and leaves crowding the space as Temple, Cali, and Yaya move back.

Right before Temple turns from them, she sees Lam take Brenda's hand. She closes her eyes before she can see them step into the fire.

They're free. And now, Temple is, too.

She turns back to the grass, dodging corpses on their way back to the path.

Temple sees a few she recognizes. Some, her father's victims. Free from their body bags that police never found, and back together in the woods. Others younger, fresher. Pale yellow T-shirts with blood splashed across the camp logo.

As the smoke builds up, the dead get harder and harder to see. The girls break free of the mask of the trees, gasping with heaving rasps of air. They're too weak at this point.

Even the fresh air can barely force its way through, and Temple collapses. She coughs into the grass, leaning over her knees with Cali right beside her, gagging on the path again.

"I've never thrown up so much"—Cali cuts off with a harsh revulsion, and she catches her breath—"in my life."

Yaya coughs. She leans over a tree, fist clutched against her forehead as she heaves heavy sighs, her back rising and falling. It's all they can do.

For a moment—until the strength in Temple's legs returns—they're once again a part of the North Point woods. Their breaths match the birds, and the birds match the bugs, and they're all clustered around the same trees and vines and leaves and dirt.

When, finally, Temple finds it in her to stand up again, her vision swims. She checks over her shoulder, for a second scared she'll find some straggler running after them. But the path is empty.

At least it's confirmed—the dead never cared about Temple at all. They just wanted peace—and her mother and dad ruined it for them.

But they have it now.

Temple watches Yaya stand and Cali gather herself. They face the path, back at each other's sides—Temple in the middle, one arm around Yaya's, one arm around Cali's.

No matter how somber their journey got, the three of them had always found something to say. But for the next half hour, they walk without speaking. Even their breathing is inaudible.

Three alive.

Ten dead.

Dawntae. Brenda. Mickaeyla. K'ran. Wynter. Natalie. Lam. Sierra. Janae. Anysaa.

Their names weigh on Temple's chest. Ten girls they have no answer for. But they have no choice but to continue to walk on.

Cali's the first to break the silence. Her soft gasp brings both Temple's and Yaya's eyes upward, and Temple makes out a sandy brown gap in the trees just as the sun fully rises in the sky.

Cali points. "Is that—"

"The highway," Temple finishes.

That little sliver of the gray-brown mist and open land peeks through the trees, just on the horizon. The mere sight is enough to fill Temple up, until she's ready to burst—and then all three of them are beside themselves.

They crack apart.

Break into a sprint.

Temple runs until her feet hit the road, the asphalt crashing against the rubber of her sneakers, kicking up rocks and dirt and grime as she claws over the metal guard. She runs into the middle of the open road, screaming up into the sky.

"The highway!" Yaya yells.

"We're alive!" Cali joins in.

Temple twirls around, the trees on either side of her and the road wide and open. There are no cars in sight as the mist rises in a haze that hides the distance. Cali and Yaya are still by the side of the road. Temple walks back to them, collapsing.

"I've got thirty years' worth of high blood pressure, now," Cali says. "My doctor's gonna be on my ass when I get my physical for cheerleading."

"I'm joining the track team again," Yaya whispers, her chest rising and falling as she closes her eyes. "I'm never getting caught up like this again."

"I'd take North Prep girls beating my ass over that bullshit any day," Temple says. Her legs are stretched out toward the middle of the road, and she scoots farther out, past the line that blocks off the shoulder. The highway's empty, but it still carries that safety of civilization she'd taken for granted.

Temple catches her breath, her eyes up on the lightening sky. "Only me and you two."

"We started out with thirteen," Yaya says. Temple turns to her as the trail of her words wobbles. "That's ten. Gone."

Cali scoffs. "What did I say? Thirties and therapy. Let's not worry before then." She rolls over, and Temple turns her head to find Cali staring down the road. "Should we, like, wait for the shuttle to come? Walk to a town? There one, like, ten miles away." She rolls back over, flat on her back. "God, I'm never going camping again."

Yaya lifts up slightly. "I always thought I'd hate camping for different reasons."

Temple furrows her brow, pushing Yaya by the shoulder as she shifts to get more comfortable. "We can't wait until our thirties to call somebody."

"Yeah, but who can we call?" Cali raises her eyebrows. "Jesus? Yaya's the only one with the number."

Yaya nods, serious even though it's a joke. A breeze flutters through, causing dust and leaves to whirl around them.

Temple jerks over, straining as she flops onto her stomach. Her butt aches from the knife in her back pocket—and something else, hard and flat. "We could always just call the police," she says. She digs into that pocket and pulls out her cell phone. Its screen is black and slightly slick with sweat, but it's otherwise in one piece.

Temple hands it over to Cali.

"What the hell are you giving me this for?" Cali asks, grabbing it despite the protest.

"It's off," Temple says.

"And mine is dead. And Yaya's is dead. I can't do any rigging if it's already gone," Cali says.

The road is more comfy and clean than a bed could be—simply for its lack of blood and body parts. But Temple still peels her back off, brushing the dirt from her hoodie. She shrugs. "It's not *dead*. It's been off the whole time. My aunt's the one that bought me that thing—I don't even use it."

Cali's mouth falls open. She must not have believed Temple, because a second later, she swears as the whoosh of her phone's speakers fills the air, cutting to life. She looks over at Temple, her hands shaking. "Temple, you beautiful ghost slayer."

Temple rolls her eyes. "Just call 9-1-1."

"I never knew you being an old man would save us," Yaya says.

Temple doesn't defend herself. She looks over to Cali, who's already hunched over the phone with her eyes narrowed. Her fingers fly over the screen.

"You've got a missed call! And text messages!" she exclaims. "Sweet texts, I missed you so!"

Temple doesn't know anybody who'd text her.

Still, Cali presses the phone into Temple's palm, saying nothing else as the brightness adjusts. There is, in fact, a single missed call. And six unread messages.

OK, one says.

Let me know if you need a ride.

Your father's dead. It's all over the news.

Temple?

Are you OK?

Be safe.

Temple's hand is frozen around her phone, feeling a ball in her throat as she reads over Aunt Ricki's texts.

Cali watches quietly, the morning breeze rustling the wispy fly-aways in her braids. "Temple," she says, "you need to call your aunt."

Temple wraps her free arm around her legs, letting gravel rub onto her jeans as she takes a breath. "I never call her." As if it's a reason not to.

A few hours ago, she thought her aunt was one of the many people she terrorized. One of the many people who think she's a monster, better off dead. Temple's always been so harsh with her—but what Cali said was right. Aunt Ricki didn't have to take her in. She knew Aunt Ricki and her mom weren't close, didn't talk. But she took Temple in anyway.

Aunt Ricki probably struggled to match the energy of some angry kid with no parents that hated everything, including herself. And if this were a few hours ago, maybe the guilt would eat Temple alive.

She'd let it seize her, as it had for sixteen years.

But Temple doesn't let the guilt stay with her this time. She isn't the same scared girl anymore.

She takes a breath.

Four in through the nose.

Four out through the mouth.

It's not about dwelling on her guilt; it's about trying to be better. Crossing her legs, she backs out of her text messages, opening her contacts. She was never as alone as she thought she was.

A single car drives by, passing the three bloody high school girls laid out on the side of the road without even a pause. Yaya, in particular, looks dead as she curls into a ball with her hair sprawled over the ground.

Cali stares blankly out in the road, the sound of her nails tapping on the hard asphalt keeping Temple present. And when Temple finds Aunt Ricki's name in her contacts list, she slides across the name and waits.

Her phone's volume is turned up to the max, and Cali can probably hear the ringing as Temple sits frozen in place.

But it doesn't ring for long. Just one, and then there's a click. Wind howls in the receiver on the other side, and Cali tenses next to Temple.

"Hello?" Aunt Ricki's voice is tight but hopeful. "Temple? Are you OK?"

Cali breaks down. No matter how muffled the answer is, it's the first response they've had in days. She's curled over in tears while Temple swallows, her mouth struggling to find the right words.

But if Cali's crying, Temple won't be far behind.

"I'm sorry I didn't call sooner," Temple says. "I—I didn't know what to do." She clenches the phone tightly, smashing it into her cheek. Her eyes feel hot. "Aunt Ricki," she sobs.

She and Cali knock foreheads as they grip onto each other. Slobber spills from her lips as she leans over, cradling the phone like it's a lifeline.

Yaya pops over to them in a second with half-closed eyes and a hand on her thigh. Temple holds her hand as she gets control of her breathing.

"Temple, please," Aunt Ricki begs. She sounds like she's crying too. "Where are you? What's happened?"

Finally, Temple takes a deep breath. Her shoulders still tremble, but she manages to force out the words. "Can you pick us up?" she asks, clutching Cali's and Yaya's hands as hard as she can. They squeeze back, and another car passes down the open highway. "Me and my friends need a ride."

ACKNOWLEDGMENTS

It was quite obvious to me, back in 2018 when I wrote the first draft, that this book would be published. It ain't happened in the timeline I thought it would, but all these years later I'm living proof that it *really* only takes one "yes."

To start, thank you to my agent, Maeve MacLysaght, who was my first "yes." Thank you for dealing with a diva like me. I will not get better, but I appreciate the patience and advocacy that you have shown me over the years. I would also like to thank my second "yes," my editor, Emily Daluga. I came in headstrong, and I'm leaving even stronger—a true testament to your editing and collaboration skills.

Thank you to Abrams, my publisher, who has shown me more support than I've gotten in the seven years before my deal combined. To Abrams team members I haven't had the chance to meet but who have enthused about my book and supported me behind the scenes: Megan Carlson, Chelsea Hunter, Micah Fleming, and Maggie Moore.

Thank you to my writing friends and my community—first, the Forkers. Truly, no words. I could name you all (dare me to, I'll do it right now), but it's overwhelming. Truly the phoenix of group chats—in the ashes of [redacted], a family grew and I love y'all. Special shout out, though, to the pitchforks who read this book: Amanda (my other brain cell) Helaelhleaer, Siana LaForest, Emily Varga, Chandra Fisher, Katie Bohn, Molly Steen, Sophia Mortensen, and Victor Manibo.

Then, there's my FAM, the Lit Squad: Susan, Maya, and Cecily. I know y'all ain't readin' this—y'all better not be—but thank you for your support and your laughs and for putting up with me being unserious 90 percent of the time and ranting about institutional racism the other 10 percent. Here's to more years of dominating together! Love y'all—FB&N!

Thank you to my numerous beta readers, who have seen this book in different forms over many years, particularly Ayala Franco, Dawning, Karissa, and Kayley Clothier.

Thank you to my supervising manager, Jael, and my executive accountant, Alea. To Shaina, too, I guess. To Mama—thank you for keeping the secret. I hope I can scream-sing at you for many more road trips.

And finally, thank you to anyone reading this. I hope you read with the lights on (figuratively).